ALSO BY JESSICA S. TAYLOR

The Seas of Caladhan Duology

The Syren's Mutiny (#1)

The Captain's Revenge (#2)

The Ocean's Mercy (prequel novella)

Standalones

Hollowed: A Sleepy Hollow Reimagining

Beyond Those Gilded Walls

Beyond Those Gilded Walls

JESSICA S. TAYLOR

BEYOND THOSE GILDED WALLS
Copyright © 2024 by Jessica S. Taylor.
All Rights Reserved.

Cover Design & Chapter Illustrations by Moonpress Designs (moonpress.co)
Map Illustration by Cartography Bird
Character Artwork by @cebanart and @panna_mara

Visit the author's website at:
https://authorjessicastaylor.com

First Edition: October 2024
Published in the United States of America

The scanning, uploading, and distribution of this book without permission is considered theft of the author's intellectual property. If you would like permission to use material from the book (other than for review purposes), please contact the author at the website listed above.

Any use of this work to "train" generative artificial intelligence (AI) technologies is expressly prohibited. No AI was used in the creation of this work, including visual and textual elements.

ISBNs:
eBook: 9798988711841
paperback: 9798988711810
hardcover: 9798988711834

Editing by Booklight Editorial
Copy Editing by Megan Records
Proofreading by Rachel L. Schade

To those who never grew out of their goth phase.
This one's for you.

And to Nebula, for always being super creepy and cute at the same time.

PLAYLIST

I cannot start a book without putting together a playlist for it. Please enjoy this selection of songs I listened to entirely too many times while writing! They are in no particular order.

For the full playlist, please visit my website.

Devil - Shinedown
Looking at the Devil - Siebold, Neutopia, Leslie Powell
Killer Inside of Me - Willyecho
Who Are You - SVRCINA
Grimstone Manor - Nox Arcana
Death of Me - SAINT PHNX
Flesh and Bone - Black Math
Dark Matter - Les Friction
Death Waltz - Adam Hurst
Don't Stop the Devil - Dead Posey
Seven Devils - Florence + The Machine
Blackest Hand - Saint Mesa
In the Woods Somewhere - Hozier
Black Cathedral - This Cold Night
Blood in the Wine - Aurora
Your World Will Fall - Les Friction
Fate of the Clockmaker - Eternal Eclipse
Masque of the Red Death - Nox Arcana

AUTHOR'S NOTE

If you haven't already picked up the threads for yourself, this story is inspired by various works from Edgar Allan Poe.

I do want to be clear, while inspired by many, this book is not a retelling of any particular story. I hope you have fun finding all of the hidden references and Easter eggs I left behind. Head to the Author's Note at the end of this book for a full list of all the inspiration!

To read all of Edgar Allan Poe's work, including the original source material that inspired this book, visit the website of the official Poe Museum at https://poemuseum.org/poes-complete-works/.

And with that, I invite you into the world of Veressia...

A Map of Castle Auretras
its noble and formidable exterior; and the notable rooms within it

Raised over four centuries prior to the present day, the castle that looms so regally above the city of Jura remains the jewel of Veressia— hosting rooms for a thousand guests, a soaring ballroom of remarkable size, and a vast underground system which connects to its cityside entrance.

the southern facade

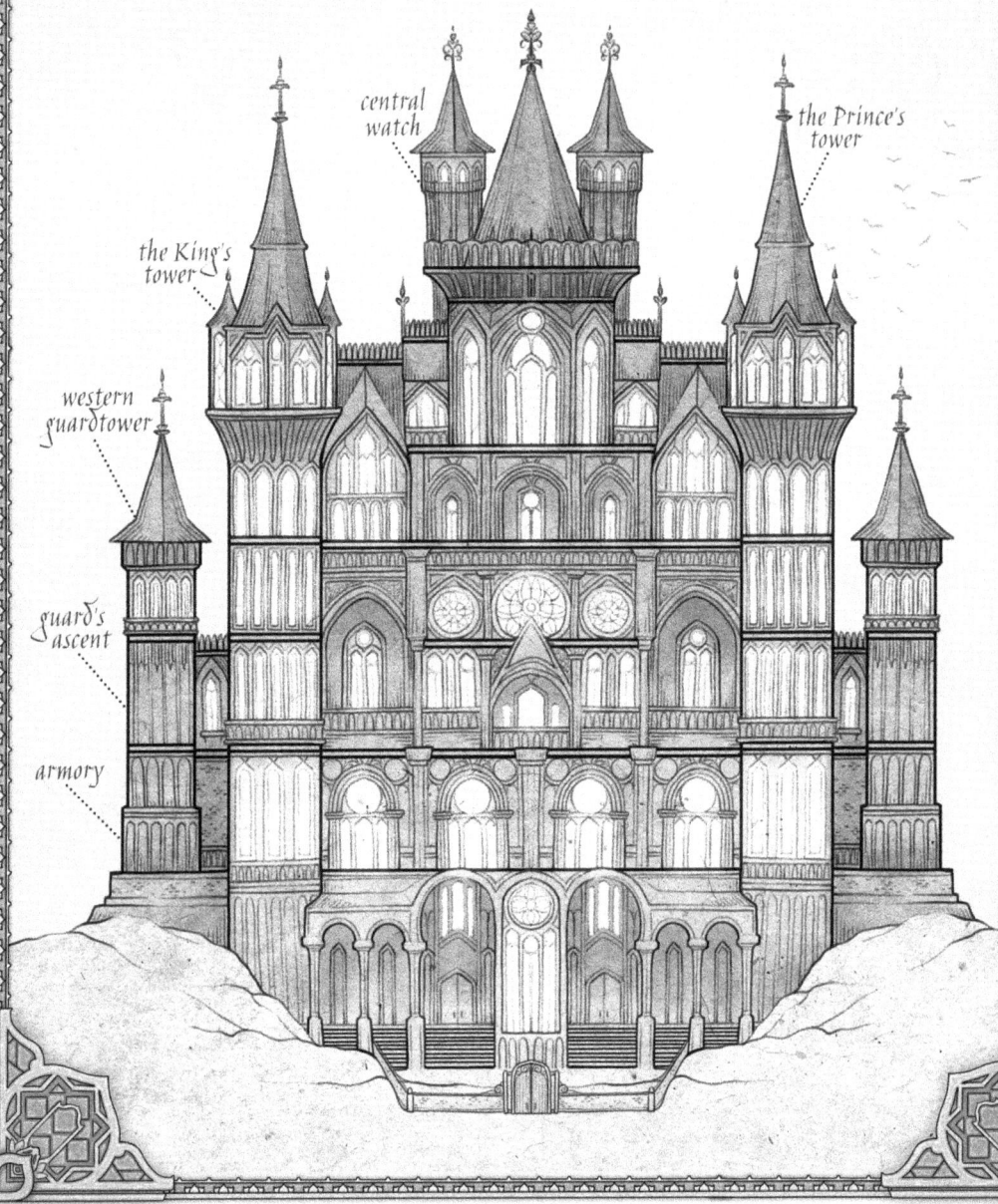

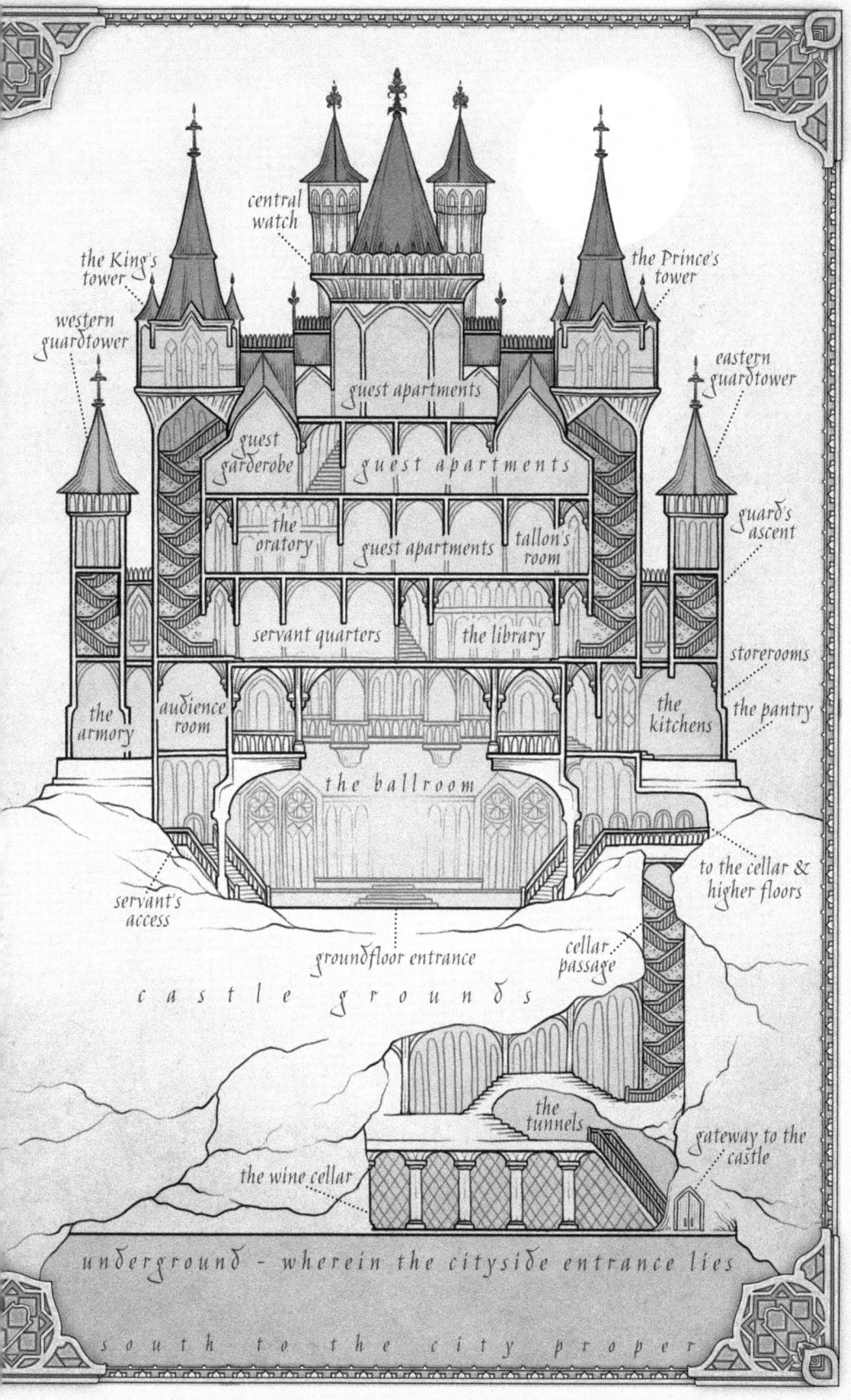

VERESSIA'S GODS

Throughout the book, you'll encounter mentions of Veressia's gods and goddesses.

While Odyssa doesn't necessarily believe in the gods (at first), that doesn't mean they aren't important to the story—or to the world as a whole.

Here is the list of the gods and their domains:

KALYX - God of Death
ALYONA - God of Life
SONYA - God of Wisdom
RATKA - God of War
JARYK - God of Wilds
ALASTRIONA - God of Seas
CETHIN - God of Shadows/Night
SERENEILA - God of Light/Day

BEFORE YOU BEGIN

This story contains dark and mature content and themes that may be triggering for some readers. BEYOND THOSE GILDED WALLS is a dark/gothic fantasy romance, but the romance is not considered dark romance. Content includes:

- Familial death, including parent and sibling (on-page and off-page)
- Pandemic/plague references (on-page)
- Body horror, blood and gore (on-page)
- Violence and murder (on-page)
- Explicit sexual content (on-page)

If you require a more detailed list of content advisories and warnings, including locations, please turn to the last page of the book or visit my website at authorjessicastaylor.com/BTGW.

*And Darkness and Decay and the Red Death
   held illimitable dominion over all.*

— EDGAR ALLAN POE

CHAPTER ONE

Death was inescapable in the kingdom of Veressia.

Brought in on a red mist that now choked the city, death lingered in the dark stains that were permanently etched into the stones that lined the streets. In the perpetual shroud of mourning that hovered over everyone who dared step out of their homes. In the coppery taste of blood coating the back of my throat that no amount of wine could ever chase away.

But above all, Death was in the specks of crimson that covered my mother's lips and chin, sputtered out during a coughing fit as she tried to expel the blood flooding her lungs.

Noctisanguis Ciuma, so named by the royal doctors, was an affliction of the blood.

We referred to it simply as the blood plague.

It seemed like a lifetime ago that the cursed plague had fallen, a distant memory of a life not caked in blood. A life not cloaked in death and misery. It was far more than a plague or a disease. It was a curse, a putrid curse that flowed through the lands on rivers of blood. The foul miasma swept through like a tide of crimson, left no corner untouched, no soul unscathed. Its origins were shrouded in mystery and its victims were chosen by a seemingly capricious whim.

It cast its shadow over Veressia like a vengeful deity.

But this haphazard curse condemned our families to death, with only days' notice, and wreaked havoc on the people of Veressia. Perhaps they would live. More likely, they would not. They would die a bloody and gruesome end.

Through the window of my bedroom, the jagged spires of Castle Auretras jutted up into the night sky like fingers clawing through the covering of mist, a deep crimson in the darkness, as if even the stone itself lamented its cursed existence. But in this land of despair, there was no sanctuary, no refuge from the inexorable march of Death's advance. If Veressia were to die choking on its blood, the castle would accompany us.

As the lamplight danced upon the aged stones, a flickering light caught my eye, beckoning from the shadowed recesses of the street below. There, amidst the shifting red mists, a spectral figure began to materialize, its form coalescing from the veiled tendrils of smoke into the semblance of a man—though what remained bore little resemblance to the living.

Wrenching my gaze up, I looked back towards the castle and away from the Soulshade, the lingering spirits who could not pass over to the Beyond and were instead cursed to walk the world they once lived in, never finding peace. Once, they'd merely been stories my mother and others who still believed in the gods and the Beyond had told us to make us behave. But after my own battle with the blood plague and coming so close to Death itself...they were now impossible to deny.

I'd learned quickly that the more attention I gave to them, the harder it was to get them to leave. Better to pretend I did not see them in the first place. Not everyone could see them—that much was obvious from the few times I had seen people walk directly through them. But it was much harder to tell who could see them than who couldn't. And I didn't dare ask.

The heavy iron gates that secured Castle Auretras were gaudy, even by the wealthiest citizens' measure. Inlaid with gold and obsidian and decorative metals that had been crafted to resemble snakes, curling around the straight iron bars and peering out at the city below, they were hardly the first reminder of what the king and his family thought of the rest of their kingdom.

Beyond the opulent facade of Castle Auretras lay a kingdom divided, its gates adorned with lavish embellishments that mocked the suffering of those beyond its walls. Prince Eadric and his ilk basked in their seclusion, insulated from the horrors unfolding in the streets below, their decadent revelries a grotesque testament to their indifference to the plight of their subjects.

It had hardly been a surprise when he locked the castle and shut the rest of the world away. In the face of such callous neglect, the once noble kingdom had descended into chaos, its streets now haunted by the anguished cries of the kingdom the crown had forsaken.

The kingdom of Veressia was dying, but my mother was dying faster.

A wet, rattling cough pulled me out of my rage and had my feet moving before I truly registered the sound. It was as common a sound as anything nowadays, since the blood plague had begun to infect us. In mere months, the entirety of Veressia had become accustomed to the sound of bloody coughs, to the stench of copper and decay in the air. The blood plague pulled our insides out with those coughs, intent on filling either our lungs or our streets with blood.

I picked up the damp rag from the bowl at my mother's bedside and wiped at the crimson dribbling from the corner of her mouth. I'd burned seven cloths already, too drenched with her blood to get the stains or the stench out. Looking down at the increasingly few clean spots, I knew this one would also need to be burned.

"Shh, Mama, I'm here," I murmured, pushing her hair back off her sweaty forehead. She was burning with fever, and her body trembled visibly. I knew in my heart that she was not long for this world, no matter what I'd pleaded to the stars.

The splotchy black marks that now decorated my arms were stark against my mother's almost bloodless skin. The marks that showed I'd outlasted Death—barely—were now permanently etched across my neck, my chest, and my right arm and hand. Swirling, patternless lines of darkness that set me apart as a survivor.

I despised them.

My mother's eyes fell on the marks and I pulled my sleeve down to cover them as best I could. We both knew she would not be getting the marks on her own skin.

"Odyssa," she wheezed, barely getting my name out before she fell into another coughing fit. I murmured soothing words as I dabbed away the new blood that she'd coughed up. "You must take care of your brothers. You cannot let your emotions control you. Your brothers are everything now."

I squeezed my eyes shut. I did not want to hear this, to hear her implore me to shove down my anger and rage for the sake of my brothers. I knew the speech by heart now, as if it had been etched into my very bones. She did not need to say it, and I did not want to hear it. It only made it real. But my comfort did not matter here. So I opened my eyes and took my mother's hands in my own. "Yes, Mama. You know I will. I have and will always put them first."

She nodded, patting my hand. Her fingers traced over the mottled black whorls etched into my skin. "You can be good,

Odyssa. I know you can be, if you try. Touched by Death himself, and yet, you survived. Alyona has blessed you, my child. You are strong. You will keep your brothers safe. Protect them where I cannot. Provide for them where I cannot."

I didn't feel strong. And the way she'd uttered my survival, as if it were a blessing from the goddess of life…if anything, I was more cursed than the rest of them. At least they had the sweet reprieve of dying, albeit not peacefully, rather than having to sift through the remains of the dead and pull the shattered pieces of my life back together each time someone passed.

Death was easy for the dead. It was nothing but a burden for the living.

"I will." I squeezed her hand before standing from her bed. Propping up her pillows, there was no hesitation as I bent and pressed my lips to her forehead. "Rest now, Mama. I will come back in a little while."

She leaned into my touch, chasing it even as I stood. I was the only one in the house who would care for her, who was willing to touch her. Though it was suspected it wasn't passed by touch, no one could be certain. There was still so much to discover about the mysterious affliction that had accompanied the reddened mist. No one was willing to take the risk they would be the next to die. Perhaps if the cure was something as simple as avoiding contact with others, it would have been easier to stomach. It certainly would have been easier to combat it.

I knew she wanted nothing more than to see my brothers, and they her, but all of us knew they could not. Even the chance that tending to her would see them ill was enough for my mother to send them away the moment she began coughing.

I had been only one of a handful that had survived the blood plague, out of the thousands who had died from it, and it was not something I was willing to chance with my younger brothers. Caring for them, putting them first, had been all I'd ever known, and I would continue doing it until the last breath expelled from my lungs.

They were safely tucked away at a friend's house, and I would send for them to return after our mother had finally passed. Looking at her from the door, I could tell it wouldn't be long now. I let my head fall against the door frame, closing my eyes briefly.

I had no more sorrow left inside me. No more energy to mourn. No ambition to curse the gods that my mother so pitifully clung to even in her last breaths. All that was left was a soul-deep weariness. And the anger.

I let myself fall into the chair at our small table in the kitchen. I needed to eat, bathe, and then return to my mother's bedside for her last moments, but I could not find it in me to move.

My gaze shifted back to the castle spires through the window, distracting me from any thoughts of food or hygiene. My fists tightened around the edge of the table, and I had to let my jaw unhinge and fall open to keep from grinding my teeth. I pried my fingers from the table, one by one, letting them instead catch my forehead as I let my head fall.

The familiar monster of my anger clawed at the back of my mind. Only my mother's coughing kept it at bay.

There were whispers from the castle, from servants sent out to the city in the dead of night to obtain more supplies for the prince and his people. The whispers passed from person to person, until everyone in the city knew that since they'd closed the gates, no one in the castle had fallen to the curse of the blood plague. Rumors of a treatment, one that would chase away the cursed affliction, began to swirl, but none of the servants who entered the city on behalf of the prince ever did it twice, so it remained merely a whisper of a dream.

Once the castle had been sealed, Prince Eadric began to

throw ridiculously opulent parties each night. Glancing at the clock, I realized that tonight's should be starting shortly. Soon, the night would fill with the sounds of revelry and decadence, the peals of laughter echoing down from the balconies as those more privileged looked down at the city they'd left to die. I could not hear much after my bout with the plague had ravaged my body, but I could hear everything that came from the castle.

Each night now, as I listened to hints of music drifting down from the castle, I dreamed of what it would be to see Prince Eadric ill with the plague he'd abandoned us to. To see rivers of red run from every orifice and watch him choke to death on his own blood. It was the least he deserved.

Even when she'd first began showing the signs of the blood plague, my mother had been adamant that I not be angry with anyone, that it was simply her time. She'd begged me to focus on her life, and not her death, to focus on my brothers, and to remember the good childhood they had with her.

But I knew she could hear the parties every night, just as I could. I knew it hurt her that we'd been deemed insignificant by the prince whose family had sworn to serve and protect the kingdom. Listening to the music and the joy spilling down from the castle kept me up at night. It fed my anger, stoking the fire inside my belly until it was all I could think about.

My mother was too good, too kind. And where had that gotten her? She was dying in the next room, and Prince Eadric was throwing a party.

Two more days passed as I cared for my mother as she slowly drowned in her own body. Blood covered nearly every surface in the room, despite how often I cleaned it. The coughing had turned to retching had turned to vomit, until all I could see was red splattering our wooden floors, crimson soaking the once-white sheets. Stains I would never get out of both the house or out of my soul.

Every sip of water or bite of food came back up on a river of blood. Her teeth were stained pink and the handkerchief clutched in her hand was near constantly pressed against her bloody nose.

It was worse than dying myself, having to bear witness to my own mother's death.

I was surprised she had clung to us so long, but it was no secret where I inherited my stubbornness from. Before she became sick, my mother had been a pillar of the community, someone everyone had relied upon and sought out for advice. Rarely was there a night when we did not have someone else joining our table for dinner simply so they could consult with my mother after. If she was not able to help herself, she did not rest until she had found someone who could.

I admired her dedication to those around her, but I cursed that same selflessness. Perhaps if she had not taken food to that last couple, caring for their dying daughter, she would have been safe from the blood plague. Perhaps she could have stayed out of the gaze of whatever curse controlled it.

My mother had scolded me for my anger at the couple and their daughter, had told me that we always cared for those we could, especially when we were better off. It was a lesson I'd taken to heart, even if my brothers hadn't been extended the same teachings. She'd reminded me that there was no way of knowing how she'd contracted the cursed illness, and that all that was left now was to make my peace with it.

Still, sitting beside her with her hand in mine, I could not turn off my anger as I watched the pauses between the shallow breaths that panted from her chest get longer and longer.

"Odyssa," she rasped, squeezing my hand.

"Yes, Mama?" I rested my hand on her forehead as I looked down at her, watching the words form upon her lips.

Death reflected in her eyes. She smiled, keeping her lips tight to cover her bloody gums. The words she could not muster the energy to utter were clear in her eyes.

"I will take care of them, Mama," I promised, my heart shattering beneath my rib cage. Tears blurred my eyes but I didn't dare pull away from her hands, instead biting down on my lip as I pushed a strand of my mother's once-silky hair behind her ear. "Beyond this world, we will meet again, Mama."

My mother closed her eyes, and they did not open again.

A single tear fell down my cheek, rolling into the corner of my mouth. It soaked into the dry skin of my lips and my tongue snuck out to catch it. My eyes fell closed at the flavor of salt-tinged sorrow.

I needed to get up. There were things to do, and I needed to send for the undertaker to collect her body, to send for my brothers to come home, to clean the house before they arrived. But I could not bring myself to move, to let go of her hands. I felt *wrong*, holding her lifeless hands. Hands that should have been warm and sure were now cold and limp.

Perhaps in the back of my mind, I had expected that my mother would survive as I had, but looking down at her now, her slackened face and her bloodstained nightgown... I knew it had been a fool's dream. Our family would not be lucky twice, and the fates had wasted our only exception on me.

Carefully, I pulled my hand away from my mother's, folding her arms over her body. I had things to do, and even in death, my mother would expect me to do them.

After I'd handled notifications and made arrangements with the undertaker, I found myself back in her room, once again staring down at her. My ears rang with a droning noise that so often filled my head when silence came, drowning out all else and making me grasp at my head in hopes it would stop. It never did; not when I wanted it to, at least.

My mother wouldn't be buried; there was no room in the cemeteries any longer. She would be cremated. My eyes squeezed shut at the thought of her body being burned.

Death was a foul, foul creature, and one I hoped to meet one day, if only to scream at them for letting the one good thing in my life be torn away like this. I should have been the one to die, not her.

My mother's voice in my head reprimanded me, telling me to stop feeling sorry for myself. I had a task to do, one she had assigned to me, and I needed to get it done. So, I pulled back the sheets from her body and threw them into a pile on the floor, followed by her ruined nightgown. Snatching one of the last clean rags in the house, I began to clean her body. Slowly, the ringing in my ears subsided as I focused on my task.

"I am sorry, Mama," I whispered as I ran the cloth over her chin. "I am sorry I could not save you."

For the first time since I began to see them, I wanted nothing more than for a Soulshade to appear. Her Soulshade. But there was no flickering mist, no taste of smoke, no droning buzz in my ears. Just silence. Damning, unending silence.

CHAPTER TWO

After the blood was cleaned from her skin, I wrapped my mother's body in a fresh white sheet in silence. I was not present in my body or my mind, even as I opened the door for the undertaker and let him take her body. I was still in that room, with my mother as she choked out her last words. I closed my eyes.

Would I always be in that room?

My mother's voice appeared again in my mind, telling me I still needed to burn the linens and scrub what I could of the blood that had stained the floorboards before my brothers came home. My promise to her tasted like ash. I had no time to mourn her, no time to process that the most important person in my life had been ripped away as I held her hand.

Falling to my knees, I began to scrub the floors.

Mourning would come later. I had a promise to keep, and so long as I had breath in my lungs, I would do whatever it took to keep my brothers alive, just as I always had since I was old enough to care for them. They were my mother's pride and joy. In her own way, I knew she was proud of me, but I had always been something different. Her helper, her right hand, not her child.

So I cleaned. Cleaned the stench of blood and the oppressive feeling of death from the house as best as I could. It wasn't enough, though, and the sharp smell of lemon and astringent burned my nose as it mixed with the lingering smell of copper.

A knock on the door told me I was out of time. This would have to do.

The fortifying breath I took was fractured, a shuddering movement that made its way over my tongue before skittering down into my fever-weakened lungs. It had hardly filled me with the strength I so desperately needed it to, but it would have to do. I had to inform my brothers of our mother's passing, and as much as I loathed the task, no one else would do it for me. Not anymore.

As I pulled the door open, my brothers' faces appeared. Apprehension filled me, wondering whether they would be overjoyed to be reunited finally, or whether they would hate my very being for tending to our mother in her last moments. It was hardly a secret that my mother had placed her hopes and dreams on my oldest brother Emyl's shoulders rather than mine.

Dread coiled around the base of my spine, pulling taut as our eyes met. Yet at the same time, hope had my shoulders creeping up towards my ears, eager to pull them both into a hug if they would allow it. They hadn't touched me more than absolutely necessary in a long time, even before I'd caught the blood plague.

Emyl rested his hands on Rhyon's shoulders, his grip tight enough to turn his knuckles white as he kept him firmly in place. "Odyssa."

The hope bled from my shoulders and the gnawing at my spine opened a pit in my heart. It seemed our mother's death had changed nothing here. Just as my mother had never truly seen me as her child, my brothers had never seen me as their sister. To them, I was merely another caretaker, another voice telling them what to do and reprimanding them for doing things they should not do.

I'd hoped it would be different after her death, now that we were all left alone together, but it had been a foolish hope. Gripping the door so tightly both my knuckles and the wood groaned, I opened it wider to allow them to enter.

Emyl had been furious when my mother had begun showing symptoms and she'd banished them from the house, and from the way his shoulder hit into mine as he passed now, that anger had not faded. I bit my tongue to keep my own temper back.

Sometimes, it amazed me that Emyl and Rhyon shared a father. My own had abandoned me while my mother was still pregnant, and later, Emyl and Rhyon's, too, had abandoned us. It had left Emyl an angry child, and the only solace that had come from it was that Rhyon was too young to know better, and he had clung to a playful curiosity of the world rather than unfettered rage.

I wondered if my mother had ever given Emyl the same speech about not letting his emotions show that she had given me so many times. Looking at the back of his head, at the tense lines of his shoulders beneath his jacket, I somehow doubted it.

She'd always held me to higher expectations, a push for perfection that had pulled me constantly throughout my childhood between wanting to be as imperfect as possible and wanting nothing more than to please her.

I'd never found the right balance, and now, I feared I never would.

Only the sound of creaking wood filled the house as we sat around the kitchen table.

Rhyon appeared ready to vibrate out of his skin, chewing on his lower lip with such an intense frown that it created deep furrows between his brows. I wanted to reach out and smooth them with my thumb, but just as I was about to reach for him, his dark eyes snapped towards me.

"Mother is dead, isn't she?"

"She is." My voice cracked on the words. My mother had long tried to train me out of crying in front of others—a sign of weakness, she'd said—but unshed tears burned at the back of my throat. "I am sorry I could not do more to save her, Rhyon."

"She's dead because of you." His words were calm, no trace of anger or even sadness. No trace of the playful child I had sent away just a week prior.

I couldn't stop my sharp intake of breath. His words were sharper than any dagger could ever dream of being, sliding between my ribs and settling deep into my heart. My tongue darted out to wet my lips, trying to string together an answer that would not make them both hate me even more.

"I—" I shook my head, unable to get the words to form.

Rhyon bit down on his lip, worrying it between his teeth as he stared at me. "Will we be next?"

"There is no way to know—" My voice cracked again, the words scratching against my throat. Clearing my throat, I continued, "I did all I could to save her."

"You should have done more. You should have taken that food to the couple like you were supposed to. You lived, why not her?" he cried, the tears welling in his eyes and spilling over his cheeks as his lip quivered with anger and sorrow. "I wish you had died instead of her."

The room fell away, black dancing around the edges of my vision. All I could focus on was Rhyon's eyes. I saw Emyl's lips moving, but the only sound was the echoing of Rhyon's words. *I wish you had died instead of her.*

In his mind, he was stating a fact, something he knew to be true, as if he were telling me my hair was black. It was worse than I'd ever feared, that my youngest brother, the child I had cared for since he was only moments old, now wished me dead.

Oh, how I wished the same. I would have rather endured a thousand days at the hands of the plague than be in this room right now.

Emyl tucked Rhyon into his chest, cooing and rocking him as if he were an infant and not an eight-year-old boy.

"I am sorry, Rhy." I did not dare reach my hand out towards him, trying instead to reach him with my words. Mother would never forgive me if I let him continue to believe this. "That is not—"

"Do not call me that." His voice was hard as ice as he stood and pulled out of Emyl's arms to glare at me. And with that final stab to my heart, Rhyon turned and stomped to his room. The slamming of the door made me flinch.

The anger that had been building in me since Mother's first cough was quenched by the sorrow in my brother's voice as he'd uttered those words.

Normally, I was quick to defend myself to others, quick to snap, but with my brothers, both of them, I was as confrontational as our front doormat. He was right, after all. I had failed to ensure our mother survived, had failed them both because of it, and I, too, wished I had died instead. I could hardly be angry at Rhyon for speaking my own thoughts aloud.

"Why did you let him do that?" Emyl's voice pulled my gaze up from the pattern of the wood I'd been absentmindedly tracing. "Mother wouldn't have let him."

"He would not have done it if she were here." I shrugged, desperately clinging to the other words that wanted to fall out, the words of anger and spite. Those were not the ones that needed to be spoken now. "He needs the outlet. A target for his anger. I was the same at his age, and it took me long after his birth to learn to hide it. If that is what he needs, to process his feelings about Mother's death, then I am happy to be that for him. I am happy to be anything he needs. Anything *you* need."

Emyl held my gaze but said nothing.

"You are my brothers. There is nothing I would not do to protect you both. Mother knew that. I can only hope you know that too." I dropped my eyes back to the table.

Silence passed between us for a moment, to the point that it grew uncomfortable. I raised my head just as the chair screeched across the floors as Emyl stood. The look on his face was one I hadn't seen before. He hesitated for a moment, rocking slightly on his feet. "I'm going out. I'll be back later."

That had me on my feet, too. "You shouldn't leave, Emyl. Where are you going?"

Emyl froze where he'd been pulling on his coat, his gaze icy. "Believe it or not, Odyssa, Mother dying does not mean you are to take her place. Where I go and what I do is none of your concern. I need a moment to myself, if you don't mind."

And for the second time in as many moments, my brother closed a door on me. Emyl hadn't slammed it like Rhyon had, but it still brought stinging tears to my eyes regardless. Not even a full day since my mother's last request, and I was already failing at it. Failing her. Whether the tears were those of sorrow or rage, I did not know. Perhaps they were both, a balancing act as it were, with one eye pouring hatred and the other pouring grief.

I wanted to scream at the sky, to rage and yank the portraits of us off the walls and hurl them into the street after Emyl. To shout and yell and convince them that they were both wrong. But it would do no good. And my anger always retreated into this twisted state of subservience with my brothers, subdued until the moment they were out of my sight.

The taste of smoke and ash filled my mouth and a flickering mist hovered in the corner of the entryway.

Wiping at my eyes, I turned back to the kitchen before it

could solidify into a Soulshade. I did not have the time nor the inclination to deal with another tortured soul begging for my attention. Not when I had my own soul to attend to.

I needed a distraction, something to keep me from sitting in front of Rhyon's door and begging him to listen to me. Suddenly, I could understand why the king had hurled himself from the towers when his wife had passed from the plague. If we had a tower, I might have done the same.

I'd known we would all mourn differently, and in some way, I'd expected the anger. But I'd not expected them both to abandon me. Perhaps I should have.

Rifling through the cold chest and the pantry, I began pulling out ingredients for a quick soup. At the very least, I could ensure they both had food when they reappeared.

Food set aside for them both, I curled up on the bench in front of the kitchen windows, looking out into the dimming evening sky. Purples and oranges shot across the clouds, dimmed by the blood-red mist that hung over the rooftops, both of them mixing to frame the spires of Castle Auretras.

Tracing my fingers across the spiderweb cracks in the glass, I let my temple rest on the wood frame. The tip of my finger caught on a protruding sliver of glass, blood welling in the small cut left behind.

CHAPTER THREE

Peace eluded me, my mind only showing me flashes of the fever dreams I'd had while I was sick. Memories of thrashing limbs, pained moans, and a cold darkness I could not escape. No matter how I contorted my body atop the seat by the window, I could not get comfortable. I couldn't bring myself go to my bedroom.

In the kitchen, though the flickering Soulshades had finally subsided from vying for my attention, the sounds of the revelry had not waned, and they wouldn't until the sun began to lighten the sky. Once it became clear Rhyon would not be coming out for dinner, I resigned to curl up on the lounge chair in the parlor.

As hard as I'd tried to close my eyes and rest while waiting for Emyl to return, the nightmares clashing with the sound of music and laughter drifting down from Castle Auretras kept me awake. Hours passed in that fashion, with me staring at the peeling paint along the crease where the wall met the ceiling, the eerie sounds of music cutting through the red mist atop the everyday fog that clung to the cobblestones in the cool of the evening.

Resigning myself to another sleepless night, I returned to the window at the kitchen, tugging a pillow into my lap and twisting my fists in it as I stared up at the towers dripping in opulence and death.

With the tolling of the midnight bells, my thoughts strayed. Back to the words Rhyon had spit, and back to the last moments of my mother's life. They ventured down that dark and twisting path of the Death marks atop my skin, remembering my own bout with the plague and how close I had come to succumbing.

My lips had been stained crimson for weeks after, and I would never forget the taste of my own blood for as long as I lived. Even now, my body still showed signs of my battle. Beyond the obvious marks, my hearing was fading, often replaced with an intense ringing taking over all sound with no warning and lingering for hours, and it was growing worse with each passing day. Perhaps the blood plague would eventually claim me after all.

Rumors of a treatment to the plague had swirled when it first began to spread. Rumors that after his mother's death at the hands of the disease, the prince had pulled in every medic in the kingdom and sequestered them away in the castle to find a way to cure it.

None of us knew if it was true, but there had been no bodies carried out of Castle Auretras to the graveyards in months, and since those had filled, no one to the incinerators either.

If only we could get past those walls, those gilded walls, covered in iron and tipped in golden spikes. If only we could get into the castle... Our people could live, and yet the prince sat, hiding away from his own kingdom, refusing to take the throne and instead letting us die. Watching the prince die would be my only wish for the rest of my life.

Perhaps that was why I'd survived the plague, so that I could live long enough to see the prince die. One could only hope.

The front door opening and closing softly pulled me out of my silent rage, though I didn't rise to go meet my brother. Eventually, Emyl shuffled into the kitchen, his eyes red-rimmed and glassy. I bit my tongue hard to keep from saying anything about his choice to drown his sorrow in alcohol.

"I was not expecting you to still be awake," he muttered, falling into the chair across the table from me.

Still holding my tongue between my teeth, I merely turned my head back towards the window, ducking down to ensure he followed my gaze before meeting his eyes once more.

His head cocked for a moment, and then understanding washed over him as the noise finally filtered through the window. "Ah."

"There is supper, if you're hungry." Those words were safe, at least, and my tone was surprisingly even despite the churning in my soul. Their approval was all I'd ever wanted, their friendship, their affection. But I'd long ago resigned myself to the truth: they would only ever see me as a caretaker, and not their preferred one.

I turned my gaze back to the window, trying to avoid looking at his reflection in the glass over my shoulder. "Rhyon did not eat. If you would try to take him some, perhaps he'll eat for you."

A heartbeat passed, and in the window I saw his fists clench at his sides before they relaxed. He crossed his arms, huffing as he slid down into his chair. For all the anger his body language exuded, his voice was softer than I'd expected. "I am sorry for leaving like that, Odyssa. This situation..." He shook his head. "I'm just so *angry*."

"And you think I'm not?" Finally, I turned back around, resting my chin on my knee as I looked at him. "I am angry every minute of every day, but Mother asked me to care for you both, to protect you both. And if that means letting Rhyon get out his anger here rather than in public, then so be it."

Emyl's shoulders slumped as he ran a hand through his unruly hair, dark like mine, but wildly curly like our mother's had been. "He does not mean it, you know. Like you say, he is angry, too, but he hasn't learned to manage his emotions yet. Not like we have."

I snorted. What a delusion. "Are we? Managing our emotions, Emyl?"

His huff of laughter was a better response than I'd hoped for.

Silence fell once more, blanketing the room until Emyl shifted his weight, frowning as he raised his chin. "What will we do now that Mother is gone? What do we do?"

The slight smile I'd managed to muster slipped from my lips along with a heavy sigh. The weight that had lessened some with my brother's laughter had returned, pressing down atop my shoulders even heavier than before. He would not like my answer—hence why I had yet to bring up the topic myself.

"Mama and I went through all the records when she fell ill, as a precaution. You know I'd been helping her already, managing the house and contributing what money I could from cleaning for others, but even I wasn't privy to all of what she did here." He straightened at that, standing and moving to the door frame, and crossed his arms again. I pressed on, the muscles of my neck tightening as the next words fell from my tongue, oily and bitter. "There won't be enough money to keep us all alive for long. You will need to find a job to help us make ends meet. Even if I begin cleaning full time, even if I could find someone willing to hire full-time help, there just be won't enough to cover the expenses for the three of us for longer than a month. Perhaps two if we truly stretched every coin."

Stone would have been more expressive than Emyl in that moment. His jaw clenched and unclenched, as if he were chewing on the words he was about to speak but he never did. I could feel his anger building, pulsing out from his body as though it were a separate being. It was in the flush across his cheeks and the way the vein running down the side of his temple throbbed.

"I am sorry, Emyl," I whispered. His anger was about to explode, ready to rip through the walls of the house and tear into flesh. It was palpable, but if we wanted to stay in this house, to keep food in our bellies, I needed him to take some responsibility and help me provide for our family.

"What about our inheritances? I know Father left money for Rhyon and me before he left us." His voice was deceptively steady, the calm before the storm. It was only a matter of time before his walls broke down. He had never been good about containing the anger—had never had to be. Twenty years old and he had never been forced to work a day in his life, while I'd been working myself to the bone in one way or another since I'd turned eight and he was born. His nostrils flared. "Can that not sustain us longer while you work more to replenish it?"

I wasn't sure whether the feeling bubbling up in my chest was a laugh or a sob, but I swallowed it down regardless. My own walls were trembling under the weight of my anger and fear, but if we wanted to live, I needed to be honest. We would weather the storm after. "It might keep us alive for a few months more if we manage it carefully, but it isn't as much as we were led to believe."

"We? That money is Rhyon's and my own. You have no claim to it, Odyssa."

My own anger spilled out before I could stop it, the first time it had truly been directed at my brother. "So, I am to work myself to the bone and then come home and cook and clean for you, while you sit here and drink yourself into oblivion off the coin of some man who did not even care enough about either of you to stay?"

"I do not need a job, Odyssa." His voice was like ice. "You do.

And you can leave the house to find one, seeing as you have already survived the plague."

"If you are willing to risk your life, Rhyon's life, so you can go out and drink, you can surely risk it to go work so we can feed and clothe him." I took a deep breath. It scraped against my throat and burned my lungs. "That money will only last you two three months at best. What will you do after?"

"Get a better job, Odyssa, and do not worry about what Rhyon and I do with our money," he said, narrowing his eyes. "I have better things to spend that money on than giving you charity. Be glad I am letting you stay in the house at all."

My anger was building in my chest, spreading like fire through my veins. The Death marks along my neck throbbed in time with my heartbeat. "I was born in this house, Emyl. Long before you. I have as much a claim to the house itself as you. Even if you wanted to, you could not evict me from it."

He stared at me, and the venom in his eyes communicated plenty what he thought of my words.

"You would truly let your family suffer and starve, just to avoid putting in an honest day's work? What were you expecting to do for the rest of your life?" The tendrils of fury were escaping the cage of my body, and I feared it would erupt if this continued a moment longer. My Death marks throbbed against my skin to the beat of my thundering heart.

"I guess we'll never know now, will we?" He made his way back to the front door, pulling on his coat once more. "Either find a better job or be looking for a second one, Odyssa. It really is the least you could do after letting our mother die. Don't bother waiting up—I don't know when I'll return."

It was a small mercy that he did not slam the door this time either.

I stood, fingers wrapping around the vase that sat in the middle of the kitchen table, and flung it across the room with a shout, letting all my anger fly with the ceramic that then shattered against the wall and fell to the floor.

Both of them believed I'd killed our mother. And perhaps I had. Perhaps she had caught the blood plague from delivering food to the last family, and it did spread by touch. Perhaps I had been the one to send my mother to her deathbed by asking her to take it instead of me, for begging off the work due to another bout of fever-induced vertigo. We would never know for sure, but just like every other family in Veressia, we had no choice but to move on, to keep living for those left behind.

But I knew, without a shadow of doubt in my soul, that if my mother were still alive, that if she had been the one to ask Emyl to help us with money and told him to get a job, that he would not have refused her.

But I also knew she would never have asked him in the first place. She would have looked to me to help her make ends meet, whatever the cost to our own souls.

Was I weaker than my mother, that I could not make ends meet without asking my siblings to assist?

My mother had loved us all dearly, in her own way, but perhaps she'd done us all a disservice by shielding them from the world. And perhaps I'd continued it by shielding my brothers alongside her.

Breathing hard, I pushed my hands through my hair. My brother would truly rather drink himself stupid than help us survive, and there was nothing I could do to convince him otherwise. Not now. We'd failed him, failed to impose any sense of responsibility in him, any sense of family. He'd always been able to do what he wished, and I feared there was nothing I could do now to fix that. I could only hope Rhyon would not fall victim to Emyl's selfishness.

My hands balled into fists, blood singing with bottled fury. I itched to hit something, to feel something else break, to destroy.

But instead, I fell to the ground and buried my face in my hands. And I cried for the first time in years.

Not even a full day had passed since I'd wrapped my mother's corpse, and I was already failing her. My chest felt tight, like a vise had wrapped around my ribs and squeezed. Tears dripped down my cheeks, running over my lips and filling my mouth with salt.

There was nothing I could do now except hope that Emyl would somehow come around on his own.

I let myself cry a moment longer, and then I dried my own tears and picked myself up.

Alone in a world that was quickly dying and alone in a home that felt like a tomb, I knew no one would help me any longer—I needed to do it myself.

CHAPTER FOUR

Rhyon still would not deign to even look in my direction, let alone utter a word to me the next morning. At last, though, as dawn broke over the city and the morning haze lifted to reveal only the shroud of red mist, his hunger had driven him from his room and now he sat at the table while I cooked, adamantly keeping his gaze on the wood in front of him.

At least he would not starve to prove his anger. Another similarity between us. I'd tried, as a child, to win arguments with my mother by refusing to eat, but she had far more experience at being stubborn than I had, and I always broke first.

The click and drag of the front door opening caught both our attention. Our eyes met briefly before Rhyon turned his gaze towards the doorway with a flush in his cheeks, as if gazing upon his own sister was a petty crime, worthy of punishment.

I watched him for a heartbeat longer, aching to go and smooth out the sleep-wild hair at his forehead. I watched as the furrow in his forehead smoothed out and he jolted from his chair, the legs screeching against the wood as he flung himself through the doorway and into Emyl's arms.

I turned back around to finish making breakfast.

"Hi, Rhy." He grunted at the end of the word, groaning as he picked up Rhyon, who giggled. The sound of their affection cut through me, my hand tightening around the wooden spoon pushing the meat around the pan. Footsteps scuffled across the floors. "Odyssa, I did not expect you to be up."

"Yes. Someone needed to make Rhyon breakfast." I didn't turn around. Couldn't. "Would you like any?"

"No, I ate already." His voice was flat, cold. I was glad I could not see his face, at least.

I bit down on my tongue to hold back the retort, swallowing down the words I desperately wanted to say. More sounds of chairs scraping and bodies falling into chairs filled the kitchen. Hushed words passed between my brothers, soft enough that I could not make them out, not that I wanted to hear what they had to say.

Even though all three of us believed me responsible for our mother's death, I would do as she'd asked me with her last breaths. I would care for my brothers, protect them. Even if they hated me for it.

My ears rang, the shrill sound drowning out all else. They did not have to love me. They just had to live.

Somehow I managed to finish cooking and plating Rhyon's food without injuring myself. Setting down the plate in front of him, my mind was already spinning through what else needed to be done today: laundry, cleaning, meeting with the funeral home about the cremation costs. My knees wavered, my hand catching the table the only thing keeping me upright.

We could not even give my mother a headstone. Even if the graveyards hadn't been pushed beyond their capacity, we would not have been able to afford it. Our mother's memory would only be honored in our home, in private. She deserved statues and monuments, and I could not give her that.

"Odyssa." Emyl's voice startled me out of my thoughts, and his hand wavered in the space around my wrist, like he'd gone to touch me but thought better of it. His fingers flexed in the air before he drew them back, reaching into his pocket and pulling out a crumpled piece of parchment. He thrust it into my hands. "Here. This was hanging up at the pub."

"What is it?" I asked, taking the paper from him. He jerked his hands back as soon as I'd grasped the edges, wiping his hands on his thighs. I balled the paper into my fist. "I am not contagious, Emyl. I cannot *give* you the plague simply because I had it nearly six months ago."

His dark eyes narrowed. "The castle is looking for new servants, and the pay is more than enough to support us all."

A quick glance down at the paper in my hand confirmed his words. My anger cracked through the careful walls I'd rebuilt overnight, and now I could not draw it back in. "On its own, barely. This would only be enough if we were very careful and only spent on the essentials. We would still need a second income source for the family if we want to continue living as we are." I smoothed the paper down on the table and pressed my fist against it, leaning in closer. My voice was quiet, though I heard the anger and condemnation leaking through it. "This is not the solution you think it is, Emyl. But anything to get out of stepping up in life, right?"

"It would be enough for Rhyon and me."

I reeled back, and the leash on my anger snapped. "Damn me to the Beyond then? Your sister who cared for *both* of you from the moment you were born. I mean nothing, and you would turn me out to die just to ensure you both survived?" I spread my arms wide, stepping back from the table. "Who will provide for you when I work myself to death, then? When I starve because the Coward Prince will not feed me?"

"Don't talk to him like that!" Rhyon screamed, pushing his plate away. "This is your fault!"

I blinked at him, red clearing from my vision only slightly. There was no way for me to say the words I wanted to. He wouldn't understand them anyway. He was on Emyl's side, and nothing I said would ever sway him.

My gaze flicked back to Emyl. "You realize that if I take this job, I would be sequestered in the castle forever. You would never see me again unless the blood plague is cured. Who would cook for you? Who would clean the house? Do you even know where to go to get food or clothing? What happens if one of you falls ill? You have never had to be responsible for yourself, Emyl, let alone for another human being. Can you care for Rhyon? Truly, do you suddenly believe yourself capable?"

"We'll hire someone." The words were hissed through his teeth.

I laughed, a harsh and broken sound devoid of any humor. There was nothing funny about this situation. Nothing amusing about what he was suggesting and failing to realize. "With what money?" I pointed down at the paper beneath my hand. "Even if I were able to send you every *penny* of this wage, even if the Coward Prince deigns to take on all my own expenses, it would barely be enough to feed the two of you and keep the house. How, then, could you afford to pay for a housekeeper? Do you even understand how much that would cost? Do you know where to go to find someone for the job?"

Emyl surged to his feet, leaning on his fists on the table now as well, his face close to mine and his lip curling up in a snarl. "I am *trying* to find a solution, Odyssa."

And with that, the mask holding back my anger shattered completely. My anger was explosive, but my rage was quiet. "I told you the solution last night, Emyl. We both contribute to raising Rhyon. We. Both. Work." I poked a finger at his chest.

"This is you being selfish, you not wanting to lift a finger, yet again. Mother spoiled you in her life, but we cannot afford for you to continue to spoil yourself in her death."

I heard the sound of skin on skin before I'd even registered the feel of his palm against my cheek. My hand flew up to the stinging skin to press hard against it. Emyl leaned in closer, his breath fanning against the back of my hand. "You will—"

I raised my gaze to his, letting the pitiful remains of my mask crumble into dust, so that all my emotions were laid bare for him to see. His eyes widened. They'd never seen my true anger before —I'd always been able to hide it behind my walls. The walls he'd just shattered when he struck me. "Think carefully about what you're about to say, brother. You cannot take it back once you do."

Rhyon made a small noise, almost like a cough he'd been trying to muffle. It grew into a small whimper that drew both of our eyes away from each other and to him. Coughing had once been a sound that faded into the background, our minds never truly registering it. But now, I heard it above all else. Emyl and I both stared at each other a moment. I broke first, turning to Rhyon and kneeling in front of his chair, ignoring how he recoiled from me. "Rhyon, was that a cough? Please be honest."

He shook his head quickly. Too quickly.

"He is fine." Emyl's voice was like stone. His eyes burned into the back of my head. "And you will go."

"Will I?" I kept my eyes on Rhyon for a moment longer, searching for any other signs he was falling ill, watching as he wriggled in his chair and looked everywhere but at me. Finally, I stood and met Emyl, lowering my voice to a whisper, a hush of words across his face, too soft for Rhyon to hear. "Would you risk yourself to care for Rhyon as he dies?"

Emyl's face contorted in pain.

"I thought not."

"He is fine."

"Will you risk that?"

"I will take care of him. If you want to take care of him, this is how you do it. You'd be taken care of at the castle, and your paycheck can come back here to us," Emyl said. "Between that and the inheritance, we will make do without you."

Silence filled the kitchen, the kind that made you itch and squirm and spill your secrets just to fill it. I bit my tongue.

Rhyon let out another soft cough and I let my eyes slide closed. He was sick. If not already, he would be soon. The rumors of the treatment inside the castle came back to the forefront of my mind. I would do anything to keep Rhyon alive, to keep Emyl alive, regardless of what they thought of me. I would not disappoint my mother.

"Mother told you to protect us?" Emyl's voice had lost all the violence of before. He pointed at the paper. "This is how."

"If I leave this house, you will both die. If not from the blood plague, then by starvation at the hands of your own arrogance."

"Then so be it. Even Death did not want you, Odyssa. Why should we?"

I would not let them see me fall apart, would not let them see the shards they'd just shattered my heart into. Pulling on every ounce of willpower in my bones, I carefully pulled my mask back into place, settling into that empty place in my heart that was filled with indifference. My face neutral, forehead smooth and lips straight, jaw relaxed, shoulders down, hands loose.

"Very well then." Despite what my mother believed, I did know when my rage had no place, and this was one of them. Anger would not change Emyl's mind, or Rhyon's heart. If anything, it would only harden them more.

Moving into the hallway, I pulled my cloak from the hook beside the door and fastened it at my throat. I stepped into my shoes, bending down to lace them tightly. There was nothing else to do now but go. Without a backwards glance or a goodbye, I stepped out of the house and pulled the door closed.

My hand faltered on the handle as another cough echoed through the last sliver of space between the door and the frame. And then the door clicked shut, cutting off the sound completely.

I froze on the front stoop, my feet unwilling to move forward. I almost wavered in my decision to leave. Almost.

But if they were unwilling to listen, I would do whatever I could to help them. The pay would be better than nothing, and if the rumors of a treatment were true, I would find it and I would get it back to Rhyon before it was too late.

The cough began again, louder this time. So loud I could hear it through the door. The only solace I took was that the cough was still dry. It meant there was a chance this was not the plague, that perhaps it was a normal sickness brought in by the autumnal dampness.

My mother's plea in my mind, I vowed I would discover the truth of a treatment. Even if they were not sick now, it was only a matter of time, truly. And I would not take any risks. My plan solidified. Secure the job, infiltrate the castle, discover the treatment, get it to Emyl and Rhyon. And try to keep us all alive in the meantime.

I let my feet lead me into town, my mind still back at our front door, listening to the sound of that cough.

CHAPTER FIVE

There were a handful of pubs that Emyl could have gone to, and searching them all would have been tedious. Thankfully—or unfortunately—it was all too easy to distinguish which pub was being used to recruit staff for Prince Eadric. In a place that had become a town of more Soulshades than people, angry crowds were no longer commonplace.

So the one forming in front of the doors to one of the more rundown pubs was a sign I was in the right place. The voices were indecipherable from the top of the street, an angry buzzing of overlapping sounds and words that made my heart climb in my throat as the noise assaulted me. Each step closer to the throng brought both volume and clarity to their protests. Before the plague robbed me of parts of my hearing, I could have heard them long before I approached. But now, I was nearly atop them before the words were decipherable. I wanted to turn and retreat, but I forced each step forward, seeking out their protests.

The words were the same vitriol that was always thrown at anyone who came into town from Castle Auretras, the same hatred for the Coward Prince that had left his people to die.

Though today, there was something *more* behind them, something reminiscent of the early days of the blood plague, when we were all still begging the crown to do something to help us.

My steps faltered. The city had been resigned in the last months. Early on, some had tried to storm the castle, but every attempt had been unsuccessful and left behind even more bodies. No one tried anymore—there weren't enough left to risk it. What had the castle's pageboy brought to the surface to renew the ire?

Approaching the pub, I realized it could hardly be considered a crowd, really, but there were more people gathered than I'd seen throughout the entirety of the last six months. People kept their distance from each other now, either a precaution to avoid any chance of spreading the plague, or to avoid connections, to avoid having to mourn one more person they knew.

"You cannot just *take* them!" someone shouted.

Ice slithered down my veins. *Take?*

The man at the doorway, a pageboy from the castle based on his embroidered jacket and fitted pants made from a shiny material that likely cost more than an entire month's wages, rolled his eyes and huffed, tugging on his sleeves. "As I have *said*, Prince Eadric will *only* turn to conscription if there are no volunteers. This is not uncommon and has been done in every city in Veressia. Certainly people still need jobs here too, yes? Send them to me, and there should be no problems."

"Why should we work for that heartless coward?"

"He has a cure. Why is he doing nothing?"

"I'll never work for the likes of him."

"He is not our king! He will not even take the throne!"

The man's nostrils flared and even from this distance, I could see how his eyes darkened. "Mind your tongues. All of you. King Gavriel did not tolerate rebellion, and neither will Prince Eadric, regardless of his choice of when to ascend the throne. You are subjects of the crown, and you'd do well to remember it." He straightened his coat, rolling his shoulders back and jutting his chin out. "Now, if you have anyone who would like to volunteer for the honor of serving their royal family, please do send them my way. If there are no volunteers by nightfall, I shall return tomorrow with the names of those selected to serve."

"How will you choose?" That spurred the crowd back into shouting once more, echoing the sentiment.

"Citizens between the ages of nineteen and twenty-nine will be placed into a lottery to be chosen at random," he replied. "Now, if that is all."

The crowd grumbled slightly as they dispersed, running back to the safety of their homes now that there was no one to direct their ire towards. The words they'd spoken were true, though those who spoke them aloud were far braver than I. Prince Eadric was certainly a coward, but there were still those in his employ who would gladly quell an uprising.

A woman brushed past me, our shoulders bumping together. I murmured a soft apology and stepped aside, eyes still fixed on the wooden door that held my fate behind it. The gasp that escaped her lips pulled my eyes down to hers, which were fixed on my neck and chest where the Death marks sprawled and coiled like serpents across my skin.

"Lovely, aren't they?" I responded, grinning wide and showing my teeth.

Her cheeks flushed as she scurried away. The smile fell from my face, trampled beneath the footsteps of all those who passed me, trying and failing to conceal their stares. I had grown indifferent to the gaping mouths and sharp inhales that my Death marks drew. They'd been etched across my skin for half a year now, and yet it felt like I'd been born with them.

Before the cursed plague swept through Veressia, I would

have withered under the attention, but now, it just made the vein in my temple throb and my jaw clench.

The first time I had braved the city streets after I'd recovered had been difficult, and I refused to leave the house for weeks after. The first person my mother and I had passed by had openly gawked at my marks. The man had glared at me and ushered his family away with a huff about how I should not have been allowed in public. I had nearly punched him in the mouth. Only my mother's calming hand on my arm had prevented it.

"You control your emotions, your actions, Odyssa," she'd told me. "Not them. Do not give them that power."

I tilted my head back and inhaled the smell of stale copper and acrid smoke. The Death marks were a punishment, a reminder that I had lived and my mother had not. But I was not ashamed of them.

Lowering my chin, I made eye contact with each person who stared at me.

I lingered as the last people left the area, waiting for my chance to enter the pub unseen. Despite the fact that my brothers had directed me here, I feared the repercussions for them if anyone saw me enter and assumed I was volunteering willingly. Once it was clear, I brushed my hair behind my ear and pulled open the door to the pub.

Before my eyes could adjust to the dim lighting inside, a hairy arm and large hand stretched across the doorway, barring me from moving any further.

"We're closed." The large man peered down at me as he pulled his arm back slowly before crossing both arms over his chest. It was a hardly necessary intimidation tactic—the circumference of his arm was larger than my head, even without him puffing them out just so.

"I watched him walk in here." I raised my chin towards the

man who'd been speaking outside. Being meek and cowering would serve me no purpose here. "I'd like to speak with him."

"So willing to serve the crown, eh?" His lip curled up in a sneer.

"I am willing to save my family, whatever be the cost."

His eyes narrowed for a moment as he sucked at his teeth. I refused to look away, refused to back down from the silent judgement. I would save Emyl and Rhyon, even if I had to drag this entire kingdom down with me to do so.

Whatever he saw in my face passed his inspection, and wordlessly he stepped aside, raising his chin towards the back corner of the pub. The castle's pageboy was sitting there in the shadows, barely visible from the light of the candles in the center of the table.

Ash coated my tongue and my ears filled with that incessant buzzing noise—my only warning before a swarm of flickering mist began to solidify at my side. My jaw clicked. Even here, I could not escape the Soulshades vying for my attention. I hurried over to the table, keeping my eyes straight ahead.

"Can I help you, young lady?" The man looked both up at me yet down his nose at the same time. "I'm quite busy."

"Oh?" I bit my tongue to hold back the rest of the sharp remark and pressed the words into my cheek in favor of a more palatable response. "I heard the prince was looking for new staff. I'd like to volunteer and was told to find you."

He studied me for a long moment over the rim of his mug. A part of me hoped he would find me lacking in some way and send me back home. Then at least I could tell my brothers that I had tried to do it their way, and I wasn't good enough for the prince.

"Why?" He put his mug down and laced his fingers together. "This city seemed content to turn to conscription. Yet you are here. Why?"

"My family needs to eat." Perhaps I should have added some emotion to my voice, but truly, there was little else I could say, and little reason to lie. Was he expecting me to say that I'd longed my entire life to be locked inside a gilded cage with an egotistical child for a prince? Hardly.

He chuffed a laugh, leaning back in his seat. "Quite right, I suppose."

"So?" *Tell me no. Tell me no. Tell me no.*

"Seeing as how you've been our only volunteer thus far, I suppose you will have to do." He stood from the table, picking up and draining his mug, smacking his lips as he set it back down. He clapped his hands. "Well? Shall we?"

I barely stopped the shock that nearly jolted my body. "Now? You said tomorrow."

"Well, yes, for those conscripted. You can go now to the castle." He raised an eyebrow at me, pursing his lips. "Unless you had something more important to attend to."

I looked back over my shoulder, as if I could see all the way back to my house and inside to wherever my brothers were. Biting my lip, I swayed on my feet. I'd not been able to say goodbye to them, and though I doubted very much they would wish to speak with me now, it still hurt. It still tore what was surely left of my soul into pieces.

Both would likely forget me, if not from the passing of time, then by choice. I could not say which would be worse.

I turned back to the man, rolling my shoulders back. There was no use in lingering. Emyl had made his choice quite clear, and if there was one thing we had in common, it was that once our minds were made up, there'd be no changing them. "No, I am ready."

His eyes narrowed and he raised a finger to point at my neck. "You survived?"

I refused to blush, refused to show any shame for surviving this hell. I kept my chin raised. "Yes. Is that a problem?"

As he stroked his chin, he let out a hum. "No, no, it shouldn't be any issue. There are other survivors on the staff." He clapped his hands once more, and I could not stop the flinch that time. "Let's be off then."

From the shadows on either side of the table, two guards stepped out, flanking us as the man turned sharply on his heel and made way for the back entrance of the pub. No more words were uttered as I followed them out of the pub and back into the streets of the city.

Each step through the winding streets was like a knife in my stomach. A reminder that I had failed at the one thing my mother asked of me. I couldn't dream of protecting my brothers while I was sequestered inside the dark hold of Castle Auretras. Maybe, if luck was on my side, I would be able to see our home from one of the windows. But I'd not been in the graces of fate thus far in my life, so expecting that to change was for naught.

I was alone. At least they had each other.

I could only hope Mother would forgive me. That somewhere in the afterlife, she would see that this was my only choice, and she would approve. If ever there was a time for a Soulshade to appear, I wanted it to be now, and I wanted it to be my mother. It was selfish, but I did not care.

Running into the back of the pageboy was my only clue that he had stopped.

"Do not speak unless spoken to. Do not make eye contact with anyone." He paused and looked me over head to toe. "Do you understand?"

I nodded. As he turned back around, I fortified the walls around my heart, around my mind, around my soul. Brick by brick, I sealed off my emotions, letting myself turn into a mere statue of a person, one unaffected by anything. Emotionless. Blank.

My mother had always told me that my forced apathy wasn't the solution to my consuming anger. One extreme was not the solution to another, and that for someone who felt everything so strongly, I would only be making things worse when those emotions finally broke through. She'd said I needed to find balance if I was to thrive in this world.

But my mother was gone, and this was all I had. This was my only weapon in this battle.

It would keep me alive.

CHAPTER SIX

The gates in front of me stood tall, laden with twisted wrought-iron bars that spanned the vertical length. At the tops and bottoms, sharp and glittering gilded spires thrust up towards the heavy iron bar that stretched across it. The guards heaved the bar up, and those immaculately gilded gates opened with a silence that shouldn't have been possible. The pageboy bowed, stretching his arm to invite me inside first.

"What have you brought me, Corbyn?" Pin-straight lengths of dark hair fell to frame the softly rounded face of the woman who crowded us before we could even step entirely through the gate. She reached forward and grabbed my chin, her long fingernails digging into the skin. I kept my eyes down and let her move my head from side to side.

She tipped my head back and tutted, pushing my face away rather than just releasing it. My stomach flipped, churning as I tried to keep from cowering in the face of that disappointed tone.

"She's marked. Visibly and far more than any of the others have been. What am I supposed to do with this? They'll think she's bad luck." She pointed her finger at me. "You. Take off your cloak."

"She can still work, Camelya," replied the man who'd brought me here. He did not look like a Corbyn to me; he carried himself too highly to have such a common name. "That was my instruction."

"See if he'll ever let you out again," she muttered. The woman snapped her fingers at me. "Off, girl."

I followed Camelya's instructions, counting the stone pavers at her feet as I undid the button at my throat to keep from looking up and meeting her eye. I was too slow, apparently, and she ripped the cloak from my hands and shoved my hair off my neck. She hummed as she inspected me, reaching out to yank my sleeves up and my neckline down.

She pushed the cloak back into my hands. "Disgusting marks, they are. But I suppose we will find a way to cover them. Your veil should do most of it. And perhaps we can get you gloves." She hummed again, and I could hear her nails clicking on her teeth as she tapped them. My blood simmered in my veins, but I forced myself to let her words slide off me like water over oil. Nothing she could say would hurt me. "You'll do. What's your name, girl?"

"Odyssa." The unsaid words, the ones protesting being called *girl,* sat heavy on my tongue, though if one cared to listen closely enough, they could hear it in my voice. Neither Camelya nor Corbyn cared enough. This was my chance to save my brothers, and my temper would not ruin things for them. For me.

"You'll do," she repeated.

I knew better than to ask what I would do *for.*

Her hand wrapped around my wrist, the delicate bones shifting beneath her tight grip as she hauled me down a corridor and further into the castle. I grimaced, but managed to catch any noise before it could escape.

Behind me, I heard the gates slam shut and the bars descend across them, sealing it once more. I'd thought my home was a tomb, but it was nothing compared to this. Castle Auretras would be my grave, and those jutting spires my headstone. I was sure of it.

My fool of a brother had just signed all three of our death notices. But at least we would be with our mother again soon.

I was ushered through hall after hall, winding deeper into the depths of the castle with every step. Stone walls arched around me, and even these insignificant basement halls were adorned with more wealth than I could have hoped to see in my lifetime. A feeling I couldn't put a name on rose up from the pit of my stomach, oily and hot as it curled around my spine and simmered in the back of my throat.

Each gilded frame, each alcove table groaning under the weight of fresh flowers, golden candlestick holders, and heavy iron sculptures, every symbol of wealth the woman herded me past was a reminder. He who elected to waste money decorating a musty corner in some forgotten hallway was the same as he who sat idle as his kingdom transformed into a charnel ground.

I would not forget why I was here. I could not afford to.

Thunder boomed in the distance, rattling a vase on the table as we passed. Something flickered in the corner of my eye beneath the table, a shadow that was there and then gone before I'd truly had a chance to see it. Nonetheless, it sent chills down my spine and raised the hairs on my arms. The taste of smoke was absent, but I could feel someone watching me despite no one else being in the hall.

"Do you know... you... here?" The woman hurled the question over her shoulder at me, not deigning to slow her pace at all, nor release my wrist. I only caught part of the words, the stone swallowing them up before I could hear them, but I had already grown used to having to fill in the gaps and I knew what she was asking.

I tore my eyes from the shadowed corners of the halls and returned my attention to the woman tugging me down the hallways towards my doom.

To find the cure and kill the prince and save my brothers from certain death. "To be a member of Prince Eadric's staff."

She snorted, the noise buzzing in my ears and settling deep into my chest in the gaping hole my brothers had left behind. The dismissal was clear as she turned back around, and while it sparked a familiar ember of anger at the back of my tongue, ready to spit and lash out, I swallowed it back. It met with the oily feeling of *something* that still clung to my throat, the anger joining the patiently waiting emotions there.

Gods help us all when whatever it was finally exploded.

"Where are you taking me?" Each word was carefully neutral, as dull and uninteresting as the mask I'd forced upon my face.

A more substantial shadow passed by the wall, walking low along the floor. It almost looked like an animal, the shadow of a cat or dog, but it was *wrong*. Too long and too angular to be either of those things. And then it was gone before I could search it out again. My heart raced against my breastbone. Was this creature part of the castle, or had it followed me in? I wasn't sure I wanted to know the answer. I swallowed hard as I focused back in on Camelya.

"The servant quarters. You'll need to be bathed, measured, and clothed. Then the other girls will prepare you for your first night."

I pulled to a stop, twisting my hand out of her grip to wrap my fingers around her wrist. The shadowy creature was long forgotten. My voice was deadly calm and as far from neutral as it could have possibly been. I knew better to ask, and yet I could not stop myself any longer. "First night doing *what*, precisely?"

She looked down at where I now held her wrist before bringing her eyes back to mine with a raised eyebrow. "So you do have a spine after all."

"I have far more than that, if need be."

"I would be cautious who else you let discover that." A heartbeat passed and then a smirk played at her lips, erasing the ominous expression that accompanied her first words. "But not to worry, you were only hired as a servant for the parties, not as entertainment."

I searched her face for any hint of a lie. Finding none, I slowly released my hold on her wrist.

There was little I would not do for my family, even though my brothers had disowned me, but my body was my own. It had been ripped apart by the blood plague and patched back together with the marks this woman had called disgusting. But it was *mine*, and only I decided what to do with it. "Good."

We continued down the halls, the only sounds our shoes against the stone and the distant claps of thunder. The atmosphere had shifted between us, now that I had let part of my mask fall. I wasn't entirely sure if it was a good thing or not.

Eventually, she came to a stop in front of a relatively plain-looking door. "This is the dressing room. You will have your own bedroom, which one of the girls will take you to later, but all the preparations for each evening are done here together. It's easier if you all get ready at the same time."

My stomach twisted itself into knots, but despite it, I forced a nod. I did not want to make friends, did not want to interact with anyone more than I had to. I was here to find how to save my brothers, kill the prince, and get the hell out. But I could not dismiss any potential advantage, coming in as an outsider. Perhaps these girls would be able to help me, whether they were privy to it or not.

The door opened and four pairs of eyes turned in my direction from inside the room. All activity paused, the other women freezing as Camelya stepped in, all but dragging me beside her.

"This is Odyssa," she introduced, giving me a slight shove on my lower back to step forward. "She'll be joining you all."

I nodded a greeting, not trusting my words to come out steady. I wanted to vomit, to run away and bang on the gates that had locked me in here, begging to be released. But there was no turning back now. This was the path I had chosen, and despite how little of a true choice it was, I would follow through. I had nothing left to lose. If I failed, my brothers would likely die regardless.

Silence met us, along with heavy stares that would have made me duck my head in another life. In this life, though, I did not care about their opinions, about their judgements. I cared about nothing apart from doing my work to send money back to my brothers and finding the treatment the Coward Prince had refused to share.

They could think whatever they liked of me. I was not here to make friends.

One of the women finally moved, setting down a hairbrush on the vanity in front of her and standing. Her strides were smooth and confident as she stopped in front of me and stuck her hand out. Across her skin were dark marks—delicate, unlike my own—that reminded me of a lightning strike stretched across the sky. She stared at me. "I am Zaharya."

I extended my own hand slowly. Again, my movements were too slow for the women in Castle Auretras, and she reached out with a huff and grabbed it, shaking it roughly before letting it fall again.

"Where are you from?" Her voice was smooth, no hint of fear or apprehension of Camelya still standing beside me.

"The city," I replied. I cleared my throat. Though my voice had not cracked, there was a weight of *something* at the back of my tongue, oppressive and uncomfortable. "You have Death marks."

She tilted her head, making the curtain of thick white hair fall over her shoulder. "You call them Death marks down in the city?"

"I—"

"Well, now that introductions are handled, ladies, please get Odyssa ready. She will just be observing tonight, but tomorrow she'll be serving, so be sure to prepare her." Camelya clapped her hands again and whirled out the door, closing it behind her before I'd even really had a chance to comprehend her instructions. My ears throbbed, still reeling from her loud clapping.

My head was swimming with emotion and thoughts, all tangled up in knots as I tried desperately to unwind them, though I knew better than to let it show. Instead, I looked out at the other girls in the room. None of them seemed harmed in any way, and though none of them were especially joyful, equally none of them seemed overtly melancholy. I did not want to know their names, but I knew I needed to remember their faces. Zaharya had white hair, bright like moonlight. There was also a tall blonde, one with hair like flames that seemed to want to make herself look as small as possible, and one with black hair like mine but with eyes that shone like sapphires.

Silence still reigned over the room, all of us watching each other and waiting for someone else to say the next words. It would not be me, that much I knew. So I stood in the middle of the room while the four other women studied me. Some of them seemed as if they were searching for any sign of weakness, but I knew they'd find none. I'd perfected the wall that hid my emotions well.

"Do you have any other clothes?"

I blinked, turning my gaze to the woman with ringlets the color of honey that cascaded over her shoulders and down her back of smooth, unblemished skin. She stood only a few inches taller than me but held herself as if she were towering above us all. I longed for that kind of confidence to take up space in the world.

It took a moment for her words to register and I looked down at myself, at the plain clothing I'd left the house in. I looked back up, taking in her own black silk dressing gown. "I was not allowed time to go back for any of my things."

"Pity," she replied, scrunching her nose up. She turned around to face her own vanity, brushing her hair back and pinning the sides up.

I bit my tongue.

"Pay no mind to Maricara. You don't need anything else truly," Zaharya said, waving her hand. She walked around behind me, putting her hands on my shoulders and guiding me towards the chair she'd been sitting in at the vanity. "Talyssa, can you go get her a dress and a veil? I'll start on her hair."

At her command, a petite woman with elegant waves of burnished copper hair that brushed against her freckled collarbones stood from where she had been tucked away in the corner, moving to a large wardrobe along the far wall. She bent and began pulling bundles of fabric out.

Beside the wardrobe, shadows flickered again. This time, though, eyes appeared, bright yellow in the gaping darkness. I blinked and they disappeared. Zaharya squeezed my shoulder. "Are you alright? You look frightened."

My heart skipped a beat at how easily she touched me, at how there was no hesitation in her movements as she swept my hair away from my neck and traced her finger over the swirling marks there.

She did not wait for me to reply to her question. "Yours are much bigger than mine."

Dread curled up my spine, an eerie feeling falling over me. I'd only heard of other survivors, heard of the marks that the plague left upon our skin. I'd never seen another's marks up close, never had been with anyone other than my family after the plague set in. But why would mine be normal, after all? I was a freak of nature, and apparently, this would be no different. Smoke curled against the back of my tongue and I fought to keep my eyes off the flickering mass of shadows in the corner. The eyes had not reappeared, but I could feel them on me, watching.

"Where are you from?" I asked, raising my eyes to meet hers in the mirror in front of us. The hair on the back of my neck stood on end and a chill swept down my spine. I wanted to run, to squeeze my eyes shut and pretend I was not seeing anything. I wanted to ask if she saw the Soulshades, too, but at the same time, I did not want to hear her say she did not. "You said you don't call them Death marks?"

"I'm from a small village outside of Jura called Konorya," she said, tangling her fingers into my hair and picking up strands of my thick, dark waves. "And they mean you did *not* die, so why would we call them Death marks? They are just marks. What does it matter how you got them?"

"Here, they mean you should get as far away from me as possible."

Zaharya hummed.

"How are they seen in the castle?" I jerked my head toward the door. "Camelya seemed displeased I was marked."

"There are others marked in the castle."

I waited for her to elaborate, but she did not. I had attended to enough of the wealthy alongside my mother that I knew the words she left unsaid. There were others, yes, but Camelya's reaction would be the norm.

The room was tense still, though some of it had started to ease around the woman weaving my hair away from my face and neck. One side of me wanted to ask about the others, to introduce myself and get to know these women I would be with, but the other part of me wanted nothing to do with any of them. Forming connections, emotional attachments, *friendships*, with any of them would only end poorly. As much as I longed for closeness, I could never have it.

"Here," the one with black hair said, coming over to us and draping the two bundles of fabric Talyssa had retrieved across a nearby chair. She leaned her hip against the vanity, looking down at me with an unreadable expression. "I am Elena. Did Camelya tell you what you'll be doing?"

I was beginning to grow tired of that question, of everyone passing me off to someone else to explain. "She said you all would." I pulled away slightly from Zaharya and turned around to look at both of them. "Please. I am here to work with you for the foreseeable future. Tell me what I'll be doing."

Zaharya sighed, moving to the other side of the vanity and resting her back against it as she crossed her arms. "If you live in Jura, no doubt you hear the parties every night. We attend to them. We serve the drinks, take away the empty glasses, do whatever is needed to ensure the guests are enjoying themselves. Tonight, you'll only be observing."

"And tomorrow, you will be helping us," Elena added. "It's quite simple, though."

"So we're to ensure they're having a wonderful time at the party while the city beneath them chokes on its own blood."

"See? You understand perfectly."

A whisper of something almost like a laugh came from the shadows at my feet. Even the Soulshades were amused by me, apparently.

CHAPTER SEVEN

"This is the last part," Zaharya murmured, lifting the sheer midnight-blue fabric. I couldn't stop the flinch as she raised her hands over my head, which had her frowning as I cursed my reaction. "I won't hurt you, Odyssa. It's a veil; we are not to have our faces visible during the parties."

I nodded, clenching my fists into the sides of the dress. It was silly, the flinch. I knew she would not strike me, and yet my body still had the memory of Emyl's hand meeting my skin. I'd have to do better.

With a wary eye, she resumed her path and draped the fabric over my head, adjusting it so it fell neatly over my face. I almost wondered what the point of the dress was, given that the veil covered me from the top of my head to nearly my feet. While it certainly bathed my vision in blue, it was easier to see out of than I'd expected. It still felt *wrong* to be wearing it. It felt like a burial shroud rather than a veil.

Perhaps it was.

"Now you are ready," Zaharya said, stepping back to pull her own veil over her body.

I did not feel ready in the least, but there was little choice. I nodded again.

"You'll be at my side for this first night. Stay close, don't linger anywhere too long, and don't speak to anyone," Zaharya said. We left the dressing room as a group and now walked side by side down another set of long hallways. I studied each turn, expanding the map in my head as I dutifully ignored the shadow along the floor that kept pace with us as we walked.

I smelled smoke, and this time I was not fast enough to look away before the Soulshade solidified. A woman appeared, and she was dressed not dissimilarly to me. She reached her hand out towards me, silent sobs shaking her shoulders. Her face never convalesced into clarity, but I also could not bring myself to look at her for long enough to truly tell.

Zaharya did not react, did not break her stride. She did not see the Soulshade. I could not tell if the feeling racing through my veins was disappointment or ease.

I focused my eyes on Elena's back in front of me, on the waves of copper bouncing with each step beneath the veil of blue. The taste of smoke faded along with the apparition, and I let my shoulders relax only slightly. Soulshades were not the only danger here, and vigilance could be the difference between life and death. Mine and my brothers'.

Finally, we reached a small kitchen. Set off into the walls as if an afterthought to the original design, it was barely functional, yet the countertops that lined three sides of the alcove were sparkling stone. No expense was spared, even on tiny kitchens, it seemed. Trays of delicate stemmed glasses and small finger foods were already waiting atop the counters when we entered.

Without a word, Elena, Maricara, and Talyssa each picked up a tray, turning to leave the small space. Their movements were effortless, unhindered by the draping yards of sheer fabric that obscured them from view. Every glance at one of these women, every glimpse of the veils, made my anger gnaw at my spine, growing the pit in my belly. Anger at the prince for hiding us away, for wasting the money on yards of expensive fabric to cover those he deemed beneath him, anger that we were here at all.

Smoke burst across my tongue again, bitter and acrid as saliva pooled in my mouth. I swallowed roughly and tried to look away as the mist flickered once, twice, thrice, by Zaharya's foot. She looked down momentarily before returning her focus to her own tray.

"Do you see that?" I blurted, cursing myself for not being able to hold my tongue. She'd reacted to it, though, unlike with the woman in the hallway.

"See what?" The veils, both hers and mine, prevented me from truly seeing the expression on her face, but they did not hide the suspicion in her voice.

I pointed down by her feet where the shadowy mass had solidified into the form of a large black cat. It sat there, looking up at me with wide yellow eyes and slowly swishing its too-long tail. "That."

She looked down again. "There's nothing there, Odyssa. I just thought I felt something."

The blood in my veins turned to ice. I looked down at the cat again, who blinked at me and then slowly, so slowly, arched its back, stretching in a way that was so wholly unnatural I could not drag my gaze away. It contorted, seeming to grow longer as it stretched, its back reaching higher and higher. Finally, it stopped, settling back down into a sitting position where it lifted its paw and began licking. Its tongue was forked.

I blinked and scuttled away, my back hitting the counter and sending a glass crashing to the floor. The cat merely blinked again at the glass before disappearing.

"What is wrong with you?" Zaharya hissed, stooping to pick up the shards of glass.

"There was…" I shook my head, unable to complete the sentence. There was no way for me to describe what I saw without being labeled insane. "I thought I saw something."

She huffed a laugh as she dropped the broken glass into a nearby bin. "What? Did you see a ghost?"

My silence lingered a moment too long.

Her eyes widened. "Truly, did you see a Soulshade?"

I nodded slowly, lifting my arms up beneath the shroud to wrap around myself in anticipation of her answer. "It looked like a cat. But I've seen others here too."

She recovered quickly, stepping up closer until our fronts were almost touching. "I would keep that to yourself, Odyssa."

"What do you mean by that?" The question was out before I could stop it. "And can you not see them?"

"This castle has secrets, Odyssa. Ones it does not want you to learn. I advise you to not go searching for them." Her warning was ominous, made worse by the fear visible in the whites of her eyes, bright even obscured by the veils. "And no, I cannot see them."

"Do you know why I can?"

She titled her head, looking a bit like a doll in the long veil that moved with her. "Likely the marks, I would presume. You came close to death, closer than I perhaps, and now you can see those who have passed on."

My tongue felt like it weighed a thousand pounds.

"How many have you seen?" She lifted her hands and spread them out. "Here, around the castle. How many Soulshades have you seen?"

"Just two so far. But there are far more in Jura."

She let out a long breath. "Well, don't go looking for any more. I mean it."

"Do the other girls have marks? Is there anyone else in the castle who has fallen ill while here and survived?" I hoped the widening of my eyes would aid in selling the innocent curiosity. I hoped the shroud would aid even more.

Silence fell over us and a chill ran down my spine like spectral fingers.

"Odyssa—"

Clanging from down the hall interrupted whatever she had been about to say. I wanted to curse whoever it was, but when Talyssa, the one with eyes like sapphires and hair like burnished copper, entered the room, already seeming to curl in on herself, I couldn't find it in me to be cross with her. I wanted to reach out, to reassure her that I meant her no harm, but I couldn't bring myself to speak. I needed that comfort for myself, I supposed.

"I apologize for interrupting, but Zaharya, we need you down there." Talyssa kept her hands clasped in front of her, her head bowed as she spoke.

"Come, Odyssa," Zaharya said, pushing back into standing. "Take one of those trays and follow my lead."

My heart thundered against my rib cage, but I wiped my damp palms on my dress and reached through the slits in the sides of the shroud.

"Wait." Her hand came out to rest on my wrist and I barely caught the flinch in time, pushing it back down into my bones before it could escape. Her touch lightened, along with her voice. "You did nothing wrong. Be calm. We need to find you gloves to cover your marks first, that's all."

I wanted to ask why they needed to be covered, why they should have to be hidden when they meant I had survived. But I said nothing, nodding instead. The prince, too concerned with his parties to even set his own coronation, would not want that reminder of the suffering he left his people to.

Moments later, my hands and arms were covered up the

elbow in lace gloves so intricate you could not tell the underlying swirls of my marks from the design of the lace. Beneath the shroud, it would be impossible to see the difference.

With my Death marks now appropriately covered, Zaharya placed a tray filled with small pastries in my hands and adjusted her own shroud before leading me out of the kitchen.

I felt the music long before I heard it, the deep notes vibrating in my bones and shaking the tray as we neared. As we entered the ballroom, I was grateful for the willpower I'd cultivated over the years. My steps did not falter and the tray did not shake in my hands, even as my mouth opened slightly and my eyes widened to take in the scene before me. The awe quickly faded and my mouth clamped shut, the vein in my forehead throbbing once more. Smoke washed over my tongue, and I kept my focus on Zaharya's back.

The midnight-blue material that covered us was clearly not a standard uniform but specifically chosen for tonight. It matched the room perfectly. The ceiling of the long arching ballroom was clearly intended to be the centerpiece of the room, adorned with swathes of deep, midnight-blue velvet drapes that cascaded down the walls, creating the illusion of a starlit sky as the room stretched out on either side of a large, raised platform, arching down on either side.

My eyes followed the fabric down to the walls, embellished with intricate tapestries embroidered with depictions of some of Veressia's gods—Kalyx, god of Death; Ratka, goddess of war; and Jaryk, god of the wilds—their likenesses interwoven with silver and gold threads that caught the light and gleamed like distant stars. Tall candelabras stood sentinel in corners, their flickering flames casting dancing shadows.

The floor, polished to a glossy obsidian sheen, reflected the starry ceiling above, and at the center of the room, a sprawling black marble dance floor, encircled by ornate wrought-iron railings resembling twisted branches.

It was beautiful. It was horrific. I could not decide how to react.

"There you are; I'm starved!" A man's deep voice behind me made me startle, but I kept hold of the tray. "Good god, you're a skittish one, aren't you? Best not let the prince see, hmm?" He swept nearly all the pastries into his large palm and spun away, disappearing back into the fray.

My anger spiked at the careless indifference of the man, and I bit down hard on my tongue to keep from responding. Already, I was threatening to break the rules Zaharya had given me. I stood there, watching as the other revelers followed suit of the man, smiling and laughing with each other as the music picked up, spitting out a lively tune. People began dancing as they laughed, entirely unhindered as they twirled around, ignorant of the bloodbath occurring just below their gilded walls.

Zaharya had moved away, now standing at one of the long tables that spanned the sides of the room. With one last glance at the growing crowd, I rushed to her side. She raised her head at my approach. "You may be wearing a veil, but you need to be mindful of your expressions, Odyssa," she murmured, resuming her task of setting out glasses on the velvet tablecloth.

I hurried to help her, ducking my head to hide my face from any curious stares.

She stretched her hand out from her veil, setting it on mine to still my movements. "I know how you feel. You cannot show it here, though."

"It's horrible," I murmured, pulling my hand away from hers and continuing to set out the items on our trays. All these people, easily numbering a thousand, were reveling in the opulence and wealth while their kingdom suffocated. It was obscene.

"It is."

"Why does he do this? Why won't he take the throne and help his people?"

"You shouldn't ask such questions where anyone can overhear." Her words were barely more than a whisper, but I heard the caution in them. An unspoken warning, and one I both appreciated and cursed. I needed information, and I could not get that by being cautious.

We lapsed into silence as we unloaded the last of the trays before she led me around the room to collect the already empty glasses from those attendees. Wine was certainly not in short supply here inside the castle, not as it was down in the heart of Veressia. Down there, outside these walls, everything was in short supply, including hope and joy. Yet, here, as with everything else, it thrived in abundance.

Zaharya appeared at my side suddenly, thrusting her own tray full of empty glasses into my hand along with my own. She leaned in close to me, her eyes flicking about the rest of the room. "Get back to the kitchens now. The prince is coming, and you should not be here for that now. You will not be able to school your reactions to him." I stood there clutching the trays, frozen, my eyes still fixed on the crowd of crooning and celebratory revelers. "Odyssa," she hissed, finally pulling my gaze to her. "Go. Now."

The sharpness of her words pierced through the haze of my stupor and I nodded once, before making my escape to the small door at the back of the room. She was right; if I was unable to school my features well enough in reaction to the prince's chosen partygoers, I certainly would not be able to control myself in the face of the Coward Prince himself.

I fully intended to go back to the kitchens, but the smoke burned my throat and my steps faltered. The cat reappeared, sitting directly at my feet. It looked up at me, tilting its head before turning and walking away. Only a few steps away, it looked back over its shoulder, once again revealing just how *wrong* it was as its head was nearly completely backwards looking at me.

"Am I to follow you?" I asked, the words coming out on a disbelieving breath.

If a cat could smile, that one did.

I followed the cat down the hall and up a short staircase until we stopped in front of another small alcove. Unlike the ones deep in the tunnels, this one had a balcony overlooking the ballroom, though it and the alcove were both cloaked in shadow and set in the back of the room. No one would see me up here from the ballroom below, and I would be free to watch them as I wished.

The cat leapt up onto the balcony handrail with ease, turning her back to the party.

A trickle of sweat rolled down my spine as I set the trays down on a small table nestled in the corner and stepped up to the balcony next to the cat. I wanted to rip the shroud from my body, to tear away the gloves. It was all so suffocating, the fabric heavy and itchy.

"Oh, little friend," a deep male voice cooed. I tensed, my eyes flicking about the alcove, but no one was there. "What are you doing here this evening?"

The feline equivalent of an eyeroll followed the rumbling voice, the cat sending me a look of exasperation that should not have been possible. And with that, the cat disappeared.

Rushing to the balcony where she'd been, my hands wrapped around the wood, the lace of my gloves scratching against my skin. I searched for the cat, but there was nothing. No flickering mist and no burning smoke on the back of my tongue.

A metallic glimmer caught my eye down on the ballroom floor. In the corner of the room stood a man dressed in all black, seemingly ignoring the theme for the night, as the rest of the partygoers were in outfits that were over the top and elaborate interpretations of the night sky. His outfit was simple comparatively. A black coat with silver buttons running up the front of it over a black shirt and fitted black trousers tucked into black boots.

The top of his face was obscured by a mask in the image of a skull, but one that had been dipped in molten silver, catching the light and casting shadows across his sharp jawline.

He stood out for more than just his attire, too, as he was the only one not dancing. Instead he stood, studying the rest of the room with a frown upon his lips. Others gave him a wide berth, dancers avoiding the bubble around him as if there were a physical barrier around him. One couple stumbled as they neared him, hands tightening on each other as they passed back into the crowd.

The small act of rebellion against the apparent norm of the ball was appreciated, but regardless of if he was enjoying himself or not, his presence here meant one thing and one thing only. He was friends with the prince, and that meant he would not be any friend of mine.

As if he felt my stare on him, his head turned and he looked up, directly at me. The frown morphed, pulling up at the corners of his lips into a crooked smirk. The smirk grew slowly as he watched me, pushing off the wall completely and turning his whole body to face me. Even from here, I could see the white of his teeth as his smirk morphed into a full-blown smile.

Every muscle in my body froze, and I was unable to look away. It was impossible. Surely he could not see me, not through the shadows I was cloaked in and the distance between us. Perhaps he felt someone looking at him, but he should not have been able to look up and find me with such immediacy. Yet he had.

"Well, who are you, little wolf?" The voice sounded as if it were right beside me, but there was no one. There was no taste of smoke and ash on my tongue, no feeling of a body beside mine. My eyes still fixed on him, I watched the masked man's lips move in time with the words I heard beside me. I felt the words on my ear, his breath washing over the side of my neck, sending shivers down my spine that I was not sure were entirely from fear. "Not to worry, I'll find out for myself soon enough."

The gasp left me before I could stop it, and I clutched at my chest and staggered back, trying to keep from making another sound. I could see him laughing down below, and for a split second, I wondered what it would sound like as his head tipped back and he raised his glass in my direction.

Picking up the ends of the fabric that kissed the floor, I whirled and all but ran back to the safety of the kitchen. An illusion I knew, given how the man had spoken to me, but my choices were limited, and at least I could convince myself otherwise for a moment.

CHAPTER EIGHT

The party continued until the sun rose, casting rays of red-tinged gold to illuminate the shame peddled in this godsforsaken place. Thankfully, I had little time to ponder the masked stranger after our first encounter. From the moment I burst back into the kitchen, I was busy. Cleaning trays and refilling them, assisting where I could, and listening to instructions barked from the others on what to remember, how to act, and who to avoid.

I would have done anything to avoid going back to the ballroom, to avoid being in the same room as him. Even the memory of his wide smile, of his breath against my ear, sent chills down my spine, and not the sensual kind. There was something as wrong with that man as there was with the cat he clearly knew.

It was a good reminder to not become complacent. Though the girls had been pleasant enough, I was on unfamiliar ground, in a castle of people who would likely watch me die for entertainment before they would lift a finger to offer any assistance. My mother needed me to focus, to remember why I was here. My brothers hated me, but I would ensure their survival. If there was a cure in this godsforsaken place, I would find it and I would get it to Rhyon and Emyl. Spite and fury fueled me, and behind my mask, behind my walls, I could embrace that.

I was ready to fall asleep where I stood, my eyelids heavy and drooping. But we had to clean the kitchens before we could sleep so that the day staff could begin their own tasks. All that remained was to gather any remaining drinkware from the ballroom.

Zaharya had nominated the two of us for the task, wanting to show me the ballroom in the predawn light.

It was far different in the golden sunrise than in the dark of night, illuminated by extravagant chandeliers and candelabras that now lay dormant. In the day, it was cavernous. Every sound echoed off the walls.

Glasses and crumbs were everywhere in the ballroom, strewn aside and discarded with little care. I should have expected it, given the lack of care the revelers exhibited towards the rest of the suffering kingdom, but the sight of the glasses twinkling in the rising sun had my fists clenching at my sides.

At least we did not have to hide beneath the veils any longer.

The prince and his ilk had retreated to their rooms as the sun had just begun to lighten the sky, the skull-masked stranger along with them. It was only the two of us in here now, and only the sound of tinkling shards of glass and hard crumbs of food being tossed into wastebins filled the ballroom.

"Where did all these people come from?" I picked up a pair of unbroken glasses, inspecting them for any cracks before setting them on the tray to be washed and reused for tonight.

"For the parties?" Zaharya did not pause from her own tasks, did not raise her eyes from the floor. She continued before I could answer. "Oh, royal advisors, friends of the king, friends of the prince. When the mist settled and they realized what it was, they pulled everyone in here for safety and planning supposedly. And then they just never left again."

"And why must we be veiled during the parties?" It wasn't a smooth transition, but I was counting on her work distracting her enough to keep from noticing.

"If they cannot see our faces, they do not have to treat us as human, now do they?" Her words were a whisper. Still, she worked and did not look up at me.

"There was a man last night," I started, trying to get the words right to get the information I needed without raising any suspicion. "He wore a mask like a skull. Do you know who he is?"

"He is the prince's right hand." Her eyes snapped up to mine, searching my face intently. Her shoulders seemed to relax as she found whatever it was she was looking for. "I will warn you now, as I have warned the others. Do not forget the people who are here, are here for a reason. And that reason is that they matter enough to the prince to offer them safe harbor in these walls. They do not care about you, Odyssa, and they never will. None of them. You cannot forget that for a moment."

"You don't need to worry. That will never leave my mind. I know why I am here, and why they are here. I was merely curious."

"You know what they say about curiosity." She paused a beat, her lip quirking up. "Maybe that's how your Soulshade cat died."

Despite my best efforts, a smile made its way onto my face as well. Zaharya had a way about her—it put me at ease despite all my defenses. I needed to be wary of it, to keep her at arm's length. I did not need her death on my heart, did not need her memory to carve another pit in my soul.

"There are rumors that no one here has ever caught ill. Are they true?"

Glass fell heavily into the waste bin and the laughter that

had lit up her eyes was gone, replaced by an altogether blank stare I knew far too well. She'd donned her mask, and I'd pushed too far. "Mind your words, Odyssa. The walls have ears, and they hunger for our secrets."

We completed the rest of our tasks in silence, cleaning and resetting the kitchens for the next ball. As we worked, I watched them, studying how they interacted with each other. Talyssa was skittish, flinching whenever someone made too loud a noise or accidentally brushed against her. Elena and Maricara worked seamlessly, even without speaking, and were obviously close. Zaharya was more challenging to understand though, which made me even more determined to puzzle her out.

"How did you all come to work here?" I did not truly want to know. The last thing I needed here was to make connections, to pave the way for grief to tear me to shreds when I inevitably lost one or all of them. But knowledge was power, and I needed all the advantage I could get to stay alive in this tomb. "Did you volunteer?"

Maricara slammed down the tray she'd been polishing. "Why would anyone *volunteer* to come to this prison? We were taken from our families, sent here and forced to work for a prince who cares more about the silver spoon in his hand than our lives."

I blinked at her. Perhaps I had found an unexpected ally in the fight against the Coward Prince.

"Did *you* volunteer?"

"Yes, I did."

She made a harsh sound at the back of her throat, like she was gargling with rocks. Her cheeks reddened and her chest rose and fell more prominently. "It will not make him notice you, you know?"

"Who? The cow—the prince? I could hardly care if he does or not." Truthfully, I also hardly cared to stand here explaining myself and my reasons either, but isolating myself from the only people I'd likely be interacting with during my stay here was far from wise. I kept my body loose and remained pressed against the wall rather than tensing up and invading her space like my bones screamed at me to do. My voice was even, a rarity when my anger began to crack through the walls. "I care that my mother died, and my younger brothers would have starved. There are no jobs in Jura that would pay enough to support us all. Except this one. *That* is why I volunteered."

"I hope you said goodbye to them before you left." A wave of blonde hair twisted in the air as she turned and left the room.

She was fortunate she'd left the room when she did, or I likely would have said something I'd regret later. At least that was one less person I had to worry about forming a friendship with.

"We were all conscripted," Talyssa added, her voice plucking softly through the tension in the room and pulling my attention to her. Her frown etched lines into her skin. "Maricara had to leave behind her daughter when she was brought here."

Bile soured in my throat.

"We all left something behind," Zaharya said. "Some of us more than others."

The others nodded their agreement.

"Now, shall we finish up here and get some rest? I think we've certainly earned it."

Our work was finished quickly, and though it was not silent, it was clear we were all treading carefully. Maricara had still not returned by the time we were finished. No one else seemed concerned by it, but I was. Had I been less tired, I might have inquired after her, might have tried to track down where she had gone. But I hardly had the energy to keep my body upright. Investigating the prickly blonde would have to wait until this evening.

Zaharya showed me to my room, and I tried to map the turns in my head, to sear the image of my new door and bedroom into my mind, but truthfully, I could not say what any of it looked like. My eyelids were heavy and my vision bleary from lack of sleep and the utter exhaustion seeping into my bones, and as soon as she closed the door behind her, I collapsed into the plush bedding that blanketed the bed.

I did not even bother locking the door. I was asleep before I drew my next breath.

CHAPTER NINE

Rivers of blood carved through towering cliffs of obsidian, cutting a path into the land. Shadows danced over the jagged rocks, turning the darkness into a veritable void. Pealing laughter clashed with agonized screams and sent me to my knees, making me clamp my hands over my ears as the noises grew louder.

The screams gained prominence, ringing through my ears and vibrating through my very bones. Icy wind whipped through the valley between the cliffs and then I was in front of the river, blood lapping at my knees and soaking into my dress.

A hand grabbed my shoulder from behind, burning cold and searing hot at the same time.

The hand yanked, and then I was falling. Falling. FALLING.

No ground beneath me, no cliffs beside me, no river in front of me, just falling into a pit of inky nothingness as the screams grew louder and louder.

I woke on a gasp, my body recalling the nightmare as if it were real. My skin was cold yet hot at the same time, sweat beading on my neck and then freezing as it rolled down into my hair. My chest was heaving and my breath was coming in pants as visions flooded me. The nightmare had been familiar, yet not, filled with ice and shadows and screams. This nightmare was no different from the others in that as soon as I woke up, the finer details slipped from my grasp, no matter how tightly I tried to hold onto them, leaving only the lingering feeling of cold and fear.

And so I lay there, staring up at the ceiling of my new room in this prison of a castle as I caught my breath. Already, the images were fading, but I knew the feelings would linger for the rest of the day. Light was shining between the cracks in the heavy curtains across the windows, tinged red by the damning mist, but bright enough that I knew I'd been asleep quite a while.

I could not shake the discomfort from this dream, the feeling of claws skittering down my neck and heavy eyes on me, the sounds of distant screaming and sobs of people I never saw. Sleep would not return today, not without immediately pulling me back into the constant hellscape of my nightmares.

Perhaps this extra time would allow me to explore the castle more while most everyone else was still sleeping.

Rising from the bed, I finally took a moment to examine my room. I'd been far too tired last night, far too tired to even climb beneath the blankets, but now, I was practically vibrating with energy. The room itself was nice, small yet still more opulently furnished than our entire house had been. Two large windows took up most of the western wall to my right, and in front of the bed was a small sitting area tucked against the wall.

A wardrobe along the other side stood between the bed and another door, which led to a bathing chamber with a large bathtub and vanity that I was certain would be the only positive of my enduring stay at Castle Auretras.

It was a room far better than most other servants could ever claim, so I supposed it would be wise to accept without fuss.

When I spun back around towards the bed, I had to clap my hand over my mouth to keep from screaming as I slammed myself back against the wall. As my mind caught up with my eyes and I recognized the cat-shaped shadow perched on the end of my bed, my heart began to slow.

"What are you doing here?" I hissed at it. My hand moved down to cup my throat, feeling my pulse skitter beneath my fingers. "How did you even get in here?"

It merely tilted its head to the side. As with everything about this strange cat, the movement was beyond the norm a cat could tilt its head, its entire head now perpendicular to the ground as if its neck had been broken and the head was just flopping over to the side. Thankfully, the motion did not linger, and it hopped from the bed and prowled past me.

My bedroom door swung open as it approached.

"I am not following you," I said as it stopped in the open doorway, looking back at me. There were many things people had called me, but stupid had never been one of them. And I knew that following a Soulshade cat out into this castle when the door opened on its own accord was the very definition of something stupid. "I will find my way on my own."

It huffed.

"I will not."

The bright yellow of its eyes seemed to glow brighter and a cold breeze rushed into the room from behind me. The curtains shifted, though I knew I had not opened the window. Unease churned in my stomach. I'd never seen a Soulshade be able to manipulate the living world before, and though I could not rule out that all of them could do it, it made me that much more apprehensive of this creature.

While leaving the room might have been ill-advised, I couldn't deny that I was curious. I wanted to learn more about this place and the people inside. Besides, disobeying the Soulshade cat seemed to be far more dangerous to my current condition than venturing out into the castle. So I straightened my dress as best I could, pulling my hair from the messy twist it had been in and smoothing it down before following the cat to the door. "Fine. But only because I was already planning to leave."

I hadn't been expecting an answer, not in words, at least. Just like the night before, the cat led me down the hallway, twisting around corners while hugging its body along the walls. It made my skin crawl, the unnaturalness of the shadowed being, so I avoided looking at it as much as possible.

After a handful of more ornately decorated hallways, it stopped in front of a set of wooden double doors with roses and thorn-covered vines carved into the facade. It sat, tail twitching as it looked up at the door handle and then at me.

"Oh, you cannot open this one on your own?" I groused. Turning the handle, I pushed the door open.

The smell hit me first. Old parchment, leather, ink. I inhaled the scents deeply, relishing them. It had been too long since I had been in the presence of this many books.

I looked down at the cat, my heart strangely soft and my eyes strangely damp. "Thank you for showing me this."

It lifted its paw and licked at it once, twice, three times before putting it straight out like it was pointing.

Following its guidance, I peered further into the library only to see a familiar figure. The broad shoulders of a man and messy dark hair. His back was to us, but I knew without an inkling of doubt that this was the man from the night before, the one who had seen me in the balcony. The door swung shut behind us, the click of a lock sounding.

I glared down at the cat. "Traitor."

"I know you are there. The cat did not need to tell me."

When I looked back up, the man had spun to face me, the corner of his lip quirked up. And then the room tilted.

My vision blurred and I blinked, shaking my head in a failed attempt to clear it. The library had turned into my nightmares, the shelves of books replaced by a barren landscape of jagged black rocks, of ice-cold air, and shadows undulating along the walls. *No, NO!*

I backed up, reaching behind me for the door handle, but there was nothing. Nothing but cold air. My heart raced and my vision began to blacken around the edges as my breathing came too fast. I needed to *wake up*.

The man clapped his hands, echoing loudly off the stone and sending vibrations through my feet.

I blinked again at the sound, and I was back in the library, the man watching me carefully. My hand rested again at my throat and the other came to wrap around my body. What was happening? He'd clapped, I thought, but otherwise had not reacted in any way. Had he not seen that?

"Odyssa, is it?" His voice was exactly as it had been last night, rich and deep, sliding like velvet over my skin. It made me want to both melt into it and run away at the same time. Just like the cat, something was not *right* about this man, and until I could put my finger on what, I needed to stay away.

I reached behind me for the handle again, but before my fingers could close around it, the man was in my space, his breath fanning softly over my forehead and nose. Shivers erupted through me, tracing down my spine like tickling fingers. His power was evident even without touching me. The mere presence of him commanded attention, and while my body was happy to give it, my mind remained utterly aware of the potential dangers of being alone with someone like this.

"Don't." His lips curled up into a smile as he stared down at me. His pale blue eyes were swirling like clouds during a storm—clouds before the mist. The marks across my skin prickled, and I fought to keep from squirming. "Don't leave yet, little wolf."

"Why should I stay?" I lifted my chin defiantly, though my hands trembled. "Who are you?"

He leaned in even closer, his warm and slightly spiced smell invading my nostrils. A strand of my hair fell across my forehead and cheek, and he smiled at it, picking it up between his fingers and toying with it before letting it drop and leaning away.

"No one important."

"I highly doubt that, given you are here."

A smile stretched across his face, one that revealed all his teeth. "You are here as well. Are you not important?"

"I am a servant," I pointed out, crossing my arms over my chest. "You are a guest here."

"Am I?"

Voices outside the library echoed off the halls, growing louder as they came nearer. Still we stared at each other. I refused to be the first one to look away. Weakness was the language this man spoke—the language of Castle Auretras—and I would not make things easy on him.

He chuffed a laugh, taking a step away and extending an arm, bending at the waist slightly and crossing his other arm over his stomach. "You shouldn't be here, regardless." He looked down at the cat. "You can take her through the back passage. She'll be unseen."

The cat perked up from its spot at my feet, the words seemingly more for it than me. As we passed by the man, I caught a glimpse of black whorls at his wrist beneath his sleeve. My eyes snapped back to his face. This man was marked. He'd survived.

"Who are you?" I repeated, more urgency in my voice this time. His marks were thick and angry like mine, not delicate like Zaharya's. I itched to find out more.

"Wouldn't you like to know, little wolf," he said with another smirk. He dropped his arms and inclined his head towards the door, where the handle rattled. "Best be off now, though. Don't worry, I will find you later. I think we have much to discuss."

The cat flicked its tail jerkily and once my attention was back on it, we were off again, weaving between the shelves of books until we reached a small single doorway. Once again, the door opened without intervention. Human intervention, at least.

I couldn't make myself pay attention as it led me back through a narrower hallway. I noticed enough to know that it was somewhere new, but my focus was back in that library with the man. Zaharya's words echoed in my head, but I needed to know more, to know what that vision was and why it had happened in his presence. Why his intervention had pulled me out of it, and most importantly, if he had seen it too.

I barely noticed we had stopped until a doorway was right in front of my face. My doorway.

This time, I pushed my own door open. The cat apparently decided it had fulfilled its duty and turned to disappear into the stone next to my doorframe. Locking the door behind me, I leaned up against it, my hand resting at my throat once more. There was no need for it, but it felt safer, like I was holding myself together from the outside.

I still had no idea who this man was, and though Zaharya's warning was at the forefront of my mind, I knew I would not stop until I'd found my answers. I'd always been a curious child, and despite my priority being the cure and my brothers' survival, I wanted to know more about him.

The cat seemed to be working with him or for him; at any rate, it continued to lead me towards him. Smarter people would stop following such a creature. I didn't know how I knew, but I felt in my bones that it was a clue, a key to figuring out what was happening in this castle.

A knock on the door moved through the wood into my chest, startling me back to standing on my own two feet. Was it the man? He'd said he would return, but it had only been moments since I'd returned to my room.

Slowly, I unlocked the door, pulling it open only a sliver. My shoulders slumped in relief at the sight of white hair.

"It is time to get ready for this evening, Odyssa." She paused, studying me. "Are you ill? You look paler than you did last night." Her eyes narrowed. "And are you still wearing your dress from last night?"

"I—"

She pushed the door open, taking sure strides to the wardrobe I'd not yet opened that sat along the far wall. Flinging it open, she turned to look over her shoulder and frowned. "You are allowed to wear the clothes in here. It's here for a reason."

"No, I know," I said, trying desperately to keep up and wave away her concerns. "I just woke up. I fell asleep last night—I mean, this morning—and slept longer than I'd planned. I haven't had a chance to change."

She hummed. "I suppose the schedule does take some getting used to. Well, in any case, it's time to go. But this room is yours. Remember that."

"I will, thank you." I followed her to the doorway. Beside the door was a key hanging from a nail. I'd not seen it before, but then again, I'd been preoccupied. Taking the key, I locked the door behind us as we left, noting the satisfied smile on Zaharya's face.

CHAPTER TEN

I had once thought there was no greater torture than having to listen to the parties from my bedroom window.

I was mistaken.

Those Prince Eadric had pulled into the castle were abhorrent people, and I was quickly realizing why Talyssa carried herself as she did. Far better to be ignored by these monsters than to catch their attention. They thrived on lording themselves over even one another. I could hardly fathom what would happen when one of us landed in their sights.

Tonight's shroud was a dusky purple, the color the evening sky had been before the red mist settled in over Veressia. My marks were more visible through the sheer material than they had been last night, but Zaharya had left my hair down, hoping the dim lights and the soft waves of my hair would disguise the marks enough.

The taste of smoke and ash was constant on my tongue as I wove through the crowd, offering drinks and removing empty glasses. It was difficult, through the purple haze of the shroud, to tell who was a solid figure and who was a Soulshade, and three times now, I'd found myself offering a drink to a spirit. Now, those three Soulshades followed me around the party, floating aimlessly behind me as I walked.

Thankfully, it seemed no one had noticed. With all the people, even though I'd offered the tray to a Soulshade, a human had ended up taking a drink from it.

"Yes, yes, Prince Eadric would never let your daughter suffer like that." My ears caught on the conversation of two of the partygoers. One, a tall blond male with a white waistcoat and pants, both adorned with gold buttons and topped with a gold filigreed mask, and a woman in a pale blue dress with a silver mask in the shape of wings across her eyes. "You know he would give you the treatment before her time runs out. You must trust in him."

Purple clouded my vision, yet all I could see was red. The blood of my mother, covering her face and my hands. The mist over the city, oppressive and damning.

The shroud was more suffocating than ever, clinging to the sweat that had begun to bead on my forehead. My fingers tightened around the edges of the tray in my hands and my entire existence tunneled until it was focused on the couple. Their words echoed in my ears, ringing like a bell toll through my mind. A treatment existed, and *the prince had it*.

I took a step towards them, intent on listening more. I hovered as they continued speaking, offering the nearly empty tray to any who passed, though my eyes and ears were fixed firmly on the two in front of me.

"What do you think he will ask for it?" the male said, fidgeting with the buttons on his coat. "I am starting to run low on funds since we arrived here."

"I'm sure it will not be unreasonable." The woman set her hand upon the man's arm.

"He—" The man noticed me and his entire presence

changed. His shoulders rolled back, a frown grew across his face, and he drew himself up to his full height as he closed the three or four steps between us to invade my space. His boots tugged on the ends of my dress. "Why are you eavesdropping, worthless servant?"

I bit my tongue before I could defend myself, remembering all the instructions not to speak. Instead, I shook my head, lowering my eyes and holding the tray out slightly.

"No, you were *listening to us*," he snarled. His meaty hand wrapped around my wrist, shoving me back away from him.

I lost my balance, and my stomach swooped, knowing I had done the one thing Zaharya had warned me not to: drawn attention to myself. I heard the hem of my dress rip from where it was still caught beneath the man's boot and I stumbled more, only to immediately bump into someone's shoulder. Or rather, *they* bumped into me. The world seemed to slow as my feet got tangled up in the fabric and I watched as the tray began to tilt.

Before it fell, a large, gloved hand reached out to snatch it from my hands, the other gloved hand catching my elbow and guiding me upright. Even through the gloves, I felt the warmth of the contact, so unlike the cold anger of the other man who'd pushed me.

The immediate vicinity had gone silent, the couple I'd been focused on included, and the partygoers stared. My eyes were level with a broad chest, and I was almost scared to look up and see who I'd collided with. But slowly, I raised my eyes, only to be met with a familiar smirk.

My heart was pounding against my rib cage. This man, whoever he was, was clearly important given the quiet whispers and full-blown stares he was receiving. He held my tray out and I quickly took it from him, bowing my head slightly. Our hands brushed against the other and I watched his eyes widen behind his mask. Whispers erupted behind us, but I could not focus enough to make the words out. He seemed startled that I'd touched him, and I wondered for a moment if this oversight, yet another one tonight, would get me killed.

As I moved to pull away, his hand tightened around the tray, flexing against mine.

"Thank you," I muttered, keeping my eyes firmly on the silver buttons of his jacket and not on the strong jawline emphasized by his mask. I tugged on the tray gently, trying to get him to give it back so I could disappear into the background like I was meant to.

More whispers struck up behind me.

The skull-masked man's jaw clenched as his eyes tracked some movement behind me. The smirk was entirely erased now, only a neutral expression in its place. One that was so neutral, I knew it had been crafted intentionally.

I swallowed hard. Gods above, now I'd done it. I would never be able to find the treatment to save my brothers. Not if I was dead.

He raised his hand, and my body reacted on pure instinct. I flinched, ducking my head and curling in on myself as my eyes squeezed shut. I should have kept them open to see when the strike would land, but I couldn't bring myself to watch his hand fly towards me. My body was tense, waiting for the blow, but it never came.

"Stop it," the man hissed, low enough that I barely heard him.

Opening my eyes, I straightened, pulling my shoulders down away from my ears.

"Go back to your business," he ordered, looking over my head. The small crowd that had gathered skittered away, leaving us alone in the throng of dancers. His head tilted as he looked back at me.

I hadn't noticed before, hadn't been this close, but his eyes were not blue, but gray. Not a blue so pale it looked gray, but the true gray of a storm cloud, of ashes in a fireplace, of a cold and bleak winter morning. The gray of a tombstone.

The tightness of his jaw eased as he looked over me, tilting his head. Studying me. He did not speak again, and I didn't dare make the same mistake twice. I would bite my own tongue in two before I would utter another word in this ballroom.

His tongue darted out to wet his lips, and his mouth opened, but his gaze once again flickered over my head. Something in his eyes changed once more, and I realized now that this man was not just important here—he was dangerous.

The look in his eyes was now like the gray of steel and iron rather than that of storm clouds and ashes. Hard and defiant. Deadly. With one last glance down at me, he nodded and turned on his heel.

Deep breaths steadied me, and I stood there until I was able to walk without feeling like my knees might buckle. I'd been extremely lucky in that encounter. My anger had made me careless, and being careless would only end with me dead.

I grasped the tray tighter and finished my rounds to collect empty glasses, focusing only on placing each foot in front of the other, holding the tray upright, and not getting in anyone's way.

Finally, after what felt like hours, the tray was full, and I had an excuse to retreat to the kitchens. I caught a glimpse of the masked man again as I made my exit, and he raised his glass at me, the smirk once again on his lips. The deadly man was gone, replaced again by this teasing one that sent my heart racing and my hands trembling.

I sped up my steps.

Safely back in the kitchens, I all but tossed the tray onto the counter, pulling at the shroud until I was free from it.

"Odyssa, what happened?" Zaharya asked, putting down the

bottle of wine she'd been using to refill glasses and coming over to my side.

I shrugged off her hand on my shoulder and pushed my hands through my hair. Even now, words refused to come out of my mouth, hiding behind my teeth instead. Ash and smoke burst across my tongue and I squeezed my eyes shut just as the cat flickered into existence at my feet.

"What's wrong with her?" Maricara's voice could hardly be described as concerned. It should have spurned my anger, but instead, all it did was pull frantic laughter from my chest until I was sliding to the floor, gasping for breath. "Well, she certainly did not last long."

"That's enough," Zaharya snapped. She and Talyssa squatted down beside me, still in their shrouds. "Odyssa, *what happened*?"

I shook my head again, biting down on my tongue. I could not tell them what had led to the events, could not admit that the man in the skull mask had looked at me with pity when I thought he would hit me.

"She bumped into Tallon and almost dropped her tray. He caught it for her and then she *spoke*." Elena's voice had all our heads snapping towards her. She stood in the doorway with her arms crossed beneath the shroud, and even through the purple fabric and the unshed tears in my eyes, I could see the frown on her face. "And then he was about to touch her shoulder and she flinched. The prince came in shortly after."

Silence held dominion over the room for one heartbeat, two, three. And then three echoing voices said at once, "*What?*"

The judgement in the collective voice was deafening. There were too many things to focus on, and I could feel the room starting to spin. Pulling my knees up to my chest, I tucked my head between them. The skull-masked man was Tallon. Elena had seen everything. Tallon had been about to touch me. The prince had come in. *Elena had seen everything.*

My mind was spinning.

"I did not mean to," I said, voice muffled by my knees. I could feel their stares on my back. Someone was looking at the marks that stretched down my neck into my gloves. Cold washed over my foot and when I lifted my head, the cat was sitting on top of my foot, looking at me. Its wide yellow eyes held something akin to concern, and for a moment, almost looked human. "Someone thought I was eavesdropping when I lingered to offer them a drink. The man got upset and pushed me into the other man. He—Tallon—caught me and the tray. All I said was thank you."

"She touched his hand," Elena added.

"You must be more careful," Zaharya said. She reached out her hand to touch my shoulder again, and this time, I did not stop her. "You are very lucky it happened before the prince entered."

"Why?" I turned my gaze away from my feet—from the cat—and focused on her pursed lips beneath her shroud.

"It would have been much worse than whatever blow you thought Tallon was going to deliver."

A chill ran down my spine. "What does that mean?"

Maricara pushed off the counter, pulling up the ends of her dress and veil, and squatted in front of my feet. I tried not to focus on how the cat scurried away and moved to my side with an irritated look and flick of its tail. "Pray to whatever gods are left that you never find out."

Beside me, the cat nodded. It rubbed its head against my hand wrapped around my shin, sending ice-cold tingles into my skin.

CHAPTER ELEVEN

Zaharya told me to stay the rest of the party in the kitchen. None of them were willing to risk someone telling the prince about my misstep, and I was grateful for the intervention.

I knew I wouldn't be granted this much grace for much longer. I needed to get my mind together, to focus on what was important and shut out all else. My mother's words about my anger being my death sentence could not come true. Other lives depended on me, and I needed to swallow my pride and leash my temper. By whatever means necessary.

Tallon confused me still. The other partygoers had looked afraid of him. Zaharya had warned me away from him, and Elena had said his name with a touch of fear in her voice. The mystery around the man only grew.

He hadn't seemed overly intimidating when I'd observed him from the balcony the night before, but he had been able to somehow see me and speak to me as if he were beside me. A trick of sound and angles, perhaps, or perhaps something more.

Whatever he was, whoever he was, he commanded fear and that put him firmly on the side of the Coward Prince.

My curiosity had already earned me a quiet reprimand from Zaharya, so I would not ask about him again. But I had to learn more. Especially now with the knowledge of the treatment. Perhaps he was the key. If I could get close to him, I could get to the prince undetected and get the treatment for Rhyon.

The bells began to toll, signaling three in the morning and the official end of the party. If the previous night was to be the pattern, the guests would take nearly another hour to completely disperse from the ballroom to wherever else they chose to entertain themselves until the sun rose.

Before long, the others had returned to the kitchen with empty trays and pulled the veils from their heads with heavy sighs and deep frowns.

"Are you feeling better?" Talyssa asked quietly. Her face held true concern, which gave me pause. She waited for my response, eyes wide and earnest.

"I'll be better tomorrow." Deflecting the attention off any emotions was the best course of action. "I apologize for letting you all down tonight. It won't happen again."

Maricara shoved two bottles of wine into my hands. "Here, then make yourself useful now. You can take these back down to the cellar for tomorrow."

I clutched the bottles to my chest, standing slowly as I nodded once, though her focus had already shifted to some other task. A maelstrom of emotions was still swirling, my mind still attempting to catalogue all that had happened. Still, I welcomed the escape and the task, though I knew it was meant to be insulting. Gathering my thoughts would be far easier without an audience, and I slipped out of the kitchens to little attention.

I'd only made it down one hallway before I stopped short. The wine cellars were not somewhere I'd gone yet, and I realized

I had utterly no idea how to get there. I looked around for the Soulshade cat, hoping that once again it would guide me through the twisting halls of the castle, but there was nothing.

Resigning myself with a heavy sigh, I turned back towards the kitchens. Asking for more help was the last thing I wanted to do, but I was not keen to waste time wandering around the castle, especially not when the party had only so recently dissipated.

My steps slowed as voices filtered out of the kitchens.

"Why did Camelya hire her?" Maricara's voice was the first one I was able to make out. "She should have been turned away before she even set foot inside this place. She's going to get us all killed."

"We needed the help." Zaharya's voice was drier than I'd heard it thus far. "We cannot afford to be choosy now."

"She will learn." Talyssa. "It's only her second party. We all had much more grace when we started."

"She was doing rather well before the incident with Tallon," Elena admitted. "But I will not get my throat slit because she cannot take a hint that someone does not want a drink."

"We're lucky the prince was so distracted tonight and was not there yet." Maricara again. "Otherwise, we might have all been punished for her speaking."

"Tallon was going to hit her, wasn't he?" Talyssa's voice was quiet, but I could still make out the words. I held my breath, waiting for the answer. "He wasn't just trying to touch her shoulder, was he?"

"Of course he was going to hit her, Talyssa. Don't be naive."

"Like Talyssa said," Zaharya interrupted. "It's only her first night serving. She was doing well before this. She just needs to be more careful. We all need to be more careful."

"I will not be killed because of her." Maricara's voice was venom. "I need to stay alive for my daughter."

"We all need to stay alive, Maricara. She will learn. Or she will die. It's how it's always been."

Murmured agreements sounded from all of them.

My fingers tightened around the neck of the bottles, embarrassed that yet again, I could do nothing right. And that yet again, all I seemed to want was their approval.

Upset with myself, I stalked back down the hallway. I would find the damned cellars on my own, and I would keep my chin high and my shoulders back as I did. Their words burned in my soul, in the gaping pit where my heart used to be. With each step that took me further into the castle depths, my anger grew, festering, throbbing, and replacing any shame as their words echoed in my head.

I'd thought Tallon had been about to strike me as well, yet he had looked confused by my flinching away. This place, these people, confused me. Nothing was making sense, and no one was doing a damn thing to help me understand. Perhaps it was by design.

Hallways turned blurry and my vision tunneled as I kept stomping my path. Before long, I came to a junction, the hallway splitting in front of me and stretching down in long arms to either side. Both choices looked exactly the same, and neither looked like anywhere that would lead to a wine cellar. I was hopelessly lost.

Frustration now took the place of anger and before I could stop myself, before I could remind myself that this castle was not safe for letting out these emotions, I hurtled the wine bottles against the wall in front of me with a cry and watched as the glass shattered.

Wine gurgled out of the remains of the bottles, pooling on the floor and spreading across the stone like blood.

Ash filled my mouth and buzzing filled my ears.

The stone that comprised the walls began to tear apart like

flimsy parchment and out of the voids Soulshades appeared, two, then four, six, until at least a dozen of them were coming down the halls towards me from both sides.

My breath caught high in my chest and my knees trembled, but I could not make them move despite every fiber of my being screaming at me to get away. The Soulshades drifted closer, but my eyes refused to focus on the details of each spirit, instead just sending me blurry flashes of their general shapes, black beginning to dot the edges of my vision.

The one nearest to me reached out, inches away from touching me when my body finally sprang to life. I whirled, expecting to run down the hallway I'd come from, but I found myself face to face with another wall, one that absolutely had not been there before.

I was trapped now in a long corridor with Soulshades stretched to either side and a wall both in front of and behind me.

The first one touched me, grabbing hold of my bare wrist. It *burned*, ice-cold instead of hot, but it still felt like my skin was melting.

I cried out, wrenching away from its spectral grasp. My fingers clambered against the stone at my back and I lunged as another Soulshade came up on my other side, reaching for me. I grasped a shard of the broken wine bottle, clasping it my hands and flinging it out.

Grabbing shard after shard, I threw them at the Soulshades. They did nothing except cut my palms. Still, I reached for one last shard.

Two Soulshades grabbed me, one on each side, undeterred by my manic glass throwing. Their touch seared into my skin and my muscles tensed up. My hand tightened around the glass in my hand and the sharp edge sliced deep into my palm and the heel of my hand.

Another cry wrenched from my lips, more of a sob, and louder than I intended.

Nearly all the Soulshades were on me now, and I was beginning to lose feeling in my right arm where two Soulshades had grabbed hold.

I squeezed my eyes shut. This would be how I would die, worthless and a failure, killed by ghosts on my way to a wine cellar. If I hadn't been in so much pain, I might have found it amusing. My breath was coming in shuddering gasps, and I almost wanted to pass out before the Soulshades were able to kill me. That would be the smallest mercy.

And then, all at once, they were gone. The phantom holds had disappeared, leaving only the burning cold in their wake. The wall at my back disappeared as well, and I stumbled backwards without the support of it. Falling to the ground, I let another cry of pain slip out as I foolishly tried to catch my fall with my hands.

The pain tore through me and all I could do was clutch the wrist of my injured hand as tightly as possible, trying to will away the pain as I panted.

What in the hells had happened here? The walls looked normal now, no ripped seams in the stone. The Soulshades had vanished without a trace.

Heavy footsteps sounded behind me.

At once, the fear of the Soulshades was replaced by an uneasy apprehension that slithered over my spine. Whoever approached was why the Soulshades had disappeared.

And I knew without turning to look precisely whose footsteps echoed off the stone.

Somehow, I could feel it, the same feeling I'd gotten when I'd seen him in the library. That uneasy sensation, like someone was watching me yet trying their hardest to seem like they weren't.

Like someone was trying to peer beneath my skin and into my very soul.

The footsteps stopped right behind me.

"What have you gotten yourself into, little wolf?"

Tallon was here.

He stepped around in front of me, still wearing his attire from the ball, apart from his mask. His coat fluttered against his calves as I dropped my gaze from his face. As he stretched his hand towards mine, my eyes once again fell to the thick black marks across the back of his hand, snaking up and coiling around his wrist before disappearing into the sleeve of his jacket. Biting down hard on my tongue, I held my mouth closed.

Between the mystery of how a Death-marked man was at the side of the prince, why the Soulshades retreated from him, and whatever was happening to the castle walls, my heart was unlikely to ever slow down from its thundering pace.

CHAPTER TWELVE

"I lost my footing; I am fine." The pain was pulsing from my hand and I had to grit my teeth to get the words out. The others' words came back, reminding me of Tallon's true purpose here. I recoiled from his reach, pulling my injured arm tightly to my chest and pointedly keeping my eyes on his feet rather than on his wrist. "I apologize for any disturbance I caused."

He snorted, squatting down beside me and poking his index finger at the gaping wound on my palm before I could register his movements and pull away.

I cried out, biting down on my lip to cut off the sound abruptly.

"Yes, you are perfectly fine." He stood and nudged away the larger shards of glass with his boot. "You really should work on that footing. We can't have you tripping over everything all the time."

My cheeks heated. Cradling my throbbing hand to my chest, I managed to stand. "Again, I apologize for any disturbance." I hesitated a moment before bowing my head, clenching my jaw against the flood of pain. "And I apologize for my actions earlier tonight. I should not have spoken, and I thank you for not punishing me or the others for my mistake."

I kept my eyes on his boots, the black leather spotted with darker stains. Wine pooled around the soles.

He said nothing, but I felt his stare, heavy on my shoulders. Finally, after a long moment, he asked, "Why would I have punished you?"

"For bumping into you. For speaking. For touching you when I took the tray back." I could have continued, but I stopped, not wanting to give any other reason he might not have considered.

"That man pushed you into me. I would not have punished you for that, little wolf." His head tilted slightly. "Did someone tell you I would?"

"I—" I hesitated, unsure if this was a trick or if he really wanted an answer.

"Tell me; I promise no harm will come to you from my hand."

"Everyone seemed to be waiting for you to punish me. They seemed startled I touched you, more so than that I had spoken."

He hummed and continued looking at me, though the gaze was far less heavy than it had been at first.

I could not bring my eyes up from the ground, but I moved my focus from his boots to the spilled wine and broken glass mixed with my own blood. My stomach twisted as I realized the damage I'd truly caused here. It was more than just my physical injury; this wine was likely *expensive,* and I'd thrown it at a Soul-shade. "Do you know who I need to report this to? I imagine the wine will need to be replaced and taken out of my pay."

"No one will miss it," he said. "You need to tend to your injuries."

"All respect intended, but I am fine," I said, fighting the urge to raise my head and snap at him. I tried to mimic Talyssa with my voice, soft and meek. "I must return to my duties."

"Stubborn little wolf, aren't you?" He bent and once more, I found myself frozen as his breath washed over my ear and neck. His whispered words were hot against my skin. The facade had fallen once more, and the voice this time was softer, though it still held a teasing lilt. "I know you did not trip. Tell me what happened and perhaps I will consider letting you tend to your wounds yourself."

Shivers exploded across the back of my neck, sending goosebumps down my spine. His marks... did that mean he could sense the Soulshades as well? I doubted someone of his obvious standing would be wandering the castle after the parties alone. Did I draw him here? Did *they*?

I swallowed hard and again fought to keep my head bowed. I could not risk anyone finding out my secrets, my vulnerabilities. It'd just been proven that there was no such thing as trust inside this gilded prison, and it would be foolish of me to forget that so soon. "Truly, I merely lost my footing. I am still growing accustomed to the length of this dress."

He remained close to me, close enough that I could smell the wine still on his breath from the ball, and too close for him to be ignorant of the discomfort he was causing. "Liar. I heard your cries."

Fingernails dug into flesh as I struggled to keep my body from reacting to his words, his voice. It would only give him confirmation that I was lying, and though he certainly seemed confident he knew, I'd be damned if I handed it to him on a silver platter.

Finally he straightened, leaning away from my space. He nodded at my hand still clutched to my chest. "You need to get that taken care of."

"I can manage, but thank you." The words were pushed through gritted teeth as the firm flesh of my palm throbbed with each heartbeat. Pain was temporary, and I'd enough experience with it to know how to work through it. I would bandage it myself later in the privacy of my room, after I'd cleaned up the spilt wine and shattered glass.

"I insist, Odyssa." He crooned my name as his hand reached to cup the elbow of my injured arm. I wanted to protest, to yank my arm from his grasp and run the opposite direction, but I knew I couldn't. Not just because my hand was *throbbing* and still bleeding, but because of our roles in this castle. I could not refuse him, not without consequences. He hummed, looking at me with that same titled head and searching expression from the party, and then he dropped his hand. "I will not hurt you, little wolf, if that is what you're worried about."

I swallowed hard around the bitter taste of my pride. He *would* hurt me if he needed to, and more, he *could* hurt me, and I needed to remember that, despite whatever promises he'd made. I was lucky he hadn't so far for my refusal and disrespect. Lowering my eyes again, I replied, "I will go with you. I appreciate your offer of assistance."

He clicked his tongue, leaning back and crossing his arms over the silver brocade buttons lining his coat. "You do not have to do that, Odyssa. The offer is just that, an offer. It is not a demand. I do not own you."

"But the prince does." The words were out before I could stop them, hanging in the air of the halls. I raised my eyes to look at him. The words were spoken. What more could I do to condemn myself now? I continued, "The prince owns me, and if you are here, he owns you too. So pardon me, I may be new here, but I understand who holds the power in this castle, and, *Tallon—*" his eyes narrowed as I said his name— "I understand it is not me."

He watched me for a moment, and I tracked every twitch of his muscles, waiting for the abrupt strike I knew was coming. It never did. Instead, a broad smile crossed his face as he nodded. "You are not what I expected, little wolf."

The fight bled out of me, dripping from the cut on my palm and falling to the floor to join the puddle of wine and blood. "What?"

"It will be difficult to clean and bandage that properly with only one hand," he said. He offered out the crook of his elbow. "Let me help you and I'll escort you back to your room."

"I must go back to the kitchens and assist with cleaning the ballroom." I did not take his arm. The floor was sticky beneath my feet as I shifted my weight. "I should also clean this up before someone sees."

"Clean what up?" he asked.

I spun around. "The—" Nothing was there. I blinked rapidly, as if expecting the wine pool to suddenly reappear, but there was nothing. Lifting my feet revealed that even the stickiness of drying wine and blood had vanished as well. My head swam, feeling like it weighed twice what it should and would at any moment tip precariously to one side or the other. "The wine bottles. Where did they go? Did you do that?"

"Come now, Odyssa, before your hand gets infected."

His words pulled me out of my stupor. I'd survived the blood plague, but it did not make me invincible, and an infection—even here in the thrice-damned halls of whatever Castle Auretras was—could very well be a death sentence.

Looking down at me with his arm still proffered, he cocked an eyebrow. Against all better judgement screaming at me to do otherwise, I sighed and nodded down the hallway, still clutching my hand. "Lead the way, my lord."

He snorted but said nothing as he dropped his arm and began our path back into the belly of the castle. Zaharya had been right about that much, at least: the walls were hungry.

FOLLOWING Tallon down the halls of the castle was an exercise in self-control. With each step we took, I wanted to both cry out in pain and run as far away as I could. But the memory of the stones ripping open like paper to let the Soulshades out sent a shiver down my spine. If they were afraid of him, or if he could control them in some way... Well, I was safer at his side, at least for the moment.

Perhaps only for the moment.

When our path began taking us up a set of stairs into one of the towers, I finally realized exactly *where* he was taking me. Only residential rooms filled the towers, not medical suites.

"I won't go to your room," I said, my voice bouncing off the walls as I drew to a stop, despite my words being barely more than a whisper. "I need to get back to the others and help. Can you please just take me back to them?"

"No."

"Why—" My words were cut off in a hiss as he picked up my injured hand, poking at the already inflamed skin around the torn flesh.

"That is why." He dropped my hand and turned, looking back over his shoulder at me. "Do not make me carry you, little wolf. I'm not above it. Put aside the needs of others for a godsdamned moment and let me help you tend to your own wounds."

I bit down hard on my tongue to keep back the retort. Swallowing the barbed words back, I tried again. "I appreciate it, but I am not comfortable going to your room alone. I don't know you, and I have work to attend to."

He turned back around to face me fully and stared, his strong brow furrowed. After a moment, he shrugged. And then I was in his arms, one of his arms behind my back beneath my shoulder blades and the other beneath my knees.

My body hummed, buzzing all the way down to my very bones. I wanted to crawl out of my skin, to get away from his touch. "Put me—"

The walls spun, like I'd lost my balance and spun around too fast. My stomach crept up into my throat and my ears popped. I fought back the urge to vomit, squeezing my eyes shut. What was *happening*? Once it felt like the room had stopped spinning, I opened my eyes.

We hadn't moved—I was certain of that—and I hadn't felt any movement or heard his footsteps across the stone. Yet here we were, in front of a set of double doors that we had not been anywhere near before. Even the halls here were different than the ones we'd been in before, these stones dark with age and moisture. My head was still swimming, and my eyes had a difficult time focusing on one thing. I shook my head, hoping to clear it, only for Tallon's fingers to dig into the skin at my side and knee.

This tower hall was empty, and if he was as important as he seemed, no one else would be in these quarters. Anger boiled in my veins, throbbing in my forehead in time with the same throbbing of the pain in my hand. I balled my uninjured hand into a fist and punched at his chest. "Put. Me. Down."

With a quirk of his brow, he set me down. Rage built and built in the pit of my chest, climbing up my throat and wrapping around the base of my tongue like a serpent.

My fingers twitched, itching to reach out and slap the smirk off his face, but I knew that my indiscretion would not be forgiven twice. I should not have let my tongue out of its cage either, but even my self-control had limits. I stepped up close to him until my injured hand was trapped between us and looked up at him, staring into his stone-gray eyes. "If you *ever* touch me without my permission again, I swear on everything in this forsaken kingdom that I *will* hurt you. I do not care who you are."

He stared back, and I searched for any sign of humor in his face. But he took me seriously, and his eyes darkened. "I think I'd like to see that, little wolf."

My fury faded some, curling back up into the black pit in my center. Now that my anger was dissipating, the throbbing in my hand was taking back my attention. I squeezed my wrist with my other hand, trying to cut off the circulation and counter the pain.

"Shall we?" he asked, turning the handle and pushing the door open for me as he bowed at the waist slightly.

A whoosh of cold air met me, and I was staring through the doorway into my nightmares. Craggy rocks lined ice-cold black stone paths, slick with something that looked suspiciously like blood. In the distance, red-tinged midnight illuminated the terrifying mountain peaks that towered over the land. And then the screams began.

He snapped to attention, pursing his lips as he looked through the door for a moment before pulling it shut. A heavy sigh escaped his lips and he twisted the handle the opposite way as before, pushing the doors open once more. This time, he did not bow as they opened.

Normal, if even more obscenely opulent, rooms awaited this time. Regardless, the quick study was only enough for me to calm my racing heart and speak again.

"What was that?" I breathed, eyes still wide as I stared into his rooms, taking in the plush fabrics and gilded decor framing a large four-poster bed. This was twice now I had seen the fields of my nightmares when around him, and it was twice too many to be a coincidence.

"Can I see your hand?" He reached for my arm and I snatched it back. My body was nearly shaking with equal parts rage and fear, and I would sooner run headfirst into that hellscape than let him touch me without answers. He huffed and rolled his eyes, stepping into his room as he called over his shoulder. Thick, heavy curtains blocked any outside light except what came from the dozens of candelabras scattered about, the miniature gas lamps on his nightstands, and the fireplace. Based on the wealth dripping from the fireplace, I wasn't sure if it or the bed was supposed to be the focal point. Likely both. "Truly, Odyssa, if I wanted to hurt you, I would have by now. Please cooperate before you drip blood all over my room."

An icy cold brushed against my leg, and I knew without looking down that the cat was back. It looked up at me, its too-long tail curling around my calf beneath my dress, the touch burning cold like a snake of ice coiled around my skin. Releasing its hold, it sauntered into the room, looking back at me with too-wide eyes. It, too, seemed to prefer coming to me in Tallon's presence. Or leading me to him.

My hand throbbed, more painful than before, and I let out a gasp before I could catch it, tears burning at the back of my throat. It did need medical attention, and despite the feeling in my bones that something else was going on here, that I had eyes on my back, this was the only way I was going to get it. Tallon had ensured that.

"Do you even know how to clean a wound properly?" I pushed the words through gritted teeth as I joined him in the plush sitting area beside his fireplace. I did not sit.

His laugh was rich and warm yet it still sent shivers down my spine with the power it exuded. It didn't *fit*. He didn't fit, in this room or in this castle. There was something dark lurking beneath his skin, behind the gray of his eyes, and he was doing a poor job of hiding it.

"Who are you?" I murmured. The Soulshades had not reappeared, but something in my soul was reacting. There was no ash on my tongue, no smoke in my throat, but the heaviness wrapped around my ribs and squeezed. "Why are they all so afraid of you?"

"That's quite a pair of questions," he replied. His coat rustled as he removed it, draping it over the back of one of the chairs. The sleeves on his shirt were cuffed just beneath his elbows, displaying his powerful forearms and the Death marks that encircled both of them. "Ones I don't quite think you're ready to hear the answer to."

The cat brushed up against my leg again, seemingly nudging me towards the chair. He was likely right, but ignorance was a death sentence in Castle Auretras. "Tell me anyways."

"Why are you not afraid of me?"

I didn't reply. I *was* afraid of him; couldn't he see that?

"You act like you don't believe me. I know what fear looks like, Odyssa. I know what it tastes like in the air, how it bends the body to its will. It's unmistakable. And you, little wolf, do not fear me." He held his hand out. "For now, let me tend to your hand."

Carefully, I laid my hand in his, wincing as the torn flesh pulled. It was deep enough for me to see it would need stitching, even in the low light from the fire. "Do you know how to do stitches?" I pulled my hand back slightly, but his grip on it was firm. "I really should just go to the infirmary."

"Just sit here and get warm," he said, rubbing at the base of my thumb. It sent tingles down my wrist and arm, uncomfortable pinpricks of irritated nerves offset by the warmth of his skin against mine. "You are not an inconvenience to me. Let me help you."

It'd been so long since another person had touched me besides my mother. I locked my muscles to keep from leaning into the touch, to keep from chasing it as he set my hand gingerly back into my lap and stood.

I let my eyes watch the fire while he rummaged in the room

behind me. Even the fire seemed wrong here, the flames too yellow and flickering like they were pretend. I wanted to thrust my hand into it to see if it was truly a flame, despite the wash of heat that breathed against my body.

"Here." Tallon's return pulled my focus back to him. The silk of his shirt rippled like waves of night when he moved to set down his supplies on the table in front of us. My eyes were stuck on his forearms still, tracing the twisting vines of black that adorned his hands, his wrists, covering more skin than they left bare. A clearing throat startled me, but he was again smirking at me, his face much closer than I'd realized. For a moment, I thought his eyes flicked down to my mouth, but then I blinked and his head was bowed, his attention on my hand. "Surely you know it's rude to stare, little wolf."

My face flushed and I ducked my head as I stuck my hand out to him, ignoring the sharp pain until it faded back into its dull throb. "Your marks…" I trailed off, not knowing how to finish the question without seeming invasive.

"What about them?" His stitches were neat, and though I could feel every pull of the needle and every slide of the thread through my flesh, I kept still and quiet as he worked. And I kept my eyes on my own skin, no matter how much they wanted to wander to look at him.

The marks on his skin were similar yet so different to mine, and I was desperate to see what they looked like. Mine were shapeless, meaningless lines like spilled ink across the pale expanse of skin. His were patterned, forming a larger shape with detailing. I had only seen a glimpse of his wrists and forearms, and based on the intricacies there, I could not imagine what lay beneath his shirt. My trail of thoughts caught up to me and I wanted to slump down and disappear into the chair. My cheeks burned hotter than the fire before us, and I struggled to overcome the urge to shift nervously in my seat. I did not need to see what was beneath his shirt, did not want to. The marks were what interested me, not him. "They look like mine."

"Do they?" His eyes flicked to my other arm. "Hmm, I suppose they do."

"How long ago were you sick?" I asked. The castle had been closed off for nearly a year now, and I was curious to know just when he'd joined the prince's collection. His needle hit a sensitive spot on my hand and I flinched.

"I apologize if it hurts," he said. He didn't raise his head from his work, and his breath was warm against my palm. "We're nearly finished."

I did not repeat my question.

He tied the last stitch with a neat knot and cleaned it before beginning to wind a bandage around my palm. It was far less neat than the stitches had been.

"Are you sure you know what you're doing?" I asked, trying to peer around his large hands to see just exactly what he was attempting to do with the bandage.

"I think I might like you, little wolf," he said, tying off the end of the bandage. "You are not at all what I thought you would be."

"What did you think I would be?"

The dark smirk was back on his face and he leaned in close. My heart hammered in my chest as he held my chin between his thumb and forefinger. "That hardly matters now, does it? You're exceeding those expectations, just trust that."

A faint scream flew in on the night wind through his open window, and it set my teeth on edge. I knew that scream, the pain in that voice that had drifted up from Jura. Someone had died.

With startling clarity that nearly made me dizzy, I realized just what I was doing. I was here, in the prince's castle, wearing clothes he'd supplied, in the room of one of his friends. All the while, my brothers were alone. They'd likely not started to starve yet, but they would soon if Emyl had not figured things out. And the cough I'd heard as I left... What if one of them was sick? And I was sitting here, imagining Tallon without his shirt.

It could not happen again.

It would not.

I would die before I let my mother down, before I left my brothers to die. I'd sworn to them before I left that I would do whatever it took to keep them alive. And not three days had passed and I'd forgotten my oath.

What a pitiful excuse for a daughter and a sister.

I pulled my hands into my lap, discretely digging my thumb into the flesh just above the stitches. The pain offered more clarity, and I knew without a doubt I needed to get out of this room.

I needed to find the treatment, get it back to my brothers before the faint cough became a bloody gag, and end the prince's reign of cruelty.

"The others must be asking after me," I said, standing abruptly. He leaned back in his chair, lacing his fingers together over his stomach. I swallowed hard and lifted my hand. "Thank you for your assistance, my lord."

I'd made it to the door before he responded.

"Odyssa?" he called.

I turned.

"I'm far from a lord."

Our stares were locked for another moment before I managed to pull away and turn my back to him.

Gods, what had I been thinking? Nothing good would come of this, and I was losing myself more and more to this place. Forgetting the reason I'd come here in the first place, forgetting *why* I had sacrificed myself to this castle.

It couldn't happen again. Wouldn't happen again.

A hand brushed my lower back. "Let me escort you. I would hate for you to get injured again on your way back."

The heat in his words washed over my neck, and I knew without a doubt that Tallon knew exactly what had happened in those halls. My heart could not decide if that reassured me or terrified me down to my very bones. I took a deep breath through my nose. Ultimately, it mattered little which one. I was here, and so was he, and if he could keep the Soulshades from attacking me, I needed to take advantage of it.

"That's very kind of you," I lied.

CHAPTER THIRTEEN

I was a failure, and yet, I refused to let myself wallow in self-pity. That would not help my brothers, would not appease my mother, and would do nothing to punish the Coward Prince.

I had a job to do, and I would not get it done if I was drowning in doubt and distracted by Tallon and his mystery.

"Do not fret about your work," he said, startling me out of my thoughts by voicing them aloud. Perhaps he could. Perhaps the walls whispered my thoughts to him. I wondered what work he was speaking of. "I'll ensure it's taken care of."

I laced my hands behind my back and dug my thumb into the center of my palm before I spoke. It centered me, despite feeling one of the neat stitches tear from my flesh and blood ooze into the bandage. I clasped my hands tighter. "That's very generous of you."

He nodded towards my door. "You should get some rest. Welcome to the castle, Odyssa."

I entered my room without replying, closing the door behind

me and leaning back against it. There would be no rest for me tonight.

As soon as his footsteps faded down the halls, I opened the door again. I needed to return to the hallway and inspect the walls. I couldn't have imagined them closing in on me, or the new wall appearing behind me to block my path. I couldn't have imagined the stone tearing open like paper to allow the Soulshades to pour out.

Could I?

At this point, I was far from confident that what had happened wasn't in my own mind. The Soulshades had never tried to attack me before, and I'd never seen them coming from the walls. They'd always just appeared, flickering in and out of existence and accompanied by the acrid taste of ash and smoke.

Every sound had me jumping out of my skin as I wound through the halls and back down towards the cellar level, retracing the path as best I could.

If I had any hopes of leaving this castle alive, I needed to understand what I was facing. Zaharya had said the walls were hungry, but I was hungry too. I would find out what was happening in this castle, and I would ensure the last of my family survived.

Someone was playing games in the castle, and whether it was magic, an illusion, or medicine, it was not a game I was keen on continuing.

Finally back in the hallway, I stooped at the crossing, letting my fingers trace over the stone where I knew without a doubt there had been a pool of wine and broken glass before, but they were smooth and dry, no longer sticky with drying wine and blood. Not even a stain darkened their facade.

Tallon had something to do with this, but I doubted I would get answers from him. He was too good at deflecting my questions with comments that he knew would draw me in. Was he the one controlling the walls? The Soulshades? He'd certainly been the one creating my nightmare illusions, for whatever reason. I vowed to confront him the next time he threw those visions at me.

The others had me wavering, thinking he would strike me for impudence. Perhaps he would. There were worse things in life than physical pain, though.

My examination took me to the walls themselves next. Rough stone pulled at the bandage around my wounded hand, but no seams were revealed. No trace of anything to hint at how the Soulshades had appeared or how the walls had moved.

Footsteps echoed down the right branch of the hall, and I froze.

"…must ensure they do not…" a male voice sounded, just this side of too faint to be certain of the words. "…too much work to do…must learn more about…"

The voices and the footsteps grew louder. "Yes, of course, Your Majesty. I will see it handled."

My blood ran cold. That was Tallon's voice, talking to the prince. While luck had been on my side in my battle against the blood plague, I had run out of it steadily since being locked inside this tomb. Who were they talking about, and what work needed to be done? I wanted to listen more, but their footsteps grew even closer and if I stayed here, I would be spotted.

Picking up the ends of my dress, I ran as quietly as I could back to safety before making my way back to my room.

Finally, I was safe back inside. I turned the locks and pressed my shaking hands to my chest as I tried to slow my breathing.

Tallon was the prince's right hand, it seemed.

I held up my own hand, the hand he had just bandaged. His kindness could be nothing but a manipulation, and I refused to be manipulated by these abhorrent people. Gritting my teeth, I dug my thumb into the center of the wound again, pressing deeply until I was gasping in pain rather than from shortness of breath.

The stinging would remind me.

"Where did you go?" Maricara demanded, lunging in front of me to meet me toe-to-toe as soon as I walked into the dressing room. Her eyes were lit like fire, and her lip curled up in a snarl.

I stumbled back a step before I could suppress my shock at the vitriol on her face. The vein in my forehead throbbed as I realized that Tallon had decidedly *not* taken care of things before he'd left me in my room. Another reminder that he was not an ally and never would be. He'd wanted this, to separate me from the others. It was part of his manipulation, to whatever end, and I despised it.

I'd planned on keeping my wound as hidden as possible, but if Tallon had wanted them to hate me, I had to earn their civility back. Their trust and their friendship were both things I cared little for, but even the perception they did not despise me would work to my advantage. So I held my hand up, showing them the bandage. "I had to go to the infirmary. By the time they were finished and let me go, you'd all gone."

Talyssa gasped, coming over to grasp my hand. Her touch was gentle as she peered beneath the bandage. "What happened? That looks very deep. Are you okay?"

Her concern almost seemed genuine. Almost, but something in her eyes betrayed her distrust.

I pulled my hand back, rolling the words on my tongue before speaking. I could not tell them the truth, that I'd broken the wine bottles defending myself from a Soulshade. But it needed to be as close to the truth as possible, without pitting them against me further. "There was broken glass in the cellar, and I tried to clean it up and cut myself."

They were all silent for a moment, all of them staring at me. I refused to shift under their collective gaze, to fill the silence with more words. I did not lie often, but I knew how to, and I knew that if I gave into the discomfort, it would give me away. I caught Zaharya's eye and held it.

"Well," she said, clasping her hands together. "We are glad you got it tended to. Let's all try to make it through the entire night tonight, hmm?"

I inclined my head, taking the words as dismissal. "What is tonight's theme?"

"Green." She turned her back to me and settled back into her station.

Taking up a swath of forest green fabric that was draped over the back of the couch, I settled into what had been assigned as my vanity station. As I twisted my long waves back away from my face and into a low bun, I watched the others in the mirror. The darted glances and hushed conversations meant they were watching me, too, but no one was going to admit to anything.

Their cowardice would be my advantage here. They did not trust me, and I did not need them to, but they would not confront me either. And so long as they did not confront me, I could continue to get information out of them.

"Does everyone in the castle attend every party?" I asked. The mirror showed Talyssa flinching at my voice as it broke the silence of the room.

"What else is there for them to do?" Elena snorted. "Yes, of course they do. It's the only respite as we all await our fates."

"How long has everyone been locked in here?" I swallowed and ensured the surprise in my tone was clear. "And no one has gotten tired of these parties?"

A hairbrush slammed down on the vanity. In the mirror, I

watched as Maricara stood and stalked over to stand behind me. Our eyes locked in the glass. "You may have wanted to come here, but the rest of us are just trying to survive. Stop meddling or you will get us all killed."

Before I knew what I was doing, I'd stood and faced her. I clenched my fists as images of my mother's bloodless body filled my eyes. Every plan to endear myself back into their graces vanished like smoke on the wind. "Let us get one thing perfectly clear. I did not *want* to come here."

"You still volunteered," she sneered, tilting her chin to keep my gaze. "You still *chose* to come here. And now you are faced with the consequences of your choice. We do not care that you are scared and want to go home. You are stuck here now, and it's time you accept it."

"I've told you why I volunteered. Volunteering for a *job* or watching my younger brothers starve to death is hardly a choice. Could you have been so selfless, or would you have let your family die with you?" My voice was barely higher than a whisper and I could feel my pulse pounding in my neck. This anger seeping from me was not a raging inferno, not a roaring fire. It was an icy blade, cutting sharply and freezing out the air in the room.

Her eyes hardened and the twitch of the muscle in her neck was the only warning I had before her hand was flying at my face, palm open. I kept myself from flinching, but the blow never landed.

Pulsing from my body was a black shadow, tendrils pushing from the Death marks and wrapping around her wrist. Her eyes widened and she struggled, but the shadow held firm to her. And then, it was gone. Her hand fell and she stumbled back, clutching it to her chest. My knees felt weak and my heart sped, but I fought to keep calm. Better they think I could control it.

"What did you just do to me?" she spat. In my periphery, I

could see the others hovering, tense and coiled, ready to jump in if they needed to separate us.

Though I was still reeling inside, I kept my voice steady and calm. "You should keep your hands to yourself."

"That's enough, both of you," Zaharya said. She hadn't risen from her vanity chair but was turned around to face us, her eyes wide at the shadows that still hovered around me. "Get ready for the party and stay out of each other's way. We cannot afford any mistakes. We've been lucky so far, and you are doing well, Odyssa, despite last night. But that luck will run out eventually. It always does."

Maricara and I stared off for another moment before she sniffed and went back to her own vanity. Taking a deep breath, I rolled my neck before allowing myself to do the same as the shadows retreated.

"What the hells was that?" Zaharya hissed. "Did you know you could do that?"

I shook my head. I had no idea where the shadow had come from, or what it was. It had emerged from my Death marks and I could *feel* it, as surely as if it had been my own hand wrapped around Maricara's wrist to stop her blow. My chest felt tight, and I forced more deep breaths. Looking down at the hairpins on the vanity, and then at my shaking hands in my lap, I knew it would be fruitless to attempt to finish my hair.

"That is not normal, Odyssa," she breathed, looking over her shoulder at the others. "I don't think I need to tell you to keep that hidden from the prince and from Tallon."

"Will the others tell?"

"No." She seemed certain; her answer was quick and firm. As much as I shouldn't, I took her word for it.

With a nod, we settled into silence. I pulled at the pins that had already started holding the style and let the waves fall in a curtain over my shoulders and down my back. The energy in the room was odd, and instead of smoke or ash, the taste of something sickeningly sweet, so cloyingly disgusting, was settled over my tongue instead. I wanted to scratch at it to remove the feeling, the layer of *something* that had taken up residence inside.

Tears stung at the back of my nose, but I would not cry. I would not falter and I would not fail. These girls had shown their hand, and I would be damned if I showed mine. My marks had set me apart since they first appeared on my skin. And from the moment I'd seen them, stark against the unnatural pallor of my skin following a week-long battle with the plague, I'd known they would not make my life easier.

Once again, I found myself wishing the bloody curse had taken me instead of my mother. But I would not wish this hell upon her either.

Cold brushed against my calf and I closed my eyes, feeling my heartbeat slow slightly. The cat was objectively terrifying, but I couldn't deny the icy coldness was comforting. Knowing that another being, whatever it was, was there. I didn't know what the cat was, or why it was following me. My eyes flew open at a realization. This was another of Tallon's manipulations, almost certainly.

I chanced a look down at it, and for a moment, the yellow eyes staring back at me flashed gray. A familiar gray, so unmistakable for anything else.

"Get away," I hissed, kicking my leg. The comfort the cat had brought was gone. At best, it was a spy for Tallon, and at worst… I knew those eyes, and after what I'd seen in the cellar halls and again in his bedroom, I was not willing to dismiss anything regarding him anymore.

I needed to get out of here, to breathe fresh air and let myself *think* for a moment without the heavy gazes of the others. Without the heavy gazes of these damned castle walls. Was I seeing things? Was this castle making me insane? The room felt like it was closing in, but the others did not shift or move, not even as the walls seemed to shift closer and closer.

Standing abruptly, I barely heard it when my chair clattered to the floor behind me. I clutched the green shroud to my chest. "I'm going to finish getting ready in my room. I will meet you in the kitchens when the bells toll."

I left before any of them could object.

CHAPTER FOURTEEN

Back in my room, I made my way for the balcony, barely stopping to throw the shroud in the direction of the bed before I flung the doors open and stepped out into the early night. I gulped down breaths, heedless of the metallic tinge of iron the air now held.

A firm grip on the balcony railing was the only thing that kept me standing.

Slowly, with each breath, my body released some of the tension it held until I was no longer shaking and was able to hold myself up as I gazed up into the red mist that blanketed Veressia.

I tipped my head down and took in the city below.

From this height, I could not make out many details of the city, and no sounds rose this high. I still searched for my house though, chasing a foolish hope that I would be able to glimpse Rhyon or Emyl.

Suddenly, I understood why the king threw himself from the spire after his wife had succumbed to the blood plague.

Would it feel like flying? Or would it only give that sick

feeling of your stomach bottoming out as I watched the ground come up to meet me? Did it matter?

A chill against my calf brushed past me to settle on my left foot. It was an odd sensation as there was no weight to the specter cat, just a coldness. I still kicked it away regardless and took it as my sign to retreat from the balcony.

The sun was setting, and I needed to get ready for the ball still.

I focused on the rough metal of the balcony railing beneath my hands, the cool breeze across my face, the uneven stone of the balcony floor beneath my feet. Anything to ground me and keep me from falling into the panic building in my chest.

For the first time since I entered those gilded gates and heard them slam shut behind me, I was grateful for this shroud. Returning inside, I stepped up to the mirror across from the wardrobe, and all I could see staring back at me were bloodshot eyes and the dark shadows beneath them. If I'd been left uncovered, they were likely to scare away any nobility who saw them, appalled at my lack of care.

While I wanted nothing more than to take a running leap from the balcony and damn the consequences, my brothers needed me. Every day here was another chance for them to contract the plague, and our family's luck would only hold once and I'd used it up. I needed the treatment the prince hoarded, needed to be able to get it and take it back to my brothers.

The emerald green dress in my wardrobe had thin straps that I knew would dig into my shoulders and a plunging neckline that would require careful movements if I wanted to keep from spilling out of it. It was wasteful, in my mind, to have these gowns hidden beneath the shrouds, when all we needed was something simple. The silk against my skin would serve as another reminder of the opulent waste of the Coward Prince. I pulled it on.

Even the deep green shroud would not be able to hide my marks in this dress, and I doubted even the addition of the gloves would make a difference. Regardless, I slipped them on before pulling the shroud over my head.

The cat sat in the balcony doorway and watched me the entire time.

I pointedly ignored it as I left the room, shutting the door firmly behind me.

THROUGHOUT THE PARTY, the constant state of looking over my shoulder was beginning to wear on me. I'd known coming into the castle that I would never be safe, that I could trust no one and nothing, but seeing those assertions laid out in front of me was far different. Between the other servants, the Soulshades, the castle itself, Tallon, and the prince... my mind was quickly turning into a near perpetual state of madness.

Everything was tinged emerald tonight, and the ballroom was decorated like a forest, complete with tall vases filled with spiraling twisted plants and ornate vines draped from the ceiling around the chandeliers. As it was the nights before, the polished onyx floors reflected the candlelight thrown from the ornate candelabras, casting shadows across the tapestries that decorated the walls.

Dutifully, I kept my eyes down as I served the drinks. Before, I'd wanted nothing more than to stay in the kitchens, but now, they were the last place I wanted to be. The kitchens would give me nothing, but here, despite the horrible stench of entitlement, I could blend into the background, forgotten. I could excel here if I forced myself to forget where I was and why I was here. I'd served my entire life, after all.

None of the partygoers minded their tongues. It was an interesting phenomenon the prince had created, however awful it was. Like Zaharya had said, take away our faces, and our humanity went with it. We were nothing more than moving serving trays to these people, and they spoke to us, about us, and around us as if we were of no consequence.

I took advantage of it, listening as closely as my damaged ears would allow. But I'd learned my lesson never to linger in one place for too long, and I kept moving, kept serving. Perhaps the only good thing about the gauzy shroud that covered me was that I did not have to fake a pleasant facade.

I'd felt eyes on me throughout the night, certainly. Some stared longer than others, trying to make out my face beneath the shroud as they studied the new addition to the castle. But it was too dark and the veil just too opaque to truly allow them to.

And though most of the overheard conversations only served to fuel my anger at the prince and his people and reinforce the disgust at the wasteful opulence, some of the words they'd uttered as I passed were extremely enlightening.

The prince was far less revered here than I'd expected. These people feared him, certainly, but they did not seem to *like* him. They were beholden to him, but even now, nearly a year into this plague, it seemed his inactions were finally beginning to grate on even his most trusted. Frustration over not claiming his title, over not being allowed out.

Most of it was trivial, but I tucked away each tidbit deep into the recesses of my mind. It might not all make sense now, but I knew eventually, someone would say something and it would all fall into place. And then, I could ensure my brothers would live and ensure my promise to my mother was kept.

Miraculously, I stayed out of trouble this time, and before long, the party was ending. As they had the nights prior, the revelers cared little for whoever had to come behind them, and I began collecting the empty and discarded glasses.

The hairs on the back of my neck prickled, but no ash coated my tongue. Carefully, I readjusted my grip on the tray before turning to see who was behind me.

Despite the others still flitting about in their shrouds, and the last of the occupants still filtering out of the ballroom, Tallon stood before me, unabashedly staring at me through his mask. A half-skull mask yet again, but different from each I'd seen before. This one was simpler, a dark green with silver-swirled filigree around the edges. The silver made his gray eyes even more piercing.

He handed me his glass, a smirk playing on his lips.

I added it to my tray with a scowl. His smirk turned into a full smile and he tipped his head back and laughed loudly, the sound echoing off the nearly empty ballroom and drawing the attention of those left behind. My chin stayed lifted as I turned. Retreating to the kitchens, I kept my steps slow and did not look back, even as I felt his eyes following my every move.

CHAPTER FIFTEEN

A knock on my door woke me at dawn. I'd just barely gone to sleep and debated ignoring the visitor, but another irritated knock pulled me from bed. Bleary-eyed, I pulled the door open to reveal Camelya, standing there clutching an envelope to her chest with a frown on her face.

Wordlessly, she thrust the letter into my hands.

I kept her gaze as I ripped it open, trying to find a clue to its contents in her face. The envelope only held my name across the front in handwriting I instantly recognized as Emyl's.

Letters filled my eyes, and my chest clenched as they formed words and sentences.

It was a multitude of words. Words telling me the worst news of my life. The news I'd been dreading yet waiting to hear ever since that cough had bid me farewell.

Rhyon had contracted the blood plague.

My eyes scanned the letter again, searching for answers, but they snagged on the date. The letter was dated two days ago, the day after I'd arrived at the castle. My head snapped up. I'd known in my heart that it was true, what the cough I'd heard the day I'd left had meant. But seeing it here, in Emyl's messy handwriting, laid out for anyone to see... "I need to go. I have to—"

He could be already dead. He was so young. The plague would kill him faster than the normal seven days, and if he'd already been sick when I left, that only left him three days, maybe four. Only left *me* three days. I'd wasted so much time already trying to find a way to earn the trust of those who knew the castle to peer beneath the secrets of the gilded walls. I'd taken too long, and now my baby brother was going to pay for my mistakes.

My mind spun, and I could not catch my breath. Camelya just *stood* there looking at me. With a scoff, I let the letter fall to the ground between us and rushed to the wardrobe, pulling out clothing. I rifled through the bottom of the wardrobe, looking for a bag, but there was none. Grunting, I slammed the doors shut. I did not need to take clothes with me; I could make do. I needed to get home as soon as possible.

Sifting through the clothes on the floor, I pulled on a clean dress and began my search for socks and boots for the journey.

Emyl could not possibly care for Rhyon, and I hardly trusted that the first thing he'd done was send me a letter. He would have spent at least a day denying that our brother, our precious Rhyon, had contracted the blood plague. But even if he'd just begun showing symptoms two days ago and Emyl had acted quickly, it could be too late. Rhyon was young, and his little body would not be able to fight it off for as long as I or our mother had.

"Odyssa, stop," Camelya said, suddenly in front of me and holding both of my forearms. "Breathe. I need you to tell me what is happening. What did the letter say?"

"My youngest brother has the plague," I said, barely choking back the sob at hearing the words aloud. Admitting Rhyon had the blood plague was a blow to the stomach, and I had to swallow back the bile that threatened to rise in my throat. "He needs someone to help him. My other brother cannot—I have to go. I need to leave, now."

Camelya bit her lip, looking nothing like the self-assured and confident woman who'd brought me into this hell. She squeezed my arms tightly as I struggled to focus on her. "I am sorry, Odyssa. But no one is allowed to leave."

The room felt like it was closing in, but this time, the walls did not sway. A sob ripped from my throat before I could stop it, and then the tears followed. Camelya turned blurry and then I was falling, my legs no longer able to support my weight. I crashed to the floor, and vaguely I felt the pain of my knees making contact with the stone, but it was nothing. The pain was nothing.

Camelya slowly knelt beside me, one of her hands tentatively resting on my back. I wanted to scream at her, to shrug off her touch, but it felt nice to have the comfort of another person. I wanted her to hug me, to soothe me and tell me everything would be alright, but I knew it wouldn't be. She barely knew me, much less was fond of me. I shouldn't be seeking comfort in a stranger, not when my own brothers were alone, suffering through this hell. No one had comforted me since I was a child; I hadn't needed it then and I would not let myself need it now.

I leaned away from her, trying to stifle the sobs. The tears flowed freely still, burning hot tracks down my cheeks and neck. "I am sorry, Odyssa," she repeated.

"What do you mean no one can leave?" I cried. "Corbyn left to get me, to get others. Surely there is a way out! I need to get back. You don't understand—he's just a *child*."

"I do understand," she said. Her voice was hard, but not cruel. "I understand more than you know, and I wish I could help you. But we cannot leave. You knew that when you joined."

"He's just a *child*." My voice broke and I buried my face in my hands. An icy touch pressed up against my thigh, and I didn't need to look to know the cat was there. Oh, how I wished it was real, that I could bury my face in its fur and let it soak my tears. I dropped one hand to the cold spot.

Both Camelya and the cat sat with me while I cried and stayed until my tears had long dried up and my fingers on my right hand had grown numb from the coldness of the cat's presence.

"It will be okay, Odyssa," she said, still rubbing long paths up and down my back. "I know it does not feel like it, and it likely won't for a long time, but death is not the end."

"It's not fair," I muttered, pressing the heels of my hands against my stinging eyes. Death could not take Rhyon—I would not allow it. "He cannot die. It's not fair. It should not be him."

She sighed. "No, it's not fair, my dear. But as is life."

I said nothing as I lowered my hands, and instead kept my eyes on the cat still pressed against my leg. It looked back at me, tilting its head and staring with those huge yellow eyes.

"If you'd like to write a response, I will have it dispatched immediately."

My head snapped up. "What good would a response do? My brother is dying and you've locked me in this hell!"

Her eyes widened and she took a step back. "Odyssa. This is not my doing."

"Every single person in this castle sits here and has no care for those on the outside. No care for those who have died choking on their own blood." I stood. "Because you believe yourselves safe here behind your gilded walls and iron gates, but you are not. You believe yourselves better, but you are not. And if it takes me to my last breath to prove it, I will die happily knowing the prince has suffered as much as I have."

Her eyes widened even more and shifted ever so slightly to my right. I kept my gaze on her. I knew what she was looking at, could feel as my marks had once again peeled away from my skin to echo into the air.

The air crackled with energy, tingling against my tongue. The hairs on the back of my neck stood and her eyes shifted to something behind me and she visibly relaxed, pressing her hand against her chest. "Oh, good, you're here. She's losing it, I fear. Is there anything you can do?"

I whirled around, only to find myself face-to-face yet again with Tallon. No smirk played on his face now as he looked at my marks and the undulating shadows that mirrored them outside my body. His brows furrowed and he reached his ungloved hand out towards me, his own marks seemingly swirling beneath his skin. "Sleep, Odyssa."

My mind tried to cling to consciousness, trying to focus on how his marks moved and what was *happening*, but blackness crept into the edges of my vision and then I was falling, powerless to keep my eyes open any longer.

In the last vestiges of my awareness, I prayed for Death to take me in exchange for Rhyon.

As sleep took a stronger hold, I felt soft pressure on my back and behind my knees and warm breath against my ear. "It is not your time yet, little wolf. Sleep now."

CHAPTER SIXTEEN

Blistering cold wind stung at my face, freezing the tears that fell onto my cheeks. It burned at my nose and ears, dried out my lips and tongue and eyes. The howling sounded like screams, and yet, over it, I could hear my name. "ODYSSA!"

An enormous gust pushed me back, knocking me off balance and sending me tumbling to the ground. Jagged rocks cut into my palms and the backs of my thighs through my dress. In front of me, twisted spires of blackened stone rose like jagged teeth from the ground, casting sinister silhouettes against the black sky. Out of the shadows at the base of the cliffs, Rhyon emerged, dressed in his night clothes and barefoot, entirely out of place in this realm of darkness and decay.

"Rhyon," I breathed. He shouldn't be here; somewhere like this wasn't safe for him. And it was too cold for him to be out without shoes and a coat. "No, you shouldn't be here."

The wind rushed from behind me now, whipping my hair around my face and obscuring my vision. Spluttering, I swiped at it furiously, only to find Rhyon now crouched in front of me, his head cocked as he stared down at me. His eyes, usually bright with laughter and a warm amber, were pitch black and soulless.

I scrambled away from him, only to cry out as I backed into more jagged rocks that had not been there before. "What are you doing, Rhyon?"

"This is my new home, Odyssa. Don't you like it?" He smiled at me, showing off his bloody teeth and gums. "Come play, Odyssa. Then we shall always be together. You and Mama and me."

"What about Emyl?"

He traced his little fingers down the patterns of my Death marks on my shoulder as he hummed. His touch was like ice, burning trails of cold fire into my skin as he followed the lines. "But these will have to go first. Then you can come play with me."

In the next breath, his fingernails sharpened to points and he gouged them deep into my flesh.

I WOKE ON A SCREAM, panting and heaving as I clambered out of bed and fell to the floor. My shoulder burned and as I clutched at it, my fingers grew slick with blood. Panic gripped my heart as I tried and failed to stand, but each time my legs too weak to hold me up.

The door burst open and the curtains parted to let in bright daylight that stung my eyes. I squinted against it, trying to see who had come in.

"Oh my god." The soft words were followed by the sensation of my sheets being pressed to my shoulder and a calloused hand on my brow. Finally, my eyes adjusted enough to see that it was Zaharya bent in front of me. "What happened?"

I still couldn't breathe, couldn't trust my voice to speak or my body to listen. It had been a *dream*, yet why was I here on the floor with my shoulder bleeding, just as he'd left me in that land of barren nothingness? Bile rose in my throat, and I pushed away from Zaharya, scrambling and barely making it to the toilet before I vomited.

Drops of spittle and vomit clung to my hair as I heaved, unable to pull it out of the way as the pain caused another wave of nausea.

A cool cloth on the back of my neck had me flinching and then vomiting again. Zaharya's nimble fingers pulled my hair back from my face, and I felt it as she twisted it and secured it at my nape. She was saying something, but I could not hear over my own heaving and panting.

It felt like hours passed before my body was finished expelling everything I'd consumed the previous day and then some. But finally, on shaking limbs, I fell away from the toilet and crumpled against the wall.

Zaharya changed out the cloth on my neck and brought another to my face, wiping at my chin and cheeks. It felt like agony attempting to open my eyes, so I stayed in the eternal darkness. I didn't want to see the way she was surely looking at me anyways.

"Does that happen often?" she asked as she continued cleaning me up. She pulled the cloth away from my face and tossed it into the bathtub, rising to dampen another in the sink before returning. This one she used to dab at my shoulder. "Did you do this to yourself?"

"I—" My voice was nothing more than a croak and my throat was raw. I sighed, leaning my head back and trying once more to open my eyes. This time was marginally more successful, and I had a glimpse of concern on her face as she wiped at my shoulder. I squeezed my eyes closed again. "I've had nightmares since I was sick." I cleared my throat, wincing at the pain. "It has never been quite this bad before."

The cloth paused on my skin where my neck met my shoulder. Her voice was carefully neutral. "Nightmares about what?"

I licked my dry lips and swallowed, trying to get moisture back into my mouth and throat. Telling her the truth, especially after what I'd heard her say before, would be foolish. But she was trying to survive, same as me.

Taking my silence for an answer, she stood, taking the cloth with her.

"Wait," I called, reaching after her pitifully. I would tell her, I would tell her whatever she wanted, so long as I was not alone. I could still see his face, feel his hands in mine, and I feared what would happen if I fell back to sleep, even from exhaustion.

"I'm not leaving," she called as she stepped back into my bedroom. Only a moment later, she returned, pressing a glass into my hands. "Here. Drink this, slowly."

I tried to take small sips so my stomach did not revolt again, but the cool water felt like bliss on my tongue and throat.

She pulled it from my hands and placed it on the floor beside me. "That's enough; you'll get sick." Gentle fingers prodded at my shoulder and I could feel them trace over torn flesh. I couldn't bring myself to look down at it, but I knew it would follow the patterns of my Death marks, just as he had done in the dream. Was it even a dream? I couldn't tell anymore. "What happened, Odyssa? Camelya said you were ill. She asked me to listen out for you."

Indignation tried to ignite, but it sputtered out and fell quiet in the face of the sorrow at reading that letter. I cleared my throat again, swallowing down the acrid taste of vomit still clinging to the back of my tongue. "She brought me a letter. My youngest brother has been infected with the blood plague."

A heavy sigh left her lips and she shuffled until she was sitting on the floor beside me, our backs against the wall. "I am sorry to hear that, Odyssa. I know you were here to try to provide for them."

"I know I have yet to prove myself to you all, and that you

believe I will put you in danger. I heard you all talking that day I went to the wine cellars," I said. Her eyes widened, but I continued. "I want it known that I would do anything for my younger brothers. *Anything*. And despite choosing to come here to give them a chance at living, I am in agony every moment. To read that letter and know the youngest has—" My voice broke and I swallowed back the burning tears. "You all may not think I am, but I promise I am trying, and I will continue trying until my last breath. I am not asking to be friends, but I am asking for understanding. I would never put anyone in danger knowingly."

Silence held for a moment. Then, finally: "I understand. We all know what it was like having to adjust here. We've all been locked in here essentially since it started, and perhaps we've grown too callous."

It was hardly a resounding victory, but given the circumstances, sitting on the floor of my bathroom, I was glad we'd come to an understanding. The dream flashed back through my mind and I squeezed my eyes shut so tightly starbursts danced in my vision instead.

"What was your nightmare about?" she asked.

Deep breaths were calming, typically, but now they shuddered and trembled through my lungs. I switched to shallow ones, the breath holding high in my chest.

"I suffered from hallucinations when I was ill. My mother thought it was the fever, but I had vivid dreams, nightmares of cold and bleak lands filled with nothing but screaming bodies and Soulshades, of cliffs that towered over rivers of blood and fire that was so hot it felt cold when it burned you." I shook my head, clenching my hands into fists in my lap. "I thought it meant I was going to die, that I was seeing what my future would hold. I have nightmares about that place constantly since I recovered. I forget what happens in them, but the setting is always the same." I turned my head to look at her, ignoring the twinge in my shoulder. "Tonight I dreamed my brother was there in that place."

"Is this the first time you've had that nightmare?" she asked. "With your brother there?"

"Yes."

"Do you think there's something more to them?" She paused. "Do you think Sonya is trying to send you a message?"

"The goddess of wisdom would surely be kinder. If it's anyone, it is Kalyx telling me my brother's fate."

She bit her lip. I'd long given up on the gods, but Zaharya, it seemed, came from a place where they were still revered rather than reviled. "Do you truly believe that? That the gods would be so cruel?"

"I don't know what to think anymore. But if they are real, if they are still with us, I have a very hard time believing they give a damn about us right now. If they cared, surely they would have intervened, no?" I sighed when she did not reply. "I came to this castle to try to feed my family. To try to find out if there really was a treatment or if it was just city gossip. And now it has all been for nothing, yet I cannot leave."

"The treatment does exist."

"I know," I said, looking up from my lap to meet her gaze. "I overheard it being discussed at the party. That was why I stopped to listen."

Head tilted back against the wall, she closed her eyes for a moment before lowering her chin and standing. She held out her hand to pull me from the floor, grasping my forearm tightly as I stumbled with the dizziness that accompanied the sudden move. "We need to clean your wounds. Do you do that often? Hurt yourself in your dreams?"

Despite the many truths I'd spilled tonight, I held back on this. She may have believed me about the Soulshades before or the hallucinations now, but if I told her that I'd been injured in my dream, by my little brother, and then woke to those same injuries... I did not need to be gifted with sight to know what would be whispered about me. "Never before."

She hummed, reaching into the cabinet beside us to pull out a wooden box I hadn't known was there. Opening it, she pulled out bandages and various bottles. Her eyes tracked my stare. "That's how we knew you were lying about the wine cellar."

I snapped my head up to look at her. "What?"

She nodded down at the box. "You said you went to the infirmary after you cut your hand. But the castle doesn't have an infirmary. Or at least not one that would tend to us. We have these kits in our rooms, and anything that cannot be treated with them...well, then it cannot be treated." She poured clear liquid from one of the bottles onto a wad of cotton and pressed it to my shoulder.

The gasp I let out shuddered through my entire body, and I yanked away from her, panting for breath as the sensation of fire burned through the wound and deep into the muscle. Before I could recover, she was affixing a bandage over top.

"I won't ask who stitched your hand. I have a feeling I already know." Bottles rattled as she packed everything back into the box. "So I will just remind you once more: you have no friends here, Odyssa. You should trust no one, but especially none who enter the ballroom willingly and not as part of a job."

I chewed on my lip. "Do you know where the treatment is kept?"

The sigh she released was long-suffering. "I knew you were going to ask."

"I do not know your story, Zaharya, but if you were in my place, what would you do?"

"I may not be in your place exactly, but I have seen the fate of those who have been, and you are following the same path." She bent to return the box to the cabinet, slamming the door closed. "And they have all been killed for it."

"Please."

She stared at me for a moment after she stood, her eyes looking deep into my soul. I did not flinch or falter and kept her gaze. Another sigh, and her shoulders slumped. "The prince demands a price for the treatment. And very few have been willing or able to pay it." Her long finger reached out, tapping my breastbone. "And that is all I will say about it."

My hand darted out to grab her wrist as she went to leave. "I need to get it, Zaharya. I will pay whatever cost."

She smiled sadly at me. "They always say that, and yet somehow, no one ever returns with the treatment." Extricating herself from my grasp, she patted my cheek. "All you can do is hope, Odyssa. Hope that since you survived, your family will too. You cannot let your grief distract you, not here. This castle, these people, they will turn your grief into a weapon and gladly wield it against you. Don't give them the chance."

I followed her silently to the door, trying and failing to grasp at the words flying through my mind.

"Try to get some more rest," she said. "I'll wake you when it's time to prepare for the ball."

The door closed softly behind her and I was left reeling, stuck inside this room, inside this castle, inside my nightmares. My shoulder smarted and I looked longingly back at the bed, but I knew if I closed my eyes again, all I would see was Rhyon's face, covered in blood. And that, I could not bear to endure again.

Yanking open the wardrobe, I pulled off my nightgown and changed into a plain black, floor-length, long-sleeved dress.

No, sleep would not come again for me tonight. And if it did, I would send it away screaming as I had before.

CHAPTER SEVENTEEN

Despite knowing that sleep would not come easily or peacefully, I tried to rest. But every time I closed my eyes and began to drift off, I was brought back with echoes of screams and howling wind.

My stomach churned, the pain and the anguish inside stirring up nausea. I never wanted to see my brother, my baby brother, in that place. And yet he'd seemed so comfortable, so at ease there. If I ever saw him again, I feared I would only see that version of him. Bile burned my throat and my skin felt too tight. I wanted to claw my way out from inside my own chest.

The balcony looked inviting, and perhaps the fresh air would help. But when I pulled back the curtains and opened the door, I was met with red-tinged sky and the wind carrying up the faint cries of someone who'd been just a different kind of victim to the plague.

I shut the doors and pulled the curtains tightly closed, drenching the room once more in darkness.

The memory of my mother's body clung to my mind. The memory of cleaning her limp body, knowing she would never open her eyes again. I desperately tried to think of anything else, trying to recall the ballroom from the night before, what the decor looked like and what outfits people wore, but nothing would stick, nothing would drive that image out.

Despite the parting words between Emyl and me, that experience was something I would never wish on anyone. I did not want him to have to clean and wrap Rhyon's little body, to have to take our baby brother to the crematorium and get him back in a jar.

My mother had asked me to protect my brothers, to care for them, and I had done nothing but fail since her body had been taken. I had thought I would have *time* to find a solution, to be able to settle and integrate into the castle before tearing it apart brick by brick beneath everyone's noses.

But fate was fickle, and death was cruel. Rhyon had no time.

Pulling on my shoes, I left my room. I would find the secrets this castle held, where the prince held the treatment, if I had to pull it out of the walls myself. Zaharya had said I would not be willing to pay the price, but she did not know me. She did not know how much I was willing to sacrifice for those I loved.

I had already danced with death. I did not fear it.

The infirmary Zaharya mentioned, the one we were not welcome to, seemed like the most logical place to keep a cure to me. But yet, if the prince hoarded it like he did everything else, perhaps it would be best to start my search in his tower. Indecision had my steps faltering at the junction in the hallway.

Voices echoed loudly down the halls before I could decide, and I jerked back into an alcove. Whoever it was would be in the hall in seconds, and it was too long of an empty stretch to escape unseen. My heart thumped wildly in my chest, and for a moment, I feared whoever was coming would be able to hear it. Pressing my hand over my mouth, I pushed back into the wall, pressing myself as far into the shadows as possible as footsteps sounded across the stone floors. It sounded like they were already here, but the footsteps still came ever closer.

Sweat beaded on my upper lip, that cold sweat that always came at the most inopportune of times and rolled down into the corner of your mouth, salty and dank.

The footsteps slowed to a stop as they neared the alcove, yet no one had passed. Bile burned at the back of my throat. I tucked my elbows into my ribs, biting down on my lip as the movement tugged at the wounds in my shoulder.

"What is it?"

A deep voice hummed. Two more steps sounded, louder than ever before, and I stopped breathing entirely.

They retreated. "I thought I heard something."

My eyes widened at the familiar voice, and I had to tense every muscle in my body to keep from jerking. Of course Tallon was here, of course he would be the one to find me. I didn't dare look, but likely the Soulshade cat was nearby, telling him exactly where I was. Now, the only question was if he would reveal me to whoever he was with. It was a male voice, for certain, but not one I recognized. Not that I would have been able to recognize anyone at this point. But Tallon's voice was unmistakable, rich and dark.

"No one is *awake*, Tallon. It was likely just the castle." An amused huff came from Tallon's companion. "By all means, please investigate, though. You know it loves when you poke around where you shouldn't be."

There was no response from Tallon, but the footsteps started up again and finally they passed. Tallon never turned his head into the alcove, and neither did his companion who was hidden by Tallon's tall frame, but the smirk that lifted the corner of his mouth as he passed told me everything I needed to know. He knew I was here.

Only once the footsteps had faded and they had to be nearing the end of the hall did I let loose my breath, sucking down air and lowering my shaking hand away from my mouth.

My thighs wavered and I clutched on to the rough stone at my back to keep upright. It seemed my journey into the castle was finished for the night. Now that Tallon knew I was out, I doubted very much that he would let me continue. Once he was finished with whatever he was doing, he would seek me out. And I did not want to be sought by him.

Ash and smoke exploded on my tongue, making me gag with the thickness of the sudden taste. I barely had time to swallow back the burning and bitter taste when an icy finger trailed down the side of my neck.

Flinching away from the wall at my back, I stumbled out of the alcove, tripping over my own feet and falling to the ground, biting my cheek to stifle the cry. Tallon and his companion were not that far away yet that they would not hear me. My eyes darted to the side, trying to see if they had returned, but I kept my head forward, focused on the Soulshade emerging from the stone I'd just been pressed against.

As it solidified, it took the shape of a woman, but instead of coming after me like the others had, she tilted her head and stared. Her mouth opened and her lips moved, but no sound came out. She stopped talking abruptly and frowned, tilting her head the other way.

Slowly, as she watched me and I watched her, I picked myself back up from the floor. Her dress was similar to the ones we wore beneath the shrouds, thin-strapped and silky, sheathing from breastbone to ankle. Long hair flowed down to her hips. But it was her neck that caught my eye. A wide gash, nearly from ear to ear, took up her entire throat.

My eyes widened as I pieced together what was happening. Biting down on my tongue to keep from speaking, I slowly backed away. I wanted to ask her, to ask her who had slit her throat. But in the depths of my pounding heart and the roiling pit of my stomach, I knew the answer.

With jerky movements, she slowly reached out towards me. My body was screaming at me to run, the wounds on both my hand and my shoulder throbbing in time with my racing heart. But every fiber of my being wanted to see what would happen, what she wanted.

Her mouth opened and then with a quickness I hadn't been expecting, she rushed towards me, and as she made contact, a burning cold washed over me. Gasping, I stumbled back further into the hallway, clutching at my chest where the icy sting had settled.

In a flash, my vision turned white and a feeling of bone-deep fear petrified me where I stood. Anger, sorrow, fear all coursed through me on rotation, changing one after the other rapidly enough to make me dizzy. Brief glimpses of memories that were not mine, from places I'd never been and people I'd never met, ran through my mind.

I felt my body, was aware of someone coming up behind me, but I could do nothing. My movements were not mine to control. My body was not mine.

Firm hands wrapped around my waist from behind. "Get out of her. Now."

The ice writhed beneath my skin, vibrating beneath the flesh and thrumming up into my throat. I gagged and retched as it crawled up further, burning at the base of my tongue as the familiar emotions yet unfamiliar memories cycled through my mind again and again, faster now.

"I said *now*."

At the command, the burning cold vanished, taking all my energy with it, and I slumped, black stars dancing in my vision. The hands at my waist caught me, taking hold of my body weight as I swayed. Back in my body, I felt both chilled and entirely too hot all at once.

Whoever it was, they'd saved me, and more importantly, they were warm pressed up against my back. I leaned back into the warmth, trying to chase away the residual cold that felt seared into my lungs. My mind was fuzzy, like someone had pulled a blanket over it and was asking me to see through it. All I could focus on was that warmth, and the residual feeling of panic and anger and loss.

The warmth rumbled and a finger traced down the side of my neck, the same path the Soulshade had taken. "You are certainly trouble, aren't you, little wolf?"

I wanted to speak, to pull away from him as my mind recognized finally who the warmth at my back was, but he was so warm, and I was still so cold. My mind was foggy, the words flitting by before I could grasp them and speak them aloud. An intense ache settled into my bones, and my eyelids suddenly felt like they weighed a hundred pounds. Perhaps I would rest against the warmth for a moment. Just a moment, and then I would push him away and question him.

All I saw next was the ceiling, and then blackness settled in once more.

CHAPTER EIGHTEEN

I woke to the sound of bells tolling. Bells that said it was midday. My head felt cloudy, like it was stuffed with cotton that had also dried up in my mouth. Clothing rustled by the window and I froze, my breath catching in my throat.

All at once, memories slammed into my mind, one after another after another until I was gasping and jolting upright to press my hands into my eyes.

"Oh good, you're awake."

Gritting my teeth against the pain in both my palm and shoulder, I drew my knees to my chest beneath the blankets and dutifully ignored the fact Tallon had taken the care to put me beneath them in the first place. The skin around the wound on my shoulder felt tight and itchy. Lowering one hand from my face, I prodded at the wound gently, hissing when I touched the tender and hot skin.

"You seem to have quite the penchant for getting injured, little wolf." Tallon stood beside the bed. Somehow, he managed to look down at me with both a playful twist to his lips and a brow pinched with concern. "How did you come by this particularly gruesome wound? You did not have that at the ball last night."

My mind was not so foggy that I would make the mistake of telling him the truth. Or of asking him why he'd been looking at me closely enough to have known that.

"What is happening to me?"

"It seems to me someone should wrap you in protective padding and lock you in a room where you cannot hurt yourself."

Flinging the blankets off my body, I stood from the bed. He blocked my path and did not move, twitching an eyebrow up along with the corner of his lips. A challenge. Eyes narrowing, I did not back away or skirt around him, instead ensuring my front brushed up against his more closely than strictly necessary. His sharp inhale had me biting the inside of my cheek in victory.

But the small sliver of joy that came with besting him was fleeting. "Why are the Soulshades coming after me here?"

The room between us grew silent and still, and for a moment, I was convinced he'd stopped breathing as he looked down at me. Reaching into his pocket, he pulled out a small tin. When he opened it, the smell of lavender and mint and something slightly spicy filled the room. He lifted it towards me, dipping a finger in the thick paste inside.

"May I touch you, Odyssa? This will help with that," he said, nodding towards my shoulder.

After only a moment's hesitation, I nodded, letting him apply the paste. It stung slightly, and then settled into a cool burning that eased the throbbing and tightness there until it was mostly numb. I didn't know what was in the paste, but if it helped this much, I also knew I likely would not want to ask.

"Did you even clean this out?"

"Zaharya did."

His hand froze, fingers still on my skin. "Did she cause this?"

"No."

He waited, but finally seemed to accept I would not offer anything further and continued until the entirety of the wound was delightfully numb. He took my hand next, spreading a thin layer of the paste over the neat stitches there as well. Wiping his hands on the sides of his pants, he tucked the tin back into his pocket.

"I asked a question before," I reminded him, raising an eyebrow. "Why are the Soulshades so intent on me? I never had this problem living in the city. What is different about the castle?"

His eyes darkened, a morning-mist gray deepening into the color of roiling storm clouds. He stepped away from me, moving with heavy steps to the balcony doors. Back to me, he shoved his hands into his pockets and looked out over the city. "There is a lot that is different about this castle, little wolf. So much."

My eyes narrowed. I rolled my neck to ease the sudden tension in my jaw and followed him to the balcony. I would not be ignored, not this time. He knew something, and if I was in danger—more danger than normal, at least—I deserved to know. Black Death marks stood stark on my pale hand resting on the black silk of his shirt as I grabbed his shoulder to turn him around. He came easily, crossing his arms and taking a step back while shrugging my hand off his shoulder.

"What is *happening*?" I asked, eyes searching for anything in his face that would give me an answer, a clue, as to why these Soulshades were trying to hurt me, as to why this castle seemed hell-bent on tasting my blood.

"You received a bit of bad news after the ball last night, did you not?"

"Yes," I said slowly. Flashes of Emyl's handwriting on the parchment came back with a shocking clarity, cutting through the fog I had not realized was still settled around my head. I shook my head to clear it further. "Yes, I did. My youngest brother has come down with the blood plague. I—" I bit my lip, cutting myself off.

"Did you have a nightmare? Is that how you were hurt?" His words were smooth, his head tipping to the side slightly as he looked down at me. The lines in his forehead had smoothed out, but for a moment, something else flashed in those gray eyes. A warning, almost. But even despite it, I couldn't help but notice how, unlike Zaharya, his wording had not implied that I had hurt myself during the nightmare.

"I—" I shook my head again, pinching the bridge of my nose, unwilling to let him distract me yet again. "No, no. You brought me back to my room after you found me in the hall. That Soulshade was *inside of me*, Tallon. How? What is happening to me?"

He looked at me with a carefully constructed mask, but instead of one made of ornate silver and filigree, it was crafted of skin and muscle. He said nothing.

I pressed my fingertips into my temples, trying to claw through the memories and the haze they were wrapped in. "Tell me the truth, Tallon."

He pulled my hands down from my head, keeping the left one in between us and letting the other fall. "Look at me, Odyssa," he said. He ducked his head to catch my gaze. "What happened in your nightmare?"

I narrowed my gaze. "A truth for a truth, then?"

A quirk of his lip broke through the mask and he inclined his head. "Certainly. You first."

"My brother died, and then his Soulshade dug his nails into my flesh and ripped it. He wanted me to stay with him." It was as emotionless as I could manage—strictly facts, and sparse ones at that—but I still heard how my voice shook. I rolled my shoulders back and met his eyes. "Your turn."

"Odyssa, truly," he said. Dropping my hand, he tilted my chin up to meet his eyes. "I have no idea why the Soulshades in this castle are after you."

"You agreed to a truth for a truth, Tallon."

"I am telling you the truth." He looked at me, an unreadable expression on his face. For a moment, I was convinced he would drop whatever ruse this was and tell the *whole* truth, but his face hardened and something shuttered over his eyes, turning them dull and lifeless. "Perhaps you need to see a medic. The prince should know if one of his staff is hallucinating being attacked in his home."

I jerked back, anger heating my face and overpowering the confusion at his sudden shift. The nightmare and the Soulshades had already wrought havoc on my mind, and now this. If this was who he wanted to be, this cold and indifferent being, then I could reciprocate. I tucked my hands behind my back and raised my chin, feeling the expression fall from my face.

His eyes narrowed slightly, but his expression did not change.

"The infirmary is not for servants. Though I think you know that."

"Do I?"

I hummed. "I cannot see how you wouldn't. Given that you are so close with the prince."

He looked at me for a long moment. I almost jumped when he moved, once again invading my space and stepping up to my side, our shoulders meeting as he peered down at me. "What a pretty mask you wear, little wolf."

"I wear no mask." It wasn't a mask; it was a wall. One that he would not break through.

"Don't you?"

I raised my chin and rolled my shoulders back. His eyes briefly flicked down to where my gown dipped between my breasts before rising back to my eyes as he licked his lips slowly.

Heat unfurled in my belly, but the coldness still in his eyes tempered it.

It was foolish to rise to the bait, but I could not resist the challenge. I rose on my toes and leaned in until I knew he could feel my breath against his neck. "If the prince wants me dead, he'll have to have you kill me yourself."

I dropped back to my heels and stepped away, watching for his reaction.

He tilted his head back and laughed, a loud sound that came from deep in his chest. A laugh like that could not be forced. It was a challenge to keep the frown from my face as he continued to laugh for another moment.

Finally, he was finished. Faster than I could track, he was behind me, his fingers tracing over the marks high on my neck behind my ear and following the lines down to my shoulder. His touch was cool against the hot skin around the wound there.

My eyes closed and I shivered, cursing my body for reacting. It would have been too easy to give in and lean back into him, to play whatever games he wanted and let myself be consumed by the storm. But nothing in my life had ever been easy.

"Odyssa, the prince does not want you dead. But if he did, he would not need me to do it."

"Why's that?"

He moved behind me and then his lips were on my skin, brushing against where my neck curved into my shoulder. The next touch of his lips was firmer, pressed against the top of the deepest gouge in my flesh. I felt his mouth curve into a smirk against my neck. "Well, you seem to be doing a remarkably good job attempting that for yourself."

The familiar heat of shame washed over me, settling in my stomach that had fallen to my knees. It had been another game. And I'd lost.

I yanked away from him, turning to face him. His eyes were

dark, nearly black as he looked down at me. "You seem troubled, Odyssa."

"Get out," I said, pointing towards the door. My voice did not waver, a feat I was utterly grateful for. It remained steady and cool despite the embarrassment and anger blazing inside me.

He'd somehow slipped between the cracks in the wall I'd built, and I'd not realized it until it was too late. I'd been willing to play his games at first, but this was not a game. Not really. This was life or death, and I would not let Tallon be the reason I failed my brothers.

"And leave me be. I do not have the time nor the energy for these games you are playing." My hand shook slightly then, and I pulled it back to my chest, palm pressing against my breastbone heavily. "I am not a toy for your amusement, only to be tossed aside once you've broken me."

He'd started towards the door at my instruction, but stopped then, coming back until there was only the smallest sliver of air between us. My eyes widened, but I'd barely had time to react before his hands were wrapped around my biceps and his face was lowering towards mine. Noses brushed and his breath washed over my lips. If either of us had so much as swayed, his lips would have touched mine. His words washed over me, breath fluttering my eyelashes. "Make no mistake, little wolf, you cannot be broken. Especially not by me. Do not forget that."

Those gray eyes flicked down to my lips and for a heartbeat, I thought he might kiss me. I thought I might want him to. His tongue darted out to wet his lips once more, and then he was gone, halfway to the door before I'd even realized he'd let go of me.

His departure renewed my anger and I reached for the nearest thing within my reach and hurled it after him. The pillow hit the closing door harmlessly, bouncing off the wood as his laughter echoed down the hall.

Frustrated tears pricked at my eyes and I ran my hands through my hair, tugging at the roots. Something was wrong. Something was happening here, and I was losing my mind. Rhyon was *dying* and I had forgotten until Tallon had mentioned it. I clung to the clarity it gave me, picturing both of my brothers as my eyes scoured the floor where the letter had fallen.

Camelya had said I could send a response. How had I forgotten that? Brushing away the tears that escaped, I finally saw the letter on the floor and rushed to pick it up. Flipping it over, I took it to the desk in the corner and began my reply. I could not risk being lost to whatever this castle was doing to me before I replied. Rhyon needed me, and despite that he would argue otherwise, Emyl would too.

Rhyon was going to die. My nightmare had convinced me of that. But there were things I could offer to make it easier on both Rhyon and Emyl, even if I could not be there myself. Chief among them was finding the treatment for when Emyl was inevitably next. Rhyon was not dead yet, but he would be, and then it would be only Emyl and me left. I would not lose my last family to this curse. I refused.

My pen scrawled until the back of the parchment was covered in my tiny, cramped writing. It wasn't enough; I had so much more to say, but it would have to do. I set it carefully flat on the desk. Tonight, once the staff were awake and beginning to prepare for the party, I would take it to Camelya. And then, I would find that damned treatment and get it to Emyl.

CHAPTER NINETEEN

The night's decor had transformed the ballroom into a golden sunset, filled floor to ceiling with gilded *every-thing,* a mockery of the vivid colors that had painted the evening sky before the red mist had descended. Through the deep orange tinge from the shroud, I watched from the hall for a moment before entering. It was objectively beautiful, a feat of decor to have made it so drastically different from the night prior, but all I wanted to do was rip it down. Everything was dripping in gold, from the chandeliers to the silverware set out along the long table at the end of the room. All of it an obscene show of just how little the prince cared for anyone besides himself.

My breath fluttered the fabric of the veil. The music in the hall picked up, and I had no more time to wait.

There would be no mistakes tonight. Whatever purpose Tallon had behind playing his games with me, he would not be able to protect me if I continued to draw attention to us. I needed to be the perfect servant, unnoticed and unremarkable. It was the only way I would be able to find the treatment, and it was the only way I would be able to get out of the castle to get it to Emyl once I had it.

I could not trust someone to take it for me, nor could I trust if I tried to smuggle it out in the mail that it would make it to the intended destination. No, if I wanted to get it out of the castle, I would have to take it myself.

I pushed the second part of my mission out of my mind for the moment. The castle and the Soulshades would likely not make my escape easy, not if they were under the prince's control. And I could not afford any apprehension. I would puzzle out my escape once I had what I was here for.

My tray empty, I returned to the kitchens to refill it and continued my path through the castle and back to the ballroom. Focus, that was what I needed. I would excel, becoming the best servant of us all. I would flit about, ensuring the happiness of these callous people while I collected information and tucked it away to be used against the Coward Prince later, to be used to save my family when the opportunity presented itself.

The bells had just begun their midnight toll when Tallon finally appeared, sweeping into the ballroom and turning every head, though they quickly looked away once they saw who had arrived. Yet still, like every night, people watched him out of the corners of their eyes. Mostly in fear, though some looked as if given half a chance, it could easily morph into desire.

Instead of his normal mask, the top of his face was visible tonight and the mask instead covered his jaw. A golden skull gilded to fit the theme. It emphasized the coldness in his eyes better than the silver mask ever could have.

His presence here at these parties was far different than the Tallon I'd experienced in private. Whether that was intentional or not remained to be seen. Likely, it was part of his games, and despite my best efforts, I kept falling right into the thick of them.

It frustrated me that I could not seem to keep away from him despite my continued promises to myself. I tightened my grip on my tray and turned back into the crowd.

Still, I felt his gaze on me for the rest of the night.

Though the ball lasted until the first vestiges of the dawn, as it did every night, this one felt as if it were over in the blink of an eye. I could hardly complain, but my skin was still crawling, too tight for my body, and I readily took over cleaning, whisking around the ballroom, gathering empty glasses and dirtied plates and anything else I could to burn off the anxious energy.

Tallon was still watching me from the same balcony I'd watched him from that first night. He wasn't trying to hide it, leaning his forearms against the banister and peering down at me. The Soulshade cat was perched on the banister at his side, its too-long claws curled around the wood as if it were a bird instead of a cat. As if it were not a spirit and needed to hold on to keep its balance.

I avoided looking up as I cleaned.

Maricara and Elena were with me in the ballroom tonight, the others already back in the kitchen. In a way I was glad for it, as it meant I could work in silence and without the pitying looks from Talyssa or the polite and stiff conversation I knew Zaharya would turn to as a way to ease the strain my nightmare had put on our interactions.

I was alone with all of them, in different ways, and at least Maricara and Elena made no disguises about it.

My tray filled with precariously piled glasses and silverware, I began my path through the ballroom and towards the kitchen.

Two sets of eyes, one pair gray and one pair yellow, tracked my every move.

Sour and bitter and heavy, ash and smoke filled my mouth at the same moment as a Soulshade appeared in front of me, fully formed. There was no flickering, no burgeoning taste to forewarn me of its convalescence. The Soulshade merely appeared in my path. I stumbled back, cursing the thick orange haze that clouded my vision. Glasses rattled on my tray as I struggled to keep it aloft.

The Soulshade tipped its head back and screamed. I struggled to not react and forced myself to keep my eyes on the Soulshade rather than searching out Tallon to see if he was reacting. Tightening my grip on the tray, I changed my path, going towards the other doorway near where Maricara worked.

I tracked its approach in my periphery, but I had no time to react before it was on me, just as the one the previous night had been. Frozen talons burned as they clawed through my chest and I faltered. Time slowed as, clutching at my breastbone through the veil, I watched the tray fall to the ground. A cascade of shattered glass echoed, falling in a maelstrom across the floor as I fell to my knees. The stone floor of the ballroom was typically frigid, but now seemed ablaze compared to the icy grip around my heart.

I could not *breathe*. My heart thumped wildly in my chest and my mind was besieged with flashing visions that were not my own.

A library's vaulted expanse and rows of wooden shelves, the silhouette of a man's nape, a goblet raised in a toast, corridors stretching throughout the castle, a return to the library, and finally, a man's hand, adorned in rings and reaching forth, clasping my throat.

The visions that ensnared me felt so real, so true, though I could still see the ballroom around me through the vision.

Maricara and Elena continued gaping at me, their lips moving, but I could not breathe, the spectral hand tightening around my throat as it did in the vision. My heart constricted in my chest, the regular thumping of my blood against my veins in my throat slowing as the cold seemed to spread, pervasive through my body.

A slightly warmer cold brushed against my leg, and then the sensation and visions were gone. I slumped forward, hands falling to catch myself and narrowly missing embedding more glass into my flesh. The cat wove its body between my arms and my knees, winding itself around my wrists in a figure eight and looking up at me.

Relief washed through me and I let my eyes fall closed.

"What is *wrong* with you?" Maricara's voice finally cut through the haze. Footsteps stomped towards me and she yanked my veil from my head. Fingers twisted in my hair and hauled me to my feet. I didn't resist her, though I likely should have.

Tallon was still watching me from the balcony. The cat hissed at her from my side.

"Did you just *hiss* at me?" Maricara demanded. She'd let go of my hair but was still in my face, her shoes crunching against the glass shards I'd spilt.

I couldn't help the smile that stretched over my lips, couldn't stop the laughter that bubbled up from my chest, uncontrollable and far from humorous. Of course she would hear that.

In a small way, I was honored the cat was defending me. This strange, wrong creature, an echo of a soul that clung to the living, was trying to comfort me. How sad that this was the first being, living or dead, that had ever defended me in my entire life. It was equally pathetic and endearing, and only made the laughter crescendo.

Not for the first time, I had an overwhelming desire to be able to pet it.

Once the laughter finally stopped spilling from my lips, Maricara and Elena were standing in front of me, looking at me curiously. "You will be the ruin of us all, and I will not stand for it. Camelya will be hearing about this."

"She already has," Camelya's voice echoed into the nearly empty ballroom from the doorway. "Odyssa, come with me. The others will clean up the glass."

I hardly questioned following her. The Soulshade had ruined the only night I'd had since I started that had not ended in some other catastrophe, and it seemed I was out of chances. Idly, I was aware that I no longer felt Tallon's gaze on my back, but I could not muster any care to turn back and search for him. He did not care about me, nor should he.

I followed Camelya into a sitting room down the hallway from the ballroom's entrance. The door swung silently on its hinges behind me, shutting us in with a soft thunk.

Camelya stood by the window, and though her attempts at dismissal by turning her back to me were obvious, they were weakened by the quick darting of her glances over her shoulder back at me, and the way her clasped hands trembled at their place at her lower back. "I understand you are grieving, Odyssa, but this cannot keep happening. Some of the others report you are being careless."

I said nothing, though I kept my head high. Observing. Perhaps it made me a bad person that I enjoyed the sight of her fear, but the knowledge was a comfort. I did not know why my Death marks had begun reacting to my emotions, why they came to life to protect me, but I was hardly in a position to wish they had not.

"If patterns hold, your paycheck will be withheld and any opportunity for communication outside the castle will be revoked." She let out a little breath on a nod, as though proud she got through her declaration without her voice shaking. "Tomorrow's party is your last chance. Any more mistakes after that will be taken to the prince."

The words resonated in my ears, but they took a moment to settle before I truly understood the implications. *If you mess up again, your brothers will pay the price and they will die without a word from you.* The letter I had written Emyl weighed heavily in my heart. It was still sitting there on my desk, waiting to be finished. Now, perhaps it never would be.

The threat of the prince held no dominion over me. There was little he could do that would be worse than that. My brothers may have written me off, but my mother watched from the land of the dead, and I would not fail her.

Slowly, I removed the shroud from my head so that I could see Camelya without the tinge of orange.

She tracked each movement closely with narrowed eyes.

"Do you enjoy being cruel? Enjoy being able to play puppeteer to these lives in your hands? Does the control make you feel powerful?" I took a step towards her with each question. To her credit, she did not flinch or back away.

"Life is cruel, Odyssa, and cruelty often keeps you alive." Her eyes slipped down to my arm again, but the marks remained still. "Loyalty is a foolish notion; we all must look after our own interests and safety."

"Be cruel unto others before they can be cruel unto you?"

She smiled wryly. "Precisely."

"How shortsighted. To be cruel unto those who would never have been cruel unto you only makes you enemies you otherwise would not have. You should be careful: one day, you might make an enemy who can be far crueler than you."

Her passive face flickered into a frown for a moment, fear flashing in her eyes before she was able to school her features back into placidness. "You are naive to think there are people who would never wish cruelty upon you. Especially in this place."

Wind whistled through the partially open window.

"Return to your duties, Odyssa. See to it that you don't mess up again." This time, she turned fully away, hands clasped in front of her.

Escape could not come quick enough, and I left the room behind, intent on returning to my room. The others could clean up the party themselves. After all, if some of them had their way, they would be without help again soon enough.

Turning the corner towards the stairway, I stopped short at the sight of Tallon leaning against the wall. His shoulder pressed against the stone, his body tilted at an angle and one ankle crossed over the other. He lifted his head when he heard me, the skull mask firmly in place across his jaw. Still in his costume, it seemed.

Neither of us moved, intent on waiting the other out.

Slowly, so slowly, he reached up and unfastened the mask behind his head with one hand, letting it fall to dangle in his fingers by the strap. "What did you see that made you drop the glass?"

He may have removed the physical mask, but the dull gray in his eyes and the tightness in his brow revealed he was still in his persona of Tallon, the prince's companion. I raised an eyebrow, the most defiance I could risk in the public view of the hall, still so close to the end of the ball. "Grief, my lord. It was merely my own grief."

His eyes narrowed. Powerful muscles carried him off the wall and into my personal space. Fingers traced up from my wrist to my inner elbow. His voice was hushed, words meant only for me. "What did she say to you in that room, Odyssa?"

Despite the shivers that erupted on my arm where he

touched me, and the heat that flared at the base of my spine, I stepped away. "Nothing out of step, my lord. A reminder of what is at stake should I cause problems again."

"And what exactly is at stake for you?"

"Besides my own life, you mean?"

"Do not concern yourself with that," he said, stepping back up into my space and twisting a piece of my hair around his finger loosely, letting it fall away. The gray of his eyes swirled, no longer flat and dull as before. He tucked the hair behind my ear, fingers trailing down my neck along the marks. "No harm will come to you under my watch."

I scoffed, pulling my shoulder back to force his hand away. "Pity you cannot be constantly watching me, then." Twice now, I had been physically injured in this castle. Twice now, I had been run through by a Soulshade, subjected to the cold burning sensation of whatever they had done to me. The latter incidents had both happened in his presence, under his watch.

"Odyssa—"

"Why do you care, Tallon?"

He stopped short, narrowing his eyes. "What do you mean?"

"Why do you care if I am harmed or not? You do not interact with any of the others, and you've said yourself that everyone fears you. Why concern yourself with me?"

I did not expect him to answer. I expected more diversion, more avoidance, but he surprised me yet again. "I told you before, you are not what I was expecting. And it intrigues me."

Somehow, the answer made me even angrier. I curled my fingers into the silk of my dress at my hips. "You do not need to feel responsible for me, my lord. I can take care of myself."

I spun on my heel and left, intent on finding another path back to my room that did not involve Tallon. Intriguing, he said. And once he'd figured me out, I would be tossed aside and left to the whims of the castle along with the others. If I survived that long.

Cold brushed against my ankle, the gruesome cat arching its back and stretching up to rub its head against my knee while still keeping step with me. Its tail curled around my calf and then it sped up, keeping a step in front of me.

A smile curled on my lips, and I followed the unnatural creature through the castle.

CHAPTER TWENTY

The cat lounged on my bed the rest of the night, though sleep was reluctant yet again to claim me. The cat was a small comfort, but it was a comfort I hadn't known I needed. It had no weight to it as it stretched across my legs and feet, but its wide yellow eyes and the too-cold patch of air reminded me of its presence. I hadn't realized how alone I was, even in a house with my mother and brothers, even knowing I was on my own here in this castle. I hadn't truly understood the depths of my isolation until this oddly shaped, once-black Soulshade cat had appeared at my side.

I did not even care that it was likely under Tallon's control or influence.

In another life, I would have cried, would have raged and thrown things and cursed at the sky until I was exhausted and calm. But now, some of the fight had bled from me, had been leeched out by grief and further stamped down by imposed responsibility I had not wanted, had not asked for. My fingers found my temples, rubbing circles to try to ease the unfettered tension that had been building there all night.

My eyes caught the unfinished letter to Emyl on the desk and I faltered, lowering my hands slowly.

The cat lifted its head, peering at me from where it lay across my shins.

I had not asked for the responsibility of caring for my family, yet I'd taken it on anyways. And perhaps that was the nature of responsibility: taking on something you do not want, yet knew you must. I'd made excuses for Emyl all his life, trying to take what little responsibility he had off his shoulders and onto mine. It had not been fair to either of us, and now Emyl would have to bear the responsibility of Rhyon's death alone.

My first instinct was to rush to the letter and apologize for failing him, for letting him evade his own growing up and leaving him so selfish. But it was far too late for that, and I suspected he was still basking in his anger. Still, I did not want the last words spoken as I left the house that morning to be the last words we ever spoke to each other. I rose from the bed and settled into the chair to finish writing the letter.

THE LETTER I'd tucked into my dress was scorching against my breast, reminding me of its presence. I was under no illusions that this letter leaving the castle would be entirely dependent on how tonight's party unfurled, and that if I failed, my words would never reach Emyl or Rhyon in time.

Entering the kitchens just as the sun had disappeared, I had little hope of the letter ever being sent. But the words had been a balm to my own soul, if nothing else. The failures, the mistakes since I'd been in the castle were my own, yet it would be foolish of me to assume that this night would be different simply because I wished it so.

The others looked at me as I entered, all of us dressed in veils of a shimmery white fitting the moonlight theme. Maricara and Elena lifted their heads only enough to glance at me before turning in dismissal.

Zaharya tilted her head as she looked at me, the movement sending ripples down the veil. "How are you, Odyssa?"

I was grateful the veil hid my frown. She did not care, not truly. The curiosity was around what edict or punishment Camelya had issued, not around my personal wellbeing. If she'd asked any other question, perhaps I would have believed her. But this one, this inauthentic inquiry into my state of mind, had me closing off. Not that I'd planned to be forthcoming with Zaharya regardless. I'd had my breakdown in front of her; there would not be another. "I'm fine."

The silence buzzed in my ears like the incessant flies that had invaded Veressia to make their homes on the corpses of those we'd lost.

If they wanted to know what Camelya had said, what my punishment would be, they would have to be brave enough to ask it aloud, without hiding behind empty, placating words and soft tones.

"Are you still..." Talyssa's words trailed off. She swallowed hard, visible even beneath the shroud of moonlight she wore. It trembled as she moved. "Will you still be working with us?"

I inclined my head. "Yes."

Maricara sighed heavily. "Tell us what happened with Camelya, Odyssa. Is there anything the rest of us need to be concerned about?"

"If you wanted to know that, you should have just asked."

"We did."

"No, Zaharya asked how *I* was. I am fine. Talyssa asked if I would still be working. I will be."

"Fine. What did Camelya say to you last night?" Her words were spat through gritted teeth. "Do we need to be concerned?"

"Further mistakes will result in my paycheck being withheld and not sent to my brothers. Not that it matters anyways, since I received a letter yesterday telling me the youngest one is infected." She flinched. I took a deep breath to calm the raging tempest inside me. I forced the next words out slowly on the exhale. "She did not mention any of you."

"You cannot let your grief manifest here," Zaharya said, her voice soft yet firm. "The castle feeds on it. It senses your weakness and it will seek them out. You leave yourself vulnerable the more emotion you feel." She paused, considering me. "You do well not to show it, but the castle cares not for whatever mask you don, Odyssa. Wherever you must go in your mind, whatever you must do, no one here will think less of you for it."

"I find that very hard to believe, considering I was judged the moment you found out I volunteered for service."

"Yes, well, that was a mistake." Zaharya turned her gaze to Maricara and Elena. "One that will not happen again."

The bells tolled, ending the conversation before a response was needed. I was grateful, as there was no response to that; I hardly believed her, after all. We gathered our trays and made for the ballroom.

A slimy, oily feeling settled in my stomach, turning it sour and heavy and causing my grip to tighten on my tray of drinks. The castle, the prince, even Tallon himself, would not make this night easy for me, I feared.

The letter burned against my skin. Vowing to let myself hear nothing, see nothing, and speak nothing, I entered the ballroom. I would be as we were intended: unnoticeable.

I was nearly able to keep my vow.

We were nearing the end of the night when I walked past a group leaning against the windows. Taking a respite from the dancing, I supposed. I did not intend to listen to their conversation as I distributed fresh drinks to them, collecting their empty ones as payment, but I heard it all the same.

"...such a messy business," one of them said.

"I hear the city is running out of room to bury their dead. It's as if people could not get out fast enough." Laughter followed.

The tray rattled slightly in my hands, but none of them noticed, just pushing their empty glasses into my clutches. My world narrowed to their laughter, mixing with the tinkling of glasses. The veil brushed against my face, and I wanted nothing more than to rip it off, to pull away the smothering fabric.

I started to leave, to take the empty glasses back to the kitchens and take a moment to breathe and settle before returning, but their lingering conversation floated over and stopped me in my tracks, unable to do anything but stare at them.

"So sad too," someone added, though they sounded like they were trading gossip rather than remorse. "Why, I heard just this morning three young boys passed. A waste of good labor, if you ask me."

The room fell away, my blood echoing in my ears. *Rhyon. Rhyon. Rhyon.* He was the only thing on my mind. I needed to get to Camelya, to have her dispatch my letter immediately, to see if she had any news from outside the walls about my brother. I turned on my heel, mind already mapping out the best way to get back to the kitchens and then to Camelya's without being seen. My eyes were unseeing, already setting my path halfway to the door as I sped up my steps.

I passed by a small crowd, only to be stopped by more people shoving their empty glasses at me. Once they'd been added to my already full tray, and my nerves were even more frayed than ever, I took a small step back, signaling to the group my imminent departure. A masked man drained the last of his drink and thrust it on my tray, wobbling the other glass atop it.

Another body brushed against my back, not hard enough to truly be considered a glancing blow, just how people might pass by each other in a crowded room. I thought nothing of it, but in combination with my limited vision due to the shroud and the precariously balanced glasses I was holding, though, the movement sent me stumbling.

I maneuvered to keep the movement from jostling the tray further, my eyes fixed only on the glass as it tilted and finally settled. Rhyon's face was the only thing on my mind—the crowd around me simply did not exist, a sea of faceless bodies.

A large hand wrapped around my wrist and pulled me around hard, sending me tumbling to the floor. The clattering of the tray and the glasses echoed through the ballroom, sending out some preternatural signal to the rest of the party as all conversation and music halted.

My eyes closed as I let my reality sink in for a moment. The letter tucked inside my dress may as well have been torn into shreds. It would never see the outside of this castle now. Rhyon's last memories of me would be the hateful words slung between us. Emyl would never speak to me again, even if I did somehow make it out of this tomb.

The silence had weighed long enough, and my fate would not be patient much longer. I raised my gaze, meeting that of a fair-haired man with an elegant half-moon mask on and rage blazing in his ice-blue eyes. The silver crown atop his head completed the portrait that sealed my fate.

Prince Eadric had been the one to bump against me.

To his side, Tallon stood, again in his silver half-skull mask, watching me with dull gray eyes and an indifference that made something in my stomach twist.

"*Who dares to touch me?*" The prince sneered down at me, his visage everything I'd expected and more, opulence and waste personified.

I did not apologize, did not point out that it was *he* who touched me as I'd been attending to his guests, but I also did not bow my head in submission. Instead, I held his gaze through the veil, daring this Coward Prince to be the devil we all knew him to be.

Cold brushed against my wrist and arm, and Tallon's eyes narrowed as they flicked down to where I knew the cat would be curled against me.

Prince Eadric's nostrils flared. "Are you truly so ignorant that you can't manage to *walk* without failing?"

I bit down on my tongue hard enough to taste blood. Every ounce of willpower I had was thrust towards not speaking and keeping my face a blank and impassive slate. I would not ruin my chances at writing to Emyl by letting my anger get the better of me. I had done nothing wrong, and though the Coward Prince would certainly not see so, I had to hope Camelya would listen to reason.

I saw his hand moving before it reached me, and even though I fought back the flinch, my body was still not prepared for the force he struck me with. The jewels on his ring caught against the fabric of the veil, tearing into it and the skin of my face beneath. Time slowed to a crawl as my head jerked around to the other side.

Blood welled in my mouth and crimson stains spread across

the white veil. Beneath it, I watched the stain grow for a heartbeat. Somehow, the blow had lessened my anger—at least, it had extinguished the anger from a raging inferno—one hot enough to melt the silver and gold that peppered this monument to arrogance—into a blistering cold fury, colder than the icy talons of the Soulshades as they clutched at my heart.

I looked up at him beneath the veil, not bothering to raise a hand to wipe the blood away.

His eyes widened, then narrowed, and he moved to strike me again. But Tallon stepped forward, gripping Prince Eadric's wrist before he could lift his arm once more. He leaned in and murmured something in the prince's ear. The gray of his eyes was no longer still and the weight of his gaze fell heavily on me even as he whispered to the prince. To his friend.

Prince Eadric leaned back, rocking on his heels as Tallon stepped back to his side. "Well, it seems as if you are new to my service." Without warning, he bent and grabbed a handful of my hair through the veil, twisting it and yanking at the roots. I bit down hard on my tongue to keep from crying out, making sure I kept my face neutral and my eyes forward. His breath was disgustingly hot and moist against my face, dampening the veil along with the blood he'd spilt. "Do not let this happen again. Or you will learn what it is like to choke on your own blood."

I already have, I wanted to tell him, but I only looked up at him.

He pushed my head away, wiping his hand on his jacket as he turned, dismissing me entirely. To the room, he bellowed to resume the party, and the musicians began their song anew.

The crowd dispersed, Tallon lingering only slightly before following the prince back into the fray.

Once everyone's eyes were off me, I pulled myself to my feet, curling my toes in my shoes and tensing my stomach to keep from falling as the dizziness took over. The Soulshade cat curled around my ankle, looking up at me, its normally large yellow eyes and wide black pupils narrowed to slits. The hair was raised on its back, but still it curled around me, trying to comfort me as I found my balance at last.

I felt the eyes of the others, faceless against the backgrounds, as good servants should be. The walk to the ballroom entrance felt like a thousand steps, though I knew it was far less. Crimson dotted my vision, and as soon as I had made my escape from the ballroom and entered the vacant halls, I tugged off the veil, letting it flutter to the floor behind me.

Prince Eadric was not a threat to me. Not anymore. I'd signed my death warrant, and I had absolutely nothing left to lose.

I would tear this castle apart and him with it if I needed to find the treatment and get it to Emyl. The letter in my dress pressed against my skin, reminding me of its presence. Pulling it out, I unfolded it carefully and let my eyes roam over the words, the words that my brothers would never get to see. I'd ruined my chances at that, and I'd have to live with it for eternity. I folded the letter back up and returned it to its place against my skin.

The cold presence of the cat seemed to vibrate, as if it were trying to purr against me as we walked. The oddness of it reminded me yet again that this cat was a Soulshade and had likely met a gruesome end inside these very walls. It filled me with a different kind of anger, the kind that was far more melancholy and sorrowful.

Perhaps I would tear everything and everyone inside this castle apart regardless.

CHAPTER TWENTY-ONE

By the time I had returned to the small solace of my room, my mind was spinning. Prince Eadric's blow had been harsh, and the wounds on both my face and shoulder throbbed with each movement, but I was hardly thinking about it. The treatment—I needed to get it now.

As I wiped the blood from the cuts on my face, I knew I could not hold out hope that Rhyon was still alive, no matter how much I wanted to. Perhaps if I had been there to care for him, he might have made it the full seven days before the blood plague took him, but with Emyl caring for him, I had to believe my youngest brother had already passed.

For a moment, I wanted to give up and surrender, leaving Emyl to whatever fate he had designed for himself. The only thing we'd ever seen eye-to-eye on was Rhyon, and all I could see now was Rhyon's face in my nightmares as he tore into my flesh and his face that day in the kitchen when he'd told me he wished I had died instead.

If Rhyon was dead, there was no use in going on with this plan.

That thought had only lingered for a moment before the voice of my mother had shaken it from my mind. *"You will protect your brothers, Odyssa,"* she'd have said. *"Both of them."*

And whatever gods had brought down the curse of the blood plague had also made it so my greatest fear was disappointing my mother. It had never been easy to win her approval, and I'd sought it wherever and whenever I could. Now was no different and, even trapped here in this living catacomb, I wanted to please her.

The voice that sounded like my mother reminded me that Rhyon might not be dead yet, as well. Giving up now would certainly ensure he would be, though.

I pushed my fingers through my hair, clasping my hands at the back of my head and letting out a heavy breath. My next step was clear: I needed to get to the prince's quarters and find the treatment. Tonight, while there was still a chance that I could get it to Rhyon in time.

The cat jumped onto the bed and stretched out long, nearly taking up the full expanse of the bed. Those wide yellow eyes peered at me, unblinking and waiting patiently for me.

"I suppose you'll tell me this is foolish," I said, sitting down on the edge of the bedspread. My hand wavered over its head, instinct pushing me to pet the creature. I pulled my hand back to my lap. "I don't suppose asking you to keep from alerting Tallon of this will do me any good, will it?"

It blinked at me.

The soul-deep weariness pulled another sigh from my lips. "As I thought."

I lingered on the bed a moment longer, but I could delay no more. If I wanted to infiltrate the rooms before Prince Eadric retired for the day, I needed to go now. Again, only hope was my companion.

The silver slip of a dress I wore beneath the veil would stand out in the dark stone halls of the castle, but changing into a different dress required far more energy than I could muster. I settled for pulling on a robe of black silk that hung in the closet, a luxury I'd thus far been avoiding. Belting it around my waist, I set out from my room and in the direction I assumed the prince's quarters would be: in the belly of the largest tower.

Music still echoed faintly in the halls as I set out, winding through the passageways with a confidence I could barely summon. I passed no one, all of them likely still in the ballroom and drowning in the fountains of gluttony and greed furnished by Prince Eadric.

Finally, I was at the base of the stairs to the tower, and without a doubt, it would lead to the prince's rooms. The doors in front were the most ornate I'd seen yet, flanked on either side by towering candelabras and fresh flowers that made my nose itch with their heavy perfume. I could think of no one else that would boast such wasteful beauty in front of a stairwell.

My journey saw no Soulshades, no burst of ash across my tongue or ringing in my ears. The cat had accompanied me, a shadow at my side, but nothing else had been amiss. Perhaps that should have been an omen.

I'd only just reached for the door handle when a large hand and arm wrapped around my waist from behind, another settling over my mouth and nose, and then I was being lifted, carried away from the door.

I kicked and thrashed, hands going to claw at those holding me, but it did no good. The grip did not falter. My heart pounded in my ears, faint dizziness following the blood rushing through my body.

"Stop struggling, Odyssa," my captor hissed in my ear. "Or I will throw you over my shoulder."

Tallon.

The threat made me stop thrashing and kicking, but I would

never stop struggling. The portrait of calm, I allowed myself to be carried down another hallway. Halfway down it, another alcove shot off to the side, this one with cushioned benches as well as a table. He set me down, keeping his hand over my mouth as he spun me around to face him.

Still in his outfit from the party, still in his mask, he looked every bit Prince Eadric's right hand. Except for his eyes, alight as they were. "If I remove my hand, will you let me speak first?"

I narrowed my eyes and gave no indication of my inclination one way or the other.

"As I thought." His hand remained over my mouth, firmly and yet intentionally careful so as not to press down on the cuts across my face, and his other hand went to my lower back to keep me from backing away, just as I had moved to do exactly that. My skin burned where he touched me, even through both my dress and robe. "Do you truly have a death wish, Odyssa? What are you doing here?"

Though I wanted to kick at him again, I raised an eyebrow as I pointedly looked down at his hand.

I'd expected suspicion to cross over his face, to narrow his eyes and for him to refuse, but what was there in his eyes was something far different. Almost concern, curiosity perhaps. He lowered his hand, though he kept it hovering in the space beneath my chin, ready to move back up in an instant. He raised a brow at me, nodding to prod me to answer his questions.

"Are you asking as Tallon, or as the prince's advisor, my lord?"

The hand that had been lingering beneath my chin moved to rest against my unmarred cheek, and the one on my back pulled me closer until we were flush against each other. My heart sped and I gasped before I could swallow it back. Heat spread up my neck and chest.

His fingers traced over the swell of my cheek before splaying wide, his thumb under my jaw. "Were I asking as the prince's advisor, little wolf, I would not be asking at all."

"And if I do have a death wish?" I asked. My thoughts were a tangle; all I could focus on were the two blazing points of his hands on me and the way our bodies fit together. My mouth was too dry, I was too warm, and yet all I could do was meet his gaze through the skull mask. I wanted to remove it. "What would you do, then?"

"I would advise you it would be far more difficult than you might think, though I suspect you would give it a valiant effort." He leaned down slightly, eyes flicking to my mouth and then lower, where I knew the robe did nothing to conceal the indecent neckline of the dress and the space between my breasts. His words were a whisper across my nose and cheeks, soothing the stinging that still radiated from the cuts on my face. "Now, what were you doing here?"

Leaning up on my toes, our lips were a breath apart and brushed ever so slightly together as I spoke. "No business of yours, my lord."

Gray eyes were nearly consumed by black. "Wrong answer, little wolf."

Hands gripped my waist and then I was upside down, my face level with his lower back and his hands now resting on the backs of my thighs. Outrage rushed through me, blending with the blood pooling in my head to make it throb as I gripped the sides of his waist and pushed myself up, trying to get down. "Put me *down*."

The only answer I received was one of his hands moving higher on my thigh, his fingers curling around to my inner thigh and squeezing as he began to walk. Every instinct in my body was coiled to twist out of his grip, even if it meant falling to the ground. The wounds on my face throbbed. Pushing up further, I shifted my hips, ready to throw myself to the side.

His hand tightened even more around my thigh and I barely caught my gasp at the electricity that furled down my spine from his touch. The warmth of his touch, the strength in his grip... I wanted to hate it, but all I could focus on was the heat radiating into my leg. His finger shifted again as he sped up his steps, inching higher again, nearing somewhere far more indecent.

My view of the ground and his back shifted, and the floor beneath his boots transformed to dark dirt and stone. A rush of cold wind speared through me, a counterpoint to the blazing touch on my thigh. A scream echoed and I flinched, closing my eyes. In the next instant, the cold and the scream were gone and I was being set on my feet.

"What—" I looked around, finding myself once again in Tallon's room, the cat now sprawled across his bed rather than mine. His room was not close enough to the prince's quarters that he could have gotten us here in only a few steps. I turned back to face him, trying to quell the anger at yet again being manipulated, and once again being taken into my nightmare world. Stomping up, I poked at his chest. "I believe I told you that if you ever touched me without my permission again, there would be consequences."

Through the skull mask, he smirked at me. "Yes, you did. And there should have been consequences for finding you attempting to enter Prince Eadric's quarters, yet here you are. Unharmed."

"Am I? You said before that no harm would come to me under your watch, and yet..." I motioned toward my face. His arrogance only spurred my frustration, but he was right, and had it been anyone else who'd discovered me, I would have already been dead. "You watched as he did this."

"You are far smarter than that, Odyssa. What did you expect me to do in front of the prince and all those people?" He raised an eyebrow and reached out to trail his fingertips over my arm. "You've only been here a short time, yet I think you'd know better than to lose your focus in that setting. What happened? What distracted you, little wolf?"

Some of the fight bled out from my body. I was not ready to reveal what had distracted me, not to him. Not when I still had yet to truly reconcile with it myself. "What do you want with me, my lord?"

"Firstly, you know my name. Use it." His voice pitched low and his head bent toward me once more. Playfulness tinged his gaze and teased at the corner of his mouth.

I reached to trace my finger along the strap that held the skull mask in place across his face. He still held himself with that regal indifference, the same emotionless statue that stood beside Prince Eadric as he struck me. "When you take off your mask and become Tallon again, my lord, I shall use your name."

His eyes shuttered, the swirling pools of gray growing still and flat as he stepped away and yanked off the mask. He stepped up closer to me, his breath whispering across my nose and cheeks as his eyes dropped to my mouth for the briefest moment. Anticipation burned in my stomach, twisting it into knots, but he did not move except to reach his fingers up to skim over the cuts on my face. "Let me clean these for you, please?"

The sudden shift left me spinning and confused, so I nodded, following him back to the same chair I'd occupied when he'd cleaned my hand. He looked at me for a moment longer before disappearing into the bathroom.

I blew out a heavy breath, running a hand over my hair to smooth both the strands and my nerves. I wasn't imagining this. He'd been about to kiss me—and more, I'd wanted him to.

Guilt clawed at my stomach and my cheeks flushed. Once again, I'd lost myself in him, forgetting about what was important and why I was truly here. He was playing a game, one I did not even know the rules to, and even though he'd removed the mask when we were alone together, he was still the prince's puppet, and I could never forget that.

His return pulled me from my thoughts. "Does it hurt much?"

"No," I replied honestly. They did not hurt now, not physically at least. They enraged me, embarrassed me, but I suspected that was the point, so that I never forgot my place in that ballroom. "I can care for my own wounds, Tallon."

He paused, about to dab at my face with the medicine-soaked cotton. His tongue darted out to wet his lips and I could not help but follow the motion as his throat bobbed on a swallow. "I know you are more than capable, Odyssa, and from what our mutual friend has told me, more than stubborn as well. But I told you last night no harm would come to you under my watch, and as you pointed out, I've failed."

I bit my tongue to keep from comforting him and to keep from asking about what else the cat had revealed.

Wounds deemed clean enough, he began dabbing that same thick cream on them that he'd used on my shoulder, keeping his eyes firmly on my skin while I kept mine on him. "Why were you trying to break in, little wolf?"

A small hiss escaped as he touched a still tender edge. It gave me the moment I needed to collect my thoughts. "I have two younger brothers. Did you know that?"

His hand faltered. "No, I did not."

"Seven days ago, my mother passed from the plague while I held her hand," I said. I waited for a moment, seeing if he would interrupt, but he did not, just continued cleaning the scratches on my cheeks. "With her dead, we would not have had enough money to live on, with just my job and my brothers' inheritances. I asked the oldest to try to find work as well, and he refused. Instead, he gave me a flyer about the castle needing new staff. Five days ago, my youngest brother, only eight years old, started coughing. We didn't know for certain if it was the plague. But it hardly mattered. I volunteered that morning. You know about the letter I received."

Finally, he looked up at me, putting aside the medicine and pulling both of my hands into his own before settling them into my lap. "Why did your brother refuse?"

I shrugged. "I won't pretend to understand his reasons. We are only half-siblings, but I raised them, and I would do anything for them."

"Would they not do anything for you, then, in return?"

My nose itched, tears burning at the back of my eyes. I looked away, fixing my gaze on his boot beside my foot, watching as the end of my dress slipped over it.

"You were after the treatment, then?" Despite the question, I knew he wasn't looking for an answer. He took my chin in his fingers and made me meet his gaze. "He won't give it to you. Not now after what happened tonight. He likely wouldn't have given it to you before either; he has been notoriously stingy with it even amongst his most trusted. And you have no hope of stealing it alone."

"Then what do I do?" I hated the way my voice cracked and the way my lower lip trembled. This was weakness, utter weakness to fall apart in front of him, yet I was powerless to stop it. He traced his thumb over the curve of my jaw, tipping my face up to look at him.

"Sleep for now, little wolf. I will protect you tonight and we will talk in the daylight." He bundled me into his arms before I could protest, carrying me from the chair to his bed and tucking me beneath the blankets. The Soulshade cat eyed us, moving to stretch along my side as soon as the blankets were drawn back up.

I closed my eyes against the burning tears. I should have fought him, should have demanded he return me to my room, but I could not bring myself to turn away the comfort of being cared for. Bundling myself into the blankets that smelled of him, I could already feel myself drifting, the nerves finally wearing off as he'd slowly brought me down from the emotional high. I doubted he was even aware he'd done it, but I would not question it. I'd failed my brothers and had failed at my last hope.

There was nothing left to lose, and if I could gain just an ounce of comfort from Tallon, I would take it greedily.

Lips pressed gently against my forehead, and it was a struggle to keep my eyes closed and not surge up and demand that he press that same kiss to my lips, to my neck and to the rest of my body, to make me forget everything but his touch. His breath was warm against my forehead, fluttering my eyelashes. "Sleep well, little wolf."

CHAPTER TWENTY-TWO

The taste of metal flooded my mouth, hot rivers of blood running down from my nose. It was thick and coated my throat, cutting off my air. I coughed, struggling to sit up and clear my airways, but my arms gave out as blood flew from my lips and I felt the spatter land on my cheeks and neck. The blood continued with no reprieve and the coughing quickly turned to gagging. I couldn't breathe, couldn't swallow.

My mother's hands ran along my shoulders, helping me struggle up to sitting, all the while I still coughed and gagged and choked on the blood filling my mouth and throat.

"Shh, shh, Odyssa," she murmured, rubbing her hands along my back. "Don't fight it."

I couldn't have fought it even if I wanted to. Blood continued to pour down my throat, and then the panic began to set in. I could not breathe. My hands tightened on the scratchy quilt, one managing to reach up and claw at my throat, grasping and squeezing as if it would clear the thick fluid from my airways.

My stomach felt hot, twisted and wrong, and my mother barely *had time to dart out of the way before I was retching, vomiting up the blood I'd swallowed.*

Everything burned; my eyes and my throat most of all. Blinking back the tears brought by the violent expulsion, I kept one hand on my throat and the other reached for my mother, for any comfort.

Her hand grasped mine. "I am here, Odyssa. You are a fighter, dear girl, but you need to make a choice. You cannot keep lingering here in the in-between; your brothers need me to return to them."

My mind swam, vision dotted by dancing black orbs. What did she mean? I shook my head, trying to clear out the bloody haze and think. A cold rag swiped across my forehead and then the rest of my face.

The cold left and my mother's hand returned. "Live or die. You must decide soon."

My entire body trembled. Die, I tried to speak, but only garbled noises came out, blood still coating my throat and clinging to my teeth and tongue. I wanted to die, to end this suffering.

At the foot of my bed, peering back at me with yellow eyes, a black cat sat atop my blankets. All at once, I was on the ceiling, looking down at my body in the bed, the cat at my feet and my mother at my side.

The cat looked up at me and tipped its head, opening its mouth, but the voice that came out of it was that of a man, old and weathered, but distinguished and elegant, like a vintage silk. "You cannot die, Odyssa. It is not in your nature."

Blood poured from my nose anew. The cat blinked at me.

My vision blurred and when it cleared, I was no longer in my room, no longer choking on my own blood, though still-wet blood covered my chin and neck, dripping down onto my nightgown. Surrounding me were towering black cliffs overlooking churning red waters.

Ice-cold wind whipped around me, whistling through my hair.

The ground beneath my bare feet was frigid and rocks dug into the soles. I did not wince as I took cautious steps forward, searching for any clue as to where I was or why I was here.

"Odyssa."

I spun, only to find myself face-to-face with Rhyon, but not the Rhyon I'd left behind. This Rhyon looked like me, with blood covering his face and neck, staining his shirt crimson. His skin was too pale and his eyes dull and lifeless. "Rhyon," I breathed. "I am so sorry."

"You let me die, Odyssa," he said, taking a large step towards me. With each step he took, I retreated, my heart thundering wildly at the look of rage upon his face. "It is your fault I am dead."

"No, no," I said, shaking my head and holding my hands out toward him. "Rhyon, no, I would never."

"You let me die. You let me die. You let me die."

My feet scrambled against the rocks, finding no purchase of ground beneath as I stumbled back. I looked behind me, only to see the edge of the towering cliff and rocks from my feet tumbling down into the river of blood below. Frantically, I turned back to Rhyon, who was still advancing. "What are you doing? Please, stop this."

"You let me die. You let me die. You let me die." He stopped abruptly, right in front of me.

His little hands stretched out, and he pushed at my stomach hard with a strength he should not have had.

Time slowed, and then I was falling, looking up at him as he peered over the edge of the cliff. I heard a scream whistling on the wind as I fell, realizing it was my own.

I hit the water.

I WAS STILL SCREAMING when I awoke, my chest heaving and cold sweat drenching my neck and back. My hand went to my throat as I tried to pull myself out of the nightmare's grasp. In my periphery, shadows danced in the night, a darker than black darkness in the room. Fingers grazed my side.

Blinking rapidly, I saw my Death marks alive again, pulsing out from my body and peeling away from my skin where they were holding Tallon down against the bed, the tendrils wrapped around his chest and the arm that was reaching for me.

He was watching me, a careful expression on his face. Unlike the others who'd witnessed my marks, he wasn't looking at them. His eyes never flitted nervously to the sides or down to where they encased his chest and arms. His eyes stayed fixed on my face, steady and sure. That, more than anything, pulled me back into reality.

The nightmare haze slowly cleared from my eyes and I realized what was happening, what I was doing to him. Horror gripped me and I scrambled out of the bed, doubling over and gasping for breath as the shadows retreated onto my skin.

"Odyssa, breathe," he said, his voice rough from sleep. The sheets rustled as he finally moved. "I am fine, little wolf. You didn't hurt me."

The nightmare still left me reeling and my breath eluded me. I shook my head, trying to clear the visions of the icy hellscape, the taste of my own blood, the cold apathy on Rhyon's face as his hands pushed me over that cliff. It was all too much.

Hands wrapped around my waist and I couldn't stop the startled noise, but as soon as I started to struggle, the touch became familiar again, warm and strong. The curtains were still pulled tightly, leaving us only a sliver of light to see by. I didn't struggle as he hauled me onto the bed, keeping my eyes focused on the skin showing at his wrists, studying the marks there as I tried to slow my breathing. But it didn't work, and I could feel my chest tightening, my vision swimming as I fought against the lingering effects of the nightmare.

"Come here, Odyssa," he murmured. He shifted us again, and

then I was sitting between his legs against the headboard with my back to his chest and his hands wrapped around my ribs, his hands so large they nearly circled the entire way around my torso. "Breathe with me. In and out. Come on now, little wolf; match my breathing. You can do it. You need to breathe."

It was a struggle to focus enough to even find his breathing to match, but his hands squeezing gently at my sides on each inhale finally guided me to it.

Slowly, my heart no longer felt like it might burst from my chest, but the fading of the feelings the nightmares had left behind were only replaced by the overwhelming warmth at my back as I realized exactly how close Tallon and I were. There was no space between my back and his front, and his legs bracketed my own, his hands consuming my torso and thumbs brushing against the undersides of my breasts.

My tongue felt like it was stuck to the top of my mouth, and no amount of swallowing could take the dryness away. Every minute shift of Tallon behind me had me tensing, not wanting to move. I needed to get up, get away from him. This was worse than merely being seen with him or the others knowing he had bandaged my hand. I should not have stayed here, should not have let my walls down enough to fall asleep in his room, let alone his bed.

Prince Eadric's right hand, whether he wore his mask or not.

Whatever calm I'd found as the last threads of the nightmare left was gone now, and my heart pounded against my chest, picking up speed.

"How long have you been able to do that?" he murmured against my ear. His hands squeezed at my ribs, feeling me hold my breath. "Breathe, Odyssa."

I sucked in another breath, trying to keep still yet also pull my body away from his. "Only since I've been in the castle."

"The night you received the letter," he said, his hands

shifting against my sides, sending shivers down my spine. Whatever progress I'd made in extricating myself from him was undone as he adjusted and pulled me somehow even closer than I'd been before. "Was that the first time they swarmed like that?"

I squeezed my eyes closed, trying not to give too much thought to how right he felt at my back. I desperately needed to get myself back under control. It had been a nightmare, and while they were horrific and left me shaking for hours, it was hardly new. I did not need the comfort he offered, but I couldn't bring myself to refuse and move away from him. "No. There was once before. The second night here."

"What happened?" His voice was softer than I'd ever heard it, and if I wasn't able to see the skull mask on the floor, caught in the path of the sliver of light the curtains let in, I might have believed it tender. One of his hands moved from my ribs to settle on my thigh, not moving, just… there.

It made it hard to concentrate.

"What happened, Odyssa? Why did they come out?" he prodded.

I swallowed hard, forcing myself to keep my eyes on the mask instead of how right his hand looked atop my dress. "One of the others, she tried to strike me. They stopped her."

I felt when he stopped breathing, his fingers digging into my thigh. His voice didn't rise, or even change really, but there was a hardness that hadn't been there before when he asked, "Who?"

"It does not matter." And it didn't, not really. We were all trying to survive here, and I could not fault Maricara for her feelings.

"It does matter."

We sat in silence for a time, breathing together. His hand relaxed against my leg, finger by finger. I tried to ignore that I had liked feeling the strength beneath his fingertips as they'd pressed into my skin. Instead, I focused on keeping my breathing even, aware that if I could sense the change in his, he could do the same with mine.

His voice broke the silence a few moments later. "What are your nightmares about, little wolf?"

A slow inhale and exhale gave me time to gather my thoughts. "Most often, they are memories from my sickness. Flashes of myself when I was feverish or the hallucinations it brought." I shook my head. "I don't always remember the details, only the feelings."

He froze behind me, a statue rather than a man, and then he was gently pushing me forward and climbing out of the bed. My back was cold in his absence, and I tried to not think about the frown that had formed without my permission. Shifting back, I pressed into the lingering warmth on the pillows against the headboard and squinted at him as he drew the curtains back and let the early afternoon sun into the room.

The sun cut across him, the dark fabric of his shirt soaking up the light. His eyes stayed firmly on me as he undid the buttons on the cuffs of the shirt and then moved to the one at his neck. My breath hitched in my throat at each button he slipped through the hole and revealed inch by inch of dark ink and tan skin. Neither of us uttered a sound as he finally slipped the shirt from his shoulders, the silk falling to the floor with a whisper.

If our marks were signals of how close we'd come to death, then Tallon had come within a breath. The inky black swirls covered both of his arms from shoulder to wrist and cascaded over his chest and stomach before dipping into his waistband. His marks did not creep up onto his neck like mine did, but instead twisted like a necklace around his collarbones and spilled over onto his back.

"There is nothing you can say that will shock me, little wolf." His voice had lost some of the rough sleep quality, but it was still heavy and deep. He did not move out of the sliver of sunlight that cut through the room, instead letting me look my fill while watching me with the same intensity. The air in the room was charged, though with what, I couldn't describe. It was like a force drawing us together, wanting me to get up and go to him. His thigh twitched beneath the tight fabric of his pants and I knew he was struggling with the same.

It was a self-imposed torture to keep looking at his torso. I wanted to trace the lines of his marks with my fingers, and the temptation was too great. Pulling my gaze to meet his, I realized looking at his face wouldn't be any better. There was no teasing in his eyes, no hint of the arrogance or the soft mockery that typically accompanied him. Just a vulnerability and a concern that looked both out of place and uncomfortable. For both of us.

Sighing, I moved until I was lying flat on my back, hands folded on my stomach and staring up at the ceiling. I doubted I'd be able to tell him about my nightmares if he kept looking at me like that—or if he kept his shirt off.

"Ever since I recovered, I've had nightmares of this place. A dark and cold place, filled with horrible creatures and screaming and rivers of blood that carve through towering cliffs. I can never escape, and the nightmares always end with me falling or drowning, or some other horrid end." I took a deep breath that shuddered at the last second. "Recently, my youngest brother has been appearing in those nightmares, in that place. He is now the one trying to kill me in my dreams, and he enjoys it, enjoys telling me how I failed him and let him die. Reminds me that I let my mother die. Warns me that I will be the cause of Emyl's death, too, and be the reason our entire family is dead."

The bed dipped slowly beside me, and despite feeling the heat radiating from Tallon's body, I kept my gaze fixed on the ceiling. The tears burning at the back of my throat would surely spill if I caught him looking at me with pity.

"Go on," he murmured.

I wiped furiously at my nose, trying to chase away the stinging. "Tonight was the same. My youngest brother tried to kill me in that place, and twice he reminded me of what I had done to my family. And then it was a memory of what it felt like to choke on my own blood. What it felt like to suffocate and cough up blood and not know if I was going to die but wishing I would so it would just be over. Then it was like Rhyon was controlling that memory because we were back in that place, and he told me it was my fault he would die the same way. That Emyl would die the same way. He tried to choke me that time." I let out a heavy breath, one that did not shake or catch in my throat this time. "And then I woke up screaming and my marks pinning you to the bed."

The room was still and quiet while my words settled down over both of us. I wanted to take them back, to grab them from where they hung in the air and swallow them down, but they would not disappear. I'd told him my greatest fears, and now I had to accept the consequences and hope that he was not using this as part of the games he played.

I did not feel the bed move again until it was too late, too lost in my own regret and embarrassment to notice until Tallon's hands were on either side of my head and his body was hovering over mine. The muscles in his arms bulged as he kept his weight off me in an easy and steady show of strength that did not shake against the unsteadiness of the soft mattress. I held my breath as he lowered, bending his arms at the elbows until only a breath kept us apart.

My eyes fluttered shut as he ducked his head to run his nose along my jaw line. There was no doubt he could feel my pulse racing against his lips as they pressed gently to my neck, just above the wounds Rhyon had left in my nightmares. Once, twice, he kissed the skin there before traveling up to my ear.

I felt like I was floating and drowning at the same time, my body too awash in the sensations to tell up from down. I wanted to shove him away and pull him closer all at once, to run out of the room screaming at myself for being so foolish to fall for whatever game this surely was, but also to hook my leg around his foot and knock him off balance just to feel his body pressing mine into the bed. I wanted it all and hated it at the same time. Hated myself.

I kept my eyes closed and tried to keep any expression at all from settling onto my face.

His breath puffed against my ear, and though they were not pressed so firmly against my skin anymore, I still felt his lips curve up into a smirk. "I would like to make you a bargain, Odyssa Duhiva. Would you take it?"

My eyes flew open to see Tallon looking down at me. His face was still open, earnest, but his eyes were dark. "I—" My voice cracked from my mouth being so dry. Licking my lips, I watched his eyes follow every movement, somehow darkening even more. His own tongue darted out to lick his lips in response. "How can I trust you?"

Some of the darkness cleared from his eyes and that smirk was back. I wanted to shift under the intensity of his gaze, but I was also petrified of the same, of what would happen if I brought any sort of attention to the rest of my body beneath his. "You shouldn't trust me, little wolf. But that does not mean we cannot make a bargain all the same."

Any doubt I had that Tallon was a normal man vanished. A normal man would have been trembling from holding himself up for so long, and yet he had not even a hint of discomfort on his face. He also had no hint of trickery, no hint of the mocking smirk he wore in the ballroom. "What is the bargain?"

"I will help you get the treatment from the prince for your brother."

I held my breath.

"In exchange, you'll spend an hour with me here in my rooms each day."

I opened my mouth to accept eagerly. There was nothing he could ask of me in that hour he wanted that I would not give, but he shifted his weight to hold himself up on one hand as he pressed a finger to my lips. "Ah, not yet. I also want a favor from you in the future. One favor of my choosing, to call in whenever I see fit."

I let out the breath and he moved his hand from my lips. "I have nothing left to lose. I accept your bargain, Tallon."

The chuckle that rumbled from his chest was dark and heavy and it made heat curl low in my stomach. "Odyssa, there is always something left to lose."

He looked at me a moment longer, and then the hand that had pressed a finger to my lips was tangled in my hair, and lifting my head to meet his and he pressed his lips to mine. A gentle kiss and short, by all accounts, but the touch lingered, his breath mixing with mine as I fought to keep from pressing my thighs together to combat the heat building.

I wanted more, and he seemed to know it too. His hand wove deeper into my hair, and the next kiss was firmer, his mouth hot and open against mine and his tongue peeking out to run over my lips in a whisper of a promise. I couldn't stop the groan that bubbled up at the touch, my breath falling into his open mouth as our lips moved in tandem.

My skin felt like it was on fire, and his hand tightened against the roots of my hair, tugging gently as he tipped my head back, exposing my throat. His mouth left mine for a moment to kiss along my jaw line, but it returned immediately, pressing one more kiss against my lips, slow and deep.

Pulling away, I was pleased to see his chest rising and falling as rapidly as my own, both of us affected. My lips tingled and I wanted to press my hand against them to see if it was in my head or if they truly were as flushed and swollen as I thought. The kisses he'd pressed to my jaw left a path of flames that still burned even though he was no longer touching me.

He fell to his side, propping his head up on his fist as he looked down at me, the arrogant smirk falling back into place as though it'd never left. "It's a bargain, then."

The hairs on the back of my neck prickled and cold washed down my spine, dousing out the arousal that Tallon had foisted upon me with that kiss. Gods, what had I done?

CHAPTER TWENTY-THREE

My sixth night in the castle, the ballroom had been transformed into a vision of deep, warm blues and rich violets. It was beautiful, enchanting even, but my mind was elsewhere, back in that room beneath Tallon. His half-mask was black tonight, as was the rest of his attire, yet all I could see when I looked at him were the sprawling marks I knew lay beneath his shirt.

I again felt him watching me, but studiously avoided him. The letter to Emyl was once again tucked into my dress, my reminder of what was at stake and why I could not let myself fall prey to such fantasies. Tallon was first and foremost the prince's right hand, and despite seeming to want to help me, I knew there was more at stake. Hours ago, when I agreed to his bargain, I just hadn't cared.

Now that the energy from the nightmare, and then from the kiss, had worn off, my mind was clearer, and it was telling me that though I had little left to lose, there was always something left for Tallon to take. My life.

The party was quickly in full swing, the music and the

dancing for once a welcome distraction. Weaving between the bodies and avoiding bumping into anyone kept my mind off other things, and so I threw myself into it. I was a frantic whirlwind about the ballroom, refilling drinks and plates as fast as they were emptied.

I had thrown myself into my work before, losing myself to the task and the instruction and tuning out everything else. Before, it had always been a welcome distraction, but this time was different, and here in the castle, I had to keep some awareness. That was the only reason I noticed the strands of conversation that cut through the music and made their way over to me as I laid out fresh treats along the table.

Looking up briefly, I immediately fixed my gaze back on the table once I realized that the speakers tucked behind a nearby column were Prince Eadric and Tallon. I continued my duties, only daring to lift my eyes infrequently and never my head. My hands shook slightly, but beneath the gloves and the veil, I could only hope it wasn't enough for either of them to notice. The task was most important, and I set out each pastry with care, slowly and methodically.

"...is happening with you?" Prince Eadric poked his finger into Tallon's chest. "You are not holding up...bargain."

"My bargain...your father."

"People...restless. The death rate...falling. This is not...you promised."

"Would you like... kill everyone, then?"

My blood ran cold, hands freezing as they hovered to set out a pastry. The violins roared as the song crescendoed and startled me back out of my stillness. As the music softened, I caught the prince's reply.

"No...do your job." The prince was silent for a moment and his empty glass landed heavily on the table. "And you need to deal with...excuse for a servant. I will not...embarrass me again."

"Understood."

I wanted to vomit. Surely I'd missed vital pieces of the conversation, because from what I had heard, Tallon had some type of sway over the blood plague. Certainly it was impossible, but the irritation of the still-healing wound in my hand raised my doubts.

The servant he discussed was me, no doubt, as I was the only one that had come near embarrassing him in recent days, and while I was sure the prince and I had far different ideas of what it meant to deal with me, I wasn't confident where Tallon fell between the two. I didn't want to find out either. Our bargain was for the treatment for my brothers, not for my own safety.

Shuffled movements indicated the conversation was over and I ducked my head as the prince bustled past me, focusing on setting out the food and pretending with every ounce of my body that I had not overheard their conversation. Thankfully, he paid me no mind.

Tallon followed behind, and unlike the prince, he hesitated momentarily when he saw me, his steps faltering. He recovered quickly, though, offering me a small nod I did not return before he followed after the prince.

Hands shaking, I finished my task and then hastily but carefully retreated to the kitchens for a reprieve.

The kitchen was not the calm place to settle my mind like I'd hoped, though it did offer a distraction nonetheless in the form of Maricara and Elena pouring glasses of wine and trading whispered words between not-so-subtle glances at me. Focusing on them took my mind off Tallon and his conversation with the prince, even momentarily. My hands no longer shook and my breath returned in full, no longer catching in my throat.

I would not let myself consider the conversation, not until after the party was over and I was safely back in my room. Another public mistake would be the nail in my coffin, and I doubted Tallon would be able to save me this time, even if he wanted to.

Once again, I'd fallen victim to his games, believing the lies he whispered and believing myself smart enough to ignore the warnings Zaharya had so adamantly given.

I was nothing but foolish and naive, and now I would pay for it. The tray piled high with food once more, I held my chin high, ignored the whispers of Maricara and Elena, and returned to the ballroom.

For the first time in my life, whatever gods were left in Veressia had listened to my unspoken prayers and I had no opportunity to consider my predicament for the remainder of the party, too busy serving those Prince Eadric saw value in and ensuring I did not humiliate myself again.

Though there was no time to linger on what it meant, I also did not miss that Tallon had been following me whenever I was in the ballroom. His gaze felt different on my back than that of the revelers: they looked through me, only seeing a servant here to bend to their every whim, whereas he was looking at me, peering through my midnight violet shroud and looking at the person beneath.

And if he was not watching me, the Soulshade cat was by my side. In a way, I was grateful for the latter, as it seemed to drive away any other Soulshades. Its company was welcome, despite knowing that it served Tallon.

The bells tolled three hours past midnight, and the guests slowly began to disperse. Finally, as the early hours of the morning saw the crimson night begin to lighten, the ballroom was empty of all but the servants. My shoulders ached from the tension I'd carried there all evening, brought on by both my attempts to not make any more mistakes and my building apprehension over the bargain I'd made with Tallon.

Though I had no firm ideas yet, I knew that if Tallon was

going to betray me to the prince, I needed to find the treatment first. He could have already told him, and the two were biding their time. Far more likely, though, was the notion that Tallon was playing another game, that my plans would be safe so long as I played along. But I had no time for games, and I needed that treatment. I would simply need to be more careful when trying to gain access to Prince Eadric's rooms.

Tallon would not be the reason I failed my family.

The ballroom was quiet as we cleaned and thankfully, I'd been assigned to work alone. The others were nearby, and despite their best efforts to the contrary, I knew they were watching me, waiting for another outburst like before, waiting for me to slip up and give them reason to have Camelya get rid of me. They bothered me, their stares, but I'd come to accept them. There was nothing I could do, and acknowledging that they bothered me would likely only make them stare more obviously.

Cold curled around my ankle, and I briefly glanced down at the Soulshade cat at my side. It looked up at me, seemingly telling me that it would keep me safe tonight. I wasn't sure how I knew that's what its slow blink and head tilt meant, but I felt it in my heart. I wouldn't question it; far stranger things had happened in this castle.

As I swept up the scattered crumbs, I felt Tallon watching from the balcony again, and my shoulders tensed up once more under his gaze. Before I realized my mistake, I looked up at him. It was only a moment, enough to see that it was him and that he still wore his mask, his hands clasped behind his back as he surveyed the ballroom from his perch. He looked more a prince than Prince Eadric could ever hope to.

I vowed not to look up at him again and returned my focus to the floor, though out of the periphery, Maricara had paused and tracked my attention. Now, I felt two gazes on me, and one was filled with far more malevolence than the other.

A mistake. Not a public one, at least, but a mistake, nonetheless. Maricara knew Tallon was watching us, watching *me*, and I found it difficult to tell myself that she would let it go without remark. No, from the renewed frequency of the glances, I knew this would not be forgotten.

I sighed, clenching and unclenching my fingers around the handle of the broom. I wanted to be left *alone*, to work and sleep and find the treatment and get out. But we hardly ever got we wanted, and given how we all came to be here, I doubted I ever would again.

The sun was half-risen by the time I left the kitchens, the cat still a welcome fixture at my side. Tallon was nowhere to be seen, and for a blissful moment, I thought I would have a reprieve. The moment was short-lived, though, as I turned the corner to get to my room and there he was, leaning against the wall beside my bedroom door.

He was a picture of entitlement, a careless slouch in his body as his shoulder rested against the stone and his legs kicked out for balance. The mask was still affixed to his face, and though he'd lost his coat, he was still far more elegant than I.

My steps faltered but I quickly resumed them, holding my chin high as I tugged the key from my dress and unlocked the door. I knew it would not be this easy, and though I anticipated it, the hand that shot out to wrap around my bicep startled me. I froze as he bent his head, refusing to turn to look at him.

"I know you were listening to my conversation with Prince Eadric tonight, little wolf," he murmured, his lips brushing my hair. "What do you think you heard?"

"I would never deign to eavesdrop on the prince, my lord."

My voice was colder than the cat curled against my leg. "If you don't mind, I am tired and need to rest."

"I do mind. We have a bargain." His fingers flexing was my only warning before he had me pressed between him and my door, one hand still holding my arm and the other resting beside my head on the door as he loomed over me.

Narrowing my eyes, I raised my chin. Whether he'd hoped to intimidate me or distract me, I had my eyes wide open and my mind clear, and I would not let him win this round of the demented game he played. His mask was still on, an intentional choice on his part given that he'd already shed his coat. "Do we, my lord?"

The emotions that flittered across his face were dulled by the mask, but I could see clearly the way his jaw flexed as he ground his teeth together. He lowered his head until his lips were level with my ear. "You choose, little wolf: your room or mine. We will not be having this conversation in the hall, but we will be having it."

I bit my tongue to keep silent. Neither option was pleasing, and I was feeling less than accommodating for the man who had been lying to me at every turn, it seemed. Groping behind me, I grasped my hand around the door handle, using the surprise of it falling open behind me to escape his grip.

I turned and rushed inside, intent on slamming the door in his face, but he was too quick, and shoved his boot between the door and the frame, wedging it open.

It was hardly an effort for him to overpower me and push the door open, closing it firmly behind him.

"That was rude."

"You deserved it."

"Likely." He stepped around me and made himself comfortable on my bed, stretching out and propping himself up with a relaxed arm behind his head. He still wore the mask.

I stood in the doorway, only able to bring myself to watch him. He looked wrong on my bed, but I remembered what he had looked like on his own bed, in nearly the same position, and that had felt all too right. I sucked my bottom lip between my teeth, chewing on it. If he had anything to do with the plague, with the deaths of my family and so many in Veressia, I wasn't sure what my reaction would be. I wasn't sure I wanted to know.

"Ask me, Odyssa."

"Ask you what?"

He sat up, reaching behind his head in the same movement to remove the mask and let it fall into the blankets. "Ask me what you have been dying to ask me since you heard the pieces of our conversation. I have felt your outrage, your pain, and your confusion all night each time your eyes landed upon me. So ask me. I'll only give this one chance."

The letter to Emyl burned against my breast. The feeling of Tallon's lips against mine and his hand in my hair burned in my memory. I'd already failed my mother, and likely failed Rhyon as well, and if I learned without a doubt that Tallon had a hand in their deaths, a hand in my own sickness, I feared what I might do.

I was already spiraling, losing myself inside this castle with each passing night. Distinguishing what was real and what my mind was fabricating was increasingly difficult, especially when each night was plagued by nightmares, and each day was plagued by Soulshades and mysterious castles and lies from everyone around me.

The doubt was enough to hold the shame at bay, to keep from wanting to scrub my skin raw at the thought that he had killed my family and then *touched* me. The doubt was enough to give spark to the hope that I had misheard and that the way he looked at me now, without the mask on and his gray eyes bright and swirling, was the truth and not another manipulation I'd readily fallen victim to.

No, I could not ask what I wanted. I could not bear to hear the truth. "I have no question for you, Tallon."

His lips curved into a slow smile, like I'd passed some sort of test and he was pleasantly surprised. With a dramatic flourish, he fell back and settled into my bedding. "Pretty lies, little wolf, but so be it."

"Would you have answered?" I blurted. "If I had asked, would you have answered?"

"Why don't you find out for yourself?"

I squared my shoulders, an anxious sweat gathering at the nape of my neck. "What were you and Prince Eadric discussing tonight at the party?"

"You can do better than that," he said, clasping his hands behind his head as he still lay sprawled across my bed. "We discussed many things tonight. The way you ask the question is just as important as the answer, perhaps more so. You can do better. Ask me again."

"When I could overhear you, you mentioned his father, and me, and a bargain. What were you and the prince discussing then?"

He hummed as he rolled over onto his side, propping his head up on his fist. The other hand patted the empty space beside him. "That's better. You must be intentional with your words, little wolf. Especially in a place like this."

I did not move toward the bed.

A sigh so heavy it fluttered the sheets left his lips. "The prince and I have a bargain, one he inherited from his father. He believes I'm not holding up my side of it. I reminded him that the specifics of the bargain were left ambiguous at best, and I am in fact keeping to it."

"And what he said about me?" I pushed, tucking away that

information for later. Tallon had made a bargain with the king, with the prince, and now with me. And he seemed bound to uphold them more by magic than by being a man of his word.

"Ah, now that one, I will not answer," he said with a smile. "Not yet."

Of course not.

CHAPTER TWENTY-FOUR

"I owe you an hour," I said. Carefully, I pulled the veil from my head and tucked it back into the wardrobe that never seemed to run out of clothing. The dress I wore beneath was like all the others, thin-strapped and deeply cut, close fitting but shapeless. Though he'd seen me in it more times now than I cared to count, it still felt too vulnerable. I pulled on the robe, cinching it at my waist before slowly pulling off each glove, finger by finger. I turned my gaze back to the bed where Tallon was staring at me, watching every move. "What *exactly* does this hour entail?"

"I believe we agreed the hour was to be in my rooms, did we not?" He had not moved from the bed, still lazily strewn across it as if it belonged to him. "But for tonight, I'll allow it to be here."

"How generous."

"I think you'll find I am quite generous."

The game was tiring, and I knew better than to let myself be within his reach, so I settled back onto the windowsill. "What do you want with me, Tallon? I won't give you my body, if that is what you're after."

He sat up and shifted to the edge of the bed, propping his chin on his fist and resting his elbow on his knee. "You intrigue me, Odyssa. I'd like to learn more about you." He leaned forward. "And I would never need to make a bargain to get you in my bed, Odyssa. I promise that."

I wanted to both scream and laugh. He did not want to know me, he wanted to control me, and for control, he needed to know what I feared. I'd already given him that, and I'd be damned if I gave him anything else to use against me. "Tell me the truth, please. If Rhyon is still alive, he needs that treatment. If he is dead, Emyl will likely be in need of it soon given our family's luck. I don't have time for these games of yours."

"I am not playing games, Odyssa." He stood from the bed and in two strides was in front of me, looming over me once more. It was a habit he seemed to enjoy far too much. His fingers reached out, and in another habit of his, he traced down my marks. Instead of stopping at my neck as he usually did, he followed the ones that dipped into the hollow between my breasts. Fire followed the path he traced, sending flames and sparks in every direction. His fingers hesitated, and then reached down into my dress, freeing the letter to Emyl I had tucked there. "What is this?"

Ignoring the tingles that still danced across my skin, I snatched it back, standing and pushing past him to set it on my desk. "None of your concern."

"If it's a letter to your brothers, why do you carry it with you, instead of having it sent to them?" His brow was pinched as he turned to take up my previous position against the windowsill, his arms crossed and genuine confusion across his face for the first time since I'd met him.

My anger stuttered in the face of it, unsure what to do now that it was clear he had no knowledge of the punishment

Camelya had meted out. "My privilege of correspondence was revoked."

"When and by whom?" His eyes narrowed.

Mine narrowed in response. "You truly do not know?"

"Believe it or not, I am not privy to every decision made in the castle. I may be one of his advisors, but I am not the prince, as I'd hope you're well aware."

I bit my tongue, choosing to ignore the dry tone. "Two nights ago, there was a mishap during cleanup, as I'm sure you saw. Camelya informed me that any further mistakes would revoke my pay and my privilege of correspondence. Last night's interaction with Prince Eadric was considered a further mistake."

He was quiet for a long moment, looking at me. I couldn't decipher the expression on his face beyond thoughtfulness. For a moment, anger flitted by on the purse of his lips, but it vanished as quickly as it came. I found myself wanting to fidget beneath his gaze, but I held my body still and kept quiet.

"If you'd like, I would be happy to send the letter out on your behalf," he finally said.

I hesitated, faltering between wanting to shove the letter in his hands and demand he take it to Emyl right this instant and wanting to question his motives further. The latter won out. "What do you stand to gain by helping me? Would you not also get in trouble if it was discovered?"

"Are you always this suspicious of those trying to help you?" he asked, a slight smile gracing his lips as he looked at me. "Because if so, I believe I am starting to understand you just that much better, little wolf."

"I'd call myself cautious."

"Paranoid."

"Wary."

"Cynical."

"Skeptical."

"Distrustful."

I snorted. "What reason do I have to trust you? I hardly know you, and what I do know does not inspire confidence that if I gave you this letter, it would actually make it to my brothers."

"What reason do you have to believe I would do something with the letter other than deliver it?"

"I—" I'd opened my mouth to speak, but realized that out of all my interactions with Tallon, none had involved him failing to do something he'd said. Lying, certainly, hiding the full truth, absolutely. But as of now, it was only my suspicion of his future betrayal that I had to stand on, and I hardly wanted to explore that in this moment. I picked up the letter and held it out.

If he chose not to deliver it, it would be no different than if I continued to carry it with me. At least this way, there was a chance of Emyl reading it. Again, I had nothing left to lose. Nothing in the letter would give Tallon any more power over me than he already had. "Fine. I would be very appreciative if you could see this makes it to my brothers."

He crossed the room and took it from me, ensuring our fingers brushed in the process, before tucking the letter into the pocket of his shirt. "I would be honored to take this to your brothers."

Again, I was torn in my reaction to him. He seemed genuine, like he truly *would* be honored to assist me, but I couldn't let myself fall into that trap. Not again. There was too much at stake for me to forget everything that had happened so far, no matter how my body responded to Tallon's. In the face of the confusion, I settled back into a familiar embrace of emotions instead. "When will you get the treatment?"

"Should we add impatience to the list of your defining characteristics?" The lilt of his voice was teasing, and it snapped whatever hold I had on my temper.

"My brother is dying," I snapped, "if not already dead. I do not have time for patience. Are you getting the treatment or not?"

His face turned serious, gray eyes a tempest of storm clouds. "I will help you get it, Odyssa. Our bargain stands. That said, even though Prince Eadric trusts me, we cannot simply waltz into his rooms and demand it, can we? It's hardly been a full day." He paused, considering me. "When I deliver the letter, do you wish to know if Rhyon has passed on?"

My voice cracked. "Please."

"So be it." He held his hand out in offering. "Come. I'm sure you'll be wanting to sleep soon. Go prepare for bed; I'll wait here for you."

My routine had always brought a source of comfort to me, but since coming to the castle, I had yet to have a night where I was able to complete it fully. Bathe, brush my hair, braid it back, lotion my skin, wash my face. It was a ritual, no doubt, and one I would allow myself to indulge in tonight, if only for the satisfaction of making Tallon wait further.

I wasn't foolish enough to believe it would count towards my hour, but it would give me a reprieve and a chance to work through my tumultuous feelings regarding Tallon and the situation I found myself in.

As the bathwater filled, I considered the man sitting outside in my room. He was an illustration of contradictions.

Since I'd met him, he'd inspired both apprehension and attraction within me, and I still wasn't sure which would be the more dangerous of the two. He was a close confidant of the prince, no doubt, but occasionally, behind the mask he wore, his face would slip, and for a fleeting moment one could think he despised the prince as much as I.

Sliding into the bath, I let out a long sigh as the hot water pulled me into its embrace. I believed Tallon's concern tonight, and other nights, was genuine, but it also made my internal battle so much more complex. Did he truly want to help me for no reason? I doubted it.

In all my life, these long twenty-seven years, I had never met someone who cared for me just for the sake of it. The value I brought to the world was what I could give to it, and they always wanted something in the end.

Tallon would be no different. His demand of a single unnamed favor was proof enough of that. And yet, I could still not deny the impact of him; the way his words, when they brushed across my skin, sent shivers down my spine not out of fear, but out of lust. The way his touch sent me leaning into it rather than recoiling away.

Idly, I wondered what it would feel like if he touched me more intentionally. A touch not out of care, or aid, but one he *wanted* to gift me. I wondered if I had the same impact on him as he did on me. Occasionally, I thought I might. His mask was well crafted and he was as well practiced as I at keeping his emotions off his face, but sometimes it slipped and sometimes he looked at me like he wanted to touch me, to press me against the wall and kiss me. And sometimes, I might have wanted him to.

My hands had slipped beneath the bathwater and were trailing across my stomach when I came back to myself, still picturing Tallon's hands on my skin. Eyes widening at the realization, I bolted up in the tub, sloshing water everywhere.

"Are you alright, Odyssa?" Tallon's voice called from *right outside the door.*

My face flushed, both from the heat of the steam curling up from the water and from my own embarrassment that I'd been about to touch myself thinking of Tallon's hands while the man himself was sitting outside in my bedroom. He most certainly would know what I'd done as soon as I stepped foot back out of the bathroom.

"I'm fine," I called, grateful that my voice was steady even though my hands trembled beneath the water. I dug my fingertips into my thighs, willing my body to calm.

"Do try not to drown in there," he teased. "It would certainly make things more difficult."

"I'm fine," I repeated. The bathwater sloshed as I shifted and sank further into the water until it covered me to the neck. The water was cooling, but it still felt too hot on my feverish skin.

"Should I come in there and see that for myself?" His tone was still teasing, but held an undercurrent of concern. The knob twisted slowly, taunting me.

I bolted upright, splashing water onto the floor. The door remained closed, but the knob stayed in its half-turned position, unlatching the door so he could push it open at any time. My voice did waver this time as I spoke. "No, I am fine, Tallon. I'll be out in a moment."

Creeping, the door opened an inch. My breath caught in my chest and I pressed my legs together as I drew my arm over my breasts, covering myself the best I could before he opened it the rest of the way. He did not say anything.

"Do not come in here," I warned. Despite my earlier feelings, the lust I'd allowed myself to get lost in for a moment, I did not want him in here. Did not want to see how he'd react to my naked and wet body. Did not want to discover if he could read my attraction for him across my face.

"As you wish." He was no longer teasing, and the door pulled shut once more with a sharp click. His voice was muffled by the door. "I'll be waiting out here."

I did not reply, instead sinking back into the rapidly cooling water as my heart came down from the thundering pace it'd set. Without a doubt, he knew exactly what I'd been doing, and what he was doing. Another game, another mark in my tally of losses. Sloshing the water as I leaned forward, I turned the taps on once more so I could splash the ice-cold water across my face. I needed to remember my place, and more importantly, I needed to remember Tallon's place—particularly his place beside the Coward Prince.

For the rest of my bedtime routine, I focused intently on my task rather than letting my mind drift to Tallon again. Nothing good would come from giving in to the attraction I felt for him. Nothing good would come from *him*.

When I finally had the nerve to reenter my room, Tallon was sitting on the chair by the window, ankle across one knee and reading a book from somewhere. I looked around, but as before, there were no bookshelves in my room. He looked up when I closed the bathroom door behind me, shutting his book and standing.

Wordlessly, he ushered me to sit down in the chair. It was still warm from his body, and I fought back the shiver that threatened to roll down my spine. I watched silently as he set his book down on my vanity, trading it for my hairbrush before returning to my side. He held it up in a silent question, and I hesitated a moment before nodding.

I knew there was more to it, as I could find no reason Tallon would *want* to brush out my hair for me. It was a part of his games, and I just had yet to see how it fit. Until I did, it was better to play along carefully, gathering as much information as possible. I bit my tongue to keep from asking, not wanting to ruin the tenuous moment. Despite knowing there were hidden motives behind the gesture, no one had ever offered to brush my hair, not even my mother, and it was something I was disinclined to pass up.

I couldn't fight back the shivers as he ran the brush through my hair, his fingers grazing my neck as he lifted the hair off my shoulders. It was calming, the slow repetitive movements, the warmth of him against my neck and back.

Too quickly, it was over, and the relaxed stupor he left me in was fogging up my mind. He tapped my shoulder gently with the brush. Coming around in front of me, he held his hand out, pulling me from the chair and then guiding me to the bed. I followed without a fight, still not fully aware of what was happening. Had there been magic in the brush, another trick of his to make me complacent? I didn't want to know. My body had never felt so relaxed before, and I had never felt so warm.

"Our time is up, Odyssa." He smiled, pulling the blankets up over my body. "Rest well, and I shall see you this evening."

I blinked at him, opening my mouth to reply, but he was already at the door, pulling it closed behind him. Settling back into the pillows, I fell asleep on my next breath.

That night, I had no nightmares, though the feeling of gray eyes lingered throughout my dreams.

When I woke as the evening bells tolled, my mind was muddy and unfocused from a sleep that was too restful. It made my body feel heavy and almost worse than it had when I was exhausted.

I also had a nagging feeling in the back of my mind, as though there had been something I needed to remember from my dreams, something that had happened while I slept, but I could not cling to it long enough for it to fully form before it slipped away, burned out of my mind by consciousness.

It wasn't an uneasy feeling, I decided, just the feeling I'd forgotten something important, so, intent on making it through this next party and continuing to confront Tallon about the treatment, I turned my mind elsewhere.

CHAPTER TWENTY-FIVE

The next night passed in much the same fashion, and as the party tonight began to wind to a close, I was nearing the end of my limited patience. Two more parties had now passed since the night in my room, and it was as if I were walking around in a haze. By some miracle, I'd avoided any further mistakes during the parties, but the only clear memories from the ballroom were visions of my hands holding a tray and weaving through bodies, all the while feeling Tallon's gaze on my back.

It worried me, how easily I could forget everything around me when I had his attention. It terrified me, how much I liked having his attention.

The haze only cleared when I stepped into the kitchens after the party was over.

Without the letter tucked in my dress to remind me, I'd been afraid the urgency of getting the treatment would be swept up in the extravagance of the parties and the bustling of trying to remain unseen by the prince, but it hadn't. It had fallen to the back of my mind, but unlike the first nights here, the castle hadn't swallowed up the thoughts entirely.

Perhaps it was good they fell slightly to the back of my mind; it prevented me from making yet another mistake born of impulsive anger.

But now, two parties had passed since Tallon had requested patience. Tonight, during our rendezvous in his rooms, I would ask again. I needed to know what progress he'd made, if he'd delivered the letter, and if he'd learned Rhyon's fate.

As I cleaned up the remaining dishes and set them out to dry, I pondered his responses. I needed to know, but I also feared what would happen if he confirmed what I already suspected and that my youngest brother was dead. Tallon was many things, including intentionally elusive and obnoxiously arrogant, but throughout all our interactions, he did not seem cruel.

"Have a good night," I murmured to the others.

Elena raised her head from where she sat, cleaning up her polishing supplies. "Will *he* be waiting for you again?"

I hesitated in the doorway. "Who?"

She rolled her eyes. "Don't play stupid. Tallon was waiting for you last night, and the past two nights he has barely taken his eyes off you. We're not fools, Odyssa."

There was no explanation I could give them that would suffice for their curiosity. And more, there was none I wanted to give them. They had not earned my secrets, nor my trust.

Zaharya caught my eye. "Be careful, Odyssa."

I nodded once, turning to escape the room and the uncomfortable stares of Elena and Talyssa. At least Maricara had not been there.

I'd been expecting him to be waiting for me outside the kitchens, as he had last night, to escort me to his rooms, so his presence further down the hall was far from surprising. What had my steps faltering now was that he was not alone against the wall.

My luck had run out, it seemed, as Maricara was with him, her veil gone and barely a sliver of space between them as she looked up at him and twirled a strand of hair around her finger. He said something, too quiet and too far away for me to make out, but whatever it was had her tossing her head back in a laugh and then she was touching him. One hand gripped his forearm and the other pressed against his chest as she leaned in closer and replied.

A flood of emotions washed over me, sending a ringing through my ears as my hands clenched into fists. My face blazed and the urge to run away and cry coiled in my stomach, heavy and sour. Anger and shame, both two emotions I was familiar with.

I had no right to the anger; Tallon could spend his time with whomever he pleased and I had no claim to him.

The shame was a product of my own foolishness, of letting his games mess with my mind and trick me into thinking I was of some import to him.

I was nothing to him. A bargain at best, and a plaything at worst.

Perhaps it was good to see this; perhaps he had intended for me to. After the kiss in his bed, perhaps this was his way of informing me that something like that would not happen again.

I wanted to say that it would never happened again, but I couldn't. I couldn't deny that despite knowing how utterly foolish it was, I'd enjoyed his lips and his body pressed against mine, and that if given the chance, I'd do it again. Consequences for myself be damned.

Consequences for my brothers, on the other hand, was a far different matter.

Regardless, I had no claims to the anger and shame burning

through me, and I needed to remember that. The gash in my hand had mostly healed, though by all accounts of my health after the fever had wrought my body, it should still be festering and sore, but yet, it brought clarity when I pushed my thumb into the wound.

Hands behind my back and my thumb digging into my palm as hard as possible, I ventured down the hall.

Maricara leaned back slightly as I approached, her lip curling up in a sneer. Tallon's eyes widened briefly beneath the mask as they met mine, but he made no move to step away from her.

I inclined my head in polite greeting and bit my tongue until I was able to turn the corner at the end of the hall. I wanted to slump against the wall, but Tallon was too close still. Retreating to my room was foolish; Tallon would eventually come looking for me, and the last place I wanted him to be after spending time with her was in my bedroom.

Cold brushed against my ankle. The cat looked up at me, an expression that could only be classed as pity etched in its feline features. I slowed to a stop, feeling the irrational anger begin to rise to the surface once more.

"Don't look at me like that," I hissed. I did not want anyone's pity, least of all that of Tallon's pet Soulshade. "If you want to help, show me to somewhere I can be left alone until he decides he's finished."

The cat blinked at me, and then offered the equivalent of a shrug that no normal cat could have done. I fell into step behind it easily, letting it guide me through the halls. Tallon's games were a mystery to me, and while I wanted to believe the moment I'd interrupted tonight was one of Maricara's machinations to remind me of my place among them, I could not dismiss that it was one of Tallon's either.

Chewing on my lip, I hardly looked to see where the cat was taking me, and that blind trust startled me out of my thoughts. I was following a Soulshade cat through a castle that had previously proven detrimental to my health and safety, and I had no problems with doing so.

The cat looked back over its shoulder at me, slowing.

If it had wanted to hurt me, it would have done so long before now, I reasoned. This cat had been the only creature that consistently offered comfort and support, and I selfishly didn't want it to leave me. Wrong and grotesque as it was, it was the only friend I had here, and the only friend I'd had anywhere in a very long time.

I shook my head. "I'm fine. Continue."

We resumed our trek through the castle, stopping at a familiar set of doors. The library. I smiled slightly as I pushed open the doors. I hadn't known where it was going to take me, but as I inhaled the weathered parchment and old leather, I was glad the cat had chosen here.

"Thank you," I whispered as I closed the doors behind me. It curled around my ankle in response before leaving to hop up on the bench in the large window bay.

It felt wrong, being here in this exuberantly stocked library, but I would relish what little comforts I could find in this place. Still, I refrained from pulling any books down from the shelves, though I desperately wanted to. I'd not been able to read for my own enjoyment in years, since I'd been a child. But these were not my books, and given the way the walls held their secrets, I would be remiss to assume the library was benign.

I settled into the window seat with the cat, looking out over the rest of the castle and the rooftops of the city beyond. The sun hadn't fully risen yet, and the morning was still in that sleepy, quiet time when not even the birds would be awake—if there were birds remaining in Veressia, that was. In another life, one not smothered by red mist, it would have been peaceful. Now, it was solemn.

The sun had finally shown its face between the valley and the far expanses of the mountains when the doors to the library slowly creaked open. I held my breath as I stared at the door, waiting to see who would enter. I hoped it was Tallon, because if it was anyone else, I would be dead before the sun rose over the mountain peaks.

My shoulders slumped as his face appeared in the crack between the doors. He still had his mask on, but I could see the odd look on his face and knew the pinch of his brow had formed to accompany the frown. He jerked his head towards the hall, an instruction for me to follow.

Despite the irritation that prickled at the command, I followed him out of the library. Our journey to his room was silent, save the sound of our steps against the stone. I hated the silence, yet could not bring myself to break it. Every word that passed through my mind was still tinged in either red or green, and I feared what response it would evoke.

Once in his room, I watched from just inside while he closed the door tightly behind us, carefully hung up his coat on the hook beside the entryway, and pulled off the mask, adding it to the hook beside the coat. He'd still not uttered a single noise as he stepped up in front of me and took my injured hand, pulling it palm up and examining it.

"Good, the salve worked well," he said, more to himself than to me as he dropped my hand. He raised his gaze from my palm. "Your stitches are ready to be removed."

I bit my tongue as he pulled me to the chairs in front of the fire. I wanted to scream at him, about both my brothers and Maricara. More, I didn't want to have to scream at him. I wanted him to find them both important enough to address on his own.

We remained silent as he carefully cut and removed the sutures in my hand. I kept my eyes on my lap or on the cat that had settled by the fire as if it could still feel the warmth. Anything to avoid where his hands held my own.

Finished, he settled back in his chair with a sigh, crossing his hands over his stomach. The frown was still firmly on his lips, and something that almost looked like hurt had settled into the lines of his face. "I expected you to have said something by now."

He was upset I had not reacted to his little game the way he'd intended, and it only made it easier to feign the indifference I so desperately wanted to be a reality. "What is there to say? You are your own person, and one of high status at that. You can do whatever you please. I have no say over you, my lord."

"Why do you call me that now? I'm not wearing my mask," he said, frown somehow deepening.

I raised an eyebrow. "Are you not? You are playing your games still, both now and in the hallway with her."

He leaned forward abruptly, resting his forearms on his thighs. The intensity in his eyes as he studied me made me want to fidget, but I held still. "Were you jealous of her, Odyssa?"

"I have no claim to you and no authority over who you give your affections to." The storm clouds that swirled in his eyes told me I'd not kept my voice as indifferent as I'd hoped.

"You *are* jealous," he breathed. In a blur, he was on his feet, hands resting on the armrests of my chair and leaning over me, caging me in. "Good."

Both eyebrows raised at that, and I did not swallow back the indignation. "*Good?*"

"Yes," he said, leaning down closer to me, his hands tightening on the armrests and making the leather creak. "I wanted you to be jealous. It infuriated me that you seemed so unaffected, that you walked past without a word or even a glimmer of emotion on your face."

"Did you plan that?" I snarled. "If you wanted to play your

games, I'd prefer you do it with someone I don't have to work with every single day."

"I am not playing a game with you." His head tilted and the silence thrummed with unresolved energy. "And I certainly did not plan that. I don't even know that woman's name, Odyssa."

"I hardly think her name matters in this instance," I replied. "If you did not plan that, did she?"

"Why would she plan that?" He raised an eyebrow. "Had anyone but you seen her, she likely would have been punished. Especially given I did push her away after you passed."

I said nothing at first. Maricara had made it clear she did not like me, and she had made equally clear she would do nothing to jeopardize her own life in this place. It did not fit, that she would do this simply to get a rise out of me when she could have gotten in trouble for it. She had wanted something from him, and he had not given it to her. "What did she ask you for?"

He frowned. "Nothing." Understanding dawned upon his face. "She'd only just approached when you passed, Odyssa."

"What did you say to her to make her laugh, then?" I knew the jealousy was leaking into my voice, yet I could do nothing to stop it. The claim I felt over him was unwarranted, I knew, but despite that, he was *mine,* and after all the warnings the others had given me about him, they could not change their minds when they decided that perhaps he did appeal to them after all.

"Nothing that should have gotten that much of a reaction from her, I swear it." He reached out a hand to rest on my thigh.

I hummed, still trying to puzzle out what either could gain from the interaction besides my jealousy. Was that what Maricara had been looking for? Or was she after something else?

The leather creaked again as he bent his elbows, bringing his nose to brush against mine. His voice was throaty as he whispered, "I did not plan it, though I cannot deny I was curious as to how you'd react once you appeared in the hall. It disappointed me, I admit."

"Oh?"

"I wanted you to be furious, to tear her apart for touching me." His breath ghosted over my lips and I struggled to keep my eyes from fluttering shut. "I wanted you to pull her away."

I shifted in the chair, clenching my thighs together at the heat that spread through my body at his voice. It was a miracle my own voice was not breathless. "You were perfectly capable of removing her hand from your body if you did not want it there. The fact you did not until after I had already passed by is indication enough that you did want it there, for whatever reason." I shifted up, until our lips brushed when I spoke. "I told you I wanted no part of your games, Tallon."

Before I could take a breath, he was hauling me to my feet and had one hand around my waist holding me against him. "Odyssa, I—"

Whatever he'd been about to say was interrupted by a knock at the door. "Tallon, are you in there?" Prince Eadric's voice called out from the hallway.

Both of us flinched, jumping apart. My eyes widened as the haze of Tallon faded and I realized my reality. The prince was here, and I was here, where I absolutely should not be. Tallon looked over at the cat, who had perked up as well at the intrusion. "Take her through the closet. Get her to her rooms and keep her safe."

It jumped to its feet, brushing up against my calf as it led me to a smaller door along the wall. I followed, keeping my eyes firmly on the cat and not looking back at Tallon. I reached to open the door the cat stopped in front of, but Tallon was behind me, reaching around to open it first. Closing my eyes for just a moment, I took a deep breath before stepping forward.

"Wait," he murmured, taking hold of my wrist and turning

me around. His other hand came up to cup my cheek. For a moment, I thought he might kiss me again, but the playfulness and the heat in his eyes from earlier was gone, replaced only by a look of worry that made my stomach churn. "Be safe, Odyssa. I will meet you in your rooms when I'm finished."

He hesitated for a heartbeat and then surged forward to plant a quick yet scorching kiss on my lips before he pushed me into the closet before I could reply, closing the door behind me and plunging me into darkness.

CHAPTER TWENTY-SIX

The moment the closet door clicked shut behind me, my first instinct was to panic. My second instinct was to press my hand against my lips and feel the tingling that Tallon's kiss had left. Instead, I cupped my throat and tried to breathe slowly and deeply. My heartbeat thundered against my palm, slowing only once my eyes began to adjust to the darkness in the closet.

I'd been expecting something small, cramped even, given that my own rooms did not even have a separate closet, but it certainly had benefits, being friends with the prince. Even in the darkness, I could see the quality of the numerous clothes that hung along the left wall, the shoes that lined the floor beneath, and the dresser along the right wall that held a tray of rings next to seven masks, lined up neatly.

It was the closet of a lord, of someone important and wealthy. Someone I would never be. Someone I never *wanted* to be.

Seeing the masks lined up neatly in a row made them seem less menacing, less powerful than they were when they adorned

Tallon's face. For reasons I cared not to ponder further, it frustrated me. The mask Tallon wore when he was the prince's advisor was physical, certainly, but seeing these masks here, lifeless and empty, was a reminder that the true mask he donned each night was one of Tallon's own creation.

And one that he could don at any time.

I tore my gaze from the masks and let my hand fall slowly from my throat. I needed to get out of here, and return to my bedroom before either Prince Eadric discovered me here, or I discovered something else that I could not ignore.

Voices outside the door had me hesitating, though. Though muffled by the door, if I got close enough, I could still likely hear what they said. I took a step back towards the door, intent on pressing myself against it, but the cat moved in a blur, settling itself between the door and me.

At my feet, the cat looked up at me, a pair of blazing yellow eyes set in a void just slightly darker than the darkness around it. It inhaled, growing unnaturally as its entire body expanded and then contracted back on its exhale. A warning.

Exhaling slowly and silently, I nodded at it, acquiescing that I would not attempt to listen in on its master.

I was calm enough now to follow the cat through Tallon's closet without shaking, though I still had no notion as to how the closet would lead us back to my bedroom.

The cat led me to the back of the closet and stopped in front of an empty space along the wall. It looked up at me expectantly and then back to the wall. The wall was just that, a wall. There was no door, no hinges, and in the low light, no seams or any other indication that I would be able to exit Tallon's room from this spot. I looked down at the cat and it held my gaze as it stuck its paw out, disappearing through the wall. It retracted its paw and blinked at me, looking between me and the wall several times.

"You want me to..." I breathed. I shook my head. It was a Soulshade; of course it could pass through walls easily. It kept looking back and forth. I flinched when Prince Eadric's muffled voice sounded outside the closet door. There had to be a secret passage here.

Leaning forward to inspect the wall in the low light, I pressed my hands against the stone, but instead of pushing to activate a hidden door, I fell right through the wall, stumbling out into the hall. I whirled around, looking back at the wall I'd just fallen through and pushing against it. It was solid stone now.

The cat brushed against my leg, reminding me that I needed to not be here. Shaking my head, trying to clear my thoughts, I cast one last glance at the wall before picking up the ends of my dress and hurrying after the cat.

There had to have been a door. Any other explanation petrified me.

The route the cat had us following was not one I'd taken before, and it led us past a set of glass doors that opened to a patio. Nestled between the stone walls of the castle, it was akin to a courtyard if it hadn't been raised on the balcony.

Rushing past it, I nearly missed the person standing there, only seeing the silhouette too late to avert my path.

From behind, the little figure looked so much like Rhyon, down to the small patches along the back of the vest he wore. I gasped, whispering his name as I slowed.

The figure turned and the world began to spin. It *was Rhyon*, but he was...wrong. Like in my nightmares, this Rhyon, this Soulshade version of him, had blood dripping down his chin and staining his shirt. A choked sob erupted from my chest, knowing that if Rhyon was here, in this castle, he was truly dead. I'd been too late.

The Soulshade of my youngest brother smiled, revealing his bloody teeth. His eyes flicked to the side of me, and I turned just as more Soulshades poured from the walls as they had that first night in the cellar.

"No!" I croaked, spinning wildly as I tried to find an opening between the apparitions, but there was none. And I would not be so foolish as to put my back against a wall again either.

The cat turned from the top of the hallway, not realizing I'd stopped. Its eyes widened and it came back towards me, assessing the surrounding Soulshades warily. Could it help me, or would they kill it too?

The first Soulshade reached me before I realized, my eyes still darting between my brother on the patio and the cat in the hall. Its icy grip tightened around my marks, burning cold and turning my knees to liquid.

Another reached for my other arm, holding taut as the cold seared through my body. I squeezed my eyes shut, praying to whatever god would listen that Tallon would come again to save me from the Soulshades. Warmth tingled down my arms and a soul-shattering scream echoed along the halls.

My eyes flew open just in time to see that my savior was not in fact Tallon but myself. The marks along my own skin had peeled away again, as they had with Maricara, and the Soulshade holding onto my right arm had vanished. The others stopped their retreat, eyeing the thick undulating strands of jagged black. My marks struck out again at the one holding my left arm. I watched, wide-eyed, as the Soulshade evaporated with another horrible scream.

In the corner of my eye, the cat stalked towards the spot in the crowd of Soulshades that only had one figure between it and me. The cat shimmered, its body shaking and trembling as it grew even larger until it towered over the Soulshade in front of it in mere seconds. With a glance at me, it opened its mouth and, with a forked tongue licking across pointed teeth, swallowed the Soulshade whole.

I blinked once, twice, and the cat was normal sized and back at my feet, looking up at me while continuing to lick its lips.

Its gaze darted to the side, and I didn't need to see past the even more wary Soulshades to know that Tallon had appeared.

"Leave now, if you know what is good for you, or I will ensure you cease to exist permanently." His voice was pure menace, but it worked. With a wave of his hand and a pulsing silver in his eyes I could see even from down the hall, the Soulshades disappeared one by one.

And then, with only the Soulshade cat for company—one I was sure reported to Tallon and could apparently grow to the size of a large man— I was alone with Tallon.

The anger radiated out of him, mirroring my shadows, but I refused to drop my gaze and cower even as my heart raced and sweat still dotted my brow. My shadows still pulsed at my side, not retreating back into my skin as I expected them to. I lifted my hand, studying the way the black mass moved with my fingers. It was intriguing, and yet terrifying at the same time. They snapped out at Tallon, and he narrowly dodged them.

"Call them back in," he said through gritted teeth. His chin jerked at the mass of black surrounding my right arm. "They're more powerful now; you must command them to retreat."

"How do I do that?" I hissed, dropping my hand back to my side. My heart was still racing, and my anger was still burning hot, only stoked by his insults. I had not called them out in the first place.

His nostrils flared. "Visualize them settling back into your skin. You control them, not the other way around, Odyssa. Quickly."

Closing my eyes, I imagined the shadows pulling back into my skin, sinking into the thick black lines across my body. Slowly, the warmth around my arm receded, and I opened my eyes just as the last of the shadows were flattening back against my skin.

They'd barely finished before Tallon had my wrist in one hand and was bending, pushing his shoulder into my stomach and hoisting me over his back.

Livid, I punched at his back, hiding my wince when my hand hit something hard at the small of his back. I cataloged it, noting the dagger there and briefly wondering how long he'd been armed and why, but I didn't stop, driving my knees into his chest and trying to pull myself down. Unlike before, he said nothing save a soft grunt when my knee connected with his stomach. The ground beneath us turned from the stone of the hallway to the black dirt and I froze, pushing myself up on my fists to look around.

My nightmare world. I was certain of it this time. I pushed up high enough to turn and get a glimpse of his face. "What is this place?"

His jaw clenched, but he said nothing, just tightened his grip on my thighs. By his feet, the cat followed obediently, looking straight ahead. The air rippled and we were back in the castle halls, no trace of the cold, black cliffs.

Tallon set me down, though he renewed his grip on my wrist as he pulled me into my room and shut the door behind us, the lock echoing. He whirled on me, and I dropped my hand, reaching around his back to draw the dagger he'd hidden there. In a moment, I had him pressed against the door and his own dagger beneath his chin.

His eyes grew dark, pupils expanding, and his tongue darted out to wet his lips. "What will you do with that, little wolf?"

"I told you the first time you mistook me for a sack of grain that I would not tolerate it." I moved the tip of the dagger to just beneath his chin, forcing him to raise it. "I warned you the second time as well. I will not tell you again."

His eyes flicked down to my mouth and he licked his lips again, though the move was much slower this time, and it had my own attention falling to his mouth.

A stupid move.

Before I could lift my gaze back to his eyes, he had the dagger out of my hand and had reversed our positions. The blade felt cold against my neck, though there was no pressure. Just a reminder of its presence.

Tallon loomed over me. He lowered his head to make our eyes level, holding my gaze as he dragged the flat of the blade against my skin and down between the valley of my breasts. He paused directly between them, lifting the knife so the point pressed into my skin, but did not break it. "If you were not so intent on getting yourself killed, I would not have to resort to such measures."

I said nothing and kept my stare on his own. Shivers ran down my spine and heat built in my belly, but still I stared. I was tired of the secrets and the lies, and I was tired of the callous indifference he had towards my demands.

Slowly, he lowered the knife and stepped back, sliding it into the sheath at his lower back where it belonged.

"What was that place? I've seen it before, with you, and in my nightmares."

He looked at me. For a moment, I thought he would actually answer me, but it never came. He turned his attention to the cat, sitting in the middle of the room watching us patiently. "What part of my instructions was unclear to you? Get her to her room. Keep her safe. That should not have happened."

The cat's tail flicked. And then it spoke. Its mouth did not move, yet I heard a voice in my mind, clear as the morning bells. *She stopped following me. I noticed too late. I am still incorporeal, Tallon. What did you expect me to do?*

My jaw fell open and I blinked rapidly. "You can *talk*?" Disregarding Tallon entirely, I rushed into the room and dropped to my knees in front of the cat. It eyed me warily.

"Yes, she can," Tallon said from behind me. The impatience and irritation in his voice was clear. "We have things to discuss, Odyssa."

I waved a hand at him, focusing on the cat. I didn't know what I felt, if it was awe or betrayal. Perhaps both. "Could you understand me this entire time?"

Yes. The cat tilted her head and stood, pushing against my leg as much as she could. *I cannot always speak, but I did always listen, Odyssa.*

"Do you have a name?" Tears stung my eyes, and for the life of me, I could not tell if they were from anger or sadness or relief. Perhaps all three. The cat was my only comfort here, and though I always knew she was in some way connected to Tallon, I wanted to know more about this little piece of darkness that made things bearable.

The cat's eyes flicked over my shoulder to Tallon before settling back on mine. *You may—*

"That's enough, Sylviana. This is serious, Odyssa. You could have died," Tallon said from behind me. Grabbing my arm, he hauled me to my feet.

The tenderness was replaced at once with ire as I smacked at his hand. "Don't touch me. I've had enough lies, Tallon. What was that place, why is Sylviana following me, and what has happened to my brothers?"

"The real question is why are you so intent on testing your aversion to death?"

I narrowed my eyes. "What does that mean?"

He stepped closer to me. "You seem to court death at every turn, Odyssa. Despite your best efforts to the contrary, you remain alive. I would not keep testing your luck."

"My brothers, Tallon. The treatment." He would not tell me

about the nightmare world, and while I was curious about Sylviana, my brothers were the priority. "What progress have you made? Did you deliver my letter?"

Whatever response he'd been about to give was cut off by a knock on my door this time. I growled in frustration and stalked to the door. "Who is it?"

"Zaharya and Talyssa. Do you have a moment?" she called through the door.

I spun around, intent on telling Tallon that it was his turn to hide and that we would finish our conversation after, but he was gone. Both he and Sylviana had disappeared in the moments I'd had my back turned. My jaw clenched and I blew out a breath, pasting on a soft but neutral expression before tugging the door open to face the women. "Would you like to come in?"

Zaharya hesitated for a moment but nodded and I opened the door wider to allow both her and Talyssa through. Zaharya stopped as she passed me. "We wanted to check on you."

I narrowed my eyes at her back as I followed her inside. "Why?"

Zaharya settled on the corner of my bed, crossed her hands in her lap, and pursed her lips, while Talyssa stood to her side, wringing her hands in front of her. I had a strong suspicion I was not going to like their reasoning. "We've noticed Tallon paying you more attention lately, and—"

I held my hand up to stop her. "I would just like to get clarity on one thing first, before you continue with what is undoubtedly another warning to keep my wits about me and stay away from him. Am I the only one being warned off, or does the warning apply to everyone? I would like to know, seeing as I saw Maricara pressed up against him in the hallway as I was leaving tonight."

Both of their eyes widened. Talyssa's face flushed and she tucked her hands behind her back as her eyes darted between Zaharya and me.

Zaharya kept my gaze.

"Truly, I understand that we are not here to make friends, and I understand that none of us *want* to be here. And believe me, I understand the dangers this castle and those close to Prince Eadric pose. I do not understand why, in the face of these dangers, it has been decided that I am some sort of threat to any of you."

The tension was thicker than the red mist outside the window. In the end, it was Talyssa who broke it. "We just wanted to make sure you were safe, that you knew what you were getting into if he continues with the attention. We didn't mean anything by it."

"I think perhaps you mean different things by coming here tonight," I said carefully. Talyssa did seem genuine, but I'd thought the same of Zaharya before I'd heard them gossiping about me that night I went to the cellars. "And while I appreciate the warning, without context, it does me no good."

Zaharya's shoulders slumped as she relaxed her rigid posture and pushed a hand through her hair. "The warning is for everyone. Maricara has been here the longest, and I..." She trailed off, shaking her head. "I do not know why she was pursuing Tallon tonight, I truly don't. I admit, I am wary of you. You've attracted far too much attention since you've arrived and I have no desire to be associated with what that attention might bring. But I did come here today in good faith, to warn you that there was a reason your services were needed."

More word games, more hidden meanings. "Speak plainly. I tire of the games."

She sighed. "As do I. We're forbidden from speaking of it directly, but I will try to tell you what I can."

"What forbids you? How would anyone know?"

"The castle knows." She sighed again, rubbing her temples. "I was conscripted into service nine months ago. There are seven attendant positions. Since I began work here, we have welcomed thirteen attendants as we welcomed you." She squinted at Talyssa.

The redhead picked up the threads of Zaharya's thought and continued. "None to my knowledge have contracted the plague. None to my knowledge were granted freedom from service."

My mind went back to the Soulshade of the woman with the slit throat and the pieces began to fall into place. My fists tightened at my sides. The other servants were dead, and it was heavily implied they'd been killed. Both women visibly relaxed as understanding dawned. My jaw ached from how tightly it was clenched. "Who? How?"

Zaharya shook her head. "I cannot say either. But please, heed our warning. Those who live here in this castle by invitation are not safe, not for us." She stood from the bed and both she and Talyssa made for the door. Zaharya clasped my arm as she passed. "I don't know what Maricara is trying to do, but I'd stay as far away from her as you can too. Whatever she thinks you have done to slight her, she doesn't forgive lightly."

"Thank you both for coming," I said after a moment of silence. Despite that they'd interrupted my conversation with Tallon, I did appreciate that they were trying to look out for me in their own way. It warmed something beneath my breastbone, and I smiled, hoping it wasn't too much of a grimace. "Sleep well."

They both murmured their own thanks and departed.

The door closed quietly behind them. I mindlessly moved about to ready for bed and drew the curtains closed before sliding beneath the covers. Pulling my knees to my chest, I stared into the darkness, rubbing at my temples. What she was implying had been clear, that Tallon had played a role in the deaths of the other servants. Camelya had implied that Tallon would be the one to kill me if I made another mistake. But

Tallon... Tallon had told me if the prince wanted me dead, he would do it himself.

Tallon could not be trusted, this much I knew already, but the bargain we'd made loomed over my head. If he'd wanted me dead, he wouldn't have made the deal, I reasoned. Unless, a small voice contradicted, it was another part of his games and he had no intentions of keeping it.

I fell back into the pillows and closed my eyes. I needed to assume the letter never arrived, that Rhyon was dead, and that Tallon had told the prince of my plans. As much as Emyl despised me, as much as I wanted to just give in and work here until I was a forgotten piece of the backdrop, I could not bring myself to break the vow I made to my mother. I'd had nothing in this life except her approval.

I would get the treatment. I would get it to Emyl. He would live.

As I was beginning to drift off, exhaustion finally catching up with me, a cold spot settled against my thigh. *Sleep, Odyssa. I am here.*

"Goodnight, Sylviana," I murmured, letting my eyes close and sleep take me under. A pair of silver eyes flashed from a patch of complete darkness by the window, but I was too far over the edge into sleep to truly see them.

CHAPTER TWENTY-SEVEN

I woke to my curtains being yanked open and the fading evening sun sending bursts of orange and red across my eyelids. Shooting up, I squinted into the light enough to see a smirking Tallon leaning against the wall by the window. "Rise and shine, Odyssa."

"What are you doing here?" I groused, rubbing at my eyes. After his disappearing act before, I was hardly in a welcoming mood. "And how did you get in my room?"

"You believe a locked door can stop me?"

"How comforting." I sighed, tugging the blanket into my lap, trying to cover my nightgown-clad body from his intense stare. "Why are you here?"

"It is time for you to get ready, is it not?" He shrugged and sat down in the plush chair by the window, spreading his hands. "I wanted to keep you company."

"Why?" I knew I likely wouldn't get an answer, but I couldn't stop from asking anyways. Tallon confused me, and until I was able to decipher his motives, his secrets, I would always be somewhat wary of him. Now, he seemed genuine and open, lighter than before, but I knew all too well how quickly he could pull his mask on and turn into a blank and cold statue.

"Why do you not dress with the others?" He raised his eyebrow and waved vaguely towards the wardrobe against the wall. "I thought there was a room for you all to get ready in."

"There is. Some of the others and I don't quite…" I paused, searching for the right word. As much as it annoyed me how Elena and Maricara treated me, I did not want any consequences. I turned my back to him, pulling the evening's clothing from the wardrobe and grimacing at the peach-colored fabric staring back at me. "We don't quite agree on certain topics. I felt it was best to get ready here."

He hummed. "What is it you disagree on?"

I shot a look over my shoulder. "Why did you leave before we finished our conversation last night?"

"You had a visitor."

"You could have waited."

"Have you always been so stubborn?" An exasperated huff sounded and I didn't need to turn around to know that he was shaking his head at me.

"No, usually I'm quite cooperative," I said, folding the fabric into my arms and turning back to face him. "Present company must bring out the worst in me."

His wry smile almost hid the amusement in his eyes. Almost.

I waved my hand at him. "Have you always been this arrogant?"

"Yes." The answer came quickly, no hesitation in his tone.

The storm in my stomach tumbled, a war waging between the soft comfort the exchange brought and the knowledge that Tallon was still lying to me about everything that mattered.

The small smile that had crept onto his lips slowly disappeared the longer he looked at me, and he let out a sigh, nodding his head at the bundle in my hands. "You should get ready, little wolf."

I waited, but he did not move. If I'd been thinking clearly, I would have moved into the bathroom, shut the door firmly between us, and changed there. But this Tallon, the one that wore no mask and whose eyes burned against my skin and lit a fire in my belly, he made me want to tease and torment. I laid the evening's clothing out across the bed deliberately. The veil, the dress, the gloves. "Well? Are you going to give me privacy to change, or do you plan on remaining there?"

It was foolish, I knew, to entertain even a hint of whatever this was burning between us, but for reasons I didn't want to explore, I couldn't resist. Zaharya had warned me about him, and I had seen it with my own eyes: Tallon was dangerous, and I should be avoiding him at all costs, but here I was, taunting him.

He raised an eyebrow and stood, keeping our gazes locked as he turned the chair around to face the wall and sat back down in it, his back now to me. "There. Is that better?"

"Much."

We drifted into silence, the only sound that of fabric rustling as I pulled off my nightgown. My eyes stayed on his back while I slipped the dress over my head. He was already dressed for the evening, his shirt stretched across his broad shoulders. I hadn't noticed before, but the hair at the back of his neck swirled into a slight point. I wanted to run my fingers through it.

"Ask me."

I startled and finished pulling the dress down, freeing my hair from the back. "Ask you what?"

"You're staring at me," he said, still facing away from me. "I assumed you had a question."

I had many questions, but I couldn't bring myself to voice any of them. Irritation sprang up suddenly, prickling hot against my cheeks. Tallon's games were never ending, and despite my best efforts to rise to his challenges, he was sweeping me away and he knew it. Yet I continued to fall for the bait. I snatched the gloves from the bed. "You can turn around now."

He stood and faced me in one smooth motion before I even had finished speaking, his eyes roving over my body before narrowing in on the black lace gloves I was pulling on. "Why do you wear those?"

Surprise halted my movements. Of all the things for him to ask, that certainly had not been one I'd expected. I searched his face for any signs this was a test or another part of his games, but found only genuine curiosity and a touch of anger. Slowly, I continued pulling on the glove. "I was told my marks would offend Prince Eadric and his guests and was instructed to keep them covered during the parties. Between the gloves and my hair and the veils, and the darkness in the ballroom, they blend in well enough to be missed."

He hummed but didn't reply immediately, watching carefully as I pulled on the other glove and picked up the veil. He nodded at the gauzy fabric and crossed his arms over his chest, pulling the maroon silk even tighter across his shoulders. "I despise those things."

I could not read his expression now. A careful answer was best. "I imagine anyone would."

Another hum, but he stayed still, arms crossed and feet apart as he stared at me. "Ask what you wanted to ask, Odyssa. You do not have to bite your tongue around me. Not when we are alone."

I only had a moment to decide if I wanted to fall deep into the well of anger or stay afloat atop the sea of incredulity. Choosing the latter, I let out a soft huff and raised an eyebrow. "That does not mean you will answer the question, Tallon."

The smile that stole across his face was bright and wide, and I knew I'd passed some sort of test. "Of course not, but you can ask it regardless."

Tugging my bottom lip between my teeth, I considered what I wanted to ask. I had a plethora, beginning and ending with the treatment and my brothers, but I hesitated as I considered it. The evasion, the secrets, the lies... they were wearing on me. If I asked again for the third time, would he tell me? I wanted an answer, for once. The truth. And I wanted the conversation to continue, and any questions about our bargain would likely end it.

As with Sylviana, who was stretched out across the bed still, watching us, when Tallon was not being an arrogant prick—and perhaps even when he was—his presence made me feel less lonely.

"How do you know the prince? You seem quite close." It *was* something I'd wanted to ask, and perhaps the answer, if he even deigned to give one, would be helpful in getting the treatment myself once I'd figured out a way to get back to the prince's quarters without Tallon's knowledge.

He tilted his head. "That is not what you originally wanted to ask me, but I'll allow it." He walked slowly to the bed, settling down on the corner of it. "I admit, I am not here at Prince Eadric's behest. I was acquainted more with his father and we had business together occasionally. I was staying in the castle to complete a job for him when he died. After he passed, Prince Eadric invited me to remain in the castle." An indifferent shrug. "I had no other plans and nothing more intriguing to attend to, so I stayed."

It took a moment for the words to settle in my mind. And then the well of anger I'd avoided earlier swallowed me whole. "'Nothing more intriguing?' You say it as if this plague is nothing more than dinnertime entertainment. As if families aren't being torn apart and the stench of death hasn't settled into the land's very bones."

His eyes flashed. "I do not know these people, Odyssa. Nor do I owe them my grief or reverence for dying. Death is a part of life, and you must learn to embrace its inevitability before your own grief tears you apart."

I felt sick to my stomach. "You are so callous. Your humanity—"

He barked out a laugh. "Humanity? Humanity has given me *nothing*. It has given you *nothing*. There was no humanity in Veressia long before this plague descended, and there will be no humanity after it is gone. I have waited, *begged* for humanity to show its face in this city, and yet here we are."

There was truth in his words, but they stung like a slap to the face all the same. "Humanity is what you give to others, not what is given to you. Your indifference will damn you, and I cannot wait to see it."

Boots echoed in the room, and then he was in front of me. "How do you know I am not already damned, little wolf? How do you know *you* are not already damned?"

"Do you even care that my brother might be dead?" I asked, my voice cracking with unshed tears born of anger more than grief. It made the anger grow, frustrated with myself and how my emotions had been so twisted since coming to the castle. "Did you even take the letter to them?"

"Why do you care more for their lives than your own?" His voice was softer, despite the tension still in his jaw and forehead.

"Did you take the letter?" My words were spat through gritted teeth. My life was forfeit the moment I stepped through the gilded iron gates, but I could still appease my mother's last wish.

Like a curtain snapping shut, Tallon's mask was on once more. Not the skull mask that sat beside the chair he'd occupied, but the one that dulled his eyes and yanked any emotion from him. "I told you I would. I did."

"Well?"

He shook his head, stepping away and moving back to the

chair where he pulled his coat on and fastened the mask around his head, settling it into place across his face. "Anything I tell you now, you will not believe. We'll discuss this later."

The bells tolled, signaling I was already late to the kitchens. Narrowing my eyes at him, I clutched the veil in my hands and ran from the room, letting the door slam into the wall behind me as I left. He could lock it behind him when he left. There was nothing polite I could say to him now.

CHAPTER TWENTY-EIGHT

I swept into the kitchens only minutes later than I should have, out of breath and sweaty. Zaharya was the only one to look up, looking at me for half a moment before sliding the tray she'd just filled across the counter.

Elena and Maricara were finishing their own trays, huddled together with their backs to us. I focused on taking deep breaths through my nose and filled the second tray Zaharya had set out. The plague had left my lungs weak, and it took far longer than I appreciated for my breathing to steady back out. By the time it had, the sun had settled behind the mountains for the evening and it was time for us to start our work.

I furrowed my brow and looked around, but there was no sign of Talyssa. Arranging the shroud and picking up my tray, I leaned in to Zaharya as we followed Elena and Maricara out of the kitchens. "Is Talyssa alright? Has someone checked on her?"

She shook her head. "No one has seen her since we left your room last night. Elena went to her room earlier but there was no answer. Camelya is supposedly looking for her."

"We can manage without her," Elena said. She tossed a

poorly disguised sneer over her shoulder at me. "We did when you disappeared."

I bit my tongue and kept walking. Talyssa was not like me; she'd seemed competent and, though timid, she seemed settled with this reality of ours. Though, given how much had been happening to me that I'd kept from the others, it was entirely possible that they all did the same. As we approached the ballroom, I wondered if that was by design, to isolate us and make us hoard our secrets and thoughts like the prince hoarded his most prized inside the castle.

The music began as we entered the ballroom, an eerie tune that crawled across the heads of those in attendance to reach us. The ballroom itself had been turned into a mockery of what the sunrise looked like before the mist descended. Swaths of vivid peach fabric draped from the ceiling, falling down the walls around golden decor and bright pink flowers. Where they had found such flowers, I didn't want to know. They'd likely cost more than an entire month's wage just for plants that would be dead at this time tomorrow. A waste.

Further into the ballroom, a set of doors opened and then closed, and then the music faltered. Only for a beat, and then it resumed, but the effect had been noticed and those in the ballroom all turned their attention to whomever had entered. I kept my head down, focused on the tray in my hands as partygoers snatched drinks from it.

People were whispering, and there was a tension in the room that hadn't been there any other night. My eye twitched, desperate to search out the cause for the whispers. As the last glass was pulled from my tray, the gap in the crowd gave me a view of what exactly had commanded everyone's attention.

Tallon.

My feet forgot how to move and I was grateful for the shroud that covered my face as my mouth fell open slightly. Tallon was standing against the wall, which was far from unusual. It wasn't his presence that had stirred everyone up, but his sartorial choices instead, it seemed. The jacket he'd had on earlier was gone and the sleeves of his shirt were rolled up, cuffed at the tops of his forearms and revealing the thick, black marks that decorated his skin. His collar was unbuttoned to the third button, revealing the matching marks that swirled across his chest as well.

It was no wonder the ballroom had erupted into whispers at his entrance.

I could see the moment he felt my stare. His head snapped up, eyes fixed directly on mine, and his shoulders fell slightly, easing down from around his ears. My cheeks flushed as that slow smirk spread across his face. His chin dipped slightly, a ghost of a nod, and then he was pushing his cuffed sleeves further up his forearms before letting his head tilt back against the wall.

I swallowed hard, eyes tracking over the curve of his neck and then trailing lower to map the muscles of his forearms beneath the thick black marks.

"It's horrid that he'd flaunt them so." Someone's whispered venom pulled me out of my trance. "Prince Eadric will not be pleased."

"It's unnatural. It's a shame the prince even let him in here."

The words spurred me back into my body, unsticking my feet and sending me along through the ballroom, people already filling up my tray with their empty glasses. I felt Tallon's eyes on my back as I worked, and I hated that I wanted nothing more than to settle into the wall beside him and return the favor.

I found myself conflicted in my feelings once more. There was no mistaking what had led him to choose tonight to forego his jacket and roll up his sleeves; it was clearly a response to our earlier conversation about my gloves and the shroud.

Had he chosen to display them in solidarity, to show me that he didn't care what those others thought of the marks that adorned our skin? I was ashamed to say it pleased me that he cared enough to reassure me he didn't mind my marks. Our marks.

It made me want to pull my gloves off and show the world that we matched, but I would never have the reluctant acceptance he was privy to. Still, the gesture sent me about my tasks with a small smile on my face.

Tallon watched me as he always did now. Unlike before, now his eyes were a welcome weight upon my back. Knowing that he cared enough to watch me, cared enough to send Sylviana in his place when he couldn't.

"Do you know why he's chosen to show off his marks for the first time since I've been here?" Zaharya murmured as she fell into step beside me. Both of us continued collecting empty glasses as we roved through the ballroom.

"He did not like my gloves," I answered mindlessly. I was too focused on my task to realize what I'd admitted to her until the words were already out of my mouth, and it was too late to snatch them back.

The disapproval radiated off her, but she only hummed in response, as if she didn't believe my answer. Without waiting for a reply, she split off and carved a path deeper into the ballroom. Returning my focus to my work, despite the growing pit in my stomach that those words would come back to haunt me, I continued until my tray was full and began to make my way to the kitchens.

"How horrid," someone said to their companion, "that he chooses to mock those who cannot show their marks without fear of Prince Eadric's response."

"Truly," the companion agreed. They both looked at me, though I kept my gaze down and did not falter as I passed. Even with my poor hearing, I heard their parting words. "Did you see her? The marks beneath her veil are covered, and yet he flaunts his. It's hardly kind, but I suppose that's the point."

Despite the happiness I'd felt earlier, the couple's words lingered, leaping into the pit that had already begun to grow in my stomach until it was a hard ball of anxiety that gnawed at my spine.

No one would dare say anything to Tallon where he could hear. No one would punish him for his marks being visible, not like they would me, and perhaps he wanted to remind me of that. Perhaps they were right, that it was a mockery rather than a show of solidarity. I knew what I wanted it to be, but I also knew that I rarely got what I wanted.

My hands ached to throw the tray to the ground, to smash the glasses against the polished stone floor and tear the tapestries from the wall. It *had* to be another one of his games, and I would not fall for this one.

Gritting my teeth, I continued my work, clearing out empty glasses, returning to the kitchen for more, and starting the cycle all over again. I tried in vain to keep my eyes off him, but I found myself watching him more times than I cared to acknowledge. And each time my gaze wandered over his body, he was watching me back.

Despite the overwhelming impulse to do so, I refrained from confronting him now and vowed to address it later. The games in private were one thing, but to bring them here where he could mock me openly and almost certainly cause me to make a mistake was unfair. He would not be punished if I made a misstep due to the distractions he caused. I would.

It felt like days had passed by the time the midnight bells finally tolled. The sigh of relief I let out fluttered my veil, but the emotion was short lived as the doors at the back of the ballroom —the ones Prince Eadric entered from—swung open. The room collectively froze and held its breath as he stomped to the stage and commanded the music to stop.

Against the wall, Tallon's fists clenched and he pushed himself upright.

My stomach sank and I tore my gaze from Tallon, searching for Zaharya instead, only to find that she was searching for me. Through the veil, her hand waved me over to where she stood behind one of the tables, pressing herself against the wall. The mood in the ballroom shifted as the doors opened and closed again.

I tucked in beside her, but from this vantage point, we could not see the stage or who had joined Prince Eadric. Tallon was still pressed against the wall, but his shoulders had tensed up, making them look even more broad. My fingers twitched, wanting to reach out—for what, I didn't know—but I felt vulnerable here in this ballroom waiting for whatever news was so grim it was distressing even Tallon.

The feeling throughout the ballroom reminded me a bit of the tension that had filled the room when Prince Eadric had been about to punish me for jostling him, but somehow, tonight the fear was even thicker. Something had happened, and the sinking feeling in my stomach spoke of nothing good.

Zaharya's fingers found mine, twining together and squeezing. She kept her face towards the stage but held on to my hand. Despite our tepid relationship, I was grateful for the support. Though perhaps it was helping her as much as it helped me.

Someone in the crowd gasped closer to the stage. Exchanging looks, Zaharya and I shared a nod, and then she was pulling me through the crowd to stand along the wall in an attempt to see better what was happening.

Prince Eadric was on the stage, his hand wrapped in a head of copper hair belonging to someone kneeling before him. Zaharya subtly strained her neck, rising on her toes, but settled back down, shaking her head minutely. She couldn't see who it was either. My stomach churned, bile sour on my tongue, but I was grateful it was not ash and smoke that coated the inside of my mouth. This person was alive, at least.

"Someone," his voice boomed, echoing over the polished walls and floors, despite the bodies and fabric. "Someone has stolen from me. Someone has decided they would rather be out *there*, at the mercy of fate, rather than in here, safe and cared for."

Our hands tightened around each other's in the same heartbeat. I didn't know why Zaharya's clenched, but my own was fear and anger. Outrage.

"See who has betrayed us!" The crowd shuffled forward and parted just so, and I saw the face of the woman Prince Eadric was holding.

It was Talyssa.

Zaharya's hand grasped mine so tightly I felt the bones shifting. The prince said something else, but ringing filled my ears, the room hollowed out, and all I could see was Talyssa's face, with an expression there I was intimately familiar with. Failure. Shame.

"Well, do enlighten us. Why did you want to leave us, my dear?" Prince Eadric asked. "What gave you the right to try to steal silver and gold from my palace? From the home I welcomed you into?"

She kept her gaze straight ahead, but I saw her jaw clench. In that moment, something in me wished I had pushed past both our walls and reached out to her more. Perhaps if it had been both of us working together, we could have made a difference. If the prince had caught me that night instead of Tallon, I had no doubt that I would have been in her place now.

Eadric scoffed loud enough to carry over the throng of bodies, and he pushed her to the floor. Zaharya stepped in front of me just as my body lurched forward. "No," she hissed. "You'll just get yourself killed with her."

"Tallon, if you will." Prince Eadric motioned for Tallon to join them on the stage.

I watched as slowly, his eyes flicked directly to me and then shuttered, flat gray even from across the room, and he sauntered to the prince's side. There was nothing of the Tallon I knew in there; every bit of him was Prince Eadric's puppet.

"Let this be a reminder to all of you of who is in control here." He nodded at Tallon. "Kill her."

My stomach dropped to my feet, and now it was my turn to squeeze Zaharya's hand. The crowd exploded into murmurs, but no one seemed particularly surprised, not even Zaharya.

"What is he doing?" I asked under my breath, leaning in as close as I dared. Tallon would kill Talyssa, I had no doubt of that. He would do anything the prince asked of him, and despite the roiling in my soul, perhaps I needed to see this more than anyone.

Cold brushed up against my leg, and for half a moment, I would have sworn I felt weight pressing against me in the same shape.

Tallon replied to the prince, bowing deeply. I was frozen in place as he raised his hand and waved it towards Talyssa. The movement was sharp, and my eyes could only track the marks that lined from his forearms as they lifted from his skin and undulated, growing into a writhing mass of black.

Exactly as mine had done.

The mass enshrouded Talyssa, concealing her from view only for a moment before retreating into Tallon's skin. Our eyes met across the room, and there was a brief glimmer of life in his eyes, a flash of *something* that broke through the mask.

The room was still for a heartbeat, and then as if it had fallen over like the shroud we wore each night, Talyssa began to bleed.

Blood poured from her nose, then her ears, mouth, eyes.

My face felt hot and I knew my breathing was more like panting now, but I couldn't stop it. My eyes were fixed on Talyssa, and the phantom taste of blood filled my mouth, the cloying thickness of it in the back of my throat choking off what breath I could manage. I was no longer only in the ballroom, but back on my own deathbed. Each choked gasp Talyssa let out mirrored my own, and my hand clawed at my throat, trying to clear the blood that was not there.

Zaharya let go of my hand to wrap her arms around my waist, pulling me tightly to her and turning me away from the stage. I felt Tallon's eyes on my back but buried my face into Zaharya's veil as I tried desperately to *breathe*.

"It will be over soon," she murmured, fighting her hold. "Hold yourself together just a while longer."

Zaharya's warm body against my own and Sylviana's cold form against my leg were the only things that kept me tethered to the reality in front of me. My heart was pounding loudly, drowning out any more words uttered by Prince Eadric. My mind darted between the image of Talyssa's body on the stage and Tallon standing above her, his hands in his pockets and his face a picture of boredom.

Prince Eadric clapped and the flinch that followed tore through my entire body, jerking me away from Zaharya. He said something, his voice booming through the ballroom, but the words did not register in my mind. The image of Talyssa's blood pouring from her body held dominion there, giving room for nothing else.

"Come," Zaharya murmured, tugging me by the hand until my feet understood her intention and followed her. She tucked a tray beneath her arm. "You need a moment. We *both* need a moment."

I let Zaharya guide me from the ballroom. Tallon remained

by the prince's side on the stage, but I felt his eyes on me still, heavy and watching me all the way until I turned the corner and entered the hall that would lead us back to the kitchens.

Zaharya pushed me into a chair in the kitchens, setting the tray down and nearly collapsing into the chair beside mine. Neither of us spoke. I wasn't sure I could have found the right words if I'd wanted to, despite questions flying through my mind. My hands shook where they rested in my lap.

"Are you well enough to continue working?" Zaharya finally asked after what felt like hours but could have been only minutes.

She squeezed my hand when I did not answer immediately, and I tore my gaze from the table. My voice was like I'd swallowed glass. "Yes." I cleared my throat, swallowing past the sour taste of shame and horror. "I can work."

Standing, she rested her hand on my shoulder. "I am sorry this is how you had to discover his truth."

Her words pulled the haze from my eyes and I looked up at her. "Why did you not just tell me from the beginning?"

"You wouldn't have believed me," she said. I saw the soft smile beneath the veil. "They never do, until they see it."

"What..." I trailed off, not really knowing what I was going to ask, or if I truly wanted an answer to it at all. I shook my head.

"I'd suggest staying away from him tonight, if you can."

"Why?" It wasn't argumentative; I agreed with her, after all. I wanted to know her reasoning, though.

"If Prince Eadric learns how close you two have gotten, he may order Tallon to do the same to you," she said quietly. "I'd prefer not to watch another one of us die like that."

"What will happen to her body?" I asked, again not really wanting to know the answer, but I couldn't bear the thought of her being left on that stage all night or of her being tossed aside like garbage.

"I told you, the walls are hungry. The castle will take her."

My thumb found its way to the still-healing wound in my hand. Yes, they were. Taking a deep breath that shuddered its way through my lungs, I stood. "They'll be missing us soon. We should return."

"Stay close tonight, please. I've seen how Tallon watches you. Tonight is not a night for any mistakes, Odyssa."

I nodded my agreement and once more, we gathered our things, new trays filled with food and drink, and returned to the ballroom.

Talyssa's body was no longer on the stage, and for a moment, I thought perhaps I'd imagined the whole thing, given how the party had resumed and those in attendance were acting as if nothing had happened. But as the crowd flitted about, I saw the pool of blood still shining on the onyx floors, and I knew it hadn't been in my head.

I kept my eyes off the stage as I worked, trying to keep my mind present and not wander. Every time I slipped up, every time I closed my eyes to regain a sense of control, red filled my vision. Sometimes it was Talyssa's body, but others it was Talyssa's face on my mother's body, in my mother's bed, and sometimes it was my mother on that stage.

Only a few moments had passed before I felt the heavy gaze on my back return. Tallon was watching me again, and I wanted to be angry at him, but nothing flared in my chest. The pit in my soul was empty, hollow of all things, even a deserved rage. Despite my lack of anger—my lack of any emotion— I refused to acknowledge his gaze and refused to let my own eyes wander in his direction.

Every time my mind conjured up Talyssa or my mother in their last moments, Tallon was now there. He'd caused Talyssa's death, caused her to die choking on her own blood just as my mother had, just as I almost had. Seven minutes instead of seven days hardly made a difference, and Tallon could control it. I wanted to vomit, to scrub my skin until it was raw and pink and had no trace of his touch on it, but just like the rage, nothing would come beyond utter apathy. So instead I hurled myself into my work.

The night faded quickly around me, and soon, the party was over. Elena and Maricara had quietly offered to clean up the ballroom, though Zaharya assured me they would not have to clean up Talyssa's blood. Following Zaharya to the kitchen, I froze as the taste of ash burst across my tongue.

The clattering of the tray falling to the floor echoed in my ears as Talyssa's Soulshade appeared in the corner she always preferred.

I lunged to the trash bin as I ripped at my veil and then promptly vomited.

Zaharya rushed to my side, and by the time I'd stopped, I was panting, eyes and throat stinging.

"What happened?" she asked, her eyes fixed on the corner. Talyssa's Soulshade was gone, and I hated that I was grateful for it.

I couldn't bring myself to tell her, so I shook my head. My heart thundered in my ears, sweat beading on my spine as cold as ice. "I'm sorry," I croaked as I ran from the kitchens. I needed out of this place.

Tallon had won yet again, and I was starting to realize that losing his games would cost me far more than my pride.

CHAPTER TWENTY-NINE

The halls were a blur as I raced through them, seeking the refuge of my room and a door that locked. It would hardly keep Tallon out if he truly wanted in—and I had a feeling he would be showing up eventually tonight—but for a moment, I would let myself believe that I had control over my room. Over myself.

Slamming the door shut behind me, I leaned against it. Only for a heartbeat, and then I was moving again, towards the center of the room as I tore the shroud from my body, followed by the dress until I was naked, only my swath of death marks upon my skin. The mirror against the wall mocked me, showing me the truth: that I had become *exactly* what my mother had been afraid of.

While Tallon's marks were more extensive, I couldn't deny the familiarity in them even as he sent Talyssa to her death. Could I do that? I shut my eyes tightly against the rapid influx of memories, both of myself and my mother as we choked on our own blood.

He'd been the cause of that. He controlled the plague.

My breath came in pants as I approached the mirror, falling to my knees in front of it and frantically tugging and scratching at the skin adorned by blackness, as if I could rub it off or tear it off. But it remained, stark against my pale skin and mocking me. Tallon had cursed me with the plague for whatever reason, and now I was like him.

Whatever he was.

He'd tricked me, and now I would have nothing left. My brothers would die because he had made them sick, and I could not count on him to get the cure to the disease of his own making.

An abrupt knock on the door pulled me from the battle with my reflection. Scratches covered my neck once more, but I tore my gaze away and scrambled for the robe I'd left across my bed. I'd only just pulled it tight around my waist when the door opened.

I'd been right—no lock would keep Tallon out if he wanted in.

"That was locked." My voice shook only slightly, but the hoarseness made it all too obvious that my emotions had yet again gotten the better of me. I couldn't bring myself to care, though, since he certainly didn't. "And I didn't invite you in."

"I didn't think I needed an invitation," he said with a careful step forward. He was still in his costume, the mask across his cheekbones and his marks back on his forearms, still and steady. "I wanted to explain."

I scoffed, anger replacing the disgust and self-loathing. "There is nothing I want to hear from you, Tallon. You *killed* her. You killed them all. You nearly killed *me*."

He flinched and bowed his head, his shoulders slumping as he tucked his hands into his pockets. "I am sorry, Odyssa."

"Why should I listen to your apologies? They will only be more lies."

"I need you to understand," he said, raising his head. The gray of his eyes had come alive, shining like molten silver and framed by the dark mask. "Please, let me explain."

"Take off the mask," I demanded, crossing my arms. If he was going to beg for my understanding, he would do it as Tallon, not as the prince's pawn, though that's exactly what he was.

Without hesitation, he yanked it off, and it clattered to the floor. Neither of us looked to see where it fell. He took a tentative step forward, and then another, and before I could react, he was in front of me, reaching out to touch me.

"No," I said, yanking my arm out of his reach. "Explanations do not require you to touch me. Tell me why. Why are you here? Clearly you're working for the prince, so why don't you just kill me now and get it over with?"

His fingers flexed into the open space where my body had been, but he let his hand fall back to his side. "Will you take off your mask as well?"

"I'm not wearing one." I was, though, and I hated that he could see it so plainly. But if I let my own mask fall, let him see how much what he'd done had truly hurt me, it would only be another weapon for him to wield against me later.

He cocked his head, and for the first time since we'd met, I saw only curiosity in his gaze. No teasing or hidden meanings. "Are you not?"

"This is not about me," I argued.

"This is about both of us, Odyssa." He stepped closer. I retreated the same. "Please, let me explain?"

I looked at him, trying to find any sign of lies in his face, but it was open, more earnest than I'd seen before. While I wanted nothing more than to scream at him, to beat at his chest with my fists and slam the door in his face, I wanted answers too. I wanted to know why he'd done this, why he was working for the prince when he so clearly hated it. Why he had sought out my company. "Fine, I will hear your explanation."

"Can we sit?" He nodded towards the bed. "It's quite a long story."

There was no reason for me to disagree, and my legs were already trembling with exhaustion and shock. Yet the mention of the bed brought my near nakedness back to the forefront of my mind and my cheeks flushed. I hurried over, settling on the far side, barely on the edge of the bed, as Tallon sat similarly on the other side.

It felt like an ocean between us, though one made of fabric rather than water.

"As I told you before, I was friends with King Gavriel. I suppose my explanation starts there." He rubbed the back of his neck and sighed. "All I wanted was to experience humanity, Odyssa. To know what it was like to *live*." He shook his head. "I am from the Beyond, a herald of Kalyx. And yet, despite all the power and comfort in the world, I did not know what living was like, and I wanted it. I wanted to know what it was like outside the Beyond."

I sucked in a breath but bit my tongue to keep from making a noise. In some way I'd known he was not human, but to hear him admit it was something else. And the Beyond... Gods, it was a real place?

My mind flickered back to my nightmares, the hallucinations I'd had while I was sick, and the places I'd seen when he carried me to his room.

"I've been to the Beyond, haven't I?"

"Yes, many times," he said, his voice strained. "And don't ask me how because you shouldn't have been able to."

"Keep going," I whispered, still attempting to rationalize this new information. I'd been to the Beyond, the world of the dead, realm of Kalyx. I'd been to the Beyond *multiple times*. I focused back on Tallon, trying to keep my breathing slow and even, despite my heart thundering against my ribs. I dug my thumb into the center of my palm, twisting it into the healing wound.

He raised his head and looked at me briefly before continuing. "I made a deal with King Gavriel, a foolish deal but one of ironclad terms. In exchange for him showing me what living as a human was like, he would have complete control over me and my magic for a period of seven years. I had nothing to lose, I thought. I was enjoying myself here in the castle, getting to meet people and live as I had seen others do. I was foolish. The deal had only been in place for a year when Gavriel asked me to release the plague onto Veressia."

"Why?" I couldn't stop the interjection, outrage amplifying my voice.

"He was losing his control," he replied with a shrug. "There is nothing like fear to reassert that. Death is inevitable, but death like this is… it induces a panic, and people look to those in charge to help save them. King Gavriel wanted that control back desperately. But he'd never used my powers like this before, he'd only given me small tasks before, like killing political rivals and criminals. His first attempts at using them for death this widespread were clumsy. I asked him who to target with the plague, and he said to do it at random. So I did. Without limitations, my magic is destructive, and I wasn't able to set those limitations myself due to the bargain. I tried to inform him that he needed to be more specific with his commands, but he refused. I'm sure you can predict what happened next."

"The queen."

He nodded. "Yes, Queen Evanya. When she died, he was furious with me, but his grief was stronger. He asked me to kill him, but the deal prevented that. We could not harm each other, lest the binding magic exact the same thing onto the other. When he flung himself from the tower, I thought the deal had been broken. But it simply transferred to Prince Eadric, and..." He took a deep breath and shook his head on a dry chuckle. "Well, let's just say the prince is far more creative than his father ever was, and far more willing to use the bargain between us to get what he wanted."

The pieces slotted into place. "You are trapped here, too, aren't you?"

He shrugged. "In theory, I could have gone back to the Beyond. But one of the first things Eadric did was make it so I could only return there for short periods of time. He blamed me for his parents' deaths, and rightfully so, but he sought to punish me for it. He said that since I wanted so desperately to know what being human was like, to know what humanity had to offer, he would throw a party in my honor. One I could not decline. He told me he would throw me a party every night until the bargain expired."

"Why is he still having you kill people?" I asked, trying to fight back the sympathy welling in my chest. "Surely he knows he won't have a kingdom to rule much longer if he continues."

He cast me a dry look. "Odyssa, he does not *care* about the kingdom. Why do you think he has not ascended to be king yet? He cares only about punishing me, about controlling me and making me his pawn. Nothing else matters to him. None of these people matter."

I chewed on my lip, considering my words. I didn't forgive him, but the hatred and betrayal I'd felt earlier had started to fade. While nowhere near as malevolent, I could relate to his plight. My mother, my brothers, all I'd ever been to them was a means to an end. Someone to get them what they wanted. All I wanted in return was their love, but Tallon had just wanted to live. My stomach churned, flashes of Talyssa's body still fresh in my mind. "My sickness. That was you."

"It was all me. I am responsible for every death from the

plague in Veressia and for every death that will come in the next days and weeks."

"And the Soulshades?" I asked.

He shook his head. "Those are something else entirely. Outside of the castle, they are just remnant spirits who would not cross over to the Beyond. But here... I don't know how, but they are part of the castle. Eadric can control them to an extent, but they aren't mine and they aren't Kalyx's." His brows furrowed. "Do you truly believe I would have set them after you and let them hurt you like that?"

I struggled with how to respond. I had thought that, though I hadn't wanted to. "I don't know, Tallon. That is why I asked." I took a deep breath and let it out slowly. "You said you wanted to explain. Keep going."

"After Gavriel and Evanya died, Eadric had me continuing the random affliction, with guidelines now of course. Lately though, he's giving me names. Specific people to afflict. He's running out of people, though, and I've told him if he doesn't slow down, the kingdom will be gone before my deal is over and he will have to begin killing off the people inside the castle."

"Why did you keep this a secret from me? Why lie to me this entire time? Were you ever going to help me get the treatment for my brothers?" I froze, icy fear washing over my body as I came to a realization. "Tallon, *is* there even a treatment?"

He nearly lunged across the bed, sprawled half on his stomach and side as he reached for my hands. I drew them back, more out of being startled than of not wanting him to touch me. His hands rested just beside my thighs, clenched tightly into fists. "Odyssa, *yes,* there is a treatment. I would never lie to you about that."

Tears stung my eyes. "Then why have you not gotten it for me yet? You *know* what I need it for. You have been stringing me along for days, Tallon. How am I supposed to trust you now?"

He shook his head, hesitantly taking my hands in his. When I didn't pull away, his grip tightened and he adjusted himself on the bed until he was pressed against my side. Warmth blazed at every point of contact and all I could focus on was his thumb rubbing across the back of my hand. "I was trying to find a way around the deal, but to steal the treatment from him would be considered breaking our terms. I kept putting it off because I hoped…" His eyes blazed silver once more, and he reached his hand up to cup my cheek. "I hoped you would be smart enough to figure it out without me."

"I almost did, but you took me away before I could."

The little snort he let out almost had me smiling. He let his hand drop from my face and rolled over onto his back, looking up at me. "He was in his study, Odyssa. If you'd gotten in, he would have killed you."

My heart sank to my stomach. "Oh."

Silence fell between us.

"Can I hold you, Odyssa?" he asked. His eyes were so open, and there was no trace of deception or hidden truths in them. He seemed almost vulnerable. "Please?"

I was moving before I realized I'd agreed, settling my body in beside his and looking up at him. His heart thumped beneath my hand resting on his chest, and his hand curled around my hip. The room was thick with tension, and I didn't want to be the one to break it. Not yet.

His eyes darted down to my lips, and I almost pushed forward to press my mouth to his, but I held back. The visions of tonight would take time to fade, even now that I knew the truth. It felt like a betrayal to Talyssa, to them all, to be here in his embrace, let alone to give in to our desire for each other. I turned my face into his chest instead, inhaling his scent and warmth.

He merely tightened his hold around me.

"What now, Tallon?" I asked. "I *need* you to help me. I understand why you've done the things you have, and that you have no control over those you afflict. But you killed my mother, you nearly killed me, and one of my brothers is likely dead already. You must help me get this treatment."

His face pinched. "Odyssa, Rhyon has already passed. He died shortly after Emyl sent you that letter."

"What?" I shot up from my place beside him, searching his face for a lie. Any sign of a lie. But there was none. My voice was a hoarse whisper, and the room spun around the edges. The images of Rhyon in what I now knew was the Beyond came back, him choking me, pushing me over the cliff, tearing through my flesh. His Soulshade on that balcony. I'd known in my heart he was dead when I'd seen it, but to hear it aloud, to hear that Emyl had waited... "No, that's not possible. Why would...why would he not send it sooner?"

Tallon sat up, climbing from the bed until he rested on his knees before me, taking my hands into his. "I don't know why he didn't send it sooner, Odyssa. Perhaps Emyl realized he was sick, too, and that's when he sent it. They were afflicted at the same time. But you must know getting Emyl the treatment for himself... it would never make him love you."

I jerked back, his words hitting the raw wound inside my heart with stunning accuracy. "Don't say that."

"You don't need to do this to get his affection."

"No," I snarled, yanking my hands from his. "He is the only family I have left. And if I save him, he will see that. He will see I'm willing to do anything for him, for our family. And you *will* help me, Tallon. We have our own bargain, and you need to see it through."

He sighed, sinking back onto his heels. "Give me a day. Let me discover when Eadric will certainly be away from his study, and I promise, I will take you there myself."

I nodded my agreement, pushing back on my hands to scoot

up the bed. The room was still charged with emotions, and I pulled a pillow into my lap, squeezing it tightly in a vain attempt to block them out. Tallon's eyes were still silver, still set on my body, and still peering into my soul.

"I am sorry, Odyssa. Truly."

"Why do you care, Tallon?" I finally made myself ask the question that had been burning against my tongue since he had pounded on the door. "Why have you sought me out?"

In a swift motion, one smooth like the silk of his shirt, he was on the bed beside me again, tugging the pillow away. I couldn't give a reason why, but when he pulled me into his lap, tucking me against his chest and resting his chin on my shoulder, I let him. His breath was warm against my neck. "You gave me what I'd been looking for all along."

"What's that?"

"You made me feel alive."

CHAPTER THIRTY

Tallon had left shortly after his revelation, telling me to rest while I could. Sleep came easily as the sun broke over the horizon, and I slept undisturbed by nightmares. I wouldn't allow myself to ponder what that meant, that I had slept well after Tallon had murdered another servant and spent hours spilling gut-wrenching truth after truth.

Perhaps I would be able to move past it. Gods knew I wanted to. He had said I made him feel alive, but he made me feel the same. Being with him made me forget all else, and that was part of the problem.

What I could focus on, though, was what would come next. Rhyon was dead, and perhaps some part of my soul had known that, had understood what the nightmares truly meant.

While my heart ached knowing my brother had passed, the grief was manageable in a way I hadn't expected. I'd expected to be angry at Tallon and the world and Emyl for hiding it, and in some way I was, but the grief felt cold, a frozen stone set atop a gaping pit of blackness rather than the raging and volatile inferno I'd come to know.

Emyl was my focus now. Despite Tallon's insistence that he'd lied—and despite my quickness to believe Tallon over believing Emyl had simply made a mistake—I was more motivated than ever to get that treatment. He was truly the only family I had left in the world. The only person who was *mine*. And he would not want me if I could not redeem myself in his eyes.

Pushing the blankets to the foot of the bed, I began to dress for the party. I wanted to trust Tallon's assertion he would help me, especially after all he'd told me just hours ago, but until I had the treatment in hand or in sight, I would always be suspicious. Despite having all the power, he had none here, exactly like the rest of us.

Another part of me—the part that did not spend the entirety of my life aching for the approval and love of a family—might have forgiven him with just those words. But I could not. My mother had not been perfect, but she had been mine, and he'd taken her, no matter whose choice it had been. He had nearly killed me as well.

I had entered Castle Auretras with a mission, one that would not be complete until I had left it and returned home with the treatment for whoever remained.

Tallon had agreed to help me, and despite everything he'd lied to me about, last night there had been nothing but truth in his eyes. And I wasn't sure what scared me more: that or the certain hells I would face going up against Prince Eadric and his possessed castle.

My steps faltered as I approached the kitchen entryway. Licking my lips and tasting no ash, I finally took the last few steps inside.

The others looked up, and the room was silent and heavy, Talyssa's death hanging over us all.

"Is anyone else planning on doing anything stupid?" Maricara asked, pinning her gaze on me. Her voice might have almost been intimidating, if it hadn't wavered on the wave of unshed tears shining in her eyes. In that moment, I knew Maricara better than she likely ever wanted me to.

"Nothing that will come back to any of you," I admitted. This truth, I could give them. Too late, I had realized that Talyssa could have been an ally, that we could have made far more progress with each other than alone. I wouldn't make that mistake again, not even for the risk of Eadric discovering our plans. I would give no details, but I could give the truth.

She startled at my honesty, covering it with narrowed eyes. "See that it doesn't."

A silent agreement passed over the four of us, and without any further words or any taste of ash and smoke, we gathered our things and made our way to the ballroom just as the music began.

Another night in hell, for everyone involved.

Each face I passed, I now wondered if they were here under their own choosing or if they were prisoners just as we were. It hardly mattered at the end of the night, but it made me curious, nonetheless. Regardless of whether they felt trapped, they relished in the opulence around them, drinking and eating their fill, dancing their worries away while the world around them suffered.

Tallon, at least, made it clear he wanted nothing to do with the opulence, choosing instead to blend into the wall each night, watching over the party like a silent sentry. Waiting for instruction from his master.

Turning my path towards the table along the wall, I had spoken of the devil too soon. In front of me, Tallon and Prince

Eadric were gathered away from the crowd, behind the table and nearly concealed by the columns once more. Yet again, the prince was upset with Tallon, and he stood there and took it.

The anger I'd been waiting for earlier, the one that spit flames into the void and consumed everything, flickered to life as Prince Eadric poked his finger into Tallon's chest. Beneath the mask, Tallon's jaw flexed, no doubt his teeth grinding together.

I loudly set the tray down, rattling the glasses on it and the surrounding table. Though I kept my head down, seemingly entrenched in my work, I felt when both of their eyes fell on me and bit back a smile. This distraction, my own show of solidarity for Tallon facing off against the prince, I could do.

It was foolish, given that Eadric could do whatever he wanted for whatever reason, but despite it, I wanted Tallon to know that I was here for him, that while I had not forgiven him, I did understand him, and we would help each other as we'd promised.

Prince Eadric huffed loudly, stomping away from Tallon. I raised my chin and met his gaze, not bowing or looking away as I should have. He froze and his eyes scanned me over, from the top of my veil to the ridiculous satin slippers beneath my dress.

"You have a meeting, Your Highness," Tallon interjected before Eadric could speak. "I will address the mishap with this servant."

He looked back at Tallon. "You'd do well to teach this *pet* some manners. Before I do."

The music reached a crescendo and swallowed whatever reply Tallon gave with his usual smirk, but as the prince stalked away, cutting his path through the crowd, Tallon made his own path to my side. I offered him a wry smile through my veil, a deep purple tonight, and continued setting out fresh glasses and food. "What did you say to him?"

"I'm sure I don't need to tell you how foolish that was, little wolf," he said, his body so close to mine I could feel the heat through the veil. "Why did you do that?"

"What did you say to him?" I repeated.

He sighed heavily, correctly realizing his question would not be answered until mine was. Beneath his mask, pink flushed his cheeks slightly. "I told him that I might like you with no manners."

If we'd been alone, I would have laughed, loudly and openly, but we weren't, so I bit down on my lip to keep from smiling too widely. "And you say *I* will get us in trouble."

His hand found mine beneath the fabric of the veil, warm even through my gloves. He tugged me away from the table to face him. "Don't do that again, please. If he ever got it in his head to be rid of you..." He grimaced. "Just don't give him ideas, please, Odyssa."

His thumb ran over my hand, tracing the line of the marks we both knew were there but were concealed by lace. The truth settled over me, and it was horrific. I couldn't let Tallon or myself stay in that headspace, thinking of all the ways he could kill me and have no choice. I squeezed his hand. "Didn't you hear, Tallon? I am quite hard to kill."

The chuckle he let out warmed my soul. "I hope you remain that way, little wolf. Now go, do your work and stay away from him. I will meet you later."

He didn't give me a chance to answer before he, too, was slipping into the crowd, following Eadric's path.

He'd barely left my side when Zaharya filled his place, snatching the tray from the table and thrusting it into my hands. "What was that?" she hissed. "Have you listened to nothing I've told you? Everyone is talking about you two, how he was holding your hand."

The blood rushed from my face, falling along with the smile that had been born of Tallon's humor. "Everyone?"

"Did you think no one was watching? They are *always* watching him." She paused from unloading her own tray. "They either want him, or they are afraid of him. And nothing good comes from being associated with either of those things."

"It is nothing, Zaharya. I am a game to him, nothing more," I muttered. I knew the words were a lie now, but before last night, they'd been my unquestionable truth, and I could still remember what holding that truth felt like. I could still emulate it to hide behind. Tallon was playing a game—we all were—but one of Prince Eadric's design, not his own.

"I suspect you are far from nothing to him, Odyssa," she said gravely. "And that's exactly what concerns me."

"I—"

"I know you see a kinship in him with the marks. I know he has been mostly kind to you. But last night should have proven to you more than anything that you cannot trust him. He is an executioner, and everyone knows it." She spun on her heel and left me standing there, speechless.

Slowly, I returned to my work, her words echoing in my head.

Now that she'd said something, I felt the eyes on me from the party, and they made my skin crawl. I could only hope my own mask was as solid as Tallon's, because based on the smirk I could *feel* him shooting my way, I was going to need it later during our hour in his room.

CHAPTER THIRTY-ONE

The party had dragged on, but now, as the night slowly began to lighten into the red-tinged dawn, it was over and the veil was finally gone. As had become his habit, Tallon was waiting in the halls outside the kitchen. Zaharya was leaving with me, and I saw how her eyes tracked him, faltering her steps.

He was leaning against the wall with that casual power he wielded so well. While he had already stripped his mask, both the physical and emotional one, I watched as he quickly built it back as Zaharya approached him.

Her finger prodded him in the chest. "You are going to get her *killed*."

Both Tallon and I were struck still by her words, by her bravery to approach him directly. He looked over her head at me only for a moment before focusing his attention on the woman in front of him.

"I assure you, I have a vested interest in exactly the opposite." His voice was smooth—Eadric's Tallon was speaking now.

"You should know better," she hissed. "Leave her alone before you get her killed."

"I believe who she keeps company with is entirely up to Odyssa," he replied. While his voice was still that smoky silk, I saw his eyes when he pulled the mask down for just a moment. To let her see the real him. She stiffened at the glimpse. "But I do admire your courage for confronting me. I shall take your words under advisement and I assure you I will do whatever I need to protect Odyssa."

"See that you do," she said. Without a backward glance at me, she stalked down the hall that would take her to our rooms.

Before me now was just Tallon, smirking after Zaharya. "I quite like her, I think."

"Yes, I think I do too," I admitted.

We both watched until she turned the corner and disappeared from our view.

"Are you finished, then?" he asked, pushing off the wall. He fell into step beside me and nodded down at my feet. "Sylviana has been complaining about missing you."

"Was she now?" I looked down at the Soulshade cat and then back at him, a wry smile on my lips. Sylviana had been tucked beneath my dress most of the night, her cold spot comforting against my ankles. "Only her?"

He hummed in affirmation. In one moment he was pulling both our gloves off, and in the next he'd clasped our hands firmly together. I nearly pulled away from the sheer surprise but managed to suppress my reaction. Tallon's focus was firmly on the halls in front of us, but there was no tension in his shoulders or jaw, no taste of ash on my tongue or any other voices in the hall, so I let my own shoulders relax and squeezed his hand gently.

It was different, certainly, but not entirely unwelcome. His hand engulfed mine, and I felt my cheeks blazing as I remembered what his touch felt like around my waist and at my neck.

Based on the quick glances from the corner of his eye, I was far from the only one feeling the rising tension in the halls as we made our way back to his room. I tried to ignore it, to push it back and remember what I needed to be focusing on, but the burn where our bodies connected had no desire to be dismissed.

Finally, his room was within sight, and I slipped my hand from his, if only to take a moment to compose myself before willingly stepping into his domain. He waved me inside, letting his hand drag a trail of blazing fire across my lower back as I passed. The door shut behind him, and once again I found myself pressed between him and the wall of his entryway.

"I've been waiting to do this all night," he said. Before I could ask, he had one hand weaving into my hair and the other cupping my hip as he tugged me to him and met my lips with his own. It only took me a moment to respond in kind, pushing up on my toes to meet him halfway.

The kiss was hot and slow, as he thoroughly plundered my mouth with his own, pressing me back into the wall and angling my head to take even more control of the kiss as he removed all space between our bodies. His fingers flexed on my hip and I clutched at his sides.

His kiss was consuming, burning me from the inside out, and all I wanted was to get closer to him. A teasing bite to my lip had me gasping, and then he was pulling back, both of us panting as he rested his forehead against mine and slowly untangled his hand from my hair to cup the side of my face instead.

"What was that for?" I asked, my voice hoarse from the fervent experience that was kissing Tallon.

He closed his eyes and groaned softly. When they opened again, they were like quicksilver. "A thank you."

It took me a moment to register his words, my attention too

fixed on the darkness in his eyes and how his lips were slightly swollen. When they did register, my brow furrowed. "Why would you thank me?"

He smiled and let his hands fall away from my body as he stepped back. I mourned the loss of his heat against me and had to press my fingertips back into the cold stone to keep from reaching for him. He pushed his hand through his hair, looking at me with a fond smile I'd never seen on him before. "You stood up for me at the party, to Eadric. It was foolish and you put yourself in entirely too much danger, but I..." He shook his head. "No one has ever done that for me, especially not at their own expense. So thank you."

And with those words, nearly all the lingering anger from the night before had faded and I wanted nothing more than to burn the castle to the ground for what had been done to him. "You never have to thank me for that."

"I do, but if I show my thanks the way I truly wanted to, we'd never leave this room. And unfortunately, I have news to share with you that does require us to leave it at some point."

For a moment, I almost let myself ask him what he truly wanted to do, but the appeal of news on our bargain won out in the end, just as he knew it would, based on the smirk across his lips. I sighed, pushing myself from the wall and moving further into the room to settle in the chair that had quickly become mine. "What news is that?"

Tallon did not follow me to the chairs as he had the past nights, instead choosing to sit on the edge of the bed and stoop to unlace his boots, kicking them haphazardly away. He stretched out on the bed and tucked an arm behind his head, reaching across his body to pat at the space next to him. "Come lie down with me and I will tell you."

I didn't even pretend to protest, just removed my own shoes and settled in beside him. He huffed a breath of a laugh and pulled me closer into his side, my head resting on his shoulder. His arms came around me to hold me in place and I couldn't stop the laugh. "If this is what having no manners gets me, I would hate to see what being polite would do."

His arms tightened around me and when he spoke, his voice was dark and smoky. "I don't think you should put the image of you saying 'please' in my head right now."

My body heated and I shifted, pressing myself tighter into his side at the same time as I pressed my thighs closer together. I cleared my throat, trying to distract myself from the images he was painting in my head. "What news do you have, Tallon?"

A tense silence, one that nearly sent us crashing even further into each other, reigned for just a heartbeat more before he sighed. "Eadric will be out of his study at midday. That will be our only chance with any certainty to enter anytime in the near future."

My body froze against his. He'd kept his word. I swallowed back the sob of relief, not wanting him to know I ever doubted him. I hadn't even realized I still doubted him, not until he laid this out in front of me. Curling deeper into his chest, I let my hand come to rest on his stomach, relishing the way his muscles flexed beneath his shirt at my touch. "Thank you," I whispered.

"I am sorry again that I did not tell you the truth sooner. I am sorry for what my magic did to you and your family." He pressed a kiss to my hair and pulled me even closer until I was nearly atop him. "I am very glad you were stronger than my magic."

I swallowed hard, not knowing what to say to his confession until the words began to spill out. "I loathe that I am in any way grateful for the events that led me here, but I find I am. In this moment, at least here in your arms, I think the darkness might not be so bad."

"I think you'll find you belong in the darkness more than you might think. You survived me; you survived death. Eadric has no hope of stopping you, little wolf, now that you know the truth." He pulled the blankets up around our waists. "Sleep now; I will wake you when it is time for us to go."

"What if I don't want to rest?" I asked, breathing in the smell of warmth and spice that clung to his shirt. The party and the cleanup and the emotions of the night were beginning to catch up to me, and now, tucked into Tallon's side and surrounded in this cocoon of warmth and security, my own confidence was blooming. I had to be sure, though, that this was not another moment he would come to pretend had not happened later. "I do not think I could sleep now if I tried."

"I suppose I could find something to occupy your time or to help you sleep." He sounded more awake now, amusement, desire, and a careful caution all equally evident in his voice.

"Oh? Such as?" Emboldened by the wanting in his voice, I let my own trickle into my words as well.

He hesitated, sweeping his hands over my back and down my arms as he pressed another kiss onto my hair. "What are you comfortable with, little wolf? What would you let me do to you? Anything you can imagine, anything you ask of me, it will be yours. Just say the words."

"Touch me," I breathed. My head tilted up so I could look at him. "Please?"

Lips split into a lazy smile and fingers flexed across my back. "I am touching you."

"Tallon." I didn't want him to tease me; I wanted him to distract me, to make me forget all the horrible things going on around us.

In lieu of an answer, he settled me on to my back and propped himself up on his elbow to look down at me. Agonizingly slowly, his hand settled across my stomach. "Did you want me to touch you like this, little wolf?"

Butterflies with wings of fire swooped through my belly at his touch. "Not quite, but getting closer."

"Perhaps you should be more specific, then." The carnal hunger in his eyes warmed every bit of my body as he looked down at me.

Once again emboldened by Tallon's easy acceptance of himself, of his desires, I gave in to my own. I took his hand in my own and slid it slowly, so slowly, up to trace the swell of my breast. His lips parting in surprise was nearly as satisfying as when he flexed his fingers against my flesh, warmth radiating through the thin gown I still wore.

"How far do you want this to go, little wolf?"

"Just touch me, Tallon. I will tell you to stop if I need it." I couldn't think, didn't *want* to think. If I did, I knew I would retreat and curl back into my feelings of unworthiness and remember what was at stake. For now, I wanted him, and I wanted to lose myself in him.

"As you wish." His touch transformed from the tentative exploration that I'd initiated into something wholly more and all his own design.

My hand fell away from his as he took the lead, sweeping his palms over my breasts and squeezing just so. He dipped his head down to press wet, open-mouthed kisses against the exposed skin at the neckline, never staying in one place too long as he travelled up my neck and nipped at the skin beneath my ear.

Before I could ask for more, his hand left my breasts to skate over my stomach, coming to a stop just below my navel. Between kisses to my neck that left me tingling and floating, he murmured, "Is this what you want, Odyssa? Can I touch you here?"

My hand found his again and, through the silk of the gown, I pushed his hand between my legs. He needed little direction, letting out a breathy groan against my neck as he cupped my center. His palm was scorching hot where it sat against my skin, rubbing softly against me, but it wasn't enough. I flexed my hips, biting my lip as I chased his touch.

"Shh, little wolf," he said. He nipped at the skin of my neck, running his tongue over it right after to soothe the sting. "I will take care of you, I promise."

A challenge sat at the tip of my tongue but was lost to a moan as he kicked the blankets down the bed and pulled the hem of my dress up in one smooth motion to expose my body all the way up to my sternum. This time, he grabbed my hand, guiding it to hold the bunched-up fabric that settled beneath my breasts.

He groaned and pressed his forehead against my shoulder briefly as his hand returned between my legs. The aching had grown almost unbearable, and I didn't try to stop myself from rolling my hips against his touch. His fingers traced over my flesh, dipping into the growing slickness only briefly.

"Have you always worn these gowns with no underwear, Odyssa?"

"There was none in the wardrobe," I admitted, my voice nearly unrecognizable with arousal. Earlier, he'd said I belonged in the darkness more than I knew, and here, pressed against him with his hand pressed against me, I agreed.

He didn't reply for a moment, his focus entirely on how his fingers moved against my body. "Are you trying to kill me?"

Thankfully, without waiting for a response I wasn't sure I could even give, his fingers dipped lower and he slid one inside me. My mind quieted, my focus narrowing to only where he touched me, to the pleasure that he wrenched from me with only a finger as he plunged it in and out of me. A second joined the first and I let out a cry I might have been otherwise embarrassed of.

"You are stunning, little wolf," he breathed, bending his head to capture my lips in a scorching kiss. He plundered my body as he plundered my mouth, his thumb reaching up to press at the nerves above where his fingers split me. Pleasure was all I knew, *Tallon* was all I knew, and I was glad for it.

My body bowed against his touch, hips rolling with his hand as he brought me higher and higher.

Murmured words brushed against my skin between his kisses, but my ears could not make them out in the ringing haze of desire. A third finger entered me and the stretch burned so good, balancing on a knife's edge between pleasure and pain.

"Give yourself to me, little wolf," he said. His fingers pressed against a spot inside of me that had me arching off the bed. I felt his smile curve against my neck as he continued sweeping over that same spot, over and over and over. "Come for me, Odyssa."

Words stuck in my throat and I was powerless to do anything but obey as his thumb pressed down on my pleasure point and his fingertips did the same inside of me. I was lost in a sea of Tallon, and I was content to drown in it as I reached my peak.

His fingers slowed as I came down, leaving my skin as he continued kissing my neck. In the clarity of the moment, I felt exposed, my dress still rucked up around my waist and my arousal shining on Tallon's fingers. I wanted to cover myself up, but as I moved to pull the dress down, Tallon raised his fingers to his mouth and licked them clean with a groan. And once more, I was struck by the depths of his desire for me.

"I shall have to taste you properly next time, I think," he said, after he'd captured every drop of me from his hand.

Heat spurred once again in my belly, though it battled with the exhaustion that was creeping up on the trails of pleasure. Before I could move, Tallon reverently pulled my dress down and the blankets back up around us.

Acting before I could talk myself out of it, I surged up to capture his mouth, tasting myself on his lips and pouring everything I could not say into the kiss. Only once we were both out of breath did I settle back into the bedding, reaching up to trace my hand across his cheek. "Thank you, Tallon."

"You never have to thank me for that," he replied. With a kiss to my forehead, he pulled me beneath his arm and settled my head on his chest. "I am proud of you, little wolf."

I jerked my head up to stare at him. I'd done nothing for him to be proud of, certainly not recently. Beyond the solidarity I'd shown in the ballroom, I had no inkling of what he was proud of me for. "For what?"

He smiled and gathered me back against his chest, smoothing a hand over my hair and rubbing my scalp. "You did something because you wanted it. You. Not anyone else. I'm proud of you for putting yourself first tonight, and I am utterly thankful you decided to use me to do it."

Words stuck in my throat and tears blurred my vision, sending me curling deeper into his side.

Thankfully, he did not seem to expect a response as he continued running his hands through my hair. The steady thump of his heartbeat was better than any lullaby, and I found myself even more tired than I'd expected. He chuckled at the yawn that clawed its way out. "Sleep now. We have quite an ordeal ahead of us, I fear."

"You will still be here when I wake?" I asked, curling myself tighter into his side even as my eyes grew heavy. I could not bear it if I woke and he was gone, not after this. Something had changed between us tonight, with his fingers inside me and our bodies pressed together, and I feared I would not survive if he put his mask back on now.

"I think you would find that nothing short of Kalyx himself could pull me from this bed right now, Odyssa."

"Good." And I fell into the embrace of Tallon's darkness and let sleep claim me, even if just for a little while.

CHAPTER THIRTY-TWO

Wakefulness came on the palms of Tallon's hands as they ran up and down my back. I relished the moment, pressing my face further into his side and chasing the warmth.

"It's time, little wolf."

"I know," I mumbled into his shirt. It was everything I'd been pushing for and yet, in this moment, in his arms, I didn't want to leave for anything. My cheeks flushed, hearing my mother's admonishment coming from the Beyond. There was everything at stake here, and failure was not an option. I had nothing left to lose and everything to gain by getting the treatment to Emyl before it was too late. "I know."

Tallon's hands stilled. "You do not *need* to do this, Odyssa."

His words were more effective than cold water splashing across my face. With a sigh I pulled out of his embrace and sat up, twisting to look down at him still sprawled out across the bed. "Yes, I do. And you will not convince me otherwise."

He raised his brow. "A feat I'd surely never attempt."

"Don't patronize me, Tallon." I moved to the edge of the bed, pushing my hands through my hair as the enormity of what I was about to finally accomplish soared through me. My stomach was a pit of anxiety, gnawing at my spine. "I cannot fail."

The bedding rustled and I closed my eyes briefly as he shifted closer to my back, his body radiating warmth into me once more. He pressed a kiss to my bare shoulder. "I did not mean to sound patronizing, little wolf. I was speaking the truth. Convincing you to do anything you do not already want to do is an exercise in futility. If you saw yourself as I see you—how you truly are—you would have taken over the castle by now."

"My brothers convinced me to come here, to leave them behind for the sake of money." I whispered my confession to the curtains. "I abandoned them to die, because I was too cowardly to stand up against them and make them let me stay."

"Did they convince you to leave? Or did you simply take advantage of the opportunity to escape from beneath their thumb?"

"You know nothing about us," I hissed, pulling away and stalking over to the window. I crossed my arms over my chest, trying desperately to hold myself together. His words had struck true, right in my heart, in my deepest failings.

"I know everything I need to know about you, Odyssa." He did not move from his place on the bed. "I know that you are a survivor, that you are a caretaker, that you would rather give away pieces of your very soul to ensure those around you want for nothing. I know what I saw in your face that night you learned of your brother's sickness. I know what I felt from you in the ballroom when I had to murder Talyssa. If you had truly wanted to stay, nothing your brothers said would have stopped you. *You* left. To prove a point, to try to earn their love, to protect them...whatever reason you want to give. But you chose to leave. And you wound up here with me. I will not allow you to feel guilty over the circumstances that led us together." He stood from the bed and tugged me into his arms, tucking a finger beneath my chin to raise my gaze to his. "I certainly will not allow you to feel guilty for what my magic has taken from you."

Tears blurred my vision and some of the anger bled out of me as I slumped against him, burying my face in his chest. "You make it difficult to hate you."

His laugh rumbled through his chest and against my forehead. "I am immensely grateful for that."

I lingered in his arms for a moment longer before stepping back and wiping at my eyes. Regardless of what he said, I did still need to do this. Emyl did not deserve to die, not like this. "How long do we have?"

"Long enough for you to bathe and change if you wish."

"I have no other clothes here," I pointed out. "Do you really want to waste time going back to my room?"

The wide grin on his face was foreign to me. Part wicked, part pure joy. "Now that you know the truth, there are much easier ways to get around."

Pieces fell into place as his implication became clear. Every muscle in my body clenched and I watched the smile fall slowly from his face as I shook my head. "No. That place is my nightmares, Tallon. It is not somewhere I would willingly go."

"I do not know why you've been able to cross into the Beyond in your nightmares, but I promise you..." He paused, taking both my hands in his. "I *swear* to you, nothing will hurt you in the Beyond when you are with me."

I shook my head again. "I won't."

He squeezed my hand. "Then we won't. Do you want me to go get you clean clothes?"

"No," I sighed. The longer we waited, the more my nerves concocted every possible way this could go wrong and I could fail again. "I want to end this. Now."

Another chuckle rumbled from his throat and he pulled me

flush against him, every inch of his body pressed against mine. "Odyssa, *this* will never end. Whatever happens here, I have found you, and I am not letting you go."

"I thought you said no one could make me do anything I didn't want to do."

"Are you saying you *want* to leave me?" He leaned down, breath brushing over my lips. "Because then I will have to call you a liar."

"Tallon," I warned, though the word came out far breathier than I intended.

His eyes flashed silver. "Don't. Do not say my name like that, my wolf."

"Why not?"

"It makes me want to find out how you taste, with your thighs wrapped around my head."

I swallowed hard, feeling the wave of heat melt through my body. Gathering all my willpower, I rocked up on my toes to press a quick kiss against his lips before pulling out of his arms entirely and stepping a healthy distance away. "We have work to do, *Tallon*." I ignored the way his eyes narrowed at me. "You made me a bargain; it's time to uphold it."

"Then we should be going."

It was nearly laughable how little resistance met us along the path to Prince Eadric's study. Unlike before when I'd attempted myself, the one guard we passed merely nodded at Tallon before turning his focus elsewhere. The ease with which we infiltrated the room stoked the anger in my belly as we entered the prince's quarters, snaking up the spiral stair and following another hallway until Tallon pushed open a heavy door.

The study was as everything else in the castle: a shrine to opulence and wealth. It only made my steps falter for a moment, though, and then I was crossing the plush rug, rich black and woven with intricate patterns in bright blues and deep purples and vibrant reds. The desk in the center of the room was clearly the focal point, made of heavy wood and laden with piles of papers and stacks of books I doubted the prince had ever opened.

My focus was entirely on that desk.

In this room, if the treatment was here as Tallon believed, it would be here, in this testament to Eadric's self-importance. My hands hovered over the scattered paperwork, eyes searching for anything that could resemble medicine, though I had no idea what I was truly looking for. It was then I realized Tallon had not passed the threshold and was watching on with a pinched expression.

My blood ran cold. "What is it? Why aren't you helping?"

He grimaced. "I...I cannot help you further. My bargain with the prince won't allow it."

The room spun as my heart pounded in my ears. I curled my hands into fists and took a slow breath through my nose. "We will work around it then. Can you tell me what I am looking for, at least?"

"A vial," he said, gritting his teeth. He stepped back into the threshold and immediately relaxed. "I will stand guard, but you must be the one to look for it."

Expressing the irritation prickling beneath my skin at the bargain's limitations would only delay us further, so I bit my tongue and nodded, turning my attention back to the desk. I picked up a pile of papers, only to freeze and look up at Tallon with wide eyes. "Will he notice if something is out of place?"

"Unlikely."

At his assertion, I resumed my search with tenacity, shoving aside papers and pulling open drawers. Tallon had said Eadric would be away from his study, but given how the castle bent to the prince's will, I doubted our luck would hold for long. The quicker I could find the treatment, the quicker we could leave. Setting the papers back to rights as best I could, I dug through the drawers next, finding nothing but gold and silver coins tossed haphazardly atop crumpled papers and random pieces of jewelry.

The pressure in the room shifted and I looked up, expecting Tallon to have moved closer to me. But he was still standing in the doorway, and I watched as Tallon's eyes widened the split second before I felt someone step up behind me. I froze in place, slowly pulling my hands away from the desk and straightening.

"What do you think you are doing in here?" Prince Eadric hissed into my ear.

I locked eyes with Tallon and immediately wished I hadn't. The look on his face told me everything I needed to know; we'd failed. I had failed. But I would rather fail my family a thousand times than die at the hands of the Coward Prince himself. I raised my chin and stood tall, refusing to shrink in on myself for this pittance of a man. "Are you asking that to be dramatic or are you truly so stupid that you have no idea?"

Tallon's face paled, but it was his eyes flashing silver that truly made me regret not biting my tongue. He had been afraid that Eadric would use him against me already, and now I'd opened my mouth and all but ensured exactly that.

Eadric tutted and walked around the desk, sitting against it and looking at Tallon. "We had a bargain, you and I. Are you truly going to break it for some pretty little servant?"

"I've broken nothing between us, Eadric. And you know it."

Eadric pushed off the desk and continued back around until he was behind me again. "What's your name, girl?"

"You'd let me into your home, onto your staff, without ever

knowing my name?" My voice was icy to my own ears and Tallon's warning frown did little to tamp down the anger.

"You saw what I made him do to the other one who stole from me?" he asked, tugging on a lock of my hair.

I pushed down the flinch that threatened to erupt. I'd failed already—the treatment was out of reach—and while Tallon was likely safe from the prince's ire, I wasn't. I had nothing left to lose, and I'd been waiting for a long time to tell the Coward Prince what I truly thought of him. "Yes, I did. It was despicable."

He paused, looking between Tallon and me before letting out a loud laugh. "Yes, he is that, isn't he?"

I turned my head to look him dead in the eye. "I meant you."

Now the prince froze, my words shocking him into a stupor. As the insult settled into the room, I vaguely heard Tallon's hiss, but my focus was on the prince, watching as his face morphed into shock, and then outrage, and finally landing on utter fury. "You would *dare*—"

"I would. You are a horrible human being, manipulating everyone around you to control your people with fear, ignoring them as they die in the streets and Veressia drowns in their blood." Stepping away from the desk, I faced Eadric with Tallon at my back. Anger thrummed through my veins, pulsing along the lines of my death marks. I'd never felt more powerful than in this state of calm rage. "You must resort to locking people inside with you to have anyone pay attention to you. You are pathetic."

My heart soared as he spluttered, his face turning red and splotchy. The words had struck true, and for the first time, I was grateful for the years at the receiving end of Emyl's sharp tongue. I'd learned from the best how to cut someone down with little more than words, and I had no reservations in turning my brother's prized weapon on this coward in front of me.

"You insolent..." He reached down into one of the drawers that I hadn't gotten to yet, and when his hand emerged, it was holding a gleaming silver knife. "I will show you what happens to those who think they know better than me. My father thought me weak and pathetic, too, and now look where he is. You will regret crossing me, *servant*, and so will Tallon."

The knife glinted in the light as he thrust it towards me, coming in towards my side at waist level. Time slowed, and I heard Tallon shout, but my focus was on the bright silver blade. My body was frozen, and just as the knife should have impacted, should have dug into my flesh, Tallon's body collided with mine. The wet sound of a blade entering flesh squelched in the room and pulled me from my almost trance-like state.

Tallon had his back to my front still, but I could see the crimson flowing from the wound in his side, spilling down his shirt and darkening the fabric as his hands clutched at his flesh, trying to keep the blood inside. My vision spotted and black danced around the edges. Only as the black grew more consuming did I realize what they were. My marks had come alive, just as Tallon's had at Eadric's command.

Prince Eadric, now pale and trembling, stumbled away from us, the knife clattering onto the floor as he dropped it. His eyes were wide and panicked, flitting about to my shadows that swirled around us, hovering over Tallon's wound. "No, no, what did you do? Who are you? No, it *can't be*." His eyes snapped to Tallon. "You told me she had no magic!"

Tallon grinned. "I lied."

The darkness converged around Tallon and me, and I inhaled sharply, my own panic rising as I struggled with what to do next. I moved in front of Tallon, pressing my hands to his side as well. He let out a pained grunt, more blood gushing from the wound. I squeezed my eyes shut, wishing we were back in his room, that we'd never left in the first place. One moment of doubt—I could give myself that—and then I would get us out of here and back to safety.

"Odyssa," he rasped.

I opened my eyes and nearly fell over. Only my grip on Tallon kept me upright as I took in our surroundings. The nightmare world, the Beyond, was in front of us now. The study, Eadric, all of that was gone, replaced by towering cliffs and jagged canyons.

"No, no, no, why are we here?" I asked, looking up at him. "Get us out of here, please, Tallon."

"I did…not do this," he panted. "You did… Imagine your destination… It will take us there."

I tried, desperately picturing his room, but nothing happened. My marks still undulated around us, flickering irritably as I clenched my fists and tried again, hands sticky with Tallon's blood. Panic began to well up, and I fought to control my breathing. "Tallon, it's not working."

He took a deep breath and pulled one hand away from his side, grasping loosely around my throat and settling his thumb into the hollow between my collarbones. "Odyssa, *breathe*."

His grip grounded me in a way I hadn't expected, my only focus on the heat and weight of his hand around my neck, the sticky wetness of his blood on my skin. My shadows flared, wrapping around us like a cocoon once more. I wanted *out of here*, but nothing was happening.

"Remember how you felt earlier in my room," he murmured, stroking his thumb along my skin. The pain was still clear in his face and his voice, but his grip was firm even as his eyes fluttered shut. "Remember how it felt to be in my arms. Imagine what it will feel like when I'm holding you again. Take us back there, Odyssa."

His words and his hand on my throat were enough to calm my panic, though they made my heart race in an entirely different way. It helped though, and on the next blink we were no longer in the Beyond but in a bedroom. But it was not *his* bedroom. The layout, the decor, even the feeling of it, were all wrong. This room felt far more personal, and held far more traces of Tallon than the room I'd been in before.

"Do you have two rooms? Where are we?" I asked, feeling panic rise in my throat. Could Eadric follow us here?

"We are safe. This is my room in Kalyx's palace, not Auretras."

Despite the knowledge of us still being in the Beyond, I slumped against the wall in relief, his hand falling from my throat as he did the same. This room was nothing like the Beyond we'd been in; it felt warm and inviting. Cozy. I wanted to explore it, to find the pieces of himself that Tallon had left lying out. While I ached to know how I'd transported us here, having never been here myself, there were far more important things and Tallon needed care.

"That was very good for your first time," he said between panted breaths. "I think I need to sit down for a moment, though."

My ears rang, a shrill noise blaring through my head and blocking out all else as I fought through my own exhaustion. I lunged towards him just in time to get my shoulder beneath his arm on his uninjured side, catching him moments before he fell face first onto the floor.

He'd thrown himself in front of a knife for me, hadn't hesitated for a moment, and holding him now as he bled sluggishly, the gaping pit in my heart that had longed for someone to care for me rather than use me began to close.

Heaving his not unsubstantial weight onto me, I quickly discovered I would not be able to get him to the bed and settled for lowering us both gently to the floor in his entryway. I let my hand settle over his chest, to feel the steady hammering of his heart against my palm for just a moment before I stood. I was covered in his blood, and though the bleeding had slowed, the wound in his side needed treating and likely stitching. He'd done the same for me before, albeit on a far less serious injury, and I could do the same for him now.

I wiped my hands on my stained and torn dress and hurried into the room, pulling open drawers and doors until I found what I was looking for: a medicine kit, rags, and water. I'd just gotten him; he would not die because he chose to protect me. I could not bear it if another person was torn from me.

CHAPTER THIRTY-THREE

Tallon regained consciousness again as I was maneuvering his body to remove the shirt and inspect the damage. "Why are we on the floor?"

"Because you are heavy." I reluctantly pulled my hands away from his bare torso and settled back on my heels as I looked at him. "I couldn't move you to the bed."

He was quiet as he looked me over, his eyes bright and alert in a way they shouldn't have been given how recently he'd lost so much blood. "We are in the Beyond, Odyssa."

"Yes, I've been meaning to ask you about that," I replied, my voice far too casual. "How did I transport us here when I've never been here myself?"

His eyes were fixed on my face, a look akin to wonder in them that sent the silver there swirling. He reached up to cup my face, wincing as he did so.

"Will you please stay still?" I asked with a sigh. When he still didn't reply, I tugged at the open side of his shirt. "Take this off, please, so I can clean and stitch your side."

"If you wanted my shirt off, there were far easier ways to

accomplish that," he said, though he assisted in getting the blood-soaked fabric off his body. It fell to the floor with a wet sound.

"Why did you step between us?" I asked, picking up the damp cloth I'd brought with me and setting about cleaning the blood away from the wound. His muscles twitched beneath my touch. This was hardly the first time I'd seen his torso, and now was not the time for my body to be reacting to the feel of the hard muscle beneath the warm skin. Not when the warm skin was covered in blood.

I focused on my task and gently wiped away the worst of the blood in silence, waiting for his answer.

He shifted, grunting softly until he was sitting up straighter, and then his hand was on the side of my face again, his fingers splaying across my cheeks and down beneath my jaw. His touch was warm and sticky with the remnants of his own blood as it transferred to my skin. For whatever reason, I didn't mind. "You need to ask?"

"Yes," I said. I gently pulled his hand away from my face and took the rag to it, using it to wipe uselessly at my own hands before I finally raised my eyes to his. There was still blood on his hands, as well as over the rest of his torso, but the rag was already saturated with blood. "You stepped in front of a knife for me, Tallon. Of course I need to ask."

He chuckled, the sound falling off into a groan as the movement tugged at his side.

"You're going to hurt yourself even more," I scolded, bending to poke at the skin around the wound. The bleeding had slowed some, now sluggishly leaking, and with most of the blood washed away, it didn't look nearly as bad as it had seemed at first. It was deep, though, deep and jagged at the edges.

"Odyssa, look at me." He tugged my hands away from his side and held them with one of his own in his lap. The other returned to my face, his thumb stroking along my cheek. "I told you no more harm would come to you in that castle, and I meant it. Do not worry about me; I will heal quickly. You would not have."

"I—"

His hand moved to my throat again, grip firm but not tight. His eyes sparkled as my breath caught. "And I may have been bleeding at the time and trying to calm you down, but don't think I didn't notice how this affected you."

His words should have stoked the fire in my belly back to blazing, but they drenched it in ice-cold water instead as the Beyond came back to my mind. He seemed to notice the change and let his hand drop slowly. I let him, but was quick to add it to the pile of hands in his lap. "We need to get your wound cared for, Tallon, before you ruin everything by bleeding on it. Can you stand?"

"I can," he said quietly but made no attempt to move.

Swallowing down a sigh, I stood, holding my hand out to him. I was surprised he took it, but he did, and together, we got him on his feet, though he still leaned heavily against me. The atmosphere in the room had changed, still charged with the aftermath of what we'd just done, but it was colder now, awkward. I hated it, even though it was likely for the best. Even though I had caused it.

"Where do you want me?" His words were rushed out on an exhale, and looking up at his face, I saw he'd grown pale again.

"Gods above, Tallon," I cursed, shifting to take more of his weight and tugging him towards the bed.

"Wrong god," he said, dragging out the last word into a groan as I settled him on his back against the pillows. He panted for a moment before attempting a smirk that was more a grimace than anything else. "Mine's just down the hall most likely, though, if you truly want to meet him."

"I don't think that would be wise." I pulled the plush bedding onto the floor, trying to keep from ruining it more than I already had just by touching it with my bloody hands. My mind kept trying to throw images of the Beyond back at me, but I pushed them away and focused on the still-weeping wound in Tallon's side. The bloody mess should have made me hesitant if nothing else, but apparently, the sight of his naked torso and his tensed muscles overcame that just slightly, and I found my cheeks flushing again and my fists clenching to keep from reaching out to touch him. "You need stitches."

He shook his head, reaching for me as I turned away to go fetch clean water. "No."

"Tallon, there's a stab wound in your side. I promise you, it does need stitches." Did he not want me to touch him, to care for him this way? I tried to ignore the way my stomach knotted at that. This was about him and the fact that he'd thrown himself in front of a knife for me while I'd been frozen in shock. If he wanted someone else to care for him, I could do that much for him, at least. "I can find someone else to do it if you don't want me to, but we need to stop the bleeding. I have done this before. I promise I won't injure you further."

"That isn't what I meant," he said, his brows furrowing. He took my hand in his, tugging me up to stand by his head. "It will heal on its own soon. I merely need to rest. You cleaned it, and that will be enough. Here, my powers are stronger. Trust me, please, Odyssa?"

I searched his face, but again, there was no sign of a lie, not like the first days at Castle Auretras. "Fine, but I am still going to bandage it. Your bedding might already be ruined, but it doesn't need to get any worse."

"I'm not bothered by a little blood." He cocked his head. "Are you? I didn't consider what memories this might bring—"

"Don't. I'm fine," I said abruptly, moving away from the bed to collect the bandages from where they sat in the entryway floor. I hadn't even considered it, the similarities between this and my mother, myself, and Talyssa. "Blood doesn't bother me. Not anymore, not like this."

"When *does* it bother you?"

I returned to his side and chewed on my lip, debating how to answer. My voice was quiet when I spoke. "When I can taste it."

He winced, closing his eyes. I berated myself; I should have been taking care of him, not making him feel guilty. I picked up the cloth to wipe away the lingering blood, but he grabbed my hand with such quickness I couldn't stop the flinch. "Odyssa, you will *never* taste blood again. I swear to you."

I couldn't look at him, focusing instead on cleaning the wound and pressing the bandage into place. "You can't promise that, Tallon."

"I certainly can promise it will never be *yours*," he said, the smirk much less of a grimace this time. He ducked his head, catching my eye and making a show of looking me over from head to toe. It ignited the heat back in my belly and my fingers itched to run over his skin. To feel his hands back on my skin. The smirk widened, mischief sparkling in the gray of his eyes. "Besides, I think I quite like you covered in *my* blood."

Of all the things I'd been waiting for him to say, that certainly hadn't been anywhere on the list. My head spun, racing through the implications of his words, and I struggled to comprehend the feelings they sent through my body. "I don't... What?"

He shrugged, trying—and failing—to hide the wince when it pulled at his side. "Perhaps it's more knowing the bloody handprint around your neck is mine, but whatever it is, I quite like it."

My breath caught in my throat, my thighs clenching together involuntarily. Apparently, I quite liked it too. It didn't matter, though, because there was nothing either of us could do about it now, while he was bleeding still. If we made it through the rest of the day alive, perhaps I would explore this more on my own in bed. The heat thrumming through my veins dimmed some, knowing that living through the night wasn't guaranteed.

"Can Eadric come after us here?"

"We are safe here in the Beyond. He cannot come here, but we cannot stay here indefinitely," he said, reaching out to take my hand again. "If you want to bathe, you can use the tub here. After I rest, we can talk about what to do next."

I didn't want to do that. The last thing I wanted was to address how I'd failed and how despite thinking I had nothing left to lose, I had lost my chance at a family with Emyl. I focused on a different part of his sentences. "Do you *want* me to bathe?"

His eyes darkened, and his grip on my hand tightened. "Don't toy with me, my wolf."

My heart lurched at the heat in his gaze. It felt so irrevocably similar to the heat in my blood. "You are hardly in a position to do anything about it if I did."

"Would you want me to do something about it?" Hunger dripped from every word as his eyes searched mine.

"What would you do?"

"Would you like me to tell you?" He released his hold on my hand and raised his hand to my face. The marks on his forearm, the ones that spiraled up his arm and spilled down onto his chest, shifted, pulling away from the skin and reaching out to caress my cheek. Their touch was warm and left a trail of tingling energy in their wake. Tallon pushed himself up on his other hand and his hand moved to my throat, placing his fingers one at a time over top of the bloody handprint I knew was already there, gripping just firmly enough that I could feel my pulse pounding against his hand. "Or should I show you?"

My tongue darted out to wet my suddenly bone-dry lips, and my voice was a ragged whisper. Standing beside his bed, him holding me by the throat and clad in only his pants, it made me *want*, but I saw when he shifted and a fresh trickle of blood oozed out of the wound on his side. "You said you needed to rest, Tallon."

More of his marks pulled away from his skin, dancing across my collarbones. Electric warmth hit my shoulders, sending shivers down my arms into my fingers as I felt the straps of my dress snap, and then the fabric was falling. My body was frozen as his magic followed the silky fabric down my body until both puddled at my feet.

"Utterly devastating," Tallon breathed. His eyes followed his magic's path back up, taking in every inch of my body before him. His hand tightened minutely around my throat and he pulled, not aggressively, but a suggestion that I move closer towards him. It was a suggestion I gladly followed as I moved with him until he was lying flat on the pillows once more and I was leaning over him. His thumb stroked over my pulse. "You're stunning, my wolf. Would you let me touch you?"

There were a dozen reasons I should have said no, should have backed away from him and retreated to the safety of the bathroom behind the locked door. But none of those reasons mattered when I looked at the swirling silver of his eyes staring at me as if I were the most delicious treat he'd ever laid eyes on. When he looked at me like that, after all we'd been through together now, there was only one answer I could give.

"Yes."

Hands and magic surged. His lips crashed to mine as he pulled me over to straddle his hips; all in one movement that left my head spinning. He swallowed down my gasp and devoured me, claiming and exploring and leaving my mind empty of everything except for him.

I was aching for him by the time we separated, panting for breath. Blood still streaked both his torso and mine, stained from where it had soaked through the fabric of my dress and left smears across my skin, but it was hardly a deterrent for either of us. From the way Tallon's eyes darkened as they roamed over my body and how his fingers dug into the skin of my thighs, I was more apt to call it an aphrodisiac instead.

Tallon fell back into the pillows, running his hands up from my thighs to rest at the curve of my waist as he stared up at me. "What do you want from me, my wolf?"

His voice was hoarse and the knowledge that I had done that, our kisses had done that, sent a thrill down my spine. I rocked in his lap, gasping when the seam of his pants, stretched across his hardness, caught just so between my legs. He grinned and his hands were back at my hips again, tugging me forward and backward on him.

My head fell back as I fought through the haze. "What will you give me?"

Quick as a snake, Tallon sat up, twisting us so I lay beneath him now. The muscles in his arm bunched as he kept himself aloft, and I didn't stop myself from reaching out to touch him, to trace over the warm skin and follow the thick lines of black that covered his body. He wedged one of his thighs between mine, pressing forward as he lowered his mouth to my ear. Slight as they were, the kisses he peppered along my ear and down my jaw and neck were far from gentle. He nipped at my collarbone where my own marks spilled over onto the skin there. Pulling back, his eyes were no less heated, but held a tenderness that made me want to hide. I felt far more naked under that gaze than I had before.

"Everything," he murmured. I was powerless to look away, no matter how his stare made me want to squirm. He kissed down my chest, stopping to lave at the bud at the peak of my breast. "Everything you want, everything I have, is yours."

"Quite an offer," I gasped out as he continued leaving fiery kisses down my stomach, sliding down my body as he went. His hands roamed my waist, dipping down over my hip and thigh. My legs fell open in silent invitation as his fingers grazed closer inside my thigh. "What do you want in return?"

"Your honesty," he said, sliding down even further to settle his broad shoulders between my thighs, pressing them apart even further and gifting an open-mouthed kiss to the inside of my thigh that made my heart jump in my chest.

"I've always been honest with you." My hands went to rest in his hair, gripping the silky strands as his mouth grew closer to my center. I could feel my heartbeat pounding against my chest, my head spinning.

"Good," he replied. "Then tell me how you like this."

His head disappeared between my thighs and the wet, slippery feel of him *licking me* erased all other thoughts from my mind. There was no reprieve from the wave of sensation that crashed down around me, pulling me teetering to the edge of a cliff of pleasure. A groan vibrated through me from Tallon's mouth straight through my center and up my spine, leaving me panting and clutching at his hair. He pulled back long enough to press another series of wet kisses to my thigh.

Looking up at me, his hands curled around my thighs, his eyes bright with his own arousal and his lips shiny from my desire…he was breathtaking. His lips curled up into a smirk. "Do you know what you taste like?"

Words escaped me as I fought to keep from plunging into the endless well of pleasure he threatened to drown me in. I managed to shake my head, running my fingers through his hair and tugging slightly to pull his face back towards that aching spot between my legs.

He followed my guidance, ducking his head to lick another stripe across my heated skin. "You taste like mine."

Lips pressed firmly to my body, and he sucked, sending me

writhing on the bed and unable to reply. A finger pressed inside me, slowly, deliciously. Another joined, and they curled inside me, stroking that spot that sent echoes of lightning up my spine. I squeezed my eyes closed against the onslaught.

And then everything stopped.

My eyes flew open, panic the first thing bubbling in my chest as I searched out Tallon, afraid that something had happened. But he was still there, his wound still oozing blood slightly on the bedding, and the smirk still firmly on his face from his place between my thighs. "Eyes on me, my wolf. Watch how I take you apart."

He continued, his lips sucking at the pleasure point between my thighs as his fingers curled inside me just as they had before. And also just as before, he brought me to the brink, poised to tumble off the cliff into a sea of pleasure created solely by him. I watched every move, relished every groan he made against my skin. Bit by bit, he drove me to madness, and then he slowed, his fingers stopping but never leaving, even as his mouth did. A quick kiss rasped against my inner thigh and he pulled back entirely.

He sat back on his heels, looming over me as silver churned in his eyes and his marks pulled away from the skin of his hands, reaching for me. He did not wipe my glistening arousal from his face as he looked down at me. The warm tingling sensation did nothing to temper my arousal as they roamed up my stomach, pausing at my breasts long enough to leave my chest heaving before pressing firmly against my collarbone. Tallon's own fingers returned to seeking out every inch inside me, relentless in his pursuit of my pleasure.

Gasping, I reached for him, wanting to touch him as well, to feel him beneath my hands and explore his body as he explored mine. He came willingly enough, our lips crashing together as I chased the taste of myself on his tongue. I wanted every inch of him pressed against every inch of me to seal us away from the horrors waiting for us outside that bedroom door and escape for just a moment. To feel for just a moment. I tucked my fingers into the waistband of his pants, tugging at them. "Take these off," I whispered, the words pushing against the pressure of his magic around my throat.

"As you wish." His smooth departure from my body left me feeling empty, aching, but more of his magic peeled away from his skin and took his place. It never entered me, but it caressed my body, mirroring his touch just enough to leave me writhing as I watched him remove the last of his clothing. He returned to the bed, his magic not sinking back into his skin, but hovering around us.

Wrapping my hands around the back his neck, I pulled him down to kiss me again. I wasn't sure what I would do next—too many options were flitting through my mind—but now, emboldened by desire, I would take what I wanted. He pressed himself back between my legs, settling his weight atop me and his erection catching the wetness pooling between my thighs. We both gasped and he pushed forward again, my own hips rising to meet his.

"Once I have you, Odyssa," he said, pulling back from our kiss just enough to speak, "I will never let you go. Eadric and his castle be damned, you are mine now."

"Then take me, Tallon." My desire was making my head swim, and in that moment, I had truly never wanted something as much as I wanted him. Heat flushed my face, and his touch ignited my blood. I wanted more. I wouldn't be satisfied until every inch of me was claimed by him, and every inch of him was mine in return. I would accept nothing less.

He'd let me in, taken off his mask and shown me who he truly was. And I'd let him see my true self in return, whether I'd intended to or not. Tallon was under my skin, in my blood, and I had a feeling not even the plague could rid me of him. I reached up to cup his cheek, letting him see all the things I could not put into words.

"You are perfect," he breathed. His lips met mine again, and his length slid against my core once, twice, three times. "I will try to be gentle. If I lose myself..." He looked down where the wound was still healing on his side, smirking yet again. "I'm sure you will think of something."

"You said before that I could not be broken," I said, pushing back against him and delighting in the way the grin fell from his face. We both moaned as the tip of his length slid inside me, stretching me just slightly. I wanted more, and he did too. My neck arched against his hand and I relished in the way his fingers tightened. "Do not take back your words now."

His smile was filthy as he surged forward, entering me with one long, smooth thrust that had us both groaning as we were finally, finally connected. Ragged breaths came from both of us, and Tallon squeezed his eyes shut. "I wouldn't dream of it."

Slowly, he rocked into me, stealing my breath entirely at the delicious twinge that meant he was mine now. My body bowed off the bed, seeking every inch of his. I barely managed to keep my hands from grabbing his waist, exactly where his injury was. At the last second, my mind cleared enough to direct one to his hip and the other to his shoulder as I clung to him. Each movement spurred something inside of me, building and building. Tallon watched, his mouth open and panting as his eyes darted between my face, my breasts, and where he plunged into me. Sweat beaded on both of us, his palm sliding against the skin of my throat.

It was everything.

"You feel so damned good, Odyssa," he breathed. His next thrust was more forceful and I couldn't stop my gasp, even louder than before. He'd been watching himself enter me, but at the sound of my pleasure, his eyes went to mine, that confident smirk falling upon his lips. "Did you like that, my wolf?"

"I think you can do better," I said, taunting him despite the lack of breath in my lungs and the burning pleasure along each and every nerve in my body.

Narrowed eyes spoke of a challenge accepted, and any sign of restraint—out of either misplaced concern for me or caution for his injury—was gone. Tallon slammed into me with abandon, taking us both higher and higher as our pleasure spiraled together. My heart was pounding; every sensation, every touch was that much more than before.

The hand around my neck tightened at the sides as his thrusts grew faster and impossibly deeper. "You are mine, Odyssa."

I nodded eagerly. Yes, yes, I was his. And he was mine. The edges of my vision blackened, but I was powerless to look away, to pull away. "Yes," I breathed.

"Say it," he demanded, his pace faltering. "Say it, my wolf."

"I am yours." Removing my grip from his hip and using the leverage of his shoulder, I pressed myself up to sitting. The change in position had us both writhing in pleasure, but I continued my path, kissing across the marks on his chest and up to claim his mouth. "And you are mine."

He stopped altogether; his chest heaved as he stared at me with wild, silver eyes. The disbelief, the vulnerability, the awe there... "Odyssa."

"You are mine, Tallon," I repeated. I kissed him again, squeezing his wrist and moving my own hips against him. A reminder of what we were doing, as if he needed it.

"I am yours," he murmured. His body pressed me back to the bed, the hand on my throat moving to my breast where he squeezed and groped on his way down to grab my thigh. Hoisting it up around his hip, he dug his fingers in as he drove somehow even deeper inside me. Faster, harder, until my own climax shuddered through me and my nails dug into his skin, no doubt drawing even more blood than already covered us.

He thrust into me for a moment more, his mouth open in silent rapture as he spilled inside of me. Panting and sweaty, he hovered above me. He was the image of a god, not his herald.

My hip ached in protest as he lowered my thigh from around his waist. He shifted back, unable to hide the wince as his hand flew to his injured side. Cursing both of us, I slid from the bed, ushering him to lie down instead.

"Foolish man, you've started bleeding again," I muttered. The bandage was spotted with red, and I cursed myself for forgetting his injury, for seeking my own pleasure in him while he was injured. I should have known better. Ignoring the feeling of his release trickling out of me and down my thigh, I peeled the bandage back, intent on replacing it with a new one.

His hand caught mine, affixing the bandage back in place. "I will be fine, Odyssa. Come lie with me, please."

"Let me change—"

He shook his head and pulled at my wrist until I was back in the bed with him, settled against his side. He wrapped his arms around me. "Let us enjoy this moment, my wolf, while we have it. Please?"

"Rest, Tallon," I murmured. My mind still warred with wanting to slip from his embrace and care for him, but that wasn't what he wanted. And if I was being honest with myself, this right here—lying in his arms and reveling in the pleasure we'd found in each other—this was what I wanted. His breathing evened out, growing deeper as his arm around me grew heavier. "I am here."

"Stay with me, Odyssa. Please?" he whispered into my hair as he finally drifted off. "You are all that I've been searching for."

I bit down on the inside of my cheek and embraced the

stinging pain as I curled deeper against his body, seeking out the warmth and comfort I'd likely never feel again. Our time here in the Beyond was running out. We would have to return to Auretras soon, and Prince Eadric and his cursed castle would never let us both out of it alive. That much I was certain of.

CHAPTER THIRTY-FOUR

"You are thinking too hard," Tallon muttered, drawing me closer to his chest. Shivers went down my spine as he ran his fingertips over my arms, tracing the marks there. "You should be resting. We will need to get up soon enough for the damned party."

"I cannot rest," I admitted, clinging to the warmth and safety of his arms before it was taken from me as everything else had been. "My mind is racing. We should not have done that."

His hands froze around me. "Why do you say that?"

My words stuck in my throat, too jumbled and messy. "I... We..." I swallowed hard, trying to fit together the thoughts swimming through my head. "I failed. Failed my mother, and now Emyl is going to die, and I'm going to be alone. No family. Nothing to show for all the sacrifices I've made. I shouldn't be allowed to have this, to feel this, to waste this time with you when I should be finding another way to save Emyl. You say you'd give me everything, but the castle would snatch it from us before we even had the chance. It already has."

"If you think I will let anyone in that castle take this from us, you do not know me at all."

"You're right, I do not. We've barely known each other a fortnight."

The muscles in his jaw flexed. "This was not a mistake, Odyssa. And it certainly wasn't a waste of time," he said as his hands resumed their path. "You deserve something good in your life. You deserve someone who thinks you worthy without you having to do a godsdamned thing for them."

"You were injured, too, protecting me because I am too weak to protect myself," I protested. His words were nice, but he couldn't mean them. Our bargain ensured I'd do something for him at some point.

He fell silent for a moment, and then shifted and I was beneath him. His knees bracketed my hips as he sat tall above me. My mouth dried out. Golden skin and dark tattoos, the herald of Death indeed. He grabbed my hand and placed it along his side where the wound had been. "What do you feel?"

I ran my fingers over the skin, but felt nothing. Where the stab wound had been, jagged skin and gaping flesh, was smooth and unblemished, albeit still bloodstained beneath my hand. "How?" I demanded.

"I told you, I heal quickly here." He traced his fingers over my shoulder where the gouges should have been. "So do you, it seems."

My hand flew up to meet his, feeling only smooth skin there as well, where there had been still-healing flesh just hours ago.

"And even if I didn't," he continued, "do you truly underestimate yourself so much that you think I would turn down a chance to have you beneath me like this?"

"Why me?"

"Why not you?"

"Don't tease me, please."

He rolled off me, settling in at my side and running his thumb over my cheek and lower lip before grasping my chin and turning my head to face him. "I felt you watching me that first night you were here, up on the balcony, and it felt different. People watch me all the time, make no mistake, but they are watching me out of caution. You were curious, but there was no fear in your gaze."

"Surely someone has been curious about you before, Tallon." I tried not to roll my eyes.

He offered a wry smile. "Yes, but much like how you say people treat you, they were only curious as to what I could do for them. What I could offer, what my magic could offer. You have never looked at me like that, even when I was avoiding my end of the bargain we made. You were curious just to know who I was. Curious for the sake of knowledge, not of anything to gain."

"And yet you tell me you'd give me everything." I shook my head, squeezing my eyes shut. As much as I wanted to believe him, to believe that this could be real, I couldn't. "We need to find out if Eadric is going to retaliate or if we will have another chance to find the treatment before Emyl passes."

"I would have given you everything, even then." Tallon sighed softly, moving off my body and letting the cold air surge in between us. I'd never felt more alone in that moment, cold air on all sides of me, but I tried to remind myself this was for the best. "He will not retaliate. He would be foolish to try anything. No, he will wait and form a strategy first."

"Your bargain with him is broken now, right?" I pointed out, looking up at the ceiling. "Wouldn't it be wise for us to strike back before he can gather a strategy? You said that if one of you hurt the other, the magic would retaliate. So he is dealing with a stab wound too. Would he heal as fast as you, or would he still be injured?"

He froze beside me, letting out a soft exhale like he'd been punched in the stomach. I turned my head to see what revelation he'd had and was met with hands gripping both sides of my face. "You are brilliant, my wolf."

The kiss he pressed to my mouth was rough and quick, though it held no less heat than the others we'd shared. He lingered for a moment, his gaze darting between my eyes and my mouth. He kissed me once more, slower this time but still brief, and then he was rolling away to turn on his stomach and look back at me over his shoulder.

"Is there still a mark at the base of my neck?" he asked, his voice muffled by the muscle of his shoulder pressing into his mouth. "Vaguely shaped like an hourglass?"

"No, there's nothing like that," I said, reaching out to touch the skin at his nape, tracing over the points of swirling black that hugged over the tops of his shoulders and draped down onto his back. His skin was warm and smooth beneath my fingers and I pressed my palm flat between the expanse of his shoulder blades, watching how his muscles flexed around my hand.

A full body shiver accompanied the goosebumps forming along his arms. I drew my hand back as he shifted.

"If you want me to believe you when you say this was a mistake," Tallon drawled, twisting to look over his shoulder more as he pressed up onto his palm, "then you *really* shouldn't touch me like that, my wolf."

My face heated, and suddenly, my lap was far more interesting than the expanse of naked flesh in front of me. "I never said this was a mistake, Tallon, just that we shouldn't have done this now, when there are more important things we should be focused on."

He turned to lie on his side, propping his head on his fist. I forced myself to keep my eyes on his face and not on the way the muscles of his stomach flexed with the movement. Based on the smug smirk on his lips, I didn't do very well. The smirk softened and he reached out to tuck his index finger into my fist, tugging slightly. "Odyssa, nothing could be more important than this, not to me. But I do understand."

I took a deep breath, nodding my appreciation. His words stirred something in my chest and made me want to hide beneath the covers with him for an eternity, but my mother's voice echoing in my head had me frozen. I nodded my head towards his neck. "Do I have a mark from our bargain? Shouldn't you have one from our bargain too?"

"You do, and so do I. They are not all in that same place," he said. He flexed the arm lying beneath his head and pointed to a spot on his inner bicep. It was tucked between the stark lines of the marks, and though it was the same inky black, it was clear it didn't belong in the pattern. More abstract, like spilled ink across a page rather than painted lines, it was shaped oddly like an hourglass. "I don't know where yours is, but you do have one. Do you want me to find it for you?"

Were it not for the lecherous grin and teasing tone that accompanied his question, I might have let him. "No, I was simply *curious*."

"Pity."

"Now that the bargain is broken between you and the prince, can you not remove the curse or the magic or whatever you call it from Emyl?"

"It doesn't work that way, my wolf. I am sorry."

"But you can help me more now, yes?"

"Of course, and I will." He tipped his head. "What are you thinking?"

"Good. We will get the treatment tonight then. You are more powerful than him and no longer bound to not harm him."

"You are more powerful than him too," he said. "But yes, we will get it tonight. After earlier, he will likely keep it on him or somewhere else, not in his study."

There were too many things in that short statement that I wanted to ask about. I opened my mouth to speak several times before finally deciding to start from the beginning. "How am I more powerful than him?"

"How long has it been since your bout with the plague, Odyssa?" he asked. "A year? Half a year? Less?"

"About five months, yes."

"It took me decades to master my magic, and I was created with that as my sole purpose."

The room began to spin slightly. "Oh."

"So yes, you are infinitely more powerful than that sniveling child prince could ever dream of being, even with the perverse hold he has over that castle."

"What control does he have over the castle? The Soulshades?" I asked. "That night you found me in the hallways, they came out of the walls, and the walls moved to block me from running away."

He frowned, the furrow between his brows running deep. "I've never been able to figure it out, myself. Dark magic, certainly, but not any that would come from a being like me."

"There are more like you?"

"The gods all need their servants, don't they?"

"Is it another god then?" I asked. "That's giving Eadric this power?"

He hummed. "Perhaps. Though I couldn't begin to guess which, given that it gives Eadric control over the Soulshades and the castle itself. The Soulshades, at least, should be under Kalyx's dominion."

"How do you know it's not Kalyx?" I asked. He seemed so certain it was not, but from the stories my mother had told me, there was little morality amongst the gods.

"It is not Kalyx. I've asked him. I sent him a letter through the

Beyond when I first realized there was something else happening there."

"And he would tell you the truth?"

"Absolutely." He shook his head, reaching up to pinch between his brows. "It is not Kalyx, Odyssa. I promise. It could be Cethin, I suppose."

"I never believed in the gods," I admitted. "Who is that?"

"The god of shadows, darkness, night," he explained. "He's the only one that would make sense to be able to give Eadric that power."

"And what do we do if he is in the castle helping Eadric?"

Tallon hesitated, looking up at the door for a moment. "Ideally, I'd want Kalyx to back us, but he is not here and we do not have time for me to search for him."

"How do you know he's not here?"

"I can sense him."

"Oh."

"If it is a god—if it is Cethin—I will get you out of there immediately and bring you back here. And we will wait until Kalyx returns, treatment for your brother be damned." He pressed a finger against my lips to stop my outraged cry. "I cannot protect you against a god, Odyssa, try as I might. I need you safe. Please don't argue on this."

My anger still simmered, but I deflated slightly at the panicked plea in his eye and nodded my agreement. The finger that was pressed against my lips traced over my cheek, and I reached up to hold it. "And if Cethin is not there?"

"Then we will kill Eadric and finish this for good."

"Can we kill him? If he's protected by Cethin?"

"Of course. It would only be more difficult if Cethin is there. But *my* god controls Death and the dead; no one can stop him forever."

I did not answer, instead settling into the knowledge that

he'd shared. I sat, here in the palace of a god in a realm that was not my own, and we were to be facing down the prince and possibly another god.

"I never believed in the gods," I repeated, shaking my head slightly. They had been a children's story for me, nothing more. Something to dream about when I was sitting alone in my room at night, listening to my brothers play. I twisted my fingers in my lap, wondering what Tallon thought of the admission, given his place at Kalyx's side.

"You should. At least one of them certainly believes in you."

My head snapped up. "What do you mean?"

"It's just a theory," he said, waving his hand. He traced the marks down from my neck all the way to my fingertips, twisting our fingers together when he was finished. "Your marks look like mine, not like any other survivor I've seen. They act like mine."

"Other survivors can't do this?" My pulse hammered against my throat. I'd assumed as much, given Zaharya's words about her own marks, but to hear it confirmed was so different.

"No, my wolf, they cannot."

"Why can I?"

"I told you, I have a theory."

"Then share it with me."

He hesitated and I pulled my hand from his, standing from the bed and pacing.

"Tallon, no more secrets. Tell me," I commanded. This was precisely what I had wanted to avoid, why I knew it was foolish to fall into bed with him, despite how much I had wanted to—still wanted to. "You do not see me as your equal, so how can whatever this is ever stand against that?"

"You are not my equal," he said, sitting up. "You are far better than I could ever dream to be."

"Then tell me the truth."

A hand pushed through his hair roughly. His other hand

joined it shortly after, resting on the back of his skull. He groaned, closing his eyes for a moment. "I do not know how much I can tell you."

"Tell me *all of it*."

"You misunderstand, Odyssa. I mean I do not know how much I can physically tell you without Kalyx punishing me for revealing secrets that aren't mine to reveal."

"Secrets?"

"The Beyond has many secrets, and not all are ones that just anyone can know. There's magic in place to keep anyone from entering the Beyond, from sharing those things. If you even knew what you had seen there, if you'd seen something that was protected, you would not have been able to tell even me."

My blood chilled at the mention of the Beyond. I'd forgotten we were here, in Tallon's rooms inside the Beyond rather than back in Eadric's castle. I stopped pacing and licked my lips. "The Beyond. Does your theory explain how I was able to transport us here?"

"It does."

"It feels different this time, than in my nightmares. Why?" I felt no fear in this room, only comfort.

"It's not a *bad* place, Odyssa. Every soul goes to the Beyond after they pass. It looks like how you will it." Tension crawled up his shoulders, and for a moment, I wondered what the rest of the Beyond looked like to him. And why it looked so terrifying for me.

"I am certainly not willing it to look like every nightmare I've ever had rolled into one, I promise you that."

He sighed, rubbing at his temple. "Perhaps you are different, then, but I cannot say. I'd need to spend time there, in our archives, to find out, time and access that I didn't have before because of the bargain with Eadric. I would inquire for you now, though, if you wish."

I bit my lip as I debated. "After we get the treatment. Then yes, please do."

"As you wish." He looked over at the tall clock in the corner and rose from the bed. "It's time to get ready for tonight. Go bathe, and when you come back I'll have something for you to wear."

My eyebrows rose. "I'll not be joining the other attendants?"

"No. I want you by my side tonight. I want everyone in that castle to see you and know exactly what you are capable of, my wolf." He stepped up in front of me and his marks reached off his skin to caress against my own. "I want them all to know you are mine, and that you answer to no one. I want them to know you are their reckoning."

I swallowed hard, electricity thrumming through my veins. "A tall order for a dress, I imagine."

"The dress is merely for decorative purposes," he said with a smirk. He nodded to the bathroom. "Go clean up now, before I take you back to my bed and convince you to forget about all of this and just stay there with me for the rest of your life."

My knees were barely able to hold up long enough to get me into the bathroom. I leaned up against it with a sigh. I wanted that desperately, what Tallon offered, but it was not mine to have. Not yet.

CHAPTER THIRTY-FIVE

I was barely holding onto my nerves as I dried off. The bath had helped tremendously, cleaning off the remaining dried blood and washing away the worst of the memories from the prince's study. Now that I had a moment alone to process everything else that happened afterward, I was practically vibrating from my skin.

Tallon was something I'd never anticipated when I entered the gilded walls of Castle Auretras, and yet he'd burrowed under my skin. I knew it would be an exercise in futility to try to excise him now, and I was not sure I even wanted to try in the first place. He said I made him feel alive—the entire reason he'd made the bargain with King Gavriel. It was a heady feeling to know that I was enough for someone like Tallon.

And he made me feel alive, too—that was the problem. I'd entered the gates of Castle Auretras content that I would likely die inside those walls. Emyl and Rhyon had shunned me, and though I had always planned to do whatever it took to get both money and treatment to them if I could, I'd not entered expecting to find a reason of my own to live.

But now, beyond that door, Tallon awaited. And together, we were going to burn Castle Auretras to the ground. We would figure out everything else between us after.

Wrapping the towel around my torso, I took another fortifying breath and stepped back into the bedroom. I was curious what dress he would have for me, and how he had gotten a dress at all in such short notice.

Tallon looked up from where he was bent over the bed, arranging a mass of crimson fabric across his dark sheets. He was dressed already, once again in a black silk shirt and tight-fitting black pants, and while I much preferred the look of his bare skin covered by the swirling Death marks that bound us together, I couldn't deny how my mouth dried at the sight of him now.

At the sight of me, still damp from the bath, his gray eyes turned molten. "You have no idea how tempting you are, do you?" he asked.

I swallowed hard. "I could say the same to you."

The smile across his face was so genuine, and it made my heart squeeze. "Better you don't, or I might keep trying to convince you to forget about all of this and stay here with me forever."

"You know I cannot do that," I murmured. Though I had to decline, it did fill me with a warmth that he continued to say that, that he continued to want me like this. Still, I could not bear to bring my gaze to his, to see the want in his eyes and the disappointment at my words. It was tiring, disappointing everyone, in one way or another. I tightened my hold around the towel and fingered the mass of fabric. "Is this for me?"

He cleared his throat. "Yes, yes. Put on the dress itself and I will help you finish."

"Finish what?"

There was the smirk. "There are multiple parts to the dress beyond just this, Odyssa."

Before I lost the nerve, I dropped the towel and pulled the mass of crimson and black fabric over my head. Tallon groaned behind me, but he did not move as I settled the dress down around my body.

High-necked, sleeveless, and an entirely open back. It hugged my torso and hips down to mid-thigh before it flared out into a dramatic skirt the darkest shade of black. A slit in the left side revealed my leg nearly all the way up to my hip bone. I felt the back gaping and despite the collared neck, the dress felt entirely too loose.

"It's…"

"Ah, I told you there's more." He lifted a golden expanse of metal and held it out for my inspection. It was fashioned in the shape of a spinal column, with tendrils of gold reaching out from all sides. "This goes on your back."

Wordlessly, I turned and lifted my hair off my neck for him to attach it. The metal was cold but warmed quickly between my skin and Tallon's. His fingers lingered along my bare back as he affixed the piece to the sides of the dress, pulling it taut along my back. It fit much nicer now.

He turned me around to face him, running a finger down my cheek. "Gorgeous, my wolf."

"Why do you call me that?" I murmured, letting myself get lost in his reverent touches.

"The first night you saw me, when you looked at me… I could sense you. All that duty, responsibility you had been burdened with. The fierce loyalty and intelligence behind your eyes. Your curiosity," he continued. He pressed his lips to mine. "Your bravery."

Tears pricked my eyes. "You truly believe that?"

"With every fiber of my being, Odyssa." Another kiss, this one lingering. "You need shoes still."

Instead of the normal satin slippers we wore with our veils, he set out a pair of sturdy, low-cut boots that looked remarkably like his own, yet were clearly made to go with the dress. Black so deep it absorbed all the light around it, yet lined with crimson gems. "How long have you had this outfit for me?"

He raised an eyebrow. "I don't believe you are quite ready for that answer, my wolf."

I narrowed my eyes, hearing the words he would not say, that he'd had this for far longer than he should have.

"You are breathtaking, Odyssa. I wish we had more time, but I promise you, after all this business is handled, I will take great pleasure in removing this dress," he said. His finger ran down from my neck all the way along my arm, leaving warm sparks in its wake. When he reached my hand, he dropped to his knees, drawing something from behind his back and shifting the slit of the skirt aside to reveal my thigh. "This is a bloodstone dagger," he explained, pulling the red-bladed knife from the sheath he wore at his back. My eyes widened, remembering when I'd held that very knife to his own neck just days ago. He grinned and reached to strap the sheath around my leg. "It can kill anything, even a Soulshade." He looked up at me, eyes flashing silver. "Use it."

I nodded, trying to keep my focus on the knife and not on the sight of Tallon on his knees before me. "What of my magic?"

He rose smoothly, shaking his head with a grimace. "We don't have the time to teach you enough to be sure you could consistently call upon it. That would take weeks and weeks of training. But if it comes to you tonight, don't fight it. Use your instincts; they will keep you alive."

The bells in the castle tower tolled nine times, signaling the start of the ball. My stomach churned as the ringing echoed through the walls. It was time for us to go. I'd said before that the study was my last chance, but truly, this was. If we failed this time, so publicly, I doubted either of us would live long enough to even feel the shame.

"Here." Tallon's voice pulled me out of my thoughts and I took the proffered mask from his hand. He secured his own, a blood-red skull that covered his forehead and eyes and then swooped down over one cheek, leaving his mouth and the other side of his face bare.

The one he offered me would just cover my eyes and was an intricate lace pattern specked with red jewels throughout that reminded me eerily of blood spatter. It was perfect, and I couldn't help the small chuckle I let out. "You certainly know how to communicate with clothing."

He smiled as I fastened it around my head, arranging my hair carefully over the straps. "Sometimes the best thing to say is nothing at all."

"Do you think Eadric will be at the party tonight? Or will he hide?" I asked. Tallon slid his own red-bladed knife into a sheath he secured at the small of his back before pulling on a black jacket with velvet brocade detailing. He looked like Kalyx incarnate rather than merely his herald. My blood thrummed just looking at him, and from the smirk on his lips, he knew exactly what I was thinking. "You're not going to show your marks?"

"He will be there. He's too arrogant not to show his face, especially once the castle tells him we've returned." He offered up the crook of his arm. "And no, the regents have already seen mine. They need to see yours tonight."

I looked down at my arms, where the expanse of the marks along my right arm were fully exposed. "They certainly will in this dress."

"Precisely the point." He ran his hand down my back, fingers catching on each of the protrusions from the corset until his palm rested at the base of my spine. "Tell me, do you not feel powerful in this dress, Odyssa? With the evidence of your strength on display for all to see?"

"I do." My voice was hoarse.

"Good." The heat in his eyes burned through my body and his eyes flicked down to my mouth, his tongue darting out to wet his own lips. His eyes shut for a moment, and when they opened again, they were bright with determination. "I know you think this—*we*—are a mistake, and I swear I will prove to you we are not—that I can be worthy of you, and that you are more than worthy of me—but I'd like to kiss you once more before we go. If you'd allow it."

My heart shattered there in my chest, and I reached a hand up to cradle the exposed side of his face. "Tallon. *We* are not a mistake. You do not need to convince me of that. It is the timing I regret, and only that. I need to prove I am worthy to Emyl first, and I have let far too many distractions slow that down. And those distractions killed Rhyon."

"You shouldn't have to prove your worth to someone who only seeks to use you," he murmured, turning his head to kiss my palm. "But I understand the sentiment, far more than you know. I will help you however you need, bargain or no bargain. I am yours to command."

"Then kiss me once more, before we dethrone the Coward Prince and save my brother."

There was no hesitation from Tallon. As soon as the words left my mouth, he was there. His hands pulled me in tightly, one still at my lower back, and the other reaching up to cup the side of my face and plunge back into my hair. It was heady and all-consuming, the way he kissed me, and I couldn't get enough of it.

All too soon, he pulled back, both of our chests heaving and our panting breaths mingling in the space between us.

"We should go," he said. It stirred a sense of pride in me, hearing how utterly ragged his voice was. *I* had done that to him.

I leaned up and pressed a final kiss to his lips, short and chaste compared to the previous one. "Yes, we should."

The moment we stepped out of Tallon's room in the Beyond and returned to Castle Auretras, we both stiffened. Something was wrong in the halls, and the feeling of being watched prickled at the back of my neck. A dark and heavy feeling pressed down on us, making my body feel like it weighed thrice what it should. Ahead of us, the walls rippled like they were made of water rather than stone. Ash and smoke burst across my tongue, so heavy it nearly made me gag.

"Perhaps he is smarter than I gave him credit for," Tallon mused. "He's set the Soulshades and the castle upon us."

"What should we do?" My hand trailed down to where Tallon had secured the bloodstone blade.

"Not yet," he said, casting a look down at my leg. "We should get somewhere more open than this hallway. Make your way towards the ballroom. The walls are not our friend, and the more space we have, the sooner we can handle this."

At his direction, we turned and rushed down the hall. The walls rippled alongside us as we moved, and the taste of ash was growing thicker in my mouth, but I didn't dare pull my eyes from in front of me.

"They're getting closer," I warned, feeling the weight of them against my back.

"We're almost there," he said, as we turned another corner. The space ahead opened into the large foyer just outside the back entrance to the ballroom—the one Prince Eadric usually arrived through—where three hallways split off from the center space and dispersed throughout the castle. He reached the center and stopped, turning back to face what had chased us. "Draw your knife."

From all sides, Soulshades poured out of the walls.

Tallon's presence was a pulse of strength beside me. He'd yet to draw his own weapon, but the aura that radiated from him was terrifying in its own right. As the first Soulshade neared, his marks erupted from his body, coiled and ready to strike down those malevolent spirits that surrounded us. At my leg, a cold spot told me Sylviana had also joined our fight.

With a shriek that pierced the very marrow of my bones, the first Soulshade lunged forward, its bloody face contorted with rage. I raised my dagger, and slashed towards it. I wasn't sure what I had expected the bloodstone dagger to do, but it caught against the Soulshade's chest as if they were a solid form, and—with another piercing scream—the Soulshade dissipated, leaving room for the next one to take its place.

Tallon leaped into action beside me, his magic slicing through the air with deadly precision that sent the Soulshades recoiling away. I mirrored him with my knife. Beside us both, Sylviana had grown into her human-sized form without me noticing and was swallowing her own portion of Soulshades.

But for every Soulshade we vanquished, another took its place. Soulshades surrounded us like a cocoon, to the point I could hardly see the walls of the castle around us. Sweat dripped from my brow and slicked the handle of the dagger.

As the battle raged on, the line between reality and nightmare blurred, and time seemed to stretch into eternity. Still, we fought on. But it wasn't enough, I knew, as my eyes took in the scene before me.

Sylviana had retreated to her normal size; her sides heaved with exertion. Tallon was quickly being overpowered by four Soulshades snatching at him, and his marks had faded into mere whisps of smoke. My own energy was fading quickly, and my arms burned from the demanding slashing motions with the knife.

Icy arms gripped me from behind, and then Soulshades were on me. At least half a dozen of them, piling on as I stumbled and fell to the floor. I slashed and stabbed, but still more surrounded us. I couldn't breathe, couldn't see, and without a doubt, I was going to die.

Warmth battled back beneath my skin, and then my marks erupted. The magic unfurled like a broken wing and grew, shifting and multiplying until it surrounded me and all the Soulshades in the onslaught. They staggered away from me, fearful eyes on the undulating mass of black that surrounded them.

At last, with a final, desperate effort, I pushed all the intent I could at the magic, screaming at it in my mind to help us, to destroy the Soulshades and get them out of the castle for good. The magic responded, growing ever larger until it blacked out the entire rotunda and I could not see anything, not even the hand in front of my face. My chest heaved, still begging the magic to continue, to not falter in the face of my exhaustion.

Finally, the magic struck. The mass of black expanded ever so slightly more and then collapsed back into my chest with a rush that sent my head spinning. If I'd not already been on the ground, I'd certainly have fallen. And when all the mass had cleared, the room bright by candlelight once more, we were alone.

The Soulshades were gone, and the eerie feeling of being watched from the walls had vanished, too, dissipated into the night like smoke on the wind. Breathing heavily, I glanced at Tallon, our eyes meeting in silent acknowledgment of the horrors we had faced and the fight still yet to come.

"Odyssa, my wolf, what in the name of the Beyond was *that*?" Tallon asked, struggling to catch his breath.

I looked up at him with wide eyes. "I was going to ask you the same. Did you know I could do that?"

He shook his head, hauling himself to his feet and straightening his jacket. "I certainly did not. Though I'm not even positive I know what it is that you actually did, to be quite honest with you."

"You can't do that? How did you banish the Soulshade who tried to possess me then?"

He shook his head again. "It wasn't a banishment, not like what you just did. I can dissipate them, but it's temporary. They always come back. When I commanded those out of you, I hardly used any magic, merely a threat of it."

My mouth fell open slightly. "You *threatened* a Soulshade to stop possessing me, and it *listened*?"

"Well, yes."

Hysteria was bubbling up in my chest but I pushed it back down, taking deep breaths to calm my racing heart. My hands trembled as I straightened my dress and mask. "I'm sure I'll have far more to say about that later, but we're likely short on time."

"Yes, that did take far longer than I was expecting it would," he said with a sigh. The bells began to toll, signaling midnight, and Tallon's face transformed, a wicked smile pulling at his lips as his shoulders melted down his back. Chills echoed down my spine. This was Eadric's Tallon—the version of Tallon I'd come to associate with Eadric, at least. And it meant nothing good for the Coward Prince, now that he no longer held the reigns of Tallon's magic. "Are you open to a slight change in plans?"

The panic that had been cresting subsided with this casual confidence exuding from Tallon now. It was a mask, I knew, but knowing that he was choosing to become this Tallon for *me*... Something in my body trusted him, even if my mind was not always so quick to do the same. In any case, this I did trust him with implicitly. Our goals were the same. "Do what you think is best. You know him far better than I."

"We should get to the ballroom then, before the bells finish."

CHAPTER THIRTY-SIX

The bells were on their last three tolls when we slipped through the private doors along the side of the ballroom that opened right next to the stage. The same doors Eadric had dragged Talyssa through.

The musicians had already begun to falter from the eerie chiming of the bells, but our presence only quickened their fall into silence. What a sight we must have made, though we fit nicely into the decor. It was almost ironic, that tonight's theme was red and black, and I was itching to spill Eadric's blood across the black mirrored floors. Fate, perhaps.

Those closest to the stage were the first to notice us, a woman giving a strangled gasp and stumbling back as she pressed her hand to her chest. It didn't take long after that. Murmurs exploded through the ballroom, traveling back through the crowd, and by the time the twelfth toll sounded, and the lingering noise reverberated through the stone of the castle, the room was silent and all its two thousand or so eyes were solely on us.

Fear radiated off the entire room in waves. For a moment, I

felt an uncomfortable prickling at the back of my neck as if someone were behind me, and I shifted minutely.

"Steady," Tallon reassured. "It is only his magic and the castle watching. There is no sign of Cethin here. Yet, at least."

"If he appears, you promise to tell me?" I asked out of the corner of my mouth.

"You would know."

I curled my toes into my shoes to keep from fidgeting. Whatever Tallon's plan, he'd certainly gotten the attention of everyone left in the castle. Along the side walls, I saw Zaharya, Elena, and Maricara standing together. Blood-red veils shrouded their faces, though I knew they were staring directly at me.

Finally, after an eon it seemed, Prince Eadric noticed us from his spot at the entire other end of the ballroom. Even from this distance, I could see his shoulders tense and his fists clench at his sides. Beneath his mask, I imagined his face growing ruddy.

"You dare show your faces here?" His voice boomed, echoing off the walls in spite of the black velvet that hung from the ceilings. The revelers flinched at his anger, and many were looking rapidly back between us and him. "You dare make a mockery of me? I shall have you hanged by dawn."

"We dare," Tallon replied. His voice was not loud to my ears, though I saw the faces of those throughout the ballroom as it carried through the room regardless. He tilted his head slightly. "And I shall like to see you try it, Your Highness."

Eadric's eyes darted to the doors to his left before returning to us. A flicker of red in my vision, and I saw Zaharya subtly moving down the wall to stand in front of the doors, her chin held high beneath her veil. Eadric's eyes snapped back to us and I let my mask of composure slip enough to allow my feral grin to appear. He would find no allies here tonight, even amongst those he'd thought were loyal.

My heart soared when Maricara and Elena followed

Zaharya's lead, moving to stand in front of the other two sets of doors. It would not stop anyone from leaving should they want to, not really. Three could not compare to a thousand. But the imagery, the imagery Eadric himself had created, was a far better deterrent than force ever could be. Three faceless figures, standing guard at the doors, shrouded in blood and oh-so-clearly on our side.

Despite the relief I felt, my panic was also growing as Eadric continued to stare at us, a slow grin emerging on his face. If we failed again, it would not just be Tallon and me that died, but the others as well. Out of my periphery, I watched Tallon, searching for a sign that Eadric's mystery benefactor had appeared, but he remained relaxed, staring back at his former employer.

The crowd's murmurs started back up, with some of his constituents looking back at Eadric with concern as they, too, waited for his response.

Emboldened by the implication of his cowardice, Eadric rolled his shoulders back and began toward the stage. It was a slow walk, one that attempted to speak of unhurried rage, but to those who cared to look closer, his hands were trembling and sweat beaded on his forehead. His eyes kept darting to the walls with each step.

"You betrayed me," he called as he meandered past the quarter-way point. "You betray me, you try to steal from me, your whore tries to kill me with your putrid magic, and yet you still have the nerve to stand here in front of me. At the ball I conduct in your honor."

"You broke the bargain, my prince." Silence fell as I spoke rather than Tallon. "You stabbed him, and you broke the control you had over his magic. You have nothing now."

"We'll see about that," he sneered, nearing the halfway length. As if on cue, a deep rumbling emanated from the stone, rattling the glassware. A vase skittered and fell off a nearby table, shattering upon the floor. Darkness seeped out of the cracks in the walls and the taste of ash burst across my tongue so thickly I couldn't hide the gag.

"Soulshades," I told Tallon as he looked at me in concern. "He's called more Soulshades."

His eyes narrowed back on Eadric, though he responded to me beneath his breath. "There is no god here; we can stop him and we can kill him."

I spat, trying to rid my mouth of the acrid taste of smoke.

Along the wall, someone screamed as the Soulshades began to tear through the wall, just as they had in the cellar when they attacked me. Voices erupted as people pushed and crowded toward the middle of the room.

"Your Soulshades are no threat to us," Tallon called. He waved a lazy hand at me. "She destroyed them all already. You can call as many as you like—it won't protect you."

Eadric's eyes widened then narrowed as he processed the new information. "It matters little. She can destroy as many as she likes, and I will simply keep calling more."

"What god did you bargain with, Eadric?" Tallon mused, still intensely casual in his stance. "To make it so you could violate the Beyond and Kalyx's realm?"

"Perhaps I bargained with Kalyx himself."

At that, Tallon tipped his head back and laughed. The sound was so genuine and carefree that even the Soulshades halted in their slow journeys out of the stone. "Truly, you must think me stupid. Kalyx would never bargain with you, not after you worked so hard to keep him out of this castle and to prevent him from getting me out of my bargain with Gavriel."

Eadric's face reddened. A tension-filled moment passed as we all waited for his response. He raised a jewel-laden hand and pointed at us. "Kill them."

My heart raced as the Soulshades lunged, but it wasn't us they lunged at. I cried out in warning, lurching forward as the Soulshades instead lunged towards the revelers, entering their bodies and making them jerk before falling utterly still. A moment of silence, so tense I might have been able to cut through it with my dagger, and then chaos erupted. People screamed, rushing toward the doors, but no one ever made it to the red-veiled sentries; the Soulshades pouring out of the walls possessed them before they could. One who did make it shoved Maricara to the floor, only to find the doors would not open regardless.

Eadric had sealed us all in here.

My blood chilled. Perhaps we'd underestimated him. I did not want to kill all these people—the ones possessed by the Soulshades and the ones who'd done nothing but cower—but if I had to in order to get the treatment and escape this place, I would. I would kill whoever stood in my path.

"This is my castle," Eadric called over the shouting as he spread his arms wide. "It, and everyone in it, is under *my rule.*"

Rage like I'd never seen before flitted across Tallon's face. He drew a bloodstone dagger from his back, larger than the one he'd strapped on my thigh. "You are a mockery of a ruler. And I will take great pleasure in killing you."

"You can certainly try, *herald.*"

I barely had time to draw my own dagger before the Soulshades were upon us.

"Kill them, Odyssa," Tallon shouted as he stabbed the first one to reach us. "They cannot be saved now."

"You saved me," I reminded him. My heart pounded as I dodged the grasp of the first Soulshade to reach me. Slashing with my knife, I aimed for non-lethal strikes still.

"That Soulshade..." he grunted as he killed another, "was not under Eadric's direct command." He shoved off a couple that had surrounded him, dispatching them both. "If you want to save these people, do what you did in the hall."

I gritted my teeth and tried to find that well of power inside me. I chased the feeling I'd had in the hall when I'd banished the others but nothing came. Only a flicker, a recognition of my request and a response that it could not oblige. "I can't, Tallon."

He glanced at me out of the side of his vision as we continued engaging with the possessed. The ones I'd merely injured before had returned, and given my lack of magic, I swallowed thickly as I aimed for their throats and their hearts. I was willing to kill to get the treatment and escape, and now, I would.

Bodies fell to the red-bladed knives we wielded, but still more and more possessed appeared. I could hear nothing over the thundering of my blood in my ears, could taste nothing but the acrid smoke, could feel only my blood-slicked grip on the dagger's handle.

"You can end this," Eadric called, breaking through the roaring in my ears. He examined his nails. "Bend the knee and swear your fealty to me and this can stop."

"I want to try something," Tallon said, pausing to look at me fully. "Do you trust me?"

"Do it." I did not hesitate. If there was something he could do to help us, he needed to do it. And as far as trust, despite our beginning, I'd never trusted anyone more.

He nodded, and then his magic was surrounding me, swarming and dark and blocking out the rest of the room. It should have terrified me, knowing what else his magic could do, but the inky tendrils that embraced my body were warm and inviting. As quickly as they'd encompassed me, they melted into my skin, pulsing along the lines of my own marks before they settled.

Power thrummed through my blood. He'd given me some of his magic, and I intended to use every bit of it. A pale-faced

Tallon nodded once, continuing his own battle with his dagger as he encouraged me yet again. Raising my hands, I directed the power out, watching as my marks surged towards the possessed, once again engulfing anything in front of me. My marks, fueled by Tallon's magic, swallowed up the possessed. And then just like before, it collapsed in a blink, rushing back into my body and sending me reeling.

I stumbled but caught my footing before I fell, throwing my shoulders back as those who had been possessed also stumbled, shaking their heads and rubbing at their eyes. They were pale and shaky, but most importantly, alive.

Fingers wrapped around mine and I almost flinched before my body caught up and realized it was only Tallon. I let him gently pry away my death grip on the handle of the dagger, my fingers aching as they unclenched. He nodded once, smiling quickly before he turned us to face Eadric and the rest of the ballroom once more.

One step closer.

The castle settled into a stillness I'd never experienced since stepping inside those gilded gates. Once more, it was merely a castle, layers of stone and wood and metal. Nothing more.

"I'll just summon more," Eadric panted, his eyes wide as he stared at me.

"There are no more." I wasn't sure how, but I knew my words were true without a doubt. There was no more evil left to draw from inside these walls. "There is nothing."

He spluttered, fingers twitching as he tried and failed to summon anything left to combat us. But nothing came to his aid. His people watched on in horror, cowering against each other with wide eyes.

"You *have* nothing," I said softly.

"What shall you do now then?" His eyes flicked to Tallon beside me. "Is now your chance to gloat, Tallon? To boast your superiority over me? Do you wish to take the throne, herald of Kalyx? You wish to be the King of Veressia?" He shook his head. "The people will never accept you."

"I have no use for a crown."

"Then why are you still here?" Eadric roared, spittle flying out and coating his lips. "Will you kill me now? Show these people who you truly are?"

"He will not kill you," I replied. He drew back in shock and returned his attention to me finally, but I continued. "I will be the one to claim the honor of ending your miserable life. And then I will take the treatment from your corpse and liberate Veressia from the tomb you shoved them into."

Eadric narrowed his eyes, and slowly he stepped up onto the stage. "I welcomed you and your ilk into my castle, offered safety and security, and this is how you repay me?"

"You stole us from our families and made it seem like an honor."

"You know I gave him the command to kill your brothers, right? The day you arrived, they were already marked for the grave before you ever set foot in this ballroom." His venom was hissed, quiet but no less deadly. He turned his gaze to Tallon, a vague smirk of victory in his beady eyes, as though the information would make me turn on Tallon.

The information on the timing of the order was a shock, but I refused to give Eadric anything to use against us. I curled my lips back over my teeth as my marks warmed against my skin, writhing and begging to be freed once more, to feast upon Eadric's blood. Tallon squeezed my hand and gave a subtle nod. His command for me to let the magic go and do what it wanted. To embrace it once more. "You're too late again, my prince. I already knew that. And now, you will pay for it with your life."

My magic lashed out, pulling away from my skin and expanding into a mass of inky darkness, all sharp edges and smoke twining together. Tallon was the only one in the ballroom who did not flinch and cower in fear.

The mass slithered over to Eadric, who—with no magic left to call upon—was petrified where he stood, and wrapped around him, squeezing tightly around his limbs, his torso, his neck, before covering his face. I did not need to see beneath the blackness to know that it was forcing its way into his nose and throat—I could feel him choking beneath the power.

Tallon reached his hand out, twining his fingers with mine. To the crowd, perhaps it was a sign of endorsement, but to me, it was reassurance. Reassurance that it was not *me* who was beginning to choke on my own blood. "Draw it back," he murmured. "He does not deserve the dignity. Let them see him die."

I imagined the swarm of shadows sinking back into my skin, warming my body from the inside out, and like a snap, they retreated from Eadric's body and did exactly that, settling back along my arm and neck. They had grown again, spreading across my chest and collarbones now and nearly reaching my other shoulder.

"You're dead, my prince," I whispered. This time, with Tallon at my side, I did not flinch or falter when blood began to pour from Eadric's nose and mouth. I did not retreat into my own mind or picture my mother's body. I watched, and I relished the Coward Prince dying by the very weapon he'd sought to control. It may not have been at Tallon's hand, but knowing we were both free now was a relief.

He clutched at his throat and choked, blood flying from his lips and splattering across his face and chin. Trembling hands reached out towards the crowd, begging someone to help him, but no one moved. Money could not buy loyalty, it seemed. Another gurgled attempt at Eadric speaking echoed across the floors. It grated on my nerves as well, his audacity to die as dramatically as he had lived. His face was both flushed and pale as he suffocated on his own blood, spitting it out with each rasping breath that only sucked more of the crimson poison into his lungs.

Sylviana curled against my leg on the side opposite Tallon, and I couldn't help the smile that formed. "It's funny," I murmured to them without looking away from Eadric, who was still trying to take his last breaths. "I'd always feared the dark before. But the two of you seem content to turn that around."

His chuckle was low and rich as he stepped ever closer, our arms nearly touching now. "Now you are the darkness. And no one will ever harm you again." He leaned down, brushing his lips against my ear. "You have never looked more stunning than now, my wolf. I cannot decide if I want to show you off across Veressia and the Beyond, or if I want to lock you in my room and never leave."

My body thrummed with both power and arousal, but I was all too aware of the slowly dying prince and his gaggle of revelers to respond the way I wanted to. We still needed the treatment, and I still needed to get to Emyl as soon as possible. "After," I promised. "You can do both, after we see Emyl."

With a last gasping choke, Eadric's body slumped to the floor, falling into the pool of blood, his unseeing eyes staring up at the bejeweled ceiling. The tomb of his own creation.

The ballroom was silent as I pulled away from Tallon and approached Eadric's body. I never faltered, stepping through the spreading mass of blood along the floors, not caring how it soaked into the bottom of my dress as I bent over his body and began rifling through the pockets of his jacket and pants. Glass clinked against glass as I moved his jacket, and I dug into the inside pocket, retrieving two glass tubes filled with crimson liquid.

I held them up to Tallon to see. "Is this it?"

He approached and nodded, but frowned and turned his

back to the crowd so only I could see his face as he squatted down beside me. "That is them, but there should be far more than two. Last I saw, there were thirteen. And in this form," he nodded at the vials, "they still need to be split apart. One vial is enough for five hundred or so people."

I chewed on my lip. I had the treatment; I could get to Emyl now if I wanted. I could even give some to Zaharya and Maricara and Elena, who still stood guarding the doors, even as the crowd began to grow restless. But this would not be enough for Veressia as a whole. A thousand people, only enough for those inside the castle walls. Never mind the perhaps seven thousand or so still on the outside, trapped in Jura and the surrounding villages, and who knew how many more beyond the mountains as well.

"How many are infected, Tallon?" I asked. "I assume you have stopped infecting new people since his hold broke, but how many are already ill?"

His face tightened with shame and he could not meet my eyes. "Too many, I fear. In these last days, he had me afflict many."

A beat of silence as I processed his words, processed the pain on his face, the shame and embarrassment that had him ducking his head.

"I am sorry, Odyssa."

"Don't. He made you do this, didn't he? You would never have done this on your own, would you?"

He looked horrified. "Of course not."

"Can you amplify my voice, the way you did with yours?" I asked, closing my hand around the two vials and standing. He still would not look at me. Transferring the vials to one hand, I lifted his chin with the other and splayed my palm across his cheek. It was a balm when he sighed and turned his face into my hand, pressing a kiss there, where the jagged scar from the wine bottle still lay. I curled my fingernails against the scruff lightly dusting his jaw. "Do you trust me, Tallon?"

"Of course." Tallon nodded and then frowned as the rest of my words settled. "Unquestionably, and with everything I have."

His words caught my breath, unexpectedly solemn. It hadn't truly been a question I needed answering, but hearing the conviction in his voice, seeing it on his face... I couldn't deny how comforting it was. And despite everything that had happened, everything he still had not told me, I trusted him too. Yet, the words stuck in my throat, and all I could offer was a nod and a grateful smile as I stepped back and lowered my hand from his face.

We both faced the anxious crowd. I took a deep breath, reaching for Tallon's hand only to find he'd been reaching for me already. My exhale settled me.

"I know there is more treatment somewhere in this castle. I also know that for nearly the past year, you have all turned a blind eye to the suffering of the people outside these walls, content to revel in the manufactured safety of this prison. You drowned yourself in liquor and plied yourself with food to ignore those you think beneath you." My magic began to lift from my skin, playing into the charade without instruction. "Whoever of you is the first to tell me where the remaining treatment is will get to live."

CHAPTER THIRTY-SEVEN

The crowd was silent for a heartbeat; no sound of breathing could even be heard in the ballroom. And then, from the side of the room, a woman spoke.

"I will show you, Odyssa." Camelya stepped through the crowd and made her way to the stage. Her eyes landed on Eadric's body before lifting back to mine. "I know where he keeps it, and I would be honored to give it all to you and Tallon."

"Camelya." Tallon acknowledged her with a deep nod. "Thank you for your cooperation."

"Thank you for freeing us," she said quietly, so no one else would hear.

I narrowed my eyes but did not reply.

She shook her head. "Think whatever you want of me. Kill me after I get you the treatment if you wish. But let me do this. My daughter is still on the outside, and I'd like to help you save her."

Turning, I looked at Tallon, searching for his opinion. He seemed to know Camelya far better than I, and of anyone in this room besides Zaharya, I trusted his judgement. He nodded. I lifted my chin and met Camelya's eyes once more. "Where is it?"

Before she could reply, there was a commotion at the back of the hall. Someone, a desperate soul, charged Zaharya and was trying to grab her and shove her out of the way. My anger snapped out and my marks took flight and soared over the crowds, striking like a viper at the man who was so foolish as to lay his hands on her. Unlike Eadric, there was no long, drawn-out moment of his death. The marks—the magic—struck once, and the man fell convulsing and bleeding to the ground.

"No one touches them." I didn't need to know that Tallon hadn't been the one to amplify my voice that time; I could feel the surprise beneath his carefully schooled features.

"The other vials are hidden in the wine cellar, Odyssa," Camelya said quietly, drawing my attention back to her.

I will accompany her and ensure she returns, Sylviana spoke. Her head turned up to Tallon. *May I show my true form now?*

There was no chance for me to ask what that meant, because as soon as Tallon offered a huff, an eye roll, and a small nod, Sylviana prowled in front of us and *changed*. As a cat, she'd been abnormally sized, too large for the features she had, but this was beyond that. Her body shifted and shimmered as she grew even larger, her features shifting out of a house cat and more into something better suited for sitting in the trees and stalking her prey by night.

Nearly sitting at my waist, Sylviana sank back on her haunches and looked up at me. The only thing about her face that remained the same was her eyes, and when she licked her chops, that forked tongue. Her yellow eyes sparkled with amusement. *Are you ready, Odyssa? They are going to see me now. It always gets a rather...visceral reaction.*

I knew the exact moment she revealed herself to the ballroom because the entire crowd let out a collective gasp, and one lady in the front screamed before fainting against her companion. It filled me with an indescribable joy that this creature, who had only ever been kind to me, exacted so much fear from these horrible people.

I nodded to Camelya, who was pale and trembling. "Sylviana here will escort you while you retrieve it."

A hushed, forced silence fell over the ballroom as they departed, the doors echoing loudly behind them as they closed. Tallon kept his eyes on the crowd, never staying on one person for too long, assessing the threat constantly. My magic may have been cooperating in the face of the current situation, but I could feel my energy fading, and if the crowd truly wanted us dead, they vastly outnumbered us.

As if thinking it brought it to life, the partner of the lady who'd fainted surged toward the stage, screaming, "Traitors!"

Before I could react, Tallon's own magic was holding the man by the throat. He slowly walked forward, his shoes clicking on the mirrored floors as he approached the man.

"You would die for your prince?" he asked the man, nodding down at where Eadric's body still lay. The man did not answer, so Tallon shrugged. "So be it."

The crowd's murmurs were almost loud enough to drown out the choking breaths of the man, but not quite. Again, I did not retreat into my own head at the sound of them. My focus remained entirely on Tallon, on the bright defiance in his eyes, on his relaxed jaw and loose shoulders. How I wished to be as at ease as him. But I would not relax until I was back in my home, until I saw Emyl with my own eyes.

He turned his back on the crowd as the man slumped to the floor and he returned to my side. A frown tugged at his lips and he reached for my hand, sending those warm tingles up my arm to settle in my chest. "It's almost over, my wolf. I swear it. And then we will get to your brother."

I nodded, but the softness in his eyes, only for me, emboldened me to add, "And then, we will have that conversation about us."

The answering smile was wicked, and his voice was like the black velvet that draped from the ceilings. "I'm not sure how much of a conversation it would be, but yes, we absolutely will."

My face and neck flushed as heat coursed through my body, and I was immensely grateful for the high neckline of the dress that would, at least, cover the worst of the redness.

His face turned serious once more. "I want you to know that I am proud of you. What you did here tonight, I understand it might be difficult. You are a good person, and this..." He shook his head as if he couldn't find the right words. "I am proud of you. Your grasp of your magic is phenomenal, and..."—he stepped up closer and bent his head to my ear, his voice turning teasing—"to be quite honest, that you have this much power is making you even more devastatingly attractive than you already were."

I couldn't find the words to reply, to tell him that it should have been hard, taking not one but two lives, but it was perhaps the easiest thing I'd ever done. If he thought it should have been difficult, I didn't know what he would think of me if he knew it hadn't been. I bit my lip. "I—"

Sylviana once again rescued me, this time by returning with Camelya, who was clutching a bulging black pouch in her hands. The crowd fell into that forced silence once more, everyone waiting for Tallon or me to say something.

Sylviana looked between the two of us, still standing close together and Tallon's back still to the crowd, with an amused expression. *What is happening here?*

Tallon narrowed his eyes at the cat. "Does she have it?"

Sylviana inclined her head.

Camelya's trembling hand held the pouch out towards me and I snatched it, pulling it tight to my chest and opening it. A quick count later, and adding the two I'd retrieved from Eadric's body, we had fifteen vials. Enough for everyone in Veressia. I swallowed back the burning tears of relief and nodded at Tallon.

"Good," he said with a smile. He nodded out toward the crowd, still gathered and waiting with bated breath for their fates. "They are yours to decide what to do with."

"Me? But you—"

He shook his head, bending to press a quick kiss to my lips. "I am having my vengeance through you, Odyssa, as you have yours. Eadric is dead. I am free. *We* are free. They are yours. Do what you think is best."

My magic flickered in that pit in my chest as I surveyed the gathered revelers, both pleased by the confidence in me and anxious to get out of the castle as quickly as possible. I hardly wanted to be responsible for these horrible people, but Tallon was right that something needed to be done with them.

They would atone for their actions, or rather their inactions, in one way or another, that much I knew with certainty.

"Your prince is dead, and now you all must make a decision," I called into the room, pulling their attention back to me entirely. Some in the front shifted nervously at the sight of Sylviana sitting protectively in front of me. "If you are still loyal to the corpse there on the floor, you can choose to die here and now. You have my word Tallon will make your deaths quick."

They looked amongst themselves, waiting for someone to speak up. No one did.

"If you are loyal to Veressia and her people, and you want to atone for your appalling behavior while protected behind your walls of lies, then you will help me distribute this treatment throughout the kingdom and help whoever you can, however you can. Whatever it takes."

The crowd came alive, small murmurs at first until people were talking loudly amongst themselves. I tensed, waiting for someone with foolish plans to try rushing us again, but it seemed the warning blows from earlier held true.

Tallon nudged my back, and I took a deep breath. "Whoever knows where the prince kept his money, I want it distributed throughout Veressia as well. To those who need it most. To those who lost the most first." I stepped forward to the edge of the stage, letting coldness into my voice. "If I discover *any* of you take *any* of that money for yourselves, you will not like the outcome."

Silence washed over the crowd on a wave of anxious shifting. Finally, someone spoke. The voice was so soft and timid I could hardly hear it through my fever-addled ears and the ringing that still filled them. "Does this mean we can leave the castle now?"

"I insist upon it." I nodded to Camelya. "Camelya is going to oversee getting the treatment split out and distributing it throughout the kingdom. *None of you are to leave without seeing her first* and ensuring you have both direction and treatment to take with you. By dawn, everyone is to be out of the castle."

"What happens at dawn?" someone shouted. "Why do they need the treatment now? It's over!"

"At dawn, Castle Auretras will become the tomb it was always intended to be." I turned my back to the crowd and let out a shuddering breath. It was nearly over. "And there are those who've been afflicted who are not dead yet. They will *not die*."

"Why me?" Camelya whispered, her eyes wide.

"This is how you make your amends," I said. "We will stay until just before dawn to help, but I have somewhere else I need to go."

She nodded and something shifted in her eyes, becoming much more like the Camelya I had known in my time here. She snapped her fingers at the crowd, and one young man jumped and rushed over, his eyes wide and flickering between Tallon and me. "Yes, Camelya?"

"Go get me that map of the kingdom from the library. Bring it here. And bring some parchment and ink, too, lots of it." She waved him off and peered out over the crowd again, finding her next target. "Luca, come here please."

An older man with white hair and wrinkled hands approached. His body held none of the unease the young man's had but did have a weariness that made him hunch slightly. "Yes, Camelya?"

"We need to split these vials into small enough doses that everyone can take some with them. Is there anything in the medical suite that can aid in that?"

Tallon and I shared a look, but he shrugged and turned his focus back on Camelya. I supposed if he had a problem with my approach, he would have told me by now. My heart was pounding still, and the events of the evening were beginning to catch up to me, my vision swimming slightly. I stepped closer to Tallon, not listening as the older man gave his response. "I am not sure how much longer I will be upright," I murmured.

"It's the magic. I wish I could take the burden from you," he replied, wrapping his arm around my waist and pulling me into his side. Offering me his strength. I leaned into it readily. "We are almost finished here, my wolf. You can make it a bit longer, I promise."

The older man disappeared through the doors into the castle as well, and Camelya turned to me. "I need the others. Can they come off the doors now?"

I bit my lip, unsure. Tallon stepped in smoothly though. "Yes,

I will watch the crowd. If anyone goes near the doors, they will be stopped."

She hesitated for a moment, and then gave a decisive nod, stalking through the crowd to fetch the others. Tallon and I both watched the crowd intently as they returned to the front of the ballroom, but no one tried for the doors.

"Take those damned things off," I commanded as soon as they were close to the stage. "You will never need to wear those ever again."

At once, all three of them ripped the red fabric from their heads. Elena and Maricara watched me suspiciously, but they lacked the usual venom in their eyes. Zaharya kept her eyes on Sylviana but still approached me, pulling me into a fierce hug. "You did it," she whispered into my ear. "We're free because of you. *Thank you.*"

"We are all free now," I replied, hugging her back just as tightly.

Separating, she went back to the others, and Camelya directed them to clear a table from the side walls and bring it to the stage. "And can we please do something with his body?" she asked while looking at Tallon.

The flicker of a smirk was so brief I almost missed it, and he nodded. "Of course."

"What will you do with it?" I asked, eyeing the bodies that littered the stage.

"Take them to the Beyond."

"Oh."

"Would you like to accompany me? I don't need to go with them, but if you'd like to see the Beyond you remember, but under different circumstances, now would be ideal while Camelya organizes everyone." His voice was soft, and I knew that if I said no, he would respect it.

Perhaps a part of me wanted to say no, but another part of

me was curious as to why Tallon was so adamant I was wrong about the Beyond being a nightmarish place. His room had been nice enough, but the craggy canyons were far different. "If I want to return, we can?"

"Of course, at any time."

"Alright, I will go with you."

"Camelya," he called. "We'll return in just a moment."

She nodded absently, still talking with Zaharya.

A wave of Tallon's hand and the ballroom disappeared, leaving only us and Eadric's corpse, now in another world. The Beyond looked similar to what I'd seen before, all dark, soaring cliffs and rivers of crimson in the carved-out canyons below. But it *was* different now.

Instead of the icy-cold wind that had whistled and pierced my skin, there was a gentle breeze, almost warm against my face. There were no screams, no imminent feeling of being watched, no pit of dread curled in my stomach waiting for something bad to happen. The cliffs did not seem daunting, and the river meandered slowly.

"How?" I asked on a shaking exhale.

"I suspect the castle was influencing things some, but most of all, I think you were afraid of the darkness inside you. You've accepted it now, accepted the truth of yourself."

"Why would you ever leave here?" I asked. "If it's so nice, why did you leave?"

"Do you see anyone else here?" He shrugged and looked around at the empty void. "Occasionally, someone would pass through. And of course, I could speak with Kalyx in the palace, but I was lonely, Odyssa. I was a herald of Death— people were not pleased to see me. They ran in terror when they discovered what my presence meant. I wanted to live, wanted to know what it felt like for someone to be happy I was with them for once."

"And Eadric just made it so everyone still feared you anyways," I murmured, my heart breaking for him.

He ran his thumb over my lower lip. "Until you."

"I was afraid of you at first," I admitted.

His laugh was like silk washing over my body and I couldn't stop from smiling with him. He moved his hand to cup the back of my head and pulled me ever closer into his body. "No, Odyssa, you were never afraid of me. You were curious, certainly. Suspicious and angry, absolutely, but never afraid."

"I should have been afraid."

"Yes, you should have. But I will be forever grateful that you weren't. You are what I've been looking for my entire existence, my wolf, and I will never let you go."

My heart soared, secretly pleased by the possessiveness in his voice. No one had ever wanted *me* before, only what I could do for them. He was what I'd been looking for, too, and what I'd never allowed myself to have. I would never let him go either; he was mine now. "Kiss me, Tallon."

His eyes flashed silver, and then he did.

When we returned to Veressia and the ballroom, Camelya had somehow formed the crowd into four long lines in front of the spread of tables across the stage, stretching back to the end of the ballroom. At the head of each line stood Camelya, Zaharya, Maricara, and Elena, each with a map in front of them and a stack of boxes at their elbows filled with tiny glass vials. I watched as each person stepped up to the table and, after a short discussion, was directed to a section on the map and given a vial of crimson from the box.

The lines moved quickly, and before long, the ballroom was only filled with people waiting to be given leave for their work. And just in time, too, as the sky began to slowly lighten. Not quite dawn yet, but near it. I looked up at Tallon, who was staring out over the room, assessing everything.

"Is this the right thing to do?" I asked, suddenly uncertain of what I'd commanded.

His gaze softened when he looked down at me. "Yes, absolutely."

"We're ready," Camelya called, interrupting only more of my hesitancy.

Before I could respond, Tallon nodded at her, and I squeezed his hand to express my gratitude. "Send them off, then. We will be leaving as well. Clear the castle and then lock the gates from the outside." He paused. "All of the gates, Camelya, even the ones to the tunnels. Once the gates are locked, throw the keys into the river. No one will ever enter this castle again."

I was practically vibrating by the time everyone had filed out of the ballroom, anxious to get out myself and get to Emyl. Every moment that passed, I felt my muscles grow tighter, coiling like a spring. Finally, *finally*, the ballroom was empty of those who'd been here as guests. It was solemn now, only us six still remaining.

Despite my anxiety, I wanted to address the others. "You are all free now, and I hope you return home and find what this castle has taken from you."

"You as well." Maricara surprised me as the first to respond. "This castle brought out the worst in us all, but it brings me hope to see how you overcame that. I hope we can all do the same."

"Be safe in your journey," Tallon rumbled from behind me.

We all said our goodbyes to each other, Tallon reminding Camelya again about his instructions. Another moment, and then Tallon and I were alone in the ballroom at last. I let my mask fall, both the physical one and the emotional one. I was trembling with the need to get out of this castle. "Emyl now, please."

Tallon nodded, pulling off his own mask as he pulled me to his side. A whirl of his magic surrounded us, and when it fell, we were in the street in front of my house, and the dawn sky was red no longer.

I swallowed back the burning tears in my throat and approached the door. Testing the handle, it gave way, unlocked.

But the smell of death and decay rushed out of the door to meet me, and I fell to my knees, unshed tears burning at the back of my throat.

I was too late. Emyl was dead.

CHAPTER THIRTY-EIGHT

Amid my grief, I felt Tallon move behind me, pulling the door closed, though the stench of death still burned in my nostrils. He did not try to pull me to my feet, instead sinking down beside me and resting his hand at the nape of my neck.

"Stay out here, my wolf. I will go in," he murmured. I did not have the energy nor the desire to fight him on his proclamation. He pressed a kiss to the side of my head and then the smell wafted out once more before the door clicked shut.

My hands were trembling, my breath shaking, and my entire body seemed to want to implode on itself. All of this for nothing. I had no family left, and nothing to show from the hell I experienced in that castle. Now, I would never be able to prove myself worthy of their love, to convince them to change their minds and see me as a sister rather than a caretaker. I'd lost my only opportunity, carried away on rivers of blood that came from the same magic that Tallon and I had wielded to make our escape.

The door opened again and Tallon exited, pulling it tightly closed. This time, he did pull me to my feet and settle me onto the bench just beside the door, kneeling in front of me on the cold stone. "I am sorry, Odyssa."

"How long?" I croaked, my voice hoarse with tears that would not fall. I finally brought my gaze up from my hands to Tallon's face. "How long has he been dead?"

He sighed, rubbing at my knee through the blood-stained dress I still wore. "Two or three days perhaps." With his other hand, he reached into his pocket and pulled out a folded piece of parchment. "This was on the nightstand. It's addressed to you."

"Did you read it?"

"Yes."

"Should I read it?"

He hesitated. "At some point, yes, but right now it would only hurt you."

I bit down hard on my lip in a failed attempt to keep it from trembling. My vision blurred and the tears finally spilled out, along with a choked sob.

Tallon cursed, shifting closer to me and wrapping his arms around my waist. "I know, my—" He faltered for a moment. "If it helps any, I don't believe he ever intended for you to read this letter. There were ones there addressed to your mother and brother as well."

"What did it say, Tallon?"

He sighed again, clearly not wanting to tell me. After a moment, he stood and sat beside me. "He blamed you for your mother, for Rhyon, for himself. He blamed you for everything that ever went wrong in his entire life. He said you ruined his family, and that as far as he was concerned, he had no sister."

It was nothing I hadn't expected, but hearing the words from Tallon's lips rather than Emyl's hurt far more than I'd ever expected. Surprisingly, no tears came this time. I was numb mostly. I'd known my brother's feelings toward me, had known them all his life, but I'd hoped I could change them. I'd hoped that by saving him, even if I couldn't save Rhyon and our mother, that I could have proven myself to him.

Tallon pulled me into his lap, tucking me beneath his chin. As if he were reading my thoughts, he murmured, "You were always worthy of their love, Odyssa. And they never should have made you feel like you had to earn it."

"I only ever wanted someone to love me. To have a family that loved me. What does it say that I could not meet their expectations? Could not earn their love?"

"That they were not worthy of your love. You gave yours without condition, without falter, and they withheld theirs from you out of some petty attempt to get you to do more for them." He lifted my chin and the unwavering *love* in his eyes made my mouth drop open. He smiled as I realized what the look in his eyes truly meant. "Does it not mean more to have someone love you when they are under no obligation at all?"

"You cannot love me, Tallon," I protested. Yet, even as I said it, I knew that if he pushed me to describe my feelings for him, there would be no word more appropriate than love. "We only just met, though, and you are the herald of a *god*. I am..." I shook my head, trying to understand what my heart and mind were screaming at me.

"You are everything," he supplied, tilting my head up to press a lingering kiss to my lips. "And do not presume to tell me how I feel about you, Odyssa. I know you feel the same, even if you cannot say it yet." He kissed me again. "You have always been worthy of love, and Veressia will always know what you did for them in that castle. You are *good*, my love."

My answer was to press another kiss to his lips, pouring everything into the kiss to show him that yes, I did love him, too, or I *would* love him, given more time.

"Well, this is charming." An amused voice startled us both apart. At the stoop stood a tall man with gray-streaked black hair, slicked back neatly to reveal his prominent cheekbones. He tugged on the lapels of his coat, black wool and heavy against the morning breeze. His eyes were dark, yet alive and churning with silver flecks. The wicked smirk across the man's lips was familiar, but I couldn't place it.

"Who are you?" I asked warily as Tallon shifted me off his lap and put himself between the stranger and me.

Tallon sighed as he stood. "Why are you here, Kalyx?"

"I have been waiting for *months* for you to be freed from that accursed place," the man—Kalyx, God of *Death*—said. He rested a booted foot on the bottom stair and peered up at Tallon. "Did you truly think I would not come see why you lingered here rather than returning immediately? I am a curious man, Tallon."

"You mean you are nosy."

"That as well, yes." Kalyx leaned around Tallon to smile at me, the mirthful smirk replaced by a genuine and warm smile. "Hello, Odyssa. It is very nice to finally meet you, my dear."

I looked up at Tallon, watching him pinch the bridge of his nose and shake his head. Suddenly, the pieces fell into place and I knew why that smirk and those eyes had seemed so familiar. I saw them every day in the mirror. Tallon's previous words came to mind. "Is this what you meant before, by your suspicions about my magic?"

"Yes. I wasn't certain until now, though." He looked between us. "Seeing you both here, together, it's undeniable you're related."

"You suspected?" Kalyx asked, raising a curious eyebrow at Tallon before looking back at me. "It seems we have a bit to catch up on."

"Pardon me for being bold," I said, remembering my manners, "but can you confirm our suspicions? I *am* related to you, aren't I? That is why my marks and my magic are so prominent compared to other survivors?"

"Yes, my dear. You are my granddaughter."

"Oh." Hearing it aloud made it far realer than the suspicions I harbored for only a moment, and just like that, my world was upended once more. He had to be my father's father, as I'd met my mother's parents once when I was younger, before they'd died. I'd never known my father, had never asked about him after learning he'd abandoned my mother. I wasn't entirely sure I wanted to ask about him now. My ears rang, and I swayed slightly from my seat as the information sank in.

"You did not come here for me," Tallon accused, his arms tightening around me. "I would have brought her to you when we returned and you know it. Why are you here *now*?"

"You and I will be having a conversation privately, Tallon—be sure of that." Violence flashed in Kalyx's dark eyes. "You made that foolish bargain and look what has happened because of it."

I jumped to my feet, wrenching myself from Tallon's embrace. "Do not blame him for that. You cannot seriously expect me to believe you could not have intervened if you wanted to. You *left* him there to be a puppet for the crown, so you cannot blame him for what they made him do."

The rage in Kalyx's eyes extinguished as he turned his gaze on me. "You are right, of course. Though had Tallon simply told me what he was seeking, making that bargain could have been avoided in the first place." He eyed us together, gaze landing on my hand wrapped around Tallon's. "I suppose it all worked out in the end, regardless."

I chewed on my lip, debating if it would be proper to ask about my brothers and mother, if they were in the Beyond and if they were happy, at peace.

"They are not," Kalyx replied, looking at me. He waved a hand. "Apologies, it's one of my powers. If someone asks about the dead, I hear it. Your family is not at peace in death, because they were not at peace in life. Though from what I am hearing from Tallon, that is a fitting punishment."

"I—" I didn't know what to say, how to react. Tallon's earlier words echoed in my ears, but it was hard to dismiss the God of Death telling me my family was not at peace. "Can you help them? Please?"

His eyes turned sad. "No, my dear. They brought upon their own afterlife in the Beyond. I am the overseer, the guardian of the Beyond, not its master."

"You are too good, my wolf," Tallon said, pulling me into his side. "Think of those you have saved; think of the lives you have changed even in that castle."

"They are my family," I stressed.

"Am I not your family?" Kalyx asked. At my sharp look, he shrugged. "Perhaps I overstep, but it seems to me that I carry about as much significance to you as you carried to them. And that does not a family make." He climbed the steps slowly until he stood in front of us on the small porch. "Death is inevitable, Odyssa. Focus your efforts on the living, not the dead. Remember them, certainly, but your life is your own now."

"And I suppose you have ideas on how I should live it." My voice rose. "My father, your *son*, abandoned my mother when she was pregnant. Abandoned *me*. What right do you have to have any ideas on how I should live my life?"

"My son is dead, Odyssa. That is why he abandoned your mother and you. My son was a fool, and an arrogant one, but he would not have left you behind if he had a choice. He was thrilled when he learned your mother was pregnant. He came home to tell me, and then, well, his past caught up with him before he could reach me." Kalyx's eyes—my eyes—were sorrowful.

"Tell me about him," I demanded. Of all the things I'd considered when thinking of my father, that he'd *wanted* me had never been one of them.

"In due time," he said with a bow. "Perhaps once we are in the Beyond." He smiled then, looking eerily like Tallon when he had an idea that he was pleased to be sharing. "And of course I have ideas on what I'd like you to do. I want you to come home. You are not the only one who has been searching for a family. I have made do with my heralds, with Tallon here especially, but they are not my blood. I'd like to pass on what I can, to help you learn your powers and grow into your magic." He stretched his hand out to me. "If you'd allow it, of course."

My head snapped up to look at Tallon, searching for his opinion. He shrugged, an easy smile on his face. "I was going to call in my favor to have you to come with me to the Beyond, regardless. It is your decision, but know that I do want you there with me." Kalyx cleared his throat. Tallon rolled his eyes and added, "With us."

"Now what will your favor be?" I asked. It should have been a sign, how easily he could redirect me from my confliction about my brothers and mother, how easy it was to forget them when I was with him.

"Perhaps I shall save it for another time."

"Please save the flirting for later. She is my granddaughter, Tallon," Kalyx sniped, his lip curled back in feigned disgust. It fell back into that warm smile. "So, will you join us in the Beyond, Odyssa?"

"I will stay with Tallon?"

"Of course."

"What will be expected of me?"

"Absolutely nothing you do not desire for yourself. You are not a prisoner, nor under my employ. You are my heir, and you will have free rein over the Beyond and those in it."

I turned to Tallon once more. "Sylviana will be there?"

"*This is where she has been?*" Kalyx spluttered. He narrowed his eyes. "Damned creature."

Tallon smiled widely. "Yes, she will be there. And don't mind him, he is just upset she favors you now. She is Kalyx's favorite."

I only hesitated for a moment. After all, I did want to learn about the magic I now wielded, and I was not ready to leave Tallon's side. Not now, when we were just discovering ourselves together. And there was nothing left for me in Veressia now. Nothing I could not live without, at least. "I will join you, then."

Kalyx clapped. "Wonderful. Shall we be off now then?"

"The castle," I remembered. "Once everyone is out, can you seal it permanently? They have instructions to throw the keys in the river, but I would feel far more comfortable if it was sealed with magic so that no brave fool could break in with brute force later."

"Of course," he said easily. "Now that the bastard prince is dead, he has no hold over the magic there. I can do whatever you'd like with it."

I wanted desperately to ask about the magic in the castle, if it was a bargain Eadric had with Cethin after all, but it didn't matter anymore. If it was gone, and Kalyx could seal it off from anyone ever entering again, that was enough. "Do it."

"And what will become of Veressia without a leader?" Kalyx inquired.

"They've been without a leader for a long time now. They will survive."

"Very well." He bowed lowly. "I shall seal it off once all have vacated it."

Tallon clasped my hand and nodded for Kalyx to proceed. We followed him down the stairs, away from my former house, which was now little more than a tomb. I jerked to a stop, needing to do one last thing before I left.

"What is it?" Tallon asked as I dug into his pocket.

Emyl's letter clutched in my hand, I climbed the stairs and propped it on the door handle. I did not need to read it, did not need to see his venomous goodbye in his own handwriting. "Goodbye, brother."

When I returned to Tallon's side, I slipped my hand back in his and squeezed. He pressed a kiss to the top of my head and returned the squeeze. A cold spot appeared near my hip, and I looked to see Sylviana had joined us. Tallon huffed a laugh and called ahead to Kalyx, who was tapping his foot impatiently. "We are ready now."

Kalyx waved his hand and a portal opened there in the street, revealing the Beyond inside, framed by whorls of black so similar to Tallon's and my own magic. Despite the apprehension pitting in my stomach as I studied the craggy black rocks visible on the other side of the portal, I stepped through with Tallon without fear.

CHAPTER THIRTY-NINE

The portal closed behind us and Tallon pulled me tightly to his side.

Breathing in the calm air of the Beyond, I was certain I was exactly where I belonged. Finally.

"I'd like to introduce you to my court," Kalyx said as the portal collapsed behind us.

The soft breeze, so unlike the cold wind from before, pressed my dress against my shins, the fabric damp with blood and reminding me just what we'd escaped. Tallon squeezed my hand, noticing my grimace no doubt. "Let us clean up and rest first, will you?"

Kalyx bowed. "Of course. I'll wait for you in the throne room. Tallon, you know the way still, yes?"

Tallon barely stifled his eye roll. "Yes, I do remember the way. I've been gone not even two years, not a century."

My grandfather waved us off with a wide, too-innocent smile and a wink to me when Tallon turned away. "Go, get clean. Rest. There's much to show you, but all the time in the world now that you're both here."

My heart squeezed at the warmth and genuine joy in his voice. He *wanted* me here. Still overwhelmed by how different this Beyond seemed, I let Tallon pull me down the black-dirt path, away from Kalyx even as I watched him over my shoulder as we departed. Finally out of his sight as Tallon guided us around a towering pillar of stone, I turned my attention back to the man who'd given me everything.

"Are you glad to be back here for good?" I asked. His hand was warm in mine, and despite the blood that still streaked both of us, I was not afraid. Sylviana fell into step beside us as we continued down the path. "And where are we going?"

"I figured we could walk to the palace, so you could see the Beyond outside of your nightmares," he said softly. "And I am very glad to be back, though I am immensely more pleased that you are here with me."

"Would you have really called in your favor to get me to come here?" I did not linger on the piece about my nightmares. He'd already proven this was a far different place when I was awake and here willingly. If he wanted to show it to me, I would be glad to see it. Besides, I was curious to see what else lay here in the Beyond.

"Absolutely." There was no hesitation, only that brazen confidence that occasionally bordered on arrogance.

"Well, I suppose you'll figure out another favor to..." My words trailed off as we turned a corner in the path. Before us lay what could only be the palace, a towering and expansive structure of gleaming black stone with jutting spires not unfamiliar in appearance to the jagged rocks that lined the cliffs it sat on. Stopping as I continued to marvel at it, I felt both Tallon and Sylviana watching me. Waiting for my reaction. "It's beautiful."

Tallon's shoulders visibly relaxed as he raised the back of my hand to his lips. "I hadn't realized how much I missed it until just now. And I am glad to be seeing it again with you."

As lovely as this is, Sylviana spoke, *you two are both covered in blood still. Perhaps a bit of urgency to wash it off wouldn't be amiss.*

"She's right. Let's get you clean," Tallon said. He ran his hands over my arms, flaking off some of the dried blood caked there. His chest inflated with a deep inhale, and on his exhale, we were back in his room in the palace. The bloody rags that I'd used to tend to his wounds not even a day ago were gone, and the room was pristine. He paused at the door to the bathroom. "Would you prefer to bathe alone, or would you mind some company? I find I'm not exactly eager to let you out of my sight right now."

Quickly growing exhaustion warred briefly with flaming desire, but before I could decide the victor, he spoke again.

"I promise, it will only be a bath and I will be on my best behavior." Despite his words, his smirk stoked the fire in my belly. "You're not used to the toll of the magic yet; you need to rest. Let me take care of you, please."

The exhaustion nudged ahead of the desire, cooling the burning in my blood as I nodded. Until he'd said something, I hadn't noticed the heaviness about my body, the ache forming behind my eyes. "A bath sounds lovely."

Stepping out of my shoes, I lifted my hair over my shoulder and turned my back to him. As reverently as he had put it on, Tallon carefully undid all the clasps along the dress, removing the spine piece and then peeling the blood-crusted dress from my body. His arms came around my waist, pulling me back to his chest as he pressed kiss after kiss along the marks that adorned my shoulder. "You are resplendent, Odyssa."

"Even covered in another's blood?" I teased as I looked over my shoulder at him.

His breath was warm as his laughter huffed against my skin. "Especially so, I find."

The sound of running water had me pulling back to look at him quizzically. "Is there someone else here?"

He kept me to his body, fighting gently as I'd moved to pull away and cover myself. "No, there's no one. Kalyx's palace is not so different from Auretras in that it's more than just a building of stone and metal. I requested it draw you a bath, and the magic responded."

"Would you teach me?" I asked. Despite the exhaustion, the magic I'd performed at Auretras still burned in my mind, and I wanted to know more. Leaning back into his embrace, I let my eyes fall closed. His touch was a comforting anchor amidst the swirling currents of uncertainty. His warmth soothed the ache of Emyl's letter that still lingered in my bones.

Tallon's lips brushed against my ear, his voice a low whisper that sent shivers down my spine. "I will teach you that and more. Anything you'd like will be yours here, Odyssa. But for now, let me get you clean."

With a gentle nudge, he guided me toward the awaiting bathtub, steam curling up from the fragrant water, filled with floating herbs and shimmering oils. Tallon held my hand as I stepped into the tub and eased myself down into the water's embrace. Immediately I felt relaxed yet also strangely energized, as if the water had peeled away the exhaustion from my body and left behind only a content state of accomplishment.

"Will you not join me?" I asked. He'd pulled my blood-soaked gown from my body, but had yet to shed his own clothes, simply rolling up the sleeves as he settled onto his knees beside the tub. "You are more covered in blood than I."

He leaned forward to capture my lips with his own, but the kiss was too brief and I chased his mouth as he pulled back, his silver eyes glittering as that smirk settled back into place. "Do not worry about me, my wolf. You first." He ran his hand through the water, bumping into my thigh as he did so. "Besides, I do not think this tub could hold us both."

I hummed, settling further into the water. He had a point, and though I'd expected his request for company to be fulfilled quite differently, so long as he stayed within my reach, all would be fine. I, too, didn't want to stray far from him. While he was comfortable here in the Beyond, far more so than I'd ever seen him at Castle Auretras, I was not.

Tallon settled onto the floor by my side, his presence a steady beacon as he reached for a washcloth, dipping it into the water before gently running it across my skin, the remnants of blood and battle fading beneath his touch. The water swirled red and I fought to raise my eyes to Tallon's face rather than watch the reminder of what we'd done. What we'd had to do.

"Relax, my love," he whispered, his voice a soothing melody that wrapped around me like a comforting embrace. "There will be plenty of time for thoughts and questions later."

Closing my eyes, I surrendered to the sensation, allowing myself to be carried away by the current of affection that flowed between us. In the safety of Tallon's watchful presence, I found solace amidst the chaos of the Beyond, knowing that no matter what trials lay ahead, we would face them together. Water sloshed and the washcloth rasped over my skin gently, but with my eyes closed, surrounded by warm water and feeling Tallon next to me, I drifted to the edge of sleep, never quite falling over.

Some time later, I was pulled from my warm drifting by Tallon's hand cupping my cheek. "My wolf, I'm afraid it's time to get out of the bath. Your grandfather has grown impatient, it seems."

Opening my eyes, I was surprised to find him in an entirely different outfit and completely devoid of blood. Now, he was dressed in a deep purple shirt with his sleeves pushed up to his elbows and left unbuttoned so I could see the way his marks dipped across his throat and collarbones. I wanted to tear the buttons off with my teeth. I blinked at him. "When did you leave?"

His smirk gave way to a full smile, one that showed his teeth and dimpled his cheeks. "You were quite out of it, my wolf. But I only left for a moment." He rose from the floor gracefully, extending his hand out to me. "Come. If Kalyx must come fetch us himself, I fear it would not be a pleasant experience."

I let him guide me from the tub and stepped into his arms as he held out a fluffy towel. Biting my lip as I grew wary, I wondered if we'd made a mistake coming back here. "What would he do?"

Tallon paused in running the towel over my body. "Oh, no Odyssa, not like that. He would not harm us, I swear it. I meant more along the lines of unbearable teasing. I apologize."

Shaking my head, I pulled the towel from his hands and continued drying myself off as I avoided his stare. "No, I'm being silly. I suppose I'm not..." I searched for the right words.

His hand cupped my elbow and brought me to standing where his gaze captured mine. "You're not used to being wanted. To being loved. It's quite alright, my wolf. We will teach you."

I dried and dressed in silence, pulling on the off-the-shoulder crimson gown that Tallon had laid out for me while trying to find the words to express just how grateful I was for him. I had no example of how to express my own love, my own want, but I wanted to desperately. To tell him exactly how much I appreciated his support and his care. Instead, I settled for cupping his face in my hands and pouring it all into a kiss. One that left my knees weak and my chest heaving.

Tallon had not fared much better. His voice was hoarse as he pulled away and tucked a strand of hair behind my ear. "We should leave this room. I certainly don't want to be made a liar, but if your grandfather comes to find us now, I worry what he'd do if he found us in bed."

At that, a laugh finally bubbled up from my chest. The absurdity of it, of me going from having no one to care what I did so long as I was useful, to having a grandfather. And one who would care enough to be upset at the thought. It was odd, but in a delightful way. "Let's go then. I'd like to learn more about this place anyway."

"We will teach you everything," he vowed. He took my hand as we left the room. "I suspect he will want to introduce you to his court. Some of the other gods might be here, but he might not call on them so soon."

My blood chilled and the smile fell from my face. "Cethin?"

"I plan to ask him about that later, but Cethin doesn't often come here." He brought my hand to his lips. "You will be safe, Odyssa. I swear, just as I swore it at Auretras, no harm will come to you."

I didn't point out that harm *had* come to me at Auretras, even after his vow. It wasn't the time, and I knew that if he'd had more authority, more power, he would have kept it. "How should I act?"

"Be yourself." His words were firm. "You do not have to wear a mask here, my wolf. Never again."

"Never again," I repeated. I liked the sound of that, though I knew it would never be as easy as he made it out to be. I'd lived my life behind a mask, and shedding it would be like shedding my skin. But I would do it. I wanted to do it.

"Ahh, my darling granddaughter has joined us," Kalyx's smooth voice boomed over the stone as we entered what could only be the throne room. Much like the ballroom of Castle Auretras, the floor was smooth black stone that reflected the lanterns that bordered it, set upon the face of black columns streaked with gold veins. It was regal in a way Eadric could have only pined for.

"She needs to *rest*, Kalyx," Tallon said through gritted teeth. "Not be paraded about. This could have waited."

"Nonsense!"

"She isn't used to expending as much magic as she did at Auretras."

"She will learn. This is important; they need to meet her."

"They can wait."

"Stop it!" I hissed, clutching my hands to my ears. Everything was too *loud*. Too much. Something had changed since we'd first arrived, and it was like everything was amplified, all the noises rushing into my head and swirling around. "What is this?"

"What's wrong?" Tallon asked, rushing to my side. "What did you do, Kalyx?"

"I merely reversed the effects of the plague on her body." The concern was clear in Kalyx's voice, but the volume was still piercing my ears. "I fixed what *you* broke."

"Take it *back*," I demanded. "There was nothing wrong with me. I don't want it. I don't want this."

"Undo it. Now."

"Fine, fine." Kalyx waved his hand, and like a blanket settling over the room, the noise was muffled. His voice sounded like it was underwater, but it was manageable. It was familiar, and it was what I'd grown accustomed to. "Is that better?"

I lowered my hands from my ears. "Much."

"You truly do not wish to be made whole again?"

"I was never made less." I raised a brow. "Do not deign to make decisions for me again, especially regarding my body. I can hear you just fine. I can breathe just fine. I can manage my way through life just fine and I do not need anyone deciding otherwise."

Tallon said nothing, but I could sense the arrogant smirk on his face directed at Kalyx, who bent his head like a scolded puppy. "Of course, my dear."

"Now," I said, squeezing Tallon's hand. "Who would you like me to meet, Kalyx? Tallon is right; I am exhausted and would like to rest, but I understand this is important to you too."

"Of course, my dear," Kalyx repeated. He bowed lowly before straightening and clapping his hands. "My court, if you will join us. I'd like to introduce my granddaughter, Odyssa. And of course, you all know my favorite herald, Tallon."

From between the columns that lined the walls, people appeared. Only a handful, and yet my heart raced in my chest. Tallon had said no mask, and yet I couldn't deny my desire to impress these people. To impress Kalyx. Tallon squeezed my hand twice, no doubt reminding me of his presence, and of his words.

"Hello," I greeted the crowd. I couldn't bring myself to offer other pleasantries, not when I was growing quickly overwhelmed by them staring.

"She is Eiran's daughter?" a woman asked, peering at me closely. Whatever she found in my face, she liked, because she straightened, and the smile she offered was near blinding. "Of course she is; I see it now. Welcome, Eiran's daughter, to the Beyond."

Eiran. I'd never known my father's name; my mother had refused to speak it. My throat was thick with tears I would not shed for a man I had not known, so I nodded in return.

"Introduce yourselves to her," Tallon ordered. He shifted closer to me so our arms brushed, and that warmth seeping from him was all I needed to find my footing once more. "She just arrived and doesn't know your names. Kalyx is a terrible host."

Several of them fought to hide smiles as my grandfather rolled his eyes. Tallon, it seemed, had embraced the removal of his own mask. I enjoyed seeing him be himself and not the instrument of Death that Eadric had wielded. They stumbled over themselves to approach me, offering their names along with small bows. The woman who'd gifted me my father's name spoke first, introducing herself as Imelda. Then, Evander. Silas. Amira. Hale. Runa. Eris. Thane.

I greeted them all, committing their faces and names to memory as best I could.

"Will she be your heir?" Hale, a slight blond man with long hair, asked.

"If she wishes to be," Kalyx replied, looking at me expectantly.

"Do not make her decide now," Tallon nearly growled. "This is enough; she needs to *rest*."

"Fine," Kalyx said with an eye roll. "Tomorrow evening then, we will have a party welcoming home Odyssa and Tallon. Once there's been a decision made by Odyssa, there will be an announcement. For now, Tallon remains my heir."

"You're the heir?" I asked under my breath as the others began to talk amongst themselves about the party. He hadn't told me that, and the last thing I wanted was to take anything away from him. He'd had enough taken.

"We'll discuss this later," he said, pressing a kiss to my hair. "I have no problem with you being heir. Besides, I'm planning on never leaving your side. Perhaps we can be co-heirs."

Kalyx's eyes narrowed on us, but before he could open his mouth, the throne room doors opened and a harried man entered, clutching his hands in front of him.

"I apologize, my lord, for the interruption," he began with a bow. "I have an urgent message for you."

"Clear the room," Kalyx ordered after watching the man for a moment. He raised a brow to me and Tallon. "You may stay."

The courtiers cleared out, leaving us with the anxious man, Tallon, and my grandfather in the spacious room. The weight of judging stares lifted, I felt more at ease and studied the man. He wore a gold brocaded jacket, heavy and certainly expensive.

"Odyssa, this is Caspian," Tallon introduced. "He is the messenger between the gods."

"Who has a message for me?" Kalyx asked, leaning forward and resting his elbows on his knees.

"Alastriona is having," he paused and grimaced, as if searching for the right word, "difficulties with some pirates off the coast kidnapping her heralds. She's requested your assistance in dealing with them."

"Of course she is." Kalyx sighed heavily, rubbing his brow. "Alright, then, tell her I will be there in a moment."

The man bowed before hastily retreating.

"And tell her I will be bringing my heirs," Kalyx called to his back. He eyed us as the doors swung shut. "Yes, I did hear that little conversation between you. We will discuss it tomorrow."

My face flushed, fearing an admonishment, but Tallon merely scoffed. "It delighted you; do not lie. Now you do not have to make a choice."

"Alastriona is...?" I asked, trying to remember the stories my mother had told me and coming up short.

"You do not have to change the subject, Odyssa. This is not like Auretras," Tallon said. "No one will harm you for having an opinion, nor for questioning Kalyx."

I nodded, grateful that again he'd seen through the mask I hadn't even realized I'd put on. I squeezed his hand. "Thank you, Tallon. Truly, though, I do not remember who Alastriona is."

"Goddess of the seas," Tallon supplied, squeezing my fingers in return as I smiled at him in thanks. He winked at me. "You will like her."

"How can you help her?" I asked Kalyx. I had to ignore Tallon's teasing even as it made my heart soar with joy, lest my questions go perpetually unanswered. "What does she want you to do?

"I'm not sure that I can help, really. If she wanted them simply killed, she could have done it herself." He shrugged, standing from his throne and adjusting his clothing. "But we are friendly, so I'll at least go see what is happening. Come with us, Odyssa. I'd like you to meet her. Tallon is right; you will like her. I have a strange feeling she will like you as well."

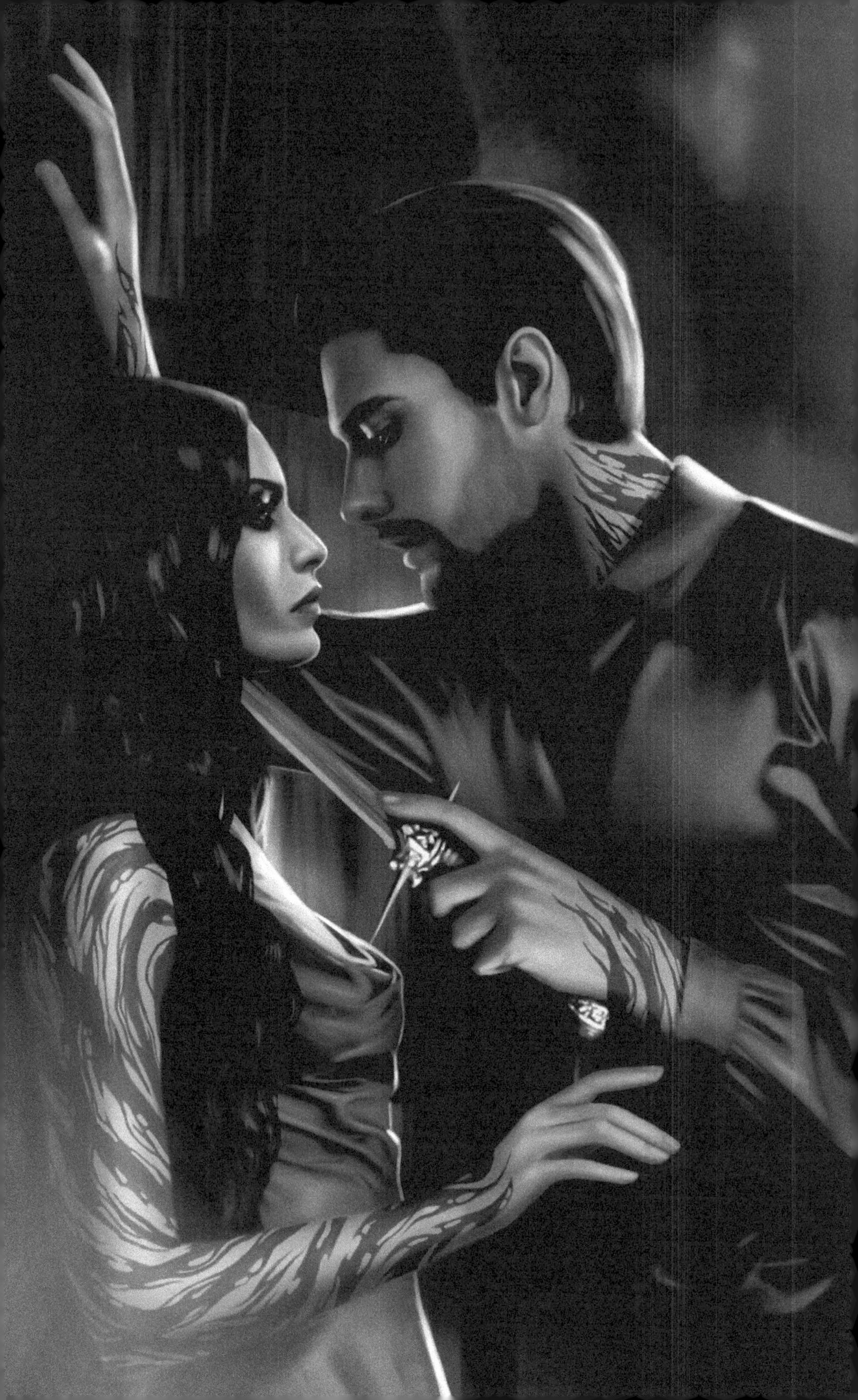

THIS IS THE END OF TALLON & ODYSSA'S STORY...

But you can still venture back into the story with this bonus chapter from Tallon's POV:

AUTHOR'S NOTE

BEYOND THOSE GILDED WALLS was inspired by a multitude of Edgar Allan Poe's works. Did you find them all?

- Masque of the Red Death
- The Black Cat
- The Fall of the House of Usher
- The Conqueror Worm
- A Dream Within a Dream
- The Haunted Palace
- The Imp of the Perverse
- Ligeia
- Never Bet the Devil Your Head
- Al Aaraaf
- The City in the Sea
- To Helen
- Lenore

LEAVE A REVIEW

I hope you enjoyed your trip into Veressia.

Please consider leaving a review for BEYOND THOSE GILDED WALLS on your preferred platform!

ACKNOWLEDGMENTS

First of all, to Jourdan, thank you for believing in this book even when I didn't.

Thank you to everyone who made this possible. This book was something different, but something I think I needed to write, and I appreciate beyond words all the support I've gotten for my spooky little baby!

A special thank you to my husband and my family, as always.

Thank you to my wonderful beta readers, who helped me shape up this story and make it the most delightful it could be.

If I had the space, I would list out every single person who's supported me with this writing thing, but that would take up it's own book. Just know, your support means the world to me, and I doubt I would be here without each of you.

Thank you to Bianca, for yet another gorgeous cover and bringing my vision to life in a spectacular way. Thank you to Rachael, for the amazing map of Castle Auretras. Thank you to Carly at Booklight Editorial for helping me while I developed this story.

And to my readers, thank you. Thank you for taking another chance on me. I love you beyond words!

ABOUT THE AUTHOR

Jessica S. Taylor (she/her) is the author of dark fantasy romance novels. Her first book, THE SYREN'S MUTINY was an ode to her childhood love of pirates and mermaids. She's since moved onto spookier things, as one does.

As a kid, Jessica devoured whatever books she could get her hands on and when that wasn't enough, she began writing her own.

Jessica was born and raised in Kentucky, but is currently residing in southern Maine with her husband and cat, Nebula. When she's not reading or writing, Jessica enjoys concerts, traveling, and spending time with her family.

Visit her website to learn more and join her newsletter to be the first to get exclusive content and updates! www.authorjessicastaylor.com

CONTENT ADVISORY LOCATIONS

- Parental death (semi-graphic, on-page) - Chapters 1-2
- Verbal and physical abuse by a sibling (brief, on-page) - Chapters 2-4
- Gaslighting (mild, on-page) - Chapters 12, 13
- Injury and body horror (graphic, on-page) - Chapters 11, 13, 16, 20
- Sibling death (mentioned, off-page) - Chapters 26, 29, 37
- Moderate to explicit sexual content - Chapters 24, 33
- Violence and murder (graphic, on-page) - Chapters 20, 28, 35, 36, 37
- Grief - throughout
- Emotional neglect by a parent (implied) - throughout
- Blood and gore (graphic, on-page) - throughout

If there is something not on this list that you are concerned about, please email me at jess@authorjessicastaylor.com to inquire. I would be happy to let you know if (and where) it is present in my book.

Milton Keynes UK
Ingram Content Group UK Ltd.
UKHW040215091024
449407UK00016BA/245/J